LADY OF CONQUEST

LADY OF CONQUEST

A Medieval Romance

A "clean read" rewrite of *Saxon Bride*, published by Bantam Books, 1996

TAMARA LEIGH
USA Today Best-Selling Author

ISBN: 1942326149
ISBN 13: 9781942326144

TAMARA LEIGH NOVELS

CLEAN READ HISTORICAL ROMANCE
The Feud: A Medieval Romance Series
Baron Of Godsmere: Book One 02/15
Baron Of Emberly: Book Two 12/15
Baron of Blackwood: Book Three 2016

Medieval Romance Series
Lady At Arms: Book One 01/14 (1994 Bantam
Books bestseller *Warrior Bride* clean read rewrite)
Lady Of Eve: Book Two 06/14 (1994 Bantam Books
bestseller *Virgin Bride* clean read rewrite)

Stand-Alone Medieval Romance Novels
Lady Of Fire 11/14 (1995 Bantam Books best-
seller *Pagan Bride* clean read rewrite)
Lady Of Conquest 06/15 (1996 Bantam Books best-
seller *Saxon Bride* clean read rewrite)
Lady Undaunted Late Winter 2016 (1996 HarperCollins
bestseller *Misbegotten* clean read rewrite)
Dreamspell: A Medieval Time Travel Romance 03/12

INSPIRATIONAL HISTORICAL ROMANCE
Age of Faith: A Medieval Romance Series
The Unveiling: Book One 08/12
The Yielding: Book Two 12/12
The Redeeming: Book Three 05/13
The Kindling: Book Four 11/13
The Longing: Book Five 05/14

INSPIRATIONAL CONTEMPORARY ROMANCE
Head Over Heels: Stand-Alone Romance Novels
Stealing Adda 05/12; 2006 (print): NavPress

Perfecting Kate 03/15 (ebook); 2007
(print): RandomHouse/Multnomah
Splitting Harriet 06/15 (ebook); 2007
(print): RandomHouse/Multnomah
Faking Grace 2015 (ebook); 2008 (print edition): RandomHouse/Multnomah

Southern Discomfort: A Contemporary Romance Series

Leaving Carolina: **Book One** 11/15 (ebook);
2009 (print): RandomHouse/Multnomah
Nowhere, Carolina: **Book Two** 12/15 (ebook);
2010 (print): RandomHouse/Multnomah
Restless in Carolina: **Book Three** Mid-Winter 2016
(ebook); 2011 (print): RandomHouse/Multnomah

OUT-OF-PRINT GENERAL MARKET TITLES

Warrior Bride 1994: Bantam Books
*Virgin Bride 1994: Bantam Books
Pagan Bride 1995: Bantam Books
Saxon Bride 1995: Bantam Books
Misbegotten 1996: HarperCollins
Unforgotten 1997: HarperCollins
Blackheart 2001: Dorchester Leisure

*Virgin Bride is the sequel to *Warrior Bride*
Pagan Pride and *Saxon Bride* are stand-alone novels

www.tamaraleigh.com

1

England of The Norman Conquest
October, 1068

"A THOUSAND TIMES I curse you!" the fallen knight shouted at the one who cradled his head in her lap, whose blue skirts were stained purple with his blood.

Trembling violently, he pulled the dagger from his chest, let it fall to the dirt road, and clawed a hand over the wound. "To eternity I curse you, Rhiannyn of Etcheverry. If you will not belong to a Pendery, you will belong to no man, your days and nights gaping pits of despair. Never again to know—"

He drew a gurgling breath, expelled it on blood that fell like crimson mist.

"Thomas," Rhiannyn whispered.

He jerked his head. "Never again to know the love of a man, never to hold a child at your breast."

Throat pained by unspoken sobs, she brushed the hair off his glistening brow. "Forgive me. Pray, forgive me."

"The devil forgive you!" He raised his bloodied hand and dug his fingers into her neck.

Though death surely crouched at his side, she knew he could strangle the life from her. Still, she did not try to free herself. It would be no less than she deserved if all ended here, and she almost wished it would. Then the torment of these past years, which had seen so many dead, would also end. For her.

As she drew breath through her constricted throat, she longed to relive these last hours. She would not run from Thomas, and he would not be dying in her arms.

Warm tears slid down her face. "I did not want this."

"Curse you!" He released her neck, dragged his bloodied hand down her bodice, and pressed his palm between her breasts as if seeking the beat of her heart. With a grating breath, he shifted his gaze to the gray sky and rasped, "Avenge me, Brother!" Then his body convulsed, lungs emptied, and arm dropped to his side.

A sob broke from Rhiannyn as she stared into sightless eyes that would never again darken with anger over her defiance. Nor would they smile.

She turned her face up. "Why?" she asked as the advancing storm rolled out its thunder. "Now more will die. Surely that cannot be Your will."

Chill droplets fell, spotting her, mixing fresh water with salt tears—gentle at first, as if heaven wept with her, then fast and hard, as if with a grief more vast than her own.

She was drenched when the sound of approaching horses reached her. Uncaring whether those who came were friend or foe, she bent nearer over Thomas.

"I will belong to none," she accepted the great emptiness to which he had banished her, an emptiness complete now that she had lost not only her family to the conquering Normans, but the family she might have made with another. "No children will I bear."

Though the voices of those who came spoke Norman French and were raised in anger, relief swept her. With the arrival of the Pendery knights, her own death was imminent, meaning she would not long be burdened with guilt.

Rhiannyn thought herself prepared for the fury, but she could not keep from crying out when hands wrenched her upright and dragged her back from Thomas.

"What have you done?" Sir Ancel snarled.

Rain pelting her face, she met the gaze of one who had been Thomas's friend. "He is dead," she spoke in his French. "I—"

The back of his hand snapped her head to the side with such force she would have flown backward had she not been supported by a man on either side.

It will be over soon, she silently counseled amid bursts of blinding white and pounding pain. He would come at her again, and within minutes, she would join Thomas upon this dirt road—for a short time. Whereas he would be taken away for a proper burial, she would share the fate of the numerous Saxons who had fallen to the Normans. No kindness in death.

Of a sudden, the men between whom she hung released her, and she dropped to her hands and knees amid the sludge of the road.

"Thomas!" Sir Ancel bellowed, and when she lifted her throbbing head and narrowly opened her eyes, she saw he approached the prone figure of his liege, around which the others gathered.

She slid her gaze to the bordering wood. It was a short distance, but though the instinct to survive urged her to run, reason told her she would not reach it unopposed. And her Norman captors knew it as well.

Peering past Thomas's men, she saw one rider had not dismounted.

With stricken countenance, Thomas's fourteen-year-old brother moved his gaze from her to the man Sir Ancel had pulled into his arms.

The youth's name was Christophe. Lame from birth, he was a gentle soul destined to know books and healing rather than weapons and lording. Henceforth, he would hate her, but he would not avenge his brother's death as bid. Of such violence he was not capable.

Though Rhiannyn longed to explain to him what had happened, she knew if she were believed, Thomas's men would seek retribution. What they considered an eye for an eye would mean further carnage of her people. Thus, she would bear the blame for Thomas's death. And since he had died because of her, it was a good version of the truth.

"Rise!" Sir Ancel commanded.

She startled to find he once more stood over her.

"Lady Rhiannyn!"

Lady because Thomas had named her one. Determined to wed her, though she had shamed him with her public refusal, he had bestowed the title upon her. After all, it would not do for a favorite of the Norman king to take a Saxon commoner to wife.

Imagining her blood would soon join with his, though not in the manner he had wished, she struggled upright to face the one who would do the deed.

Short-cropped hair plastered to his head, face contorted, Sir Ancel demanded, "Who did this to our lord?"

She lowered her eyes to more easily tell the lie. "I did it."

He grabbed her shoulders. "No more of your Saxon lies. I want the truth!"

"I have told it!"

"Do you think me a fool? It was your lover who put a dagger through him."

He spoke of Edwin, the second son of the Saxon thane who had ruled Etcheverry before the coming of the Normans. Edwin, whose bitterness kept the enmity alive between the conquering Normans and the vanquished Saxons. Edwin, who was not her lover, though he would have been her husband had the Normans not claimed this land to which they had no right.

Though she would never admit it, he had aided in her escape this morn, and it was he who had fought Thomas and been wounded by his opponent's blade. But it was not Edwin who landed the deathblow. After Thomas had sliced through Edwin's sword arm, a dagger had been thrown from the wood.

Thomas's cry, mingled with Edwin's angry shout, returned to Rhiannyn as she stared through Sir Ancel. She saw herself take Thomas in her arms, saw the disbelief with which he regarded her as Edwin urged her to her feet, saw Edwin's contempt as he berated her for refusing to leave with him, saw the injured arm Edwin pressed to his chest as he struggled to mount his horse. And then Thomas's sightless eyes.

Blinking Sir Ancel to focus, she said, "*Non*, it was I who killed him."

He sneered. "Where is your weapon?"

What had become of it? She lowered her chin and searched for a glint of silver. The dagger hid itself well, and she had to drop to her hands and knees and scrabble in the wet earth to find it.

She regained her feet and raised the weapon toward Sir Ancel. Though the blade had drawn the mud of the earth, the red spilled from Thomas's veins was yet visible amid the recesses of the intricately carved hilt. "This is what I used."

Disbelief continued to shine from the knight's face and the faces of those behind him.

Did they not believe her capable of the atrocity—that she did not possess the stomach or strength required to kill a man?

She stepped forward. "God is my witness," she said, promising herself she would repent later.

Sir Ancel knocked her hand aside, sending the dagger into the rain-beaten grass alongside the road. "Lying Saxon. It was the coward, Harwolfson, who did it!"

As she clasped her pained wrist to her chest, Sir Guy retrieved the dagger. When he looked askance at her, she averted her gaze.

"It was Harwolfson!" Sir Ancel insisted.

She shook her head. "You are wrong. I hated Thomas."

"*Non!*" Having dismounted, Christophe hobbled forward. "You did not hate my brother, and even had you, you could not have done this."

"I am responsible," she asserted, which was true whether it was she who had wielded the weapon or the unseen one in the wood.

"Fear not, Christophe." Sir Ancel grabbed Rhiannyn's wet hair and forced her head back. "Justice will be done."

Quelling the impulse to struggle, she said, "Do it now."

"That would be too merciful."

Mind ripe with imaginings of what he would do to her, she began to fully feel the chill of clothes soaked through. Or did fear make her shudder? "Do with me as you will," she said through chattering teeth.

"Be assured, I shall." He thrust her from him.

She threw her hands up and felt her palms tear when they met the muddied road. Prostrate, she silently prayed, *Dear God, be here, be merciful, be swift.*

A hand gripped her arm and, with effort, pulled her to her feet.

It was Christophe. Wondering how it was possible to find no smudge of hatred amid the pain upon his face, her burning eyes brimmed.

He smiled sorrowfully. "Lady Rhiannyn—"

"Do not call her that, boy!" Sir Ancel snapped. "She is no longer a lady—indeed, never was."

Christophe Pendery, who knew most believed he was undeserving of his surname, looked around. "She was to have been my brother's bride."

"*Oui*, and Thomas was a fool to think he could trust her." The man jabbed a finger at where two knights arranged their lord's body over a horse. "Your brother is dead."

Christophe lowered his chin, closed his eyes, and fought emotions that sought to unman him before knights who would scorn him for showing a woman's weakness.

He had to be strong. With Thomas gone, the estates fell to him, he who would never train for knighthood, whose destiny had been to serve as his brother's steward. He did not want the responsibility, nor the struggle for power that would ensue. But what other course? Of the four sons born to Lydia Pendery, but two survived, himself and the eldest.

He opened his eyes. "Maxen," he whispered. He to whom all would have belonged had he not pursued a different life. A *far* different life.

But would he come back out into the world? If so, would he stay?

2

His demons quieted, the lone figure rose from before the high altar and lifted his tonsured head to consider the holy relics—sole witnesses to his prayers.

"Answer me, Lord," he said. And waited, as he did each time he prostrated himself in the chapel, but again he was denied deliverance from memories that had made him seek this place.

Disdained by God who was not yet ready to forgive him his atrocities, he strode from the chapel. He would try again on the morrow, and the morrow after, and one day there would be peace for his soul. God willing.

Paying little heed to the cool wind and its whispers of winter, he left his head uncovered and crossed to the cloister where his studies awaited.

It was Brother Aelfred who intercepted him. "A messenger from Etcheverry is here to speak with you," he said from deep within his hood.

All of Maxen went still. For two years there had been silence, as he had directed upon entering the monastery. What was so important Thomas should break his vow to leave him be? Had ill befallen the house of Pendery?

"The man awaits you at the outer house," Brother Aelfred prompted.

Maxen inclined his head and changed course. As he approached the building, he saw the one who stood to the right of it. Facing opposite, wind sifting short black hair and ruffling fine garments, the man appeared to be appraising a section of the monastery's outer wall. But as if sensing he was no longer alone, he turned.

Maxen halted, causing his heavy clerical gown to eddy about his feet. "Guy."

The knight who had fought beside him at Hastings grinned. "No other." He strode forward and gripped his friend's arm. "It is good to see you."

Demons roused, Maxen demanded, "Why have you come?"

Guy blinked, released his arm, and donned an impassive expression. "Let us talk inside."

"Something is amiss at Etcheverry?"

"It is. I would not have come otherwise."

"Thomas sent you?"

"*Non*, Christophe."

As Maxen was a dozen years older than the youngest Pendery, that would make his brother a mere fourteen years of age. Thus, it boded ill that it was he who had directed Guy to the monastery.

"What of Thomas?" Maxen asked.

A long silence, then, "I am sorry. Your brother is dead."

Maxen's chest constricted. Another brother destined for the dirt. Another taken too young.

Memories he had struggled to bury rising from their graves, he saw the sloping meadow of Senlac, the strewn, ravaged bodies. He heard the Norman battle cries of *Dex aie!* and *God's help!*, the Saxon cries of *Holy Cross!* and *Out! Out!* He smelled the spilled blood and felt the heat of bodies pressing in upon him. And then...Nils.

He wrenched himself back to the present. Thomas was dead, the same as Nils. Of his three brothers, only Christophe remained. "How did he die?"

"A Saxon woman. She whom he wished to wed."

"A woman?" Maxen barked.

As if uncertain of how to deal with this man of God who, in that moment, must look anything but, Guy took a step back. "She claims she was the one, but Sir Ancel believes her rebel lover murdered Thomas."

Maxen knew he should distance himself by accepting his brother's death and returning to the chapel to pray for him, but he had to know. "For what did she betray Thomas?"

"Rhiannyn is the daughter of a villein who died at Hastings. She blames the Normans for the deaths of her father and two brothers in battle, and of her mother during a raid upon their village before the fighting." Guy shook his head. "Thomas thought he could make her forget her loss by bringing her into the castle and grooming her to become his wife."

Hands concealed in the long sleeves of his robe, Maxen closed them into fists in an attempt to squeeze the breath out of emotions he had not thought to experience again. "It was Thomas who lost," he growled. "Everything."

"So he did. Rhiannyn refused to wed him, and though he might have gained her consent by threatening her people, he was determined she would come to him willingly."

"And she never did."

Guy shook his head. "She slipped free of the castle a sennight past. Though the wood teems with Saxon rebels, Thomas rode after her without awaiting an escort. When we found him, he was dead—put through with a dagger."

"What of the woman?"

"Rhiannyn was there. She claimed she killed your brother, but it is unlikely she possesses the strength or skill to down a warrior."

"She protects her rebel lover."

"Edwin Harwolfson, to whom she was betrothed before William claimed England's throne."

"Who is he?"

"The second son of the thane who possessed the lands King William awarded Thomas. As the only survivor of his family, he claims rights over Etcheverry, refuses to acknowledge a Norman as his overlord, and leads the Saxon rebels who abound in the wood of Andredeswald."

"He murdered my brother for revenge."

"For which he is more than qualified. A worthy adversary."

"Is the uprising restricted to Etcheverry?"

"No longer. It touches other Pendery lands, and many villages are dying as the young and strong leave to join the rebellion. There are not enough to work the land and tend—"

"Tell me more of Harwolfson."

Guy drew a deep breath. "He was a royal housecarle to King Edward before his death. Next, he served the usurper, Harold."

Surprise sprang through Maxen. A housecarle who had not died with his king? According to Saxon tradition, no housecarle should leave the battlefield alive if his lord was killed. There could be no worse disgrace.

"Harwolfson does not limit his foul deeds to Normans who pass through the wood," Guy continued. "He leads attacks against Etcheverry Castle and its sister castle, Blackspur. The first year, he set fire to both so often Thomas began replacing wood with stone."

Returning to what was yet unknown, Maxen asked, "How is it Harwolfson did not die at Hastings?"

"The Saxons say that while Harold expired a hundred feet away, an old witch pulled Harwolfson from beneath the dead and breathed life back into him. Afterward, she took him from the battlefield and healed his wounds with magical words and herbs."

"What do the Normans believe?"

Guy's brow was momentarily disturbed, as if he was tempted to point out Maxen was also Norman. "They say Harwolfson is a coward and ran to the wood when his king fell."

"What do you think?"

"Word abounds of his courage. And with my own eyes I have seen the wound he is said to have gained while fighting to protect his king. Though I dare not say it too loudly, methinks he did not take to flight."

Maxen wondered if he had met the man. By invitation of the now deceased King Edward, who'd had a particular fondness for Normans, the Penderys had resided on English soil for nearly a quarter century. For this reason, the first language of the Pendery offspring was

Anglo-Saxon, though they were equally fluent in Norman French. But following King Edward's death, the Penderys had not supported Harold Godwinson's claim to the throne. Instead, as commanded, they had taken up arms for their liege, Duke William of Normandy. So much bloodshed...

The images sharpening, as if yesterday he had thrust his sword into the blood-soaked soil of Senlac and walked away, Maxen silently raged. *Curse Thomas for his obsession with the Saxon wench! Curse him for dying and leaving none but Christophe to take control of the Pendery lands!*

"There is none but you," Guy said.

Maxen jerked. "What speak you of?" Not that he did not know. He just did not care to know.

"Christophe cannot do it, nor does he wish to. If what belongs to the Penderys is to remain theirs, you must come out."

Leave his refuge that with prayer might someday free him of his demons? "I cannot. My vows are spoken. My life is here."

"A petition has been dispatched to King William. If he agrees, which he would be a fool not to, you will be freed of your vows—at a price, of course."

Further reminded of who he was and what he had done, Maxen struggled to contain emotions that might once more make of him an animal. When he had entered the monastery, he had determined he would never again know the outside world in which he had become merciless and bloodthirsty—as had been expected of him to prove his family's allegiance to Duke William. More, he had given himself to the Church to ensure the world beyond these walls would never again suffer him.

"Christophe sent the petition?" he growled.

Guy swallowed loudly. "I did—with your brother's blessing."

Maxen stepped toward him. "You?"

"I had to, not just for our friendship, but because I could not bear to see all lost."

"But Christophe—"

"I have told you. He is not fit to lord Etcheverry, nor Trionne once your father passes on. If you do not come out, it will be Sir Ancel Rogere who controls Pendery lands. At best, Christophe will be a figurehead."

"Rogere?"

"Thomas's friend, whom he intended to make lord of Blackspur Castle. Surely you remember him?"

He did. Thomas had become acquainted with the Norman prior to the Battle of Hastings. A landless noble, Rogere had sought his fortune fighting alongside Duke William in the quest for the English crown. However, it was told he had fallen early in battle, and a handful of coins had been his only reward.

"Continue," Maxen ordered.

"It is he who sits at high table in Christophe's stead. He who directs the household knights and to whom the steward answers. He who intends to seal his power by gaining your father's permission to wed your sister."

Maxen turned away. All was lost. Just as duty had bound him to defend his family's holdings at Hastings, he must do so at Etcheverry, even at the cost of the soul he had struggled to save these two years. Suddenly so weary he longed to drop his head between his shoulders, he asked, "When do you expect the king's reply?"

"He should have my petition in hand by the morrow. Thus, his answer will likely arrive within a sennight."

Maxen knew William would not dally over the decision, nor did he question what the decision would be, for the king had conferred the barony on Thomas after Maxen had refused it and entered the monastery.

"Does Sir Ancel know what you do?" Maxen asked.

"He does not, my lord."

My lord. So, neither did Guy doubt what William would decide.

Maxen's anger flared, and though he forced it down, it simmered beneath his surface.

"I will ready myself." He pivoted.

"Maxen?"

He looked over his shoulder.

Guy's smile did not reach his eyes. "It is for the better."

"For the house of Pendery. But for me?" He shook his head. "This is where I belong, Guy." And she who had forced him from his sanctuary would pay for her faithlessness. "The woman," he said, "tell me she yet lives."

"She does. Sir Ancel would have put her to death, but it is the one thing upon which Christophe will not be moved."

"Why?"

"Regrettably, he is as enamored of her as was Thomas."

Foolish boy. Directly or not, she was responsible for their brother's death. "She yet dwells within the castle?"

"She does, though no longer in the comfort Thomas provided her. Sir Ancel holds her in a prison cell."

Rightly so, Maxen mulled and realized the Maxen of old had edged out the Maxen he had struggled to become. In that moment, the vows he had taken seemed hollow. All because of a treacherous woman.

So be it, he conceded. *If I must give up the monastery, forget compassion, charity, and forgiveness. Forget every last one of the kindnesses I have sought and been taught. Forget all!*

And God help the Saxon wench.

3

⚜

Rʜɪᴀɴɴʏɴ sᴘʀᴀɴɢ ᴛᴏ her feet, but there was no refuge within her prison and no possibility of getting past the man-at-arms advancing on her.

Pressing herself back against a wall, she demanded, "What do you want?"

He smirked and clamped a hand on her arm. As he dragged her from the cell, she twisted and dug her heels into the dirt floor.

Naming her the vilest thing one might call a woman, he heaved her onto his shoulder.

Lungs nearly emptied of air, she clawed at his back, a puny defense which seemed not to affect him. Defeated—for the moment only, she promised herself—she lifted her head, and through her tangled hair, saw the cell recede and the dim passageway open wide as if to swallow her.

Preferring her own darkness, she squeezed her eyes closed and did not open them again until she was dropped onto a stool. Grabbing the splintered seat to keep her balance, she tossed her head back. "What is this?" she demanded.

The man-at-arms stepped aside, revealing she sat in the center of an unlit room, and amid the shadows ahead was the figure of a man.

"Bind her," that one said in Norman French.

Rhiannyn leapt up.

And was shoved back down. As she resumed her struggle, the man-at-arms forced her arms behind her, clasped her wrists together, and lashed them with coarse rope. Holding her to the stool with a hand that bit into her shoulder, he came back around and pulled a ragged piece of cloth from beneath his belt.

He thrust his face near hers. "Unless you wish me atop you, wench, you will be still." He released her shoulder and began binding the cloth around her eyes.

Though horrified at being denied her vision, she did not move, certain he would take pleasure in stretching himself upon her.

Is this to be my end? she wondered. Though she knew she deserved no better for the part she had played in Thomas's death, she silently counseled, *Wait, Rhiannyn. Wait and listen and be ready.*

Hearing the man-at-arms' retreat, straining to see through the blindfold's dense weave, she waited.

The long silence was broken by the heavy tread of boots, evidencing the man in shadow was of good size.

The nearer he drew, the more her skin prickled, and when he halted before her, the sensation was so strong she thought it possible he touched her.

"Comfortable?" he asked in Norman French, his voice warming her ear, the scent of sweat and horse and leather filling her nostrils.

She turned her head, and against her cheek felt the rasp of a lightly bearded jaw. "Who are you?"

"Who do you wish me to be, Rhiannyn of Etcheverry?"

Was that harsh, dark voice truly his? Or did he affect it to frighten her? "It matters not what I want. You are Norman. Thus, we are enemies."

"Norman or no, I have the power to be your judge. Or your champion."

The latter was a lie, but she would play the game. "Which will you be?" she asked. "Norman or no?"

"It is for you to decide."

He wanted something from her, doubtless the same as Sir Ancel. But though he dangled her life before her, she would not give him Edwin.

His hand closed over her lower jaw, thumb pressed into the hollow beneath her cheek. "I would know where your lover dwells."

Heart quickening in anticipation of brutality, she prayed it would be no worse than Sir Ancel's visits to her cell that left her bruised and aching.

"As I have no lover, I know not of whom you speak," she said and steeled herself for the blow.

"Edwin Harwolfson."

"Not my lover. Nor do I know where he is." Now the blow, the snap of teeth, the bloodying of lip and nose.

"Methinks you lie."

Not with regard to her virtue. Further agitated that he had yet to strike her, fearful the blow would be tenfold worse for the delay, she said, "If it is Thomas's murderer you seek, it is not Edwin you want."

"Truly? Then enlighten me."

Dear Lord, she silently entreated, *he will make of me a bloody mess. Or a corpse.*

But if it ended her soul-tearing remorse and Sir Ancel's beatings, his attack would be welcome, would it not?

She drew breath through her nose. "You want me. *I* killed him." And now she would feel the spit of his obscenities, the back of his hand, the punch of his fists, mayhap a long fall into darkness out of which she would not escape.

Derisive laughter made her startle. "A wee Saxon wench downed an esteemed knight of King William? You profane Thomas's memory with such tales, Rhiannyn."

It was that or the massacre of her people.

"No matter what you tell," he continued, "you will not convince me Harwolfson did not kill him."

She shook her head. "I vow, he did not—could not have. Thomas did great injury to Edwin's sword arm and was about to put him through when…" There was the truth. Here was the lie. "…I planted the dagger."

"Do you think me a fool?"

She did not, but why could he not simply punish her and leave the others be? Accepting she wasted her breath, she asked, "Why will you not let me see you?"

No response.

"Are you so unsightly none can stand to look upon you?"

Naught.

"Are you Thomas's father?"

He drew so near his mouth brushed her ear. "*Non*, Rhiannyn, I am not our father."

It took her no moment to understand, but she did not believe it. "It cannot be. Christophe and his sister are all who remain."

He stepped nearer, and she felt his leg alongside hers. "There is also Maxen Pendery."

If what he said was true, why had there been no mention of another brother besides the one killed at Hastings? Neither Thomas nor Christophe had spoken of this one.

Rhiannyn was about to challenge his claim when she remembered Thomas calling upon his brother to avenge him. She had thought it was gentle Christophe to whom he had cried out, though it had made no sense. But this day, sense was made. He had summoned Maxen. And Maxen had come.

"I give you a choice, Rhiannyn. Yield up my brother's murderer, or your people will suffer."

Meaning he would pursue and slay those who took refuge in Andredeswald, the very thing she had tried to avoid by claiming she had killed Thomas. Sir Ancel had threatened the same, but she feared this man's threat more. And yet, it changed nothing. If she revealed an unseen person had murdered his brother, he would not believe her and still work his revenge upon the Saxons.

"I will hunt them down," he continued. "I will not rest until I am certain Thomas's murderer is among those whose lives I take."

Her chill deepened as if death walked past her. Wishing her arms free so she could hug them about her, she said, "It will be innocent lives you spoil." Like her mother's life, which had been taken in the Norman raid upon their village.

"The same as Thomas," Maxen Pendery said.

True. His life had been lost for no other reason than the desire to possess her. "Thomas was innocent," she agreed. "He should not have died."

The air stirred with her captor's retreat, and she heard his long strides carry him away.

She blinked behind the blindfold, marveling that he had not struck her. Surely he wanted to, but something in him that was not in Sir Ancel denied him the indulgence.

"Maxen," she called.

His footsteps halted.

"I say again," she unthinkingly slipped into her own language, "your revenge should be against me. My people are not responsible for what befell your brother."

When he finally answered, it was in French. "You will speak my language if you speak at all. Your language is dead."

It was then she realized his accent was so thick it bore little resemblance to Thomas's or Christophe's. It was more like that of Sir Ancel who had been raised on the continent. "Do you not know our language?" she asked in French.

He returned to her, and this time when he spoke, it was from high above. "Unlike my brothers, I was raised in Normandy. Thus, I do not embrace your vulgar Saxon tongue."

He meant to offend her, but she understood his feelings for a language not his own. She had been barely conversant in French before Thomas had come to Etcheverry, but he had insisted she learn, and she'd had little choice living amongst those who spoke only French—excepting the Penderys who were equally conversant in Anglo-Saxon.

"You did not understand what I said?" she asked and startled when his hand settled at the base of her neck, reminding her of when it was Thomas's hand there.

"I do not need to." His grip was firm, but not so firm air was denied her. "Responsible you may be, but I want the one who spilled his blood."

"You have the one!"

"When you break—and you will—whomever you protect will be mine."

He did not know her, she assured herself. Ever she had been told she was more headstrong than a woman ought to be, and Maxen Pendery would learn it soon enough.

"You must desire this Harwolfson very much," he said.

She told herself not to dignify his taunt with a response, but protested again, "He is not my lover!"

"Then you will not grieve overly much when I take his life."

"Only a fool would be so certain it will fall that way," her tongue once more defied her. "Take care lest he kills you first, Norman pig."

His grip tightened slightly. "His death or mine, Rhiannyn, you and I will see it together."

Determined to speak no more, she seamed her lips.

"One thing more," he said. "By your deceit, I am lord of Etcheverry and beyond, and you will show me respect. Thus, you will address me as *my lord*, and nevermore speak my given name."

As if her time with him might stretch to years.

"Do you understand, *Rhiannyn?*"

Do not challenge him! warned the cautious side of her.

"Mayhap *you* ought to understand something, *Maxen Pendery,*" her other side triumphed. "Never will I accept you or any Norman blackguard as my lord." She thrust backward and wrenched out of his hold.

If he had not snatched hold of her arm, pressing fingers into one of several bruises Sir Ancel had inflicted, she would have landed at his feet. As she suppressed a whimper of pain, he righted her on the stool.

Releasing her, he said, "You *will* accept me as your lord."

Once again, he retreated, and when his footsteps went silent, she slumped.

All for naught. As none believed her capable of murdering Thomas, she had given herself into the hands of the enemy only to become a pawn to a Norman bent on blood. And her people would pay with their lives.

Another's approach brought her head up. As evidenced by a powerful odor, it was the man-at-arms who had delivered her here. Like the man before him, his fingers bit into her bruises.

"Where are you taking me?" she asked as he pulled her from the room.

"Depends."

"On what?"

He pushed her up against a moist wall. "On whether or not you would like company." He fit his body to hers, causing the meager contents of her belly to churn.

She swallowed hard, and when fairly certain she could hold down the bile and gruel, lifted her chin. Staring into the blindfold, she said, "I would rather keep company with the rats!"

She felt him tense and braced herself for the blows Maxen Pendery had held in reserve. But neither did this man strike her. For fear of denying his new lord the privilege which, heretofore, had belonged to Sir Ancel?

"As you wish," he said and wrenched her forward.

Fool, Maxen silently chastised as he watched Rhiannyn disappear around a bend in the corridor. A misplaced sense of gallantry had tempted him to defend her, and if the perverted guard had not pulled back, he would have aided her. A mistake, for the Saxon woman would have discovered his weakness—that the *blackguard* in him was sometimes more gray. He must not forget who she was and what she had done.

But neither could he forget the bruises, cuts, and scratches the torchlight had revealed. When he had caught hold of her arm to prevent her from falling, he had felt her response to the press of flesh made tender—likely, by Sir Ancel who had been unable to disguise his rancor when Maxen had arrived at Etcheverry hours past. The man's power over Christophe having been wrested from him, the embittered knight would have to be watched closely.

Maxen returned his thoughts to Rhiannyn. She was different from what he had expected. He had come prepared for a female expert at using her body to further her lies. Instead, she had gained his grudging respect by wielding her sharp tongue, rather than abundant wiles—full lips which would be softly inviting outside the ravages of imprisonment, long hair which promised gilt-colored tresses beneath the filth, well-proportioned curves which not even her foul, torn garments could disguise.

Had she lain with Thomas?

He ground his teeth. Though he began to understand his brother's obsession, he would not share it. And yet—

"Almighty!" he growled and told himself she deserved the punishment Ancel had dealt her. And more. He had seen the dark stain across her bodice that was surely Thomas's blood. So what were bruises and scrapes when she, not his brother, lived?

A semblance of enmity restored, he flexed his shoulders. Though from his teachings at the monastery, he knew vengeance was God's, his impatience would not allow him to wait for however long the Lord might take. And Rhiannyn would provide the means by which Thomas was avenged. Soon she would lead him to the murderer. Then Harwolfson, his kith and kin, would suffer the full extent of the Pendery wrath.

4

A RHYTHMIC SCRAPING tugged at Rhiannyn where she dwelt in the haze between sleep and wakefulness. Narrowly opening her lids, she peered across the cell and waited to discover whether the sound was imagination or truth.

Truth. Torchlit face uncertain, Christophe peered through the grate in the door. "Lady Rhiannyn?"

She sat up. "What do you here, Christophe?"

"I have come to help."

Unfolding her stiff body, she rose and took the two steps to the door. "Help?" She went up on tiptoe to look nearer upon Thomas's brother.

He lifted a hand to reveal a key. "I have come to free you."

Her first thought was it must be a trap, but she could not believe he would be so deceitful.

She gripped the bars. "You know I was Thomas's downfall."

"I do not blame you as…" He pressed his teeth into his bottom lip.

"As Maxen does," she finished what he feared to speak.

His eyes sprang wide. "He has not hurt you, has he?"

"He has done me no harm." Not exactly true, but neither could she define what he had done to her.

"But he may." Christophe's eyebrows pinched. "No matter how he presents himself, he is foremost a warrior."

"He does not know you are here?"

He shook his head. "Like Sir Ancel, he has forbidden me to see you."

Rhiannyn considered the key and what it offered. To see again the blue of the sky, the gray of a day filled with rain, the moon and stars, to breathe fresh air and touch the morning dew, to feel the warmth of the sun…

Selfish, she silently chastised. In an England ruled by grasping Normans, freedom meant little more than survival. For her, it would mean warning Edwin and his followers of the revenge with which Maxen Pendery intended to smite them.

"When your brother discovers me gone," she said, "what punishment will be yours?"

"He will not know it was I who released you."

"And if he learns it was you?"

Though worry flashed in his eyes, he said, "I can see after myself."

Nay, he could not. If she was to escape, she must do it in a manner that would not cause Christophe to suffer his brother's wrath. Turning away, she rubbed her chilled arms. "I cannot."

"You must! The desire to avenge our brother eats at him. Are you prepared for what he could do to you?"

She returned to her corner, lowered to the floor, and wrapped her arms around her knees. "If the choice be you or me, I must stay."

A key scraped in the lock, and the door swung open, letting in more torchlight. With a quick, uneven gait, Christophe crossed the cell.

"Clothes to conceal your person." He dropped a bundle beside her.

Rhiannyn grabbed it, scrambled upright, and thrust it at him. "Return these whence they came."

He crossed his arms over his chest. "You will need them to slip free."

Bewildered by a resolve she had rarely glimpsed in him, she dropped the bundle at his feet. "Leave now and no more concern yourself with me."

"Think of your people, Rhiannyn. If you sacrifice yourself—"

"If I escape, it will be without your aid."

He laid a hand on her shoulder. "Then you will not escape. Many were the lives Maxen took at Hastings, and just as he showed no mercy there, none will he show you."

"So be it."

"My lady, do you not remember the ballads sung of The Bloodlust Warrior of Hastings?"

One could not forget those verses raised to the rafters by Thomas's men while consuming great quantities of drink. They were triumphant, crude, and frighteningly vivid in their accounts of the Norman warrior who had slain Saxon after Saxon, earning himself Duke William's high regard.

"I remember," she said and waited for what she hoped Christophe would not tell.

"The ballads are of Maxen."

Fear cramped her belly. "They are but songs——"

"They are not. It was hardly more than a game—albeit deadly—Edwin and Thomas played. But now there is Maxen, and a more worthy opponent Edwin will not find."

It took most of her resolve not to stagger, and what remained of it to accept she had no choice. If she did not leave this day and warn Edwin, there might not be another chance.

"End the bloodshed that has already taken too many lives," Christophe pleaded. "Once you are returned to Edwin, he will take you far from here."

Would he? Would he accept her back amongst their people? When she had refused to accompany him into the wood after Thomas fell, he had accused her of siding with the Normans. And like Thomas, he had cursed her.

"You will do it?" Christophe pressed.

Regardless of whether or not Edwin yet had feelings for her, he had to be warned. But would he listen? Could he be convinced to turn from a life bent on vengeance? There was one way to find out.

"I will do it," she said.

Christophe sighed. "You must take your leave now, whilst Maxen is with his steward."

"But the guard——"

"—sleeps well." He smiled sheepishly. "With some help."

Christophe was dabbling in herbs again. And not their healing aspects.

"I have tethered a horse in the grove," he said. "It is not very worthy, but neither will it be missed for some time."

Rhiannyn dropped to her knees and opened the well-worn mantle he had bundled around other clothes. She drew out a peasant's gown.

"Too large," Christophe said, "but it is all I could manage."

"It will be a fitting disguise."

"Had I time, I would have brought your own garments."

"Worry not," she said. "It is a wood to which I go."

"But still you should have the gowns that were made for you."

She smiled sorrowfully. "As long as Normans rule England, I have no need of fine garments."

He looked away.

Wishing to console him as she had done in the past, Rhiannyn stood and captured his hand. "I will not forget you. You have been a good friend."

He colored, and his eyes shone with tears. "As have you." He lifted her hand, pressed his lips to it, and turned away. At the door, he peered over his shoulder. "Was it your betrothed who did it, my lady?"

Knowing it was useless to maintain she had murdered Thomas, and there was nothing to be gained in allowing him to think Edwin guilty, she said, "He did not."

He nodded and exited the cell.

"God be with you," she whispered when the forlorn youth, whose transition to manhood he had fought this past year, went from sight. Then she readied herself for escape.

5

As Andredeswald drew her deeper into its embrace, Rhiannyn wondered for the dozenth time at the sense of being watched.

She halted her horse, closed her eyes, and concentrated on the sounds—small animals scuttling for cover, the drone and buzz of insects, air puffing at the leaves, the huffing of her horse.

Though she did not believe this feeling of being watched was unfounded, she detected nothing untoward. Opening her eyes, she tipped her head back and searched the trees for one of the lookouts Edwin would have set about his camp.

She sighed. Wherever he was, the man was not ready to show himself.

Urging the horse forward, she worked the fingers of one hand through her snarled hair. Would any recognize her? she wondered, having earlier caught her reflection when she had paused to drink from a stream.

It had not seemed her face. Dark circles rimmed dull eyes that had once shone warm brown. Hollows beneath her cheeks made her face appear gaunt. Pressed lips looked as if they had never known a smile. Tangled, filthy hair hid all evidence of the golden tresses Thomas had so admired. Eight and ten years aged, yet she might be nearer thirty.

Just as well, she told herself as she guided the horse around bramble. If she had been old and unbecoming when Thomas first laid eyes on her, he would not have desired her. He would be alive, and Maxen Pendery would remain in whatever dark place he had crawled out of.

A whispered rush of air brought her chin around a moment before something struck the back of her neck and pitched her from the saddle.

Her cry silenced by her meeting with the ground, consciousness dipping toward darkness, she dug her fingers into the soil and tried to raise herself to her hands and knees. Failing that, she lifted her head and strained to make sense of the jubilant voices. Though their words eluded her, there was no doubt they were Anglo-Saxon.

Shabby, cross-gartered legs approached, and a few moments later, rough hands flipped her onto her back.

"Looks familiar," one of two men said.

Rhiannyn shifted her gaze from him to a gap-toothed, bearded face. "Aethel?" she whispered.

"Indeed," her departed father's friend said, and she knew it was he who had slung the stone, hitting her exactly where he had aimed. This once, it would have been nice had he been less accurate.

"Is it her?" the other man asked.

"Aye, Peter. 'Tis Rhiannyn whom Pendery stole from Edwin."

She sighed. It was beyond good to hear Anglo-Saxon spoken again.

"Traitor," Peter spat. "Norman whore."

Aethel straightened to his enormous height and seized the other man by the neck of his tunic. "Keep your tongue about you, lad, else I'll cut it from your mouth!"

As Peter stammered, Aethel returned to Rhiannyn. "You have come alone?"

She nodded, the movement making her grimace. "Escaped."

He lowered to his haunches and probed the swelling at the back of her neck. "Had I known 'twas you, I would have received you more kindly."

"I hurt."

"'Course you do."

"Edwin..."

"I will take you to him."

"He needs to know——" She cried out when his arms came around her.

"I have hardly touched you, little one," he said as he straightened and settled her against his chest.

"My ribs. Are they broken?"

His concerned face dipped near hers. "We shall let the white one be the judge of that."

Dora. The old, unnaturally pale woman who, two years past, had appeared in the Norman-ravaged village of Etcheverry. Though the survivors had feared one of such white countenance, a handful—Rhiannyn among them—had come forward to peer into the cart bearing their dead thane's son.

Although Edwin's torn and broken body had been testament he would not be much longer among the living, Dora had promised the villagers a miracle. She would return Edwin to life, and in him they would have a leader capable of taking back their lands.

None had believed her, for even if Edwin's body could be mended, all knew his will would thwart her. As a housecarle, it had been his duty to die alongside his king, and to live would mean disgrace. But Dora had persisted in nursing an enraged Edwin, and true to her promise, he had lived.

The thump of Aethel's gait lulling Rhiannyn into a state of rest, she distantly heard the discourse between the men and felt the rare burst of sunlight through thickening shadows. Occasionally, she peered through narrowed lids and beheld Aethel's wiry gray beard and sparsely leaved branches above his head. But like the vaporous haze swirling above the floor of the wood, much was a blur.

It was Edwin's voice that roused her. Turning her head, she saw her betrothed was flanked by numerous men and women.

Though his face was shadowed by unkempt black hair falling past his shoulders and a beard in need of clipping, the dark anger expressed there most detracted from his looks. Mouth compressed, hawkish nose flared, green eyes narrowed, he appeared hard and dispassionate.

She had feared he would be this way, but had hoped that with the passing of weeks he would come to understand why she had refused to flee with him. Not because she had not wanted to, but because leaving Thomas to face death alone would have been cruel.

"Rhiannyn," he said.

She swallowed against a dry throat. "Edwin."

He shifted his gaze to Aethel. "How did you come upon her?"

"She nearly came upon us. Says she escaped the Normans."

"Set her down."

"She is not well. My rock struck her—"

"She will stand, else lie where she falls!"

Aethel lowered her. "Steady, now," he bid as her feet touched the ground.

She braced her legs apart, and when his hand fell away, remained upright. Feeling the rake of Edwin's gaze, she lifted her head and noted the frayed sling supporting the arm Thomas had wounded.

"How did you know where to find me?" he demanded.

"A good guess," she said, wishing her voice were stronger. "'Tis where I would have come." Where, as children, she and others had ventured to enjoy the warm pools of water springing from deep within the earth.

Edwin clamped a hand around her forearm. "Do you betray me again? Have you brought the Normans with you?"

"You know I would not."

"Do I?"

She could not avert her tears. "I would never harm you, nor my people."

He sneered. "I know not whether you speak of Normans or Saxons."

Though tempted to slap him, she said, "The Normans stole me away, but I am still one of you."

"That you will have to prove."

"I intend to."

The steel in his gaze did not soften. "What changes are wrought at Etcheverry since Thomas Pendery's death?"

"Another of his brothers has claimed the demesne. His name is Maxen, and he is dangerous."

Edwin's eyes lit. "The rumor is true."

She was surprised by his seeming lack of concern. If he had received word of Maxen Pendery, surely his reputation had also been told.

"What know you of him?" Edwin asked.

"He vows he will not rest until Thomas's murderer is found. He says—"

"You have spoken with him."

She moistened her lips. "He came to me ere my escape."

"Why?"

"To learn your whereabouts."

"He believes I killed his brother."

"Aye, though I told him I did it."

Harsh laughter burst from Edwin. "Ever the martyr, Rhiannyn."

"But I feared he would—"

"Did he believe you?"

She shook her head.

"Then your fears are founded."

"Not if we leave Andredeswald. We could go north—"

"Run?" Edwin looked about him. "Hear that, men? The *lady* thinks us cowards."

Rhiannyn stepped forward and gripped his arm. "Do not speak thus, Edwin. 'Tis peace I seek. If you continue to fight, more will die—on both sides."

"I can think of no better cause than driving the Normans from our lands and avenging the deaths of our men, women, and children."

He did not speak of Hastings, but of the village in which he had been returned to life. Much of it had been burnt to the ground and most of his people murdered—all because they would not yield their food supplies to the contingent Duke William sent out prior to the confrontation between himself and England's King Harold.

"This Maxen is said to have killed many at Hastings," Rhiannyn pressed on. "He—"

"And I did not kill many?" Edwin growled. "Hastings was about death, Rhiannyn. Everyone killed, some even their own."

"Listen to me! Maxen Pendery is The Bloodlust Warrior of Hastings. He did not just kill, he slaughtered. This has to end!"

Edwin pried her hand from his arm. "'Twill end when the Normans are dead." He pushed her toward Aethel and started to turn away. Pausing, he asked, "How did you escape?"

She pressed her shoulders back. "Christophe released me from my prison cell."

Edwin frowned. "You did not consider it could be a ruse?"

"He would not do that."

"Spineless whelp!" His upper lip curled. "But mayhap that child's heart of his will be the Penderys' undoing." He nodded as if to himself and strode opposite.

Rhiannyn would have liked to go back into Aethel's arms, but she bore the stares of those she had grown up amongst—Saxons who refused to crop their hair or shave their faces in the Norman style. Some looked upon her with accusation, others with suspicion, and yet others regarded her with uncertainty. All because she had shown heart for a dying man.

Was Thomas's murderer among them? Had Edwin discovered the one responsible?

Dora broke the silence, muttering as she pushed her way among the others with surprising speed for one whose body was so bent. She halted before Rhiannyn and squinted up from beneath the hood which draped her white hair and protected her pink eyes from light. "You are returned to us."

"She is injured," Aethel said.

"Looks fine to me. Nothing a scrub and good meal cannot make right."

"She took a knock at the back of her neck—"

Dora waved Aethel to silence. "I do not remember Rhiannyn ever having trouble speaking for herself. Let her tell me."

Rhiannyn had every intention of denying her ailments, proving she was of good stock and fortitude, but her swaying body did not agree.

"I am fine," she gasped when Aethel's arms came around her.

"'Course you are," he said. "Just keeping you close."

Dora stepped nearer, with cool, bony hands touched Rhiannyn's neck, felt up the sides of her face, and pressed her brow. She leapt backward. "A curse is upon you! I feel it to my bones."

Thomas's curse, that if she would not belong to a Pendery, she would belong to no man.

Rhiannyn told herself it was foolish to give the curse any credence, but how could the old woman know?

Quieting the others' murmurings with the flap of a hand, Dora prompted, "'Tis true, aye?"

Though Rhiannyn reminded herself she did not believe in curses, justifying her acceptance of Thomas's by telling herself it was his due, a part of her was still turned that way. And it frightened her. "I am not cursed," she said.

Eyes sparkling amid the shadow of her hood, Dora said, "You lie like a Norman," then jutted her chin at Aethel. "Bring her. If I am to lift the curse, there is much to be done ere night falls."

6

"WEAK!" EDWIN DENOUNCED.

Perspiration running into her eyes and salting her lips, Rhiannyn spun around. Arm strained by the sword with which she had been practicing, she stared at Edwin.

A blade propped on his shoulder, the sling that had supported his injured arm recently abandoned, he swept her with a look of distaste.

"Weak?" she said, struggling to maintain the composure that had held her in good stead this past fortnight of trials and troubles, suspicion and ostracism.

"Aye, like a woman."

"I *am* a woman."

He raised his eyebrows. "What I should have said is you are weak like a woman bred of Normans."

It was best not to engage in such talk, but she said, "Again, I remind you I am Saxon."

"As you are fond of stating, though you have yet to prove it."

Rhiannyn released the sword to the ground and threw her hands up, revealing blisters. "This past sennight, I have swung a sword half again as heavy as your own, and yet you say I have not proven loyalty to my people?"

Though she knew he had set her to learning the sword as punishment, in the camp were several women who trained in the use of weaponry. It was not because there were not enough men. Rather, it was thought trained women would be useful against unsuspecting Normans.

Edwin grabbed one of her hands and examined the palm. "Nay, you have not proven loyalty." He released her, retrieved her sword, and extended it. "Take it, and nevermore let me see it cast upon the ground."

Inwardly, she groaned. Made for training, the sword was more unwieldy than those used in combat, its purpose being to accustom a man to the weapon and develop his muscles. Thus, going into battle, a soldier's sword would feel relatively light and easily maneuverable. When Rhiannyn had asked Aethel the reason she alone practiced with this one, he had said with apology that no others were out of favor with Edwin.

She sighed, squared her shoulders, and took the sword.

Edwin motioned her to the pel, a wooden post protruding from the ground that displayed the marks she had made this day in her attempt to master the swing of the blade.

She stepped forward and struck it hard. Though the impact jolted her head to toe, she struck again. The second blow fell short of the first by inches, and the next by several more. Still, she ignored Edwin's mutterings and persisted in proving him wrong.

She was beginning to fear she would collapse in a sweat-stained heap when urgent shouts were heard. She swung around and watched as four riders burst upon the glade, all but one recognizable as a follower of Edwin.

On a horse whose better days were scarcely within memory, the stranger was out of place. Wearing a shabby russet-colored mantle, under which the skirts of a robe could be seen, the large man sat his horse with unease. More than his garments and his awkward carriage, his tonsured head with its fringe of hair set him apart from Edwin's rebels. The Saxons had brought a monk into their midst.

Rhiannyn propped the sword against the pel and followed Edwin across the glade to where the men had dismounted.

"Found him wandering the wood," a stout Saxon said. "Told us the Normans are after him."

"Aye, and meant to kill him," another added.

Though it was not unusual for Saxons fleeing Norman oppression to seek refuge in Andredeswald and join the rebellion, swelling its ranks to more than ninety strong, Edwin would be skeptical. Placing himself before the monk, he asked, "You are Saxon?"

The monk inclined his head.

"By what name are you called, Brother?"

"Justus." The man's voice was resonant, without hint of foreign accent that might put lie to his claim. "Brother Justus of St. Augustine."

A peculiar sensation pricked Rhiannyn—a feeling she had encountered this monk before. She swept her gaze up his great height, across his broad shoulders, and onto his rugged yet attractive face. A long nose, with a slight bend that testified to its having been broken in the past, yielded to prominent cheekbones. Lower, lightly stubbled planes revealed a hard jaw, and in his chin was a cleft so deep its shadow appeared to be a dark smudge on his skin.

Working her way back up, she picked out blue eyes fringed by lashes the same dark brown as the hair growing out of its severe tonsure cut. Aye, a handsome man, but she had not met him. She would remember one of such size and countenance, especially a monk.

"You say the Normans make after you?" Edwin asked.

"Aye."

"For what purpose?"

Brother Justus gave a sorrowful shake of the head. "The clergy arriving from Normandy think naught of impugning the reputation of the saints, of scattering the relics of centuries past, of…" He turned his hands up. "In my anger, I challenged them, and have been marked a heretic."

"You flee them."

The monk nodded and clasped his hands before him. Large, powerful hands, as if fashioned for weapons rather than prayer. Might they be more familiar with a hilt than a psalter?

"It is my shame I run from them," he said, "but it was that or death."

"Why Andredeswald?"

"In the open, 'tis not difficult to spot a man of God. I thought to take refuge a short time in the wood, but wandered astray and could not find the way out."

"Which is how we came upon him," the stout Saxon said.

Edwin looked to the men who had brought the monk. "Was he followed?"

"We waited to see if 'twas so," one answered, "but there are no signs of others. Still, I left Uric and Daniel behind to keep watch."

Edwin returned his attention to Brother Justus. "As you can see, we are outcasts ourselves—Saxons who wish our lands free of the heathens who have stolen them."

The monk moved his benevolent gaze over the faces before him. However, when his blue eyes met Rhiannyn's, they turned fiery. But then he blinked and, gaze once more mild, looked higher to her hair straggling from its thick braid.

Only when he returned his attention to Edwin did she realize she held her breath.

"Continue," Brother Justus said.

Edwin widened his stance. "As we are without spiritual guidance, mayhap you would join us."

"And minister to these good people?"

"Good?" Edwin scoffed. "Perhaps once, but now our days are filled with every manner of sin." He smiled. "Aye, minister to them, hear their confessions and absolve them of their misdeeds, but do not try to make them good—not yet."

The monk's brow furrowed as if he deliberated the offer.

"There is but one answer," Edwin said.

Brother Justus arched an eyebrow. "What is that?"

"Acceptance."

"And if I do not accept?"

Edwin smiled broadly. "As I said, there is but one answer."

He did not trust the monk and would not allow him to leave, Rhiannyn realized.

"Then I must needs accept," Brother Justus said.

Edwin stepped forward and clapped him on the shoulder. "Welcome to Andredeswald." He pivoted and strode toward Aethel who stood to Rhiannyn's left.

"What is your name?" Brother Justus called to him.

Edwin looked around.

The monk shrugged. "I must call you something."

"I am Edwin."

The man inclined his head, and when he lowered his gaze, Rhiannyn's misgivings swelled.

Edwin continued forward and drew Aethel aside. "Watch him closely," he said low.

Relieved to find his good judgment held, Rhiannyn turned toward the camp and her mind to imaginings of the pallet that awaited her weary body.

"Rhiannyn!" Edwin called. "You are not finished with the sword."

She halted, struggled against the impulse to name him things most foul for trying to reduce her to tears, and came back around. "Lead on."

Maxen, now Brother Justus to the Saxons, watched Rhiannyn cross the glade behind Edwin Harwolfson. At first sight, he had been uncertain she was the same woman who had spent weeks in a prison cell, her resemblance to that creature fairly distant.

But it was she, and more lovely than he had imagined she would be beneath the dirt, grime, and bruises. Hair that had barely whispered of gold gleamed, the cream of her skin was accented by the flush of roses in her cheeks, and a shape that had promised much beneath her tattered bliaut had more than fulfilled that promise in the belted tunic and hose she wore to practice the sword. She was easily capable of luring men to their deaths, and given the chance, she would do so again. He had felt her resolve and seen it in her stiffening spine when Harwolfson had called her back to task. A small woman with the strength of many.

But he would break her.

Harwolfson was now instructing her where they stood before a pel, sweeping his arm from on high to low as if he wielded a sword, then stepping back and motioning her forward.

As she assumed the proper stance, angling her sword in readiness for a mock attack, Maxen wondered if the Saxon rebel had lain with her. But then Rhiannyn dealt the wooden post an admirable blow, speeding his thoughts elsewhere.

Perhaps she had spoken true. Perhaps she *had* murdered Thomas. He pondered it a long moment before once more determining it was another.

He swept his gaze over those who had returned to training. Their swings strong, aims sure, they promised a well-matched battle when next they set themselves to take back what they claimed was theirs.

It is theirs, a voice reminded.

Was theirs, he countered.

Regardless, he must not forget his reason for coming into Harwolfson's grim world. It had been a restless two weeks since he had allowed Rhiannyn to escape. That day, he had followed her here, thanking God none of the sentries had spotted him. Knowing if he appeared too soon after her arrival it would cast greater suspicion on him, he had returned to Etcheverry. As Rhiannyn had revealed the way to the camp, it would have been expedient to immediately bring his men against it and stamp out Harwolfson's rebellion, but that would not necessarily deliver Thomas's murderer to him—not directly.

Though Maxen had listened in on Rhiannyn's conversation with Christophe and heard her tell it was not Harwolfson who had killed Thomas, he had not believed it until he had himself seen the injury to the man's sword arm. As she had said, it would have been impossible for him to throw the dagger after receiving such a serious wound. But then, which of these men had bled out Thomas's life?

The fire in him growing, Maxen saw the approach of the one Harwolfson had surely ordered to keep watch over the monk and lowered his gaze so the hulking man would not see what was surely in his eyes.

Soon, he told himself, *every one of Harwolfson's rebels will know the yoke of Norman rule, including Rhiannyn.*

First, though, he must discover Thomas's murderer.

7

⌘

"THIS TROUBLES ME."

Until he spoke, Rhiannyn had not known Edwin was behind her. She had been too engrossed in the gathering before the campfire to heed his approach.

"What do you mean?" she asked, keeping her back to him.

"There is something about Brother Justus. I do not trust him."

"As you do not trust me?"

He laid a hand on her shoulder and began kneading the strained muscles there. "Perhaps."

Having expected something different—scornful words, a reprimand, even rough handling—Rhiannyn was surprised by his gentle touch. And unnerved. Did it mean the trials to which he had subjected her were at an end? Was this forgiveness?

"He speaks the word well," she said, having discovered a liking for Brother Justus's deep, cultured voice, and especially his message.

"That he does."

"Still, you are suspicious."

"Are you not? I saw it in your eyes yesternoon when he arrived."

"Aye, but he does seem genuine."

"He has been here not even two days," Edwin reminded her, "and yet you would toss caution aside and embrace him?"

"Not entirely." She wished Edwin would take his hand from her. Considering all he demanded of her, this small intimacy made her uncomfortable, and not a little resentful. In the next instant, his breath brushed the side of her neck, next his lips.

"Do not!" She lurched forward.

He caught her about the waist and pulled her back against him. "None can see, Rhiannyn."

True, for she had chosen to watch Brother Justus's oration from a distance—in back of the others and from among the bordering trees. But this was not the reason she protested. Simply, it felt wrong, especially since she had accepted Thomas's curse that she would never know marriage or motherhood.

"'Tis improper," she hissed.

"We are betrothed."

"Are we? That is the first I have heard of it since I arrived."

He chuckled near her ear. "Of course we are. That has not changed."

It had, but the time was not right to tell him. Latching on to the one thing certain to douse his desire—a question she had put to him several times—she said, "Have you discovered Thomas's murderer?"

He tensed. "Leave it be, Rhiannyn. Whomever it was, 'tis done."

She turned and peered into his hard, flushed face. "It is not done. Were it, Maxen Pendery would not be planning our deaths."

She spoke of the bits she had overheard from those who spied on the Penderys. It was said the castle was being fortified, great blocks of stone arriving to replace the wooden palisades. The training of knights and men-at-arms lasted far into the night, and the steady ring of metal testified to the forging of weapons.

"My goal is no different," Edwin reminded her, the mouth that had tenderly touched her flesh now a thin line. "The Normans will leave England, and those who do not will possess no more than the soil in which their bodies rot."

Deciding it best to remove herself from him, she stepped back. He let her go, but as she moved toward her tent, a high-pitched wail sounded. She swung around.

Wan hair flying, old Dora swooped upon those assembled before the fire. "A traitor amongst us!" she screeched. "I have seen it."

As something crept beneath Rhiannyn's skin, warning her to make herself scarce, Edwin swept past her.

"A Judas!" Dora cried, searching the faces that turned from the monk to her. "Our downfall."

Some of the Saxons rose to their feet, while others cowered and looked away as if fearful she might name them the betrayer.

Dora lurched near Brother Justus and demanded, "Where is she, oh man of a god who is not?"

"There is only one God," he said solemnly. "The God of the Christians. And He *is*."

"Liar!" She set herself at him, but he stepped aside, and she clawed only air.

"Dora!" Edwin called.

She snapped around. "I have seen it, Edwin." Moonlight glistened on spittle wending a path from one corner of her mouth to her chin. "So clear!" Her eyes rolled. "The ruin of our people."

As if to gentle a child, he put a hand on her shoulder. "No more, Dora."

"But I have seen it!"

He took her arm and urged her away. "Come. You are not feeling well."

Her shoulders slumped, but when she caught sight of Rhiannyn, she leveled a bony finger at her. "She is the one!"

Rhiannyn longed to flee, but even when Dora broke from Edwin and rushed at her, she could not move. Before she could think to brace herself, the wild-eyed woman toppled her to the ground.

As Rhiannyn threw her arms up to defend herself against the nails raking her neck, Edwin hauled the old woman to her feet.

"She has come to feed us death," Dora cried. "She is the one who will betray us."

Pressing a hand to her scored flesh, Rhiannyn sat up. "Never would I betray you!"

Dora strained against Edwin's hold, bared her teeth. "It is seen. If you do not bleed now, you will end our bid to oust the Normans from our lands. *You* will be our undoing."

Dear Lord, she means to kill me, Rhiannyn thought as the voices of those gathered around rose, evidencing their Christian beliefs had yet to unseat superstition, especially in the presence of one believed to have worked miracles.

"By my hand and my words," Dora continued, "I will make all things right, even if I have to call upon darkness—"

"Dora!" Edwin barked. "I have told you, sorcery has no place here."

She took hold of his tunic. "I speak true! Rhiannyn will betray us. And not alone."

He closed the mouth he had opened to further rebuke her, and when he spoke again, there was interest in his voice. "What do you mean not alone?"

"I was given the sight of another who will betray us, a faceless one who will make a child on Rhiannyn and—"

Edwin thrust her from him. "She will be my wife and lie with me. Dare you accuse me of being a traitor?"

Dora raised hands that looked almost prayerful. "Though you wish it, she will never lie with you, Edwin. 'Tis another she will fornicate with. And for that, she must die."

"Silence!"

Dora stepped toward him. "Did I not breathe life back into you?" At his hesitation, she said, "Deny the power with which I have been gifted, but without it, there would be no Edwin Harwolfson. Without it, there would be no hope for our people."

Those words proved the undoing of a handful of men. They surged past Dora and Edwin and seized Rhiannyn.

"Traitor," one spat.

"Harlot!" cried another.

More joined them and began dragging her away.

"Edwin!" Rhiannyn cried.

He took a single step toward her.

Despairing of him, she sought and found the big man who stood back from the others. "Aethel!"

Though his face reflected struggle, neither did he move.

It was Brother Justus who answered her pleas by placing himself before the swell of Saxons intent on carrying out Dora's sentence. "In the name of our Lord, I order you to release the woman!"

They halted, and the babble of voices lowered to murmurs.

"Are you pagans?" Brother Justus demanded. "Do you believe the ramblings of one who is of the devil, rather than He whom I spoke of this eve? There is no place in Heaven for those who follow the beast. Are you, then, content with Hell?"

Rhiannyn was as awed by his words and austere countenance as the others, for in this moment, there was something terribly holy about him—something that might make one believe had they not before.

The silence grew oppressive, then the hands holding her opened, and she fell to the ground. Pained by the ribs injured when Aethel had knocked her from her horse, she bit back a cry.

"Do not listen to him!" Dora screamed. "He has not seen what I have seen, does not know what I know! Take her now!"

When none moved to do her bidding, she darted to Rhiannyn's side, grasped her arm, and began dragging her upright. "She must die!"

Brother Justus strode forward and pried her fingers from Rhiannyn's arm. "Away with you, witch!"

Dora sucked air, but before she could spit in his face, he thrust her back. She stumbled around to face Edwin. "See what the outsider does! I warn you, kill the betrayer and send this man away, else your battle is done!"

Edwin momentarily closed his eyes. "He is right, Dora. We are Christians."

"Death upon us!" she cried and dropped to her knees. "Death to the proud Saxon race!"

Edwin walked wide around her and halted alongside Brother Justus. "You are without injury, Rhiannyn?"

She touched a dirt-scuffed palm to her clawed neck, held it away, and considered the crimson lines. "I am," she whispered.

He reached down and cupped her chin. "Betray me, lie with another, and your fate is decided. Understood?"

She nodded.

He released her and strode to where the old woman writhed on the ground. "Come, Dora, you need sleep."

She hissed, rolled up onto her feet, and ran toward the cave where she spent most of her days and few of her nights. Where she went after dark, no one knew.

When Edwin followed her, Rhiannyn dropped her head and squeezed her eyes closed, remaining thus until Brother Justus said, "Give me your hand."

She looked from his broad palm to an unreadable face that might have shone with condemnation for all the compassion she saw there. The holiness he had exuded a short while ago seemed to have fled, his eyes sparkling with something she could not name, though it disturbed her.

She shifted her gaze to those who had remained following Dora's fit. Furtive glances revealing their misgivings, they slowly withdrew.

"Your hand," Brother Justus repeated when they were alone.

She placed it in his, and he raised her without effort. Doubtless, beneath his robes he was as solid as she had supposed from his appearance.

"Know I believe you," he said, his fingers remaining closed around hers.

Once more, strange sensation coursed through her. Once more, she wondered if they had met before.

She pulled her hand free and rubbed her sore ribs. "Why do you believe me?" she asked.

His blue gaze dark in the night, he said, "As I would not forsake our people, neither do I believe you would."

"But Dora—"

"Are you not Christian enough to put your faith in God, rather than a crone who speaks heretical madness?"

A crone who knew things others did not, Rhiannyn considered, a crone who had brought Edwin back from the dead.

"I fear her," she murmured.

"Then mayhap you are not well with God. Would you care to speak of it?" At her hesitation, he added, "'Twill do your soul good."

Her soul. Memories of Thomas and her role in his death assailing her, she stared into the face upon which firelight danced. "Think you I yet have one, Brother Justus?"

A slight smile moved his lips. "Why would you not?"

Could she speak to him of God? Might it ease her burden?

Taking a chance that surprised her, she said, "There is much that weighs upon my conscience."

"Let us speak of it." He motioned her to precede him, and Rhiannyn crossed to the fire and seated herself on a log.

The monk lowered beside her, the folds of his robe all that prevented their legs from touching.

She started to scoot farther down the log, but movement among the trees stilled her.

"Now," Brother Justus said, "tell me—"

"There." She lifted her chin toward two figures standing close, partly in shadow, partly in moonlight. "Do you see them?"

"Aye."

"Know you what they do?"

After some moments, he said in a voice edged with what sounded like disapproval, "They speak vows, this night shall be made one."

Rhiannyn turned her face to him. "You think it wrong?"

He gave her his gaze, and it was so probing, she wished he had not. "It is the Saxon way of things."

"You say that as if you are not Saxon yourself."

"As I am a man of God, I am first of the Church."

The Church that, though a marriage required only the consent of both parties and consummation to be valid, had begun to press for priests to stand witness to the making of man and wife—even when there were witnesses aplenty. This eve in Andredeswald, beneath the heavens and in sight of God, the only other eyes upon the two who pledged their lives to each other were those of Rhiannyn and Brother Justus. And they were surely unseen.

Returning her gaze to the couple, Rhiannyn said, "I think it a beautiful thing."

After some moments, the monk said, "It is, though those of the nobility who would pass property to their children ought not to risk a clandestine marriage."

Or Saxon women who wed Normans, she mused, having heard how easily one marriage had been undone when the husband tired of his wife.

"Now speak to me of your soul," Brother Justus prompted.

Rhiannyn held up a staying hand until the couple had kissed and walked deeper into the wood, then she leaned forward and peered into the fire. "I fear for it, that there may be no way of saving it."

"You are wrong."

Her thoughts returned to her first night in Andredeswald when Dora had pronounced Thomas's curse lifted following an oft-repeated incantation and a drink so bitter Rhiannyn had feared her throat would swell closed.

She shook her head. "I know I should not believe in curses, and mostly I do not, but I deserve to be cursed. And I have been."

The monk was so quiet, she glanced sidelong to confirm he had not slipped away.

"By whom?" he said.

"The man whose death I am responsible for."

Maxen stared at Rhiannyn's profile, containing the anger bounding through him with the promise he would free it at a better time and place. He must remain calm, else he might never know what she held close.

"Have I shocked you?" she asked.

He clenched his hands beneath his long sleeves. "Only in that you have staked your soul to the belief God serves man by working curses upon others—that words spoken in anger grant divine power over one who is wished ill."

Maxen waited on her response, but after minutes passed, he said, "Tell me how you are responsible for this man's death."

She gripped her hands in her lap. "I ran from him, and when he gave chase…" She raked her teeth over her bottom lip. "I should not have fled."

Maxen put a finger beneath her chin, lifted her head, and delved eyes bright with tears. Her sorrow touching him, he hardened himself and said, "Though you claim responsibility for his death, surely you did not kill him?"

Her eyes widened, "Ah, nay."

"Who, then?"

"I…"

He saw the moment something bid her to keep her secret, and berated himself for being so eager he had not guarded his own eyes. Likely she had seen a light in their depths that had nothing to do with the fire that crackled and breathed warmth upon them.

She stood and stepped away. "It matters not. He is dead, and nothing can change that."

Forcing an expression of puzzlement, Maxen rose. "But it does matter—if I am to help you."

She shook her head. "I thank you for coming to my aid, and you have been kind to listen, but I have no further need of assistance."

She turned from him, and he threw out an arm to detain her. However, he pulled it back, fearing that to allow another glimpse of the man beneath the robes would prove his undoing.

"Good eve," he called as she hastened to her tent.

Once she slipped inside, he left the camp and strode to the distant glade where the pel was set in the ground. Seeking an outlet for his emotions, he took up the sword Rhiannyn had left alongside the wooden post, made his grip, and in the light of a moon crossed by clouds, swung at earth and air. Again. And again.

"The one."

As the hoarsely spoken words snatched Rhiannyn from sleep, her mouth was forced open and something was shoved inside.

She screamed against the gag and fought hands that bound her wrists and ankles. It was too dark to identify her assailants, but she knew Dora led them, she who had pronounced death upon Edwin's betrothed.

Dear Lord, Rhiannyn prayed, *let this be but a terrible dream from which I may awaken.*

Hands gripped her ankles, dragged her off her pallet, and out into a moonlit night just beginning to yield to day. Frantically, she searched beyond the four figures surrounding her, but no others were in sight.

Certain her struggle for life would be a solitary one unless she could alert others, she reached to the gag with her bound hands.

Immediately, her arms were forced above her head.

She writhed and screamed into the wadded cloth, but it was not likely enough to rouse anyone.

"Carry her," Dora hissed.

One of the figures lifted Rhiannyn and dropped her over his shoulder, pinning her arms under the weight of her own body. Then he began a jarring walk out of the camp.

"Hurry," Dora urged.

When Thomas had died in her arms, Rhiannyn had thought she would welcome death as an escape from the pain and misery caused by the coming of the Normans, but no longer. Regardless of what her future held, she wanted one. She wanted to live.

As she was carried deeper into the wood, she strained and bucked and kicked, and did not stop when the one carrying her halted.

"Cast her in," Dora ordered.

That stilled Rhiannyn, but before she could fully accept the meaning of those words, the man swung her off his shoulder and began to lower her.

Shrieking around the gag, she snatched hold of his tunic, but the weight of her descending body tore it from her fingers and she slammed to the bottom of a pit.

As the musty smell of freshly cut earth assailed her, the soil loosened by her descent sprinkled on her in a cruel mockery of what was to come. She lifted her joined hands, pulled the gag from her mouth, and loosed a scream so thin, it barely carried above her head.

Desperately working her tongue to return moisture to her mouth, she reached up, searched the walls on either side of her, and latched onto a frayed root. Dragging herself to sitting, she screamed louder and was quieted by a fist to the temple that dropped her onto her back.

"Nay!" Dora protested. "She must feel her death. Bring the stone."

Though dazed, Rhiannyn managed to turn onto her stomach in the narrow space and rise to her knees, but before she could get her feet beneath her, a hand slammed into her back and knocked her facedown, catching her bound hands beneath her. Then something painfully heavy was laid across her back and lower body.

"Nay!" She strained against the weight, scraping her hands and tearing her nails as she scrabbled at the earth in an attempt to push herself upright. "Oh, Lord," she cried, "not like this. Pray, not like this!"

"He does not hear you," Dora said with sickening satisfaction.

Rhiannyn snapped her head to the side and looked up.

The woman's white hair and pale face a blotch against the dark sky, she continued, "But I hear you, and I say death upon you." Then she straightened, motioned to the faceless men, and began chanting strange words.

As dirt poured down on Rhiannyn, she filled her lungs and emptied them on high-pitched wails, calling to the only one who could help her now. But still the dirt descended—shovelful by shovelful burying her alive.

And giving Thomas's curse its due.

8

Aʀɪsɪɴɢ ᴛʜʀᴏᴜɢʜ ᴛʜᴇ haze of uneasy sleep, Maxen thought it a bird, but when it cried out again, he knew it was human. Rhiannyn?

He thrust off the pel he had dozed against and surged upright. Sword in hand, he sprinted across the darkened glade.

The monk's gown hindering him, catching between his feet and legs, he halted, dropped the sword, and dragged the garment off. Going into battle armored only in long braies and undertunic, he reclaimed the battered sword and thundered into the wood.

With the next scream, he corrected his course, veering to the left into thickening trees whose gnarly branches raked his exposed flesh. Deeper he ran until he heard the grunting of men, the old witch's voice, and another scream ending on a whimper.

He bellowed and vaulted into the clearing. Instinct guiding him more than the dawning light, he struck the first man alongside the head with a blade so dull, it had naught but impact to prove itself worthy. But it served well enough, as evidenced by the crack of bone.

"The false monk!" Dora cried where she stood alongside a gaping hole. "Kill him!"

The shadow beside her divided into two men, both wielding weapons.

Blood boiling, as in days past when he had first and foremost been a warrior, Maxen lunged at the larger of the two, knocked aside the spade swung at him, and countered with a blow to his opponent's midriff. As the man doubled over, Maxen turned his efforts upon the other who aimed a branch at his head.

An upward sweep of the sword sent the primitive weapon flying, but it did not stop the one who wielded it. He hurled himself at Maxen, and they fell together.

The sword ineffective in such close quarters, Maxen released it and captured the man's descending fist in his palm, then thrust his weight to the side and rolled the Saxon beneath him. "It is done," he growled and placed his hand over the man's face and wrenched it hard left. The snapping of the Saxon's neck coincided with a burn in Maxen's side.

He lurched back onto his knees, and as he stared at the dagger protruding from him, the dead man's spasming fingers released the hilt. An instant later, Maxen saw the shadow creeping over him and felt death on the back of his neck.

He pulled the blade from his side, twisted around, and threw it at the Saxon who had first come at him with a shovel. It caught the man high in the shoulder and staggered him back. For a moment, he stood unmoving, then he turned and fled.

Pressing a hand to his side to stem the blood, Maxen stood and swept his gaze over the area.

On hands and knees, the old woman labored to push dirt into the hole.

"Witch!" Maxen shouted, and forgetting the fire in his side, bolted forward.

She sprang upright. "The death of us!" she screeched and ran.

Though he longed to pursue her, Rhiannyn was a more immediate concern. The grave being too narrow for him to go into, he flattened himself beside it and reached for the still figure beneath loosely piled dirt.

Had he come too late? Telling himself the dread he felt was for the secret she might take with her into death, he caught hold of her shoulders and managed to raise her several inches before meeting resistance.

He thrust aside the dirt, slid his hands over her facedown body, and found the stone. It was awkward, positioned as he was above her, but he hefted it off. Grasping her beneath the arms, he pulled her from the grave and lowered her onto her back.

"Rhiannyn!" he called, wiping dirt from her face.

She did not respond.

He pressed a hand between her breasts. No rise and fall, no fluttering heartbeat.

Fury flooded him. He had not killed two men to rescue a dead woman!

Gripping her shoulders, he shook her, but she made no protest.

"Lord," he rasped, "let not the wickedness in me forever shadow any good."

It was then he recalled the words Guy had spoken at the monastery—that an old witch had pulled Harwolfson from beneath the dead and breathed life back into him.

Maxen lowered Rhiannyn's jaw and placed his mouth over hers. He blew once and again, but his breath immediately returned to him by way of her nostrils. He pinched them closed. It took four more breaths before, miraculously, he captured her groan his mouth.

Hardly able to believe he had returned life to her, he held her as she coughed and spat dirt. Finally, she sank against him and narrowly raised her lids. "What...?" she whispered. "I do not..."

"Dora tried to murder you," he said, resenting how protective he felt.

Her clouded eyes cleared, only to widen with horror. Beginning to shake, she gasped, "They buried me. Alive."

Maxen fought the impulse to comfort her. And lost. He smoothed the hair back from her brow and pressed a palm to her cheek. "You live," he said as her tears wet his hand. "You are well."

Am I? Rhiannyn wondered, chest tight with sobs she longed to loose. *Will my mind hold after this?*

Recalling the dirt falling down around her, straining her head back to keep her mouth clear for the breath needed to scream to those who did not hear, she said, "I called, but no one came."

"I came," Brother Justus said.

Thus, she lived, but how had he saved her? He was but a monk against the four who had taken her.

Lowering her gaze over him, she noted the absence of his clerical gown. Stretched across a broad chest and shoulders half again as wide as hers, he wore only an undertunic woven of such light cloth the perspiration causing it to cling outlined the muscles beneath.

"The false monk," she murmured. "I heard her call you that." She returned her gaze to his. "Are you false, Brother Justus?"

His lids narrowed, and he jutted his chin to a place beyond her. "I have killed as a man of God should not do."

She saw a body ten feet from her, and another farther out. Two men dead. What of the third? What of Dora? Were they in the trees awaiting another opportunity to kill them both?

She sniffed back tears. "There were three with Dora. I see two."

"The third was wounded. Had he not run, I would have taken his life as well."

The monk had killed to save her, and though she was grateful, her unease deepened. "Are you truly a man of God?"

He pulled away and stood. "I was, and now no more."

"But—"

"We must go. Dora will return with others, and if we are here, it could mean both our deaths."

She pushed to sitting. "Where will we go?" she asked. Where would a woman named a traitor and hated by Saxons and Normans alike, and a monk turned murderer, be welcome?

"I know a place," he said and strode to one of the dead.

The sound of tearing fabric startled Rhiannyn, and a moment later she saw the reason for the destruction of the Saxon's tunic. Thinking she must be in a state of shock not to have noticed the blood draining from the monk's side, she exclaimed, "You have been hurt."

"I will live." He wound the material around his waist, tore off another strip, and secured it as well. Shortly, he crossed to the other body—a man more his size—and divested him of his clothes. After donning the rough garments, he returned to her.

"Your hands," he said.

She raised them, and winced as the flat of a blade touched the insides of her wrists. Her fetters fell away, and as she rubbed the blood into her hands, he severed the rope binding her ankles.

"Come." He pulled her to her feet.

Head reeling, she staggered against him. "A moment, please," she beseeched.

"Do you wish to live?" he demanded.

"Aye, but—"

"Then move your feet. Now!"

9

"We will rest here awhile," Brother Justus said.

Rhiannyn walked to the stream that had beckoned hours earlier when they had first begun following it, and lowered to her knees. She dipped her hands in the water and splashed it over her face and neck. Gasping and blinking, she savored the cold trickling over her heated skin, then scooped more handfuls until the front of her perspiration-dampened tunic was soaked through.

Heart beating briskly from the pace the monk had forced upon her, she lifted the hem of her tunic to dry her face. And paused over her distorted reflection.

On the surface of the water was something of the young woman she had been, the layers of age and wear peeled away to reveal herself to her again. Granted, she appeared older than her ten and eight years, but much fresher than the thirty she had looked upon escaping her prison cell. And she was alive.

Shying away from remembrances of what had transpired hours earlier, she buried her face in the tunic and rubbed vigorously—as if doing so would banish those memories. But they were there when she lifted her head.

"Leave me be," she whispered. It was not her pleading, but a movement on the water that caused the memories to slip away. Looking nearer upon it, she saw it was the reflection of the one who stood behind her.

Brother Justus's mouth was a thin line, eyes dark with what seemed accusation.

The sensation that had bothered her when he had first come into the rebel camp—a feeling she knew him—beckoned her back in time and closed fingers around her throat.

She gasped and leapt to her feet.

"Something is amiss?" he asked, reaching to steady her.

She sidestepped.

"What is it?" His expression was one of concern, a poor fit for the man she had glimpsed in the water, a man who, with the shedding of his clerical gown, appeared to have shed the last of his holiness as well.

"Naught. I…" She lowered her gaze, and the peculiar sensation turned to shame when she saw her wet garment was molded to her chest.

Hoping Brother Justus had not noticed, she glanced up and discovered the carelessness with which she had cooled herself *had* captured his interest. He did not regard her with monk's eyes, but with the eyes of a man not forbidden the fruit of women.

Rhiannyn clapped a hand to her chest and lifted the material from her skin. "I have not thanked you for saving my life. I owe you much."

"Aye, you do."

His slow, deliberate agreement summoned forth that which shame had sped to the back of her mind, and she began to shiver. This sensation was remembrance of when Maxen Pendery had stood before her blindfolded eyes at Etcheverry.

But could it be? She searched the monk's face, looked higher to his dark hair. In no way did he resemble Thomas or Christophe. The hair coloring was different, his features too defined. And his voice—she detected none of the thick French accent, nor the strained, rasping quality with which that man had spoken. Too, Christophe had said his eldest brother was a warrior, and this man was undoubtedly trained in the ways of the Church.

But he had also killed as a warrior, surely something no man of God would do.

"I know you," she said, and caught her breath at the realization she had spoken aloud.

Something appeared in his eyes that pried loose her desperate hold on doubt—the predator.

And I am the prey, she realized. Maxen Pendery had carefully laid his deception by denying facility with the Anglo-Saxon language, feigning the thicker French accent of one who had not been raised in England, and allowing her to escape the castle so he could discover the location of Edwin's camp. Then he had come to avenge his brother's death. And he would likely have achieved that end had he not answered her cries for help.

Why had he not sacrificed her? More, what of Edwin and his followers whom she had placed in jeopardy? She had to warn them, even if they killed her for it.

She turned and ran, but within moments, he took her to ground.

Pinned beneath him, she swept her hands through the fallen leaves in search of something with which to defend herself and closed a hand around an embedded rock. Resisting Maxen Pendery's efforts to turn her, she strained and clawed at her weapon. When it came free, she fell onto her back and swung the rock toward his head.

He captured her wrist, forced her arm above her head, and pressed his thumb hard at the base of hers until her hand cramped and fingers uncurled.

"Nay!" she cried and raised her free arm and struck him alongside the head.

He grunted, seized that wrist as well, and pinned it with the other.

With only her legs to defend her, she brought her knee up and into his side.

Though she had not targeted his injury, she knew what she had done when an oath rushed out on the air he expelled. But it did not move him off her.

"Enough!" he barked.

His monk's pretense entirely abandoned, the savage visible in every line of his face, Rhiannyn stilled. "I do know you," she said again, and added, "Maxen Pendery."

His smile was wry. "Nay, you do not. But you shall." Her wrists caught in one hand, he straddled her, felt down his side, and considered the blood on his palm.

Preferring a show of contempt over fear, Rhiannyn said, "Know this, Norman, as you have killed, so will you be killed."

He returned his gaze to her, and she saw his pupils had spread wider, obliterating all color save a dark ring of iris more black than blue.

"You will die," she recklessly pressed on, "the same as—"

"Thomas," he snarled, "and Nils."

It was not his lost brothers she had intended to name, but the great number of his countrymen who, despite their victory at Hastings, had pooled their blood with that of the Saxons.

Maxen felt every beat of his heart as memories returned him to Hastings. He saw himself pull his sword from a Saxon, lift an arm to wipe the blood from his eyes, turn to search out who would die next. And there was Nils—barely alive, though treated as if dead. Without honor, without glory, beyond deplorable.

He yanked himself back to this moment that was not entirely different from the place to which he had briefly gone. Blood was also spilled across this day, not just by those he had prevented from burying this woman alive, but him. And just as Thomas had survived Hastings only to die for her, he might himself.

"Heed me well, Rhiannyn of Etcheverry," he said. "Your life is no longer your own. It belongs to me, to do with as I please. Give me no excuse to see the end of you, and you may live to become a wretched old woman. Give me good cause, and I will do what Dora could not."

Her eyes flashed. "I am no man's possession. You may imprison me, but never will I belong to you."

He raised an eyebrow. "Already you do. Your tears are mine, the secret you hold near is mine."

"Secret?"

"I will have Thomas's murderer. And soon you will deliver him."

She shook her head.

"Soon," he repeated. "Now, we must resume our journey. Will you resist?"

"All the way."

"Then you bring this upon yourself." He untied the rope from his waist, lashed her wrists together, and wrapped the opposite end around his hand. "Your prison awaits," he said as he rose.

She stared up at him. "You do not frighten me."

"Aye, I do." He jerked the rope, a warning he would drag her. "And that is good."

Her defiant expression briefly softened into what seemed despair, then she got her legs beneath her.

"Better," he said.

She raised her chin. "You think so? Do not be so sure, Maxen Pendery. Andredeswald still holds you, and it belongs to Edwin."

He reeled her near. "*My lord,* to you, or have you forgotten?" It was the same as he had ordered her to title him in the dungeon.

"'Tis you who has forgotten," she challenged, "but I will say it again. *Never* will I accept you as my lord."

He smiled. "By the morrow, you will be addressing me properly."

She opened her mouth as if to argue further, closed it, and looked at the blood spreading across his tunic. "Do you intend to reach the castle alive, *Maxen,* we had best not dally."

In this, she was right.

Two things Rhiannyn knew for certain. The first, that the only benefit of trading Dora for Maxen Pendery was that she lived—for now. The second, that she was alone in a world she had not realized was so heavenly before the Normans had crossed the channel and conquered her people.

The curious commoners, the workers on the wall, the men-at-arms atop the gatehouse, and the knights summoned from the donjon all stared as their injured lord led his captive over the drawbridge.

Head high, she fixed her gaze on Pendery's back, refusing all the pleasure of seeing her cower. It was no easy thing with fear bounding through her, but anger—even hatred—helped.

Remember your father and brothers, their lives brutally taken at Hastings, she silently counseled as she passed beneath the gatehouse's portal. *Forget not your mother's death when the roof set afire by Normans collapsed upon her. Feel the terror of your flight into the wood when they sought to defile you. Imprint this moment on your mind—the humiliation to which Pendery subjects you, the chafing of your wrists, the hatred Normans and Saxons alike cast upon you. Remember, Rhiannyn, who is no longer of Etcheverry. Remember.*

Inside the inner bailey, she was presented with another challenge. Sir Ancel, eyes glimmering with satisfaction, nearly withered her resolve. Well she remembered his handling while he had overseen her stay in the dungeon, how he had beaten her and named her the foulest of things female. And now he separated from the other knights to step into her path.

Forced to a halt, she resisted the strain of her lead and met his gaze.

"Saxon whore!" he proclaimed.

She sucked a breath. *Saxon whore. Norman whore.* Ever named, but neither was she. She was Saxon, and that was all, her virtue intact despite what any thought of her.

Though Maxen Pendery was blocked from her view, she felt his gaze though Sir Ancel. Undeterred, she leaned toward the knight and returned the insult. *"Nithing!"*

Coward. It was one of the few Anglo-Saxon words he knew well. It had been shouted at the Normans during the battle of Hastings, and Rhiannyn had spat it at him when he had visited her cell.

Knowing the edge to which she pushed him, she steeled herself for the blow. But though he drew his arm back, Pendery caught it, twisted it behind the knight, and barked, "Stand down!"

Words sputtered from Sir Ancel, and his face flushed, but he had no means of reprisal. "My lord," he grudgingly acceded.

Pendery shoved him aside.

For once, punishment was given elsewhere, and it stunned Rhiannyn. What did it matter if another struck her? Might there be a spark of humanity in The Bloodlust Warrior of Hastings? Or did he simply reserve for himself the pleasure of her suffering?

"Ready yourselves," Pendery ordered his knights. "We ride within the hour."

Rhiannyn pressed her lips to keep from crying out. Though she had prayed his injury would prevent him from going after Edwin and his followers this day, giving them a chance to flee, it was not to be.

When he looked to her, she said, "I beg you, do not."

His eyebrows rose. "Begging is good. But ineffective."

No humanity. Not a spark.

Forgoing the rope, he gripped her arm and pulled her toward the far tower of the gatehouse.

She peered up the great stonework structure. Though its primary function was to guard the castle's entrance, the towers on either side of the portal housed several small rooms intended for captives of higher status than those who were tossed in the cells beneath the donjon.

Surely he did not mean to imprison her here when the alternative better served his revenge?

"Maxen!"

Pendery turned Rhiannyn with him, and she watched Christophe's ungainly approach.

What had not struck her before now did. Christophe had played an important role in his brother's deception, aiding in her escape so Maxen Pendery could discover the location of Edwin's camp. But had he done so knowingly? Or had he also been deceived?

Christophe's expressive eyes begged her to believe he had not known of his brother's plans, but it was not necessary. In her heart, she knew the answer. He had been deceived.

"What is it you wish, Christophe?" Pendery asked.

"You have been injured!" Concern tightened his face as he considered the blood staining his brother's tunic. "Perhaps I—"

"You did not come to discuss my injury, did you?"

Christophe shifted his weight. "I did not, but . . ." He shook his head. "If you would allow it, I would speak with Lady Rhiannyn a moment. A-alone."

"She is a prisoner, and no lady. Return to your books and squander no more time on her."

"But——"

"I have spoken."

Christophe's shoulders sank, and he retreated.

Indignant over Pendery's treatment of his brother, Rhiannyn said, "He is not a child and should not be treated as one."

"Not a child? What, then? A man?"

"Soon—if you show him respect and not beat down his voice."

As if deeming her unworthy of such a discussion, Pendery spun her around to enter the tower.

As the stairway was narrow, there was but one place for her—behind him. In her attempt to keep pace, she stumbled during their ascent, and it was his steely grip that kept her from falling on the steps.

Upon reaching the uppermost floor, he threw open the door and pushed her inside. "Your new home."

Standing in the center of the small, rectangular room, she noted it was empty except for a pallet and basin, its stone floor without benefit of rushes. But it was more livable than the dungeon cell. Why?

She turned and caught the shadow of pain and fatigue in Pendery's eyes before he narrowed them. Though he disguised well the extent of his injury, he had been cut deep and lost an amount of blood that would have laid down most men. She nearly pitied him.

"Why not the dungeon?" she asked.

He thrust his chin at the opening in one wall that threw a wedge of light on the stone floor. "The dungeon has no windows."

With foreboding, she asked, "For what do I require a window?"

He smiled. "I would not wish you to miss the sunrise. It can be quite spectacular when not hidden by English clouds." The smile flattened. "And it will be spectacular. I promise you."

Doubtless, he took pleasure in her misgivings, but soon enough she would know what she did not wish to know. "How thoughtful of you," she said and lifted her bound hands. "And this?"

He strode forward and began loosening the knot. "So simple, Rhiannyn," he said. "All I require is a name."

One she did not have. And it would be futile to continue the lie she had killed Thomas. However, she had to ask, "If I give you the name, will you leave the others be?"

"Harwolfson's followers?"

"Aye."

"*Non.* The rebels cannot be allowed to continue their assaults. Be it by bloodshed or Norman rule, they will be stopped." He pulled the knot free and unwound the rope. "The choice is yours."

Stepping back, she rubbed her wrists.

"As told before," he said as he bundled the rope, "keep your secret and scores will die. Tell me, and they may live."

"I cannot."

"Then it is decided." He crossed the room, stepped out onto the landing, and closed the door.

Hearing the bar fall into place, she whispered, "Run, Edwin. Run, ere 'tis too late."

10

HOLDING HIS SHOULDERS straight, though they ached from the weakening in his side, Maxen approached the far end of the hall where the lord's chamber was situated.

Of course, it could hardly be called a chamber, he thought as he regarded the screen behind which the simple trappings lay. The modest cell he had occupied at the monastery had provided more privacy. Granted, the lord's chamber at Etcheverry was of greater size than the cell, but all that separated it from the rest of the hall was a wooden, many-paneled screen held together by articulating leather hinges. What happened behind the screen could be hidden from eyes, not ears.

Telling himself he must remember this since his knights had last served Sir Ancel and, thus, might remain loyal to the man, Maxen stepped around the screen. Once inside the chamber, he lifted the coarse Saxon tunic he had donned after the struggle with the witch's men and began peeling away the crude bandages. However, the bloody flow having been stemmed, the material stuck fast to the wound.

He dropped the tunic and stepped around the screen to call for water and fresh bandages, but Christophe had anticipated the need. His sideways hitch prominent, he approached alongside a woman servant who carried a basin of water and long strips of linen that fluttered to the rhythm of her swaying hips.

A Saxon woman whose face knew more expression than a glower, Maxen mused as he received her inviting smile. It was a welcome change after Rhiannyn, but not enough to make him want to take her to bed.

Although two years of celibacy made his body ready to know a woman, *he* was not. But eventually he would, for if he must live the sinful life of man, there seemed no reason he should not live all of it. The same as before Hastings, though this time with memories between.

"Sit," Christophe said. "Theta and I will tend you."

Maxen raised an eyebrow. "I did not know you had taken an interest in healing."

"There was a need, and I filled it." Christophe dropped the bag he carried onto the bed.

"What mean you?"

"With the continual warring between Saxons and Normans, there must be someone to care for the sick and fallen."

"There are others trained for that work."

Christophe met his gaze. "There was one, but he is dead."

"How?"

"Murdered." He turned his attention to the contents of his bag.

"Continue," Maxen ordered, annoyed at being forced to rise to his little brother's bait. "What do you wish me to know?"

Christophe came back around. "He was a Saxon, his name Josa, and he was a good man. Much of what I know of healing I learned from him."

"And?"

"He had the misfortune of continued loyalty to his own. In an attack upon the castle when it was first being raised, several Saxons fell. After all quieted, and Josa had finished tending Thomas's injured men, he slipped outside the walls to see if any among his people lived. There was one, and Josa was attempting to aid him when Sir Ancel struck him down with a blow to the head. Murdered."

Though Maxen longed to harden himself against the injustice, he asked, "What of Sir Ancel?"

"You wish to know if he was punished?"

"*Oui.*"

"Thomas was angered, but he did nothing to prevent Ancel from doing the same in the future."

"Then you blame Thomas."

Christophe drew a deep breath. "I am not saying our brother was bad. I am saying he was not good—and certainly not blameless for all the ill that has befallen the Penderys."

Maxen dragged the tunic off over his head. "I have listened," he said, "and I am finished." He lowered to the chest at the foot of the curtained bed to await his brother's ministrations.

"You are a cold man," Christophe said and began removing the dirty bandages.

Though tempted to send him away, Maxen quelled the impulse. If the wound was to be cleansed of any infection that had set in, he needed his younger brother. If he died later, so be it, but not before he had done what he had come to do.

The wound was cleansed, stitched closed, and smeared with a salve so pungent Theta grimaced as she re-bandaged it.

"Rhiannyn is well?" Christophe said, eyes luminous with concern that made Maxen want to shake him.

"As you saw, she lives," he said, then finding the woman servant's fingers too inclined to caress, he took the bandage from her and finished winding it around his waist.

Christophe stepped nearer. "I did not ask that."

Displeased by his championing of Rhiannyn, Maxen said, "Regardless, 'tis your answer."

"Then I shall see for myself."

Maxen caught his arm. "I will not have her work more of her deceit upon you," he growled, distantly aware they were not alone—that the Saxon woman stood nearby, and his retainers were on the opposite side of the screen. "You will stay away from her."

The youth's attempt to pull free was unsuccessful. "Before I sent for you," he said, "*I* was lord of Etcheverry. *I* ruled all you have come to claim."

"You, Christophe? Need I remind you it was not of my choosing to shoulder the responsibilities of the heir, that it was Sir Ancel who lorded Etcheverry in your stead?"

Hurt flitted across the youth's face. "I had thought you would be different after the monastery."

The words struck a chord in Maxen that was better left unplucked. Fighting an inner battle, he squeezed his eyes closed. "So had I."

"Then—"

"Do you forget Thomas lies cold beneath the earth?" Maxen exploded. "That the woman you call *lady* is responsible for his death?"

Christophe took a step back, and Maxen regretted the words he had been holding in for weeks. Though he had come near to speaking them many times, he'd had enough presence of mind to contain them. Until now.

Releasing Christophe, he harkened back to his journey to Etcheverry. Throughout, he had hoped his brother could be groomed to become the heir, thus freeing Maxen to return to the monastery. But it seemed a false hope. Not long after his reunion with the youngest Pendery, he had accepted it was unlikely Christophe could shoulder such responsibility. He was too gentle, too innocent, and too determined to remain so. The bitterness that came with that realization ran too deep for Maxen to keep it hidden forever, and now it was known.

Christophe's voice broke through Maxen's torment. "It was a trick, *oui?*"

Maxen knew to what he referred. He had not revealed his plans for Rhiannyn to anyone, allowing all to believe she had truly escaped. And when he had departed three days past, he had told none of his destination. Now they knew.

"Christophe," he began, and out of the corner of his eye saw the Saxon woman cock her head with interest. "Leave us!" he growled.

"Harmless," Christophe said as she retreated. "She speaks little French."

"No Saxon is harmless," Maxen retorted, "especially those who wish to bed a Norman."

Christophe pushed a hand through hair far too long to show any resemblance to the preferred Norman style. "You have not answered me. You tricked me, did you not?"

Maxen had, but it did not absolve Christophe of what he had done, nor of what he might do in the future. "I did, and you betrayed me."

"By aiding Rhiannyn?" He shook his head. "It cannot be called betrayal if I did something you wanted. In fact, it is just as well said that I followed your instructions."

"You are saying you would have done it had I asked?"

"*Non.*"

Maxen turned opposite, threw open the chest containing the garments that had been Thomas's, and removed the quilted jerkin he would wear beneath his dead brother's hauberk. "Betrayal, then," he concluded. "By my design or no, you acted to betray me."

"I acted to save a woman innocent of the crimes of which she is accused."

Innocent. If Maxen could grab the word from Christophe's mouth and throw it to the floor, he would grind it beneath his heel. "We have had this discussion before."

"Discussion! Nothing is discussion with you. It either is or is not, according to what you wish it to be."

Maxen used the time required to don the jerkin to cool his anger. "As I am lord," he said, "it should come as no surprise."

"It does not, but still I would have my say."

Maxen nearly denied him, but Rhiannyn's warning that Christophe would become a man only if he was shown respect and his voice not beaten down, flew at him. Though it angered him to give credence to what the woman had said, he inclined his head. "Have your say, and be quick about it."

Christophe blinked in surprise. "You are wrong about Rhiannyn. Though she tried to make Thomas think her bad, she is good of heart. Never would she knowingly harm anyone."

Maxen stepped around the screen and ordered a languishing squire to deliver him the great hauberk. "The Saxon woman has duped you, young Christophe," he said, coming back around, "the same as she did Thomas."

"I do not believe it."

"You do not think she betrayed you in leading your brother to his death?"

"She but wished freedom. She could not know running from Thomas would bring death upon him."

"It is Thomas you blame?"

"I do. Had he allowed Rhiannyn to return to her people, he would not be dead."

"If you think to convince me she is not responsible, you will have to do better than that."

"He as good as caged her, Maxen—imposing clothing, manners, and a title she wanted nothing to do with."

"He would have made her his wife," Maxen said between his teeth, "not the bed warmer she deserved to be."

Christophe shook his head. "She did not love him."

"What fanciful notions have been put in your head? Many are the marriages made without love. Such foolish emotion is not required to unite warring families, to increase a family's holdings, to breed children of good stock to carry on the name."

"But she did not want that."

"And look what her selfishness wrought," Maxen growled. "Another brother dead at the hands of the Saxons and my chosen life stolen from me."

Christophe turned on his heel and limped away. "It is you who are selfish," he tossed over his shoulder. "You who could make all right, but will not even try."

The hard truth of his words stole the rejoinder from Maxen. At an impasse, he watched his brother go, then closed his eyes and prayed for guidance. In the end, there was nothing—only growing enmity toward the woman who had disturbed his carefully laid plans.

From the narrow window of her tower room, Rhiannyn watched Maxen Pendery ride out from the castle with a garrison of more than a hundred men, a third of whom were fully armored and mounted. The men-at-arms marched behind.

As she stared at the one who sat a horse far better in the raiment of a soldier than that of a monk, anger tumbled through her. Yet another of his deceptions. And there would be more.

Their destination Andredeswald, their mission massacre, Rhiannyn stared after them as Pendery and his men grew distant. She could do nothing to prevent the deaths. Nothing to stop the warring between the conquered and the conquerors.

Still, she cried, "Nay!" and did not stop, even after Maxen Pendery disappeared from view. Later, she pounded her fists and feet against the door, and when food was brought to her, she flung it against the wall.

Not until it was past dark and exhaustion caused her to collapse on her pallet, did she quiet. But then she dreamed—nightmares in which she plunged to the bottom of her grave, heard Dora's chanting, and tasted dirt. Almost as disturbing, each time she awakened, she frantically searched the dark for the one who had delivered her from death.

11

~⚬~

AT THE LANDING before the door to Rhiannyn's tower room, Maxen paused to unbuckle his chain mail hood. He pushed it back, causing the numerous links to ring as they settled around his neck. When they quieted, he listened for other sounds, but there was only silence, as if Rhiannyn had gone.

Although he did not believe escape possible, especially since Christophe had been given no choice in accompanying the war party into Andredeswald two days past, and a sentry had been posted to ensure no others attempted to free her, Maxen quickly lifted the bar and pushed the door open.

He stared at the slight figure curled on the pallet across the room. Knees hugged to her chest, tunic up around her calves, hair spilled over her face, she slept.

During his exchange with the sentry, he had been told of her outbursts. She had screamed, pounded on the door, kicked it, and hurled the basin and food. And again the next day, though of less duration. Doubtless, she was exhausted.

He strode across the room and dropped to a knee beside her. Ignoring the pain shooting through his side, he reached to shake her awake. And left his hand upon the air as something warmer and brighter touched her first. Through the small window, sunlight slanted its first rays across her legs.

Attraction gripped him as he looked from tender-fleshed ankles to firm calves, from a softly rising and falling chest to a lovely neck that invited kisses forbidden him as a monk. But if he turned his back on all he had been taught as a man of God, it was forbidden no longer. And his body knew it.

Why Rhiannyn? he wondered. Why not the servant, Theta? Why this one who was Thomas's downfall, the sight of whom ought to make his fingers convulse with deadly intent, rather than restrained desire? More and more he understood his fallen brother's obsession. Hate her, certainly, but want her...

That, too.

He swept the hair back from her face and looked from lashes shadowing dark circles begot by wakeful nights, to a mouth full and waiting for the man who sold his soul to her.

But even as he berated himself for not heeding the voice urging him to put distance between them, he brushed a thumb across her lower lip, trailed fingers down her jaw, and settled them at the hollow of her neck.

Innocent, Christophe said, but he was wrong. Had to be.

Desperate to vanquish her from his thoughts, Maxen closed his eyes and silently recited prayers he had not spoken since before Guy had brought news of Thomas's death.

Light where there had been dark. Warmth where there had been cold. Breath where there had been none.

The night melting into blacks and grays and streaks of crimson that ran down the sky into a clear, sparkling stream, Rhiannyn realized it was a dream. The grave was not real. The wood was not real. But neither was the stream real, nor the man standing over her whose vengeful face rippled in the water. He was gone.

So why do I feel him so strongly? she wondered, then told herself to ignore the sensation, the easier to remain in this less terrifying dream. Far better here than all the waiting within prison walls that were silent but for her fits of frustration and anger.

But the feeling of him grew, causing the sunlit stream to blur and darken. Determined to stay beside it, she commanded her hands to carry its cool water to her lips, to splash it on her heated skin—

That last was a mistake, wrenching her up through the thin veil of sleep and opening her eyes wide.

And here was the reason she felt the presence of Maxen Pendery. Eyes closed, lips moving slightly as if in prayer, he knelt beside her—his hand at her neck.

Fearing he intended to strangle her, she forced herself to remain still. *Think!* she silently urged. *Look!*

She slid her gaze down his chain mail to his sword, then to his dagger. The sword was out of the question, but not the latter.

Help me, Lord, she prayed and swept her hand forward and pulled the dagger free.

One moment Pendery's hand was at her neck, the next it encased the fingers she clenched around the hilt. "Give over," he growled.

She thrust back against the wall, kicked both legs forward, and slammed her feet into his chest.

It moved him only inasmuch as he surged upright, and still gripping her hand upon the dagger, dragged her with him and onto her toes.

"Accept your defeat gracefully," he said between his teeth.

"And die gracefully?" she spat, the burning in her strained shoulder nearly making her cry out.

He stepped onto the pallet, pushed her back against the cool stone wall, and held her there with the press of his body. "Upon my word, *you* will not die this day."

She knew to heed the emphasis that *she* would not die, but he was too close and she was too easily broken to give it more thought. "I am to believe it was not your intent to steal the breath from me?" she demanded.

"You tempt me," he said, "but I vow you are quite safe."

Safe with this man? Never. Still, she said, "For how long?"

"For now."

"That is supposed to reassure me?"

"I offer no more. Hence, will you give over, or do you prefer I take the dagger from you?"

She tilted her head farther back and considered her childlike hand engulfed in his and the blade jutting from it. In the latter, she saw her distorted reflection beneath Pendery's towering shape. As difficult as it was to accept another defeat at his hands, she had lost all advantage. Thus, a token struggle was all that was left to her, one that could leave her broken and long in healing.

She eased her grip.

"Wise," he said and took the dagger and released her.

As he returned the weapon to its sheath, Rhiannyn considered the open doorway. If she could make it past him and get the door closed and the bar dropped into place, might she escape? How many would she have to elude?

Too many, and Maxen Pendery would be the first to give chase. She glanced back at him and found him watching her.

"Again, wise," he said, as if he knew her thoughts.

She lowered her gaze and noticed the dark streaks coloring his armor. Doubtless, the blood of Saxons.

"Why have you come?" she asked.

"There is something I wish to show you." He took her arm and pulled her toward the window where she had two days earlier watched him ride out from the castle.

Dreading what awaited her there, certain it would evidence he had accomplished what she had prayed he would not, she allowed him to position her before the window that was too narrow for them to stand side by side.

"Watch," he said.

Acutely aware of his breath stirring her hair and his mailed chest against her back, she struggled to put him from her mind, but he would not budge—not until a clamor arose from the wood.

Emerging onto the clearing surrounding the castle, Pendery's soldiers rode on either side of scores of Saxons whose trudging feet hazed the air with the dust of their defeat.

"I always keep my word," Pendery said near her ear. "As promised, the sunrise is most spectacular."

For Normans, but not the Saxons whose land this was—whose children would be reared in the knowledge they were born to a beaten people if the conquerors were not ousted from England.

She struggled to hold back tears, but they fell, and a shudder moved through her.

"Rhiannyn." It was so softly spoken, it nearly slipped past her. Pendery pulled her around and lifted her chin. "It does not have to be this way." His voice was gruff, as if he were also pained. But if he was, his ache was rooted in something distant from hers.

Swallowing convulsively, she stared at him through tears.

He inclined his head. "I but require a name."

Were it as easily produced as he believed, could she speak it? She would have to, for the one he sought was not only responsible for Thomas's death, but would be responsible for the fate of the Saxons who were now Pendery's prisoners.

With anger wrought of helplessness, she swept up a hand and slapped his face. "Death upon you," she said as his skin flushed red. "Villain! Cur! Nithing!"

It was the last—*coward*—to which he responded. He caught the wrist of her offending hand and the other when she raised it to land a second blow. "Let it be, Rhiannyn!"

She narrowed her lids. "If I do not?"

"Then chain and manacle will be your constant companions."

The thought of being bound made the breath go out of her and her anger slip sideways.

"Good." He loosed her and stepped back. "Now, we talk."

She clasped her stinging palm with the other and waited.

"The destiny of those men and women"—he jutted his chin toward the window—"is in your hands. Reveal which of them murdered Thomas, and the rest will live. Hold to your secret, and their lives will be wiped from Norman soil."

Ignoring his reference to the land of the Saxons, she said, "You would take the lives of all for one?" She shook her head. "I do not believe you would welcome the slaughter of so many innocents upon whatever conscience lingers in the deepest of you." Rather, she did not wish to believe it.

His eyebrows soared. "Innocents? Under Harwolfson's direction, they pillage and kill no less than those they accuse of doing the same."

"Who *have* done the same!"

"Regardless, by one or all, justice will be done. And if you think to test me, their deaths will be upon your conscience, not mine."

Defiance once more opened her mouth. Helplessness closed it. Lowering her gaze, Rhiannyn stared into the emptiness between them. "Do I tell the truth, you will not believe me."

"If it is the truth, it will hold."

She shook her head. "Only a lie you are willing to believe will satisfy."

"Who killed my brother?" he pressed.

She raised her chin to better brave his anger. "Thomas had just wounded Edwin when a dagger flew from out of the trees. I did not see, and I do not know, who threw it."

His shoulders rose with the breath of what she prayed was patience. "Better a lie I would be willing to believe," he said, "than the pitiful one you have told." He closed a hand around her arm. "Come, see what you have wrought."

As he pulled her out of the room and down the stairs, her pleas fell on ears deafened to the truth, albeit a truth she had made seem a lie by withholding it.

Between the gatehouse and the causeway leading up the motte to the inner bailey and its donjon, Pendery pulled Rhiannyn in front of him so she faced the drawbridge over which the Saxons would be herded.

Feeling the curious regard of those on the walls who had paused to watch them, she tried to turn to Pendery, but his hands held her firm.

"Watch," he said.

"Maxen, I beseech you—"

"My lord!" he corrected.

It burned her to address him as such, but if it allowed her to reach him, it would be worth the sacrifice. "My lord," she choked, "on my life, it is the truth I tell." She peered over her shoulder. "Hear me. I—"

"Even if it were the truth," he said, eyes on the drawbridge that took the first footfalls of the approaching party, "the end would be the same, for to let Thomas's murder go unavenged would be the downfall of all that is Pendery. I will not allow it. This day, the Saxons learn who is master and who is not. Now watch."

Heart beating so hard it hurt, she looked back and saw the first of the captives step onto Norman ground. Having obviously discovered during the clash in Andredeswald that Pendery was not the monk he had pretended to be, they focused their attention on her. Displayed as she was—as the traitor she was not—their eyes felt like daggers.

Quelling the impulse to declare she had not betrayed them, Rhiannyn clenched her hands as the Saxons, bound one to another, many clutching at wounds, entered the bailey.

When all were within, her searching eyes revealed the unexpected. Edwin, Dora, and several others were not among those taken prisoner. Dead, then?

"Where is Edwin?" she asked.

"Escaped."

She jerked her head around. "You did not tell me!"

"With good reason."

Then he had thought if she knew of Edwin's escape, she might try to save these lives by putting the blame on one whom Pendery could not lay hands to. He understood the workings of her mind—rather, her desperation.

The Saxons herded before Rhiannyn made her want to slip out of her skin. Even Aethel regarded her with everything opposite fondness. None believed her innocent. If the Normans did not kill her, her own might.

Pendery released her and strode toward the conquered. "I seek the murderer of Thomas Pendery," he raised his voice for all to hear. "Deliver him, and your lives will be spared. Deny me, and all will suffer."

The silence was so thick with hatred, it was hard to breathe.

"When your brother welcomes you to the fiery pit, pretender of God," Aethel finally spoke, "he will tell you who did it!"

"Death to the murdering Normans!" another yelled.

A woman stepped forward, straining her bonds. "Death to Rhiannyn the betrayer!"

Frenzied shouts rose from others, but as Rhiannyn was assailed with imaginings of her demise, the men-at-arms closed around the prisoners.

Mouth grim, Pendery returned to Rhiannyn. "It falls upon you," he said. "Which one?"

"I do not know."

"You lie." He took her arm and drew her nearer the Saxons, making her suffer a closer look at their hatred. "One last chance, then there is bloodshed."

Throat constricted, she looked from face to face and wondered if the sacrifice of one could be justified to save the others. And who would bear the burden of that sacrifice?

She shuddered. "I do not know," she said again and lowered her gaze. It fell on Pendery's fists, so tight the knuckles were white.

"That is your answer, then," he said, "and soon you will have mine." He called to a knight, and when the man stepped forward, pushed Rhiannyn toward him. "Return her to the tower."

As she was led away, she heard him call out his commands. The Saxons were to be divided, the young and uninjured incarcerated in the cells beneath the donjon, the others—comprised of women, the aged, and the wounded—quartered in the outbuildings of the lower bailey. In the center of that bailey, a gallows would be erected by noon on the morrow.

Alone in her tower room, Rhiannyn was tempted to loose her emotions as she had on the days past. Instead, she tucked herself tight in the corner of her pallet, and with knees pulled to her chin, prayed for the lives that would soon be forfeited.

And prayed.

And prayed.

Amidst the commotion caused by the disbanding of the Saxons, Maxen called Guy to his side.

"Aye, my lord?"

"I seek among the rebels one who bears a shoulder wound."

"Many are wounded," the knight reminded him, "and several likely bear such injuries."

"This injury will be days old. Too, the man is much my size."

His task made easier, Guy said, "If he is among these Saxons, I will bring him to you."

If, Maxen mused. The one who had escaped when Dora had sought Rhiannyn's death might be among the dead left behind at Harwolfson's camp. Or he could have fled with his leader. But if he was here, he would be the first to suffer.

12

CURSE RHIANNYN! CURSE her closed mouth! Curse her for testing me! Curse this flesh for desiring her!

Waves of anger swept Maxen. But it was not anger alone that wrung moisture from his body where he lay on the bed, clothed in undertunic and braies, covers thrown to the floor. Nor was it anger that made his thoughts turn on drivel. Something else had awakened him from a vision of Rhiannyn clothed in golden hair.

Heat. It moved beneath his skin, scraping at him with fiery claws as if to dig its way out.

He sat up. Swaying as he peered into the darkness hanging over his chamber, he slapped a hand to the mattress to steady himself and found it damp. He lifted his other hand and slid its palm down his slick chest.

Was this heat—this malady—another dream? Or as Christophe had warned, had the wound become infected?

He searched along his side for the bandages his brother had applied over two days past. In all that time, they had not been tended to in spite of Christophe's urgings. Now would Maxen pay the price of ungodly obsession? Would the Saxons—and Rhiannyn—stand triumphant over his grave?

He dropped his feet to the floor and stood, grabbed the bedpost, and staggered against it. Hating himself for his weakness, he bellowed for Christophe.

Beyond the screen arose the sounds of grunting and grumbling, the screech of benches and hurried footsteps.

"My lord?" Guy asked as he came around the screen carrying a torch.

"Where is Christophe?" Maxen demanded.

"Likely tending the Saxons' injuries." Guy's brow furrowed. "What has happened? Are you ill?"

"Send for him!"

Guy turned to the half dozen knights who had followed him around the screen. He repeated his lord's command to summon Christophe, and the gathering thinned by the two who hastened away.

Maxen, knowing he had revealed too much of his ailing body to knights who were not yet fully under his control, attempted to level his gaze on their wavering faces. "Slaver elsewhere," he said. "All but Sir Guy!"

They scattered.

As Guy fit the torch in a wall sconce, Maxen released the bedpost and collapsed on the bed.

Christophe must have run with all that was in his lame body, for he soon appeared, the knights sent for him following—Sir Ancel and another Maxen could not put a name to, as well as the servant, Theta.

"There is infection," Maxen spoke in the language of the Saxons.

Christophe laid a hand to his brother's arm. "God's rood! A fire burns in you."

"Then put it out."

"I…" Christophe shook his head. "I can but try."

"Then do!"

Christophe quickly removed the bandages, revealing the diseased flesh. "Aye, infection," he murmured. "Some of the stitches are torn, and there is much—"

"What say you?" Sir Ancel demanded in Norman French.

"Is he dying?" the other knight asked.

Christophe looked over his shoulder. "It—"

"Do not interpret for them," Maxen snapped, then ordered the two knights from his chamber.

Though the one complied immediately, Sir Ancel lingered.

Several times, Maxen had glimpsed challenge in the man's eyes. But this time, it was wide open.

"My lord." Sir Ancel dipped his head in mock deference, pivoted, and made a leisurely exit.

"I may have to kill him," Maxen murmured.

"Theta," Christophe called, "bring my bag."

Hips swaying, the woman approached and set it on the mattress.

"Guy," Maxen called.

The knight circled the bed to avoid interfering with Christophe's ministrations. "My lord?"

"Did you find him?"

Confusion furrowed Guy's brow before understanding smoothed it. "Regrets, but the Saxon you seek is not amongst those captured in Andredeswald."

Then the witch's man had either escaped again or met his death.

Maxen lowered his lids, but feeling himself drift out of consciousness, opened them and called, "Guy! Bring Rhiannyn to me."

Christophe's head jerked up. "For what?"

"And a chain," Maxen continued, "an iron at each end."

"What do you intend?" Christophe demanded.

"Do it now, Guy!"

"Aye, my lord."

"What do you?" Christophe asked again following the knight's departure.

Maxen pushed a hand up his damp brow and plunged quavering fingers into his hair. "So hot. As if I am in hell."

Christophe leaned near. "You are not going to tell me?"

"You will see."

"If you hurt her—"

Maxen bolted to sitting, forcing Christophe to step back. "You will do what? Allow me to die?"

Christophe's eyes widened, and his mouth silently worked before words emerged. "*Non*, Maxen! You are my brother. I but wish to know your intentions."

Maxen dropped back upon the mattress. "You shall," he rasped. "Soon."

Rhiannyn did not turn from the cloudy night she stared into. Pendery's coming was of no surprise. She had heard the stirring within the bailey, the talk upon the walls, the scrape of boots on steps, and the ring of metal on metal. He came for her, though why he wore chain mail and what he wanted were questions to which she feared the answers.

Her skin did not prickle when he stepped into the room, and even before he said, "I am to bring you to my lord," she knew another had been sent in his stead.

She turned from the window to the knight whose face was lit by a torch carried by the squire who accompanied him. It was Sir Guy, and he wore only tunic and hose—not the chain mail she had thought she heard. In Thomas's time, the knight had not been friendly toward her, but neither had he been harsh.

"What does he want of me?"

He frowned. "That is for him to tell."

Knowing it would be useless to resist, she crossed to the door. "I will follow."

"You will be led." He captured her arm.

As if escape were possible, she silently scoffed.

The squire stepped aside to allow the knight and Rhiannyn to descend ahead of him. As he did so, she heard again the ring of metal she had believed was chain mail, and saw the young man had a chain looped over his arm.

Her heart sped, but she did not falter in step, nor inquire into it.

She was led to the donjon and into the hall where the knights had roused from their beds. Some sitting, others standing, they spoke in hushed tones until she came to their attention. Amid the silence, she walked with her chin high beside Sir Guy.

The sight that awaited her when they came around the screen made her falter.

Guy corrected her course and guided her to the far side of the bed, opposite where Christophe and Theta bent over Pendery whose chest glistened with perspiration. Of greater note was the redness and swelling around the wound he had received while rescuing her from death.

She looked to Christophe.

He met her gaze, and there was fear in his eyes.

In saving her life, might his brother give his?

"My lord," Sir Guy said, "I have brought the Saxon woman as ordered."

Pendery's lids lifted. After what seemed a struggle to bring her to focus, he shifted his gaze to his knight. "The chain?"

"I have it."

He closed his eyes, nodded.

The silence stretched until Sir Guy asked the question not answered. "What would you have me do, my lord?"

"One iron on her...one on me."

Rhiannyn caught her breath.

"*Non,* Maxen," Christophe exclaimed, "you cannot mean to chain her to you."

"Now you know," he mumbled, eyes remaining closed. "Do it, Guy."

The knight waved the squire to him, took the chain, and reached for Rhiannyn.

She turned to flee, but the squire caught her around the waist. Ignoring her yelp, he tossed her onto the bed alongside Pendery and held her there while Sir Guy fit the iron on her wrist. However, she proved too fine-boned, and it slipped off over her hand.

Muttering, Sir Guy dragged the chain lower and fastened the iron around her ankle.

"Why?" Christophe found his voice, though it broke as the child in him overwhelmed the man.

"To ensure…" Pendery rasped. "…she is here when I recover."

"The tower room will serve as well."

"Under whose watch? Yours, Christophe?" Dry laughter. "Finish your ministrations, Brother."

Tight-lipped, Christophe took the bandages from Theta and began binding them around Maxen's waist.

"My wrist," Pendery said and lifted it to receive his end of the chain.

Sir Guy did as bid, and asked. "What of the key?"

As the squire continued to hold Rhiannyn down, she stared at the scrap of metal.

"I entrust it to you," Pendery said.

Sir Guy opened a pouch on his belt and dropped the key in it. "I will keep it with my life."

Pendery turned his face to Rhiannyn, narrowly opened his eyes. "Freedom is in the length of chain, and that is all I give you." He swallowed loudly and moved his gaze to the squire. "Release her."

The squire obeyed, and Rhiannyn scrambled off the bed and fell to her knees on the floor. The clattering chain followed, snaking across the mattress and pooling on her thighs. She thrust it off, lunged to her feet, and retreated as far as the links allowed—three short strides from the bed.

Christophe's eyes, large in the torchlight, offered an apology, but she looked away. Though certain he had been his brother's unwilling pawn, the trust she had placed in him had proved beyond detrimental to the Saxons awaiting death on the morrow. And looking upon him was too much a reminder of that.

She heard his pained sigh, but kept her gaze averted.

"You must not move overly much, Maxen," Christophe warned. "If there is any chance of preventing the infection from going to rot, these stitches must stay." No response. "Did you hear me?"

"I heard," Pendery mumbled.

"Good. The herbal I am giving you should ease the pain and heat. Can you lift your head?"

Pendery complied, a frown his only reaction to the medicinal pressed upon him.

"Now sleep," Christophe said and retrieved the torch from the sconce and motioned for Theta to precede him from the chamber.

"I will keep watch over him," Sir Guy said.

Before Christophe could reply, Pendery said, "I have no need of a keeper. Leave me to my rest."

"But Rhiannyn—"

"A mere woman. Go!"

Sir Guy threw her a warning look, and he and the others departed.

For long minutes, Rhiannyn did not move where she stood back from the bed. Though the dim light cast by the torches in the hall revealed the shape of Pendery, she could not know if he slept. If he did, she had no wish to awaken him.

When she finally moved—but a slight shifting of her weight—the chain rattled. Pendery did not react, but as she began to relax, a clatter not of her making sounded, and the chain grew taut.

She resisted, the flesh of her ankle chafing from the strain of the iron, but Pendery's strength in sickness remained greater than hers, and she was reeled toward the bed. Lest he tried to pull her onto it, she dropped to her knees when she came alongside. And there he was, his shadowed face above hers where he had levered onto an elbow.

She thrust her hands against his chest, and as he dropped onto his back, she registered the damp and heat of his body.

"You burn," she whispered.

She heard his labored breathing, and after some moments, he said in her language, "Most bright. Think you I approach…hell?"

Perhaps he did, for what hope had he of living if the fever did not soon break? How long before the fire consumed him?

"You wished death upon me," he slurred, "but does it take me, 'twill not save your people. Only I and…the one you protect, can do that."

Remembrance of the words she had tossed at him jolted her. Was it possible—

Nay, they were but words. As he himself had told in the guise of a monk, no power did she possess to bring them to fruition. If he died, the blame would rest with her, though not because she had wished it on him. No matter his purpose in rescuing her from Dora, he had taken a dagger to save her.

An ache at her center, she touched his shoulder. "Sleep, Maxen."

"Lights," he said low. "And colors. Never have I seen so many."

Did the fever worsen? Might he succumb this night?

She told herself it did not matter. But it did.

A short time later, his breathing deepened. Slowly, and with as little rattling of chain as possible, she lowered herself. Sitting on the hard floor with her back against the bed, she joined her hands before her face and began praying for something it seemed God alone could provide—peace for England and no more deaths upon her conscience. Including that of Maxen Pendery.

13

THE CONVULSING OF Maxen's body and the rattle of chain pulled Rhiannyn from sleep. She straightened from where she had slumped against the bed and rose to her knees.

The dawn filtering through the windows set high in the wall confirmed the fever had not abated. Maxen was flushed, and so heavily perspiring that moisture beaded on his face, and his undertunic clung like a second skin.

Rhiannyn put her knees to the bed and took his heated face between her hands. "Maxen!" she called.

Eyes tightly closed, he shouted something, then wrenched his head to the side. Convulsing again, he kicked at the coverlet that had ridden down around his braies.

She dropped her feet to the floor and shouted for Christophe as she stretched the loudly protesting chain as far as it would go. It brought her up short at less than half the distance to the screen. But as the links settled, she caught the sound of hurried footsteps, familiar because of their uneven nature.

When Christophe came around the screen, she said, "He is worse. He throws himself about and is so very hot."

He leaned over his brother, and as she watched, lifted each eyelid. "Maxen!"

Given no response, he grasped his brother's shoulders and shook him.

Maxen shouted something that ended on a growl, jerked aside, and dropped onto his stomach.

Face fearful, Christophe looked to Rhiannyn. "I will need assistance in turning him. Will you help?"

After a moment's hesitation, she moved toward the opposite side of the bed.

"I will do it," Sir Guy said.

Surprised by his appearance, she halted.

The knight brushed past her and leaned over Maxen.

Rhiannyn was grateful it was he who aided Christophe in turning his lord, and more so when it was he who suffered Maxen's fist.

"God's wrath!" Sir Guy gripped his jaw and shifted it side to side.

Once Maxen stopped resisting and settled on his back, Christophe drew the coverlet up his chest. "Keep him still," he said. "I will return shortly with a draught to ease his restlessness."

On his way out, he pressed a hand to Rhiannyn's shoulder. "Not your fault," he said and crossed the room and disappeared around the screen.

It surprised her that he continued to hold her blameless, though Thomas was dead and his oldest brother well on his way. Strangely, she almost resented that he refused to hate her. It would be easier if none showed her kindness. Then perhaps, she could harden herself as Maxen did—feeling nothing for anyone and using deceit as a weapon without thought of the innocents who might fall beneath it.

"If not your fault," Sir Guy said, looking over his shoulder, "whose?"

Though she knew his taunting was not without justification, she said, "You have but to look to Duke William for your answer."

His mouth tightened. "King William."

A sore point, but she would not argue it.

He returned his attention to his lord who had begun to strain again. "I do not care to have you hovering at my back, Rhiannyn," he said. "Go around to the other side so I can see you better."

She stood straighter. "What cause have I given you to fear me?"

Her words had the effect one expected from a warrior whose bravery was questioned. "Now!" he snapped.

She pulled the chain with her to where Christophe had stood, and as she drew alongside, Maxen resumed his thrashing.

Sir Guy gripped his lord's shoulders, leaned his weight on the bigger man, and managed to keep him down long enough for the fit to pass. Then he put his mouth so near Maxen's ear that Rhiannyn had to strain to catch his words.

"Fight it, Maxen. Fight it!"

That his loyalty appeared more than mere fealty surprised Rhiannyn. Was Maxen capable of returning friendship? Did he? "You are friends?" she asked.

The knight's expression told she had overstepped, and though he need not have added words to it, he said, "I would hear no more of your deceitful voice."

Shortly, Christophe reappeared with Theta and two other women whose arms were filled with all manner of items. Though Theta met Rhiannyn's gaze, the other two—Mildreth and Lucilla—looked elsewhere. Both were from Rhiannyn's village, and taken by Thomas at the same time as she. They were as close to friends as Rhiannyn had, but she knew that as long as they suspected she had betrayed her people, she would be denied the solace previously found in their company.

As for Theta, Thomas had taken her from a village near Hastings. For some months before Rhiannyn was brought into the castle, the woman had regularly shared his bed, and though he had not wed her, it was said she had greatly pretended the role of lady. But all had changed with Rhiannyn's arrival. Though she herself had refused to be coaxed into Thomas's bed and rejected his subsequent offers of marriage, Theta had been displaced and made no pretense of her feelings for Rhiannyn.

"Lady, the water and washcloth are for you," Christophe said, nodding to the items placed atop the chest, "and the garments."

She raised questioning eyes to him.

"Uncleanliness spreads disease," he said. "If you are to share this chamber with my brother, you must be clean."

She glanced down her front. Her early grave, the trek through Andredeswald, and two days in the tower had left her slovenly.

"I understand," she said.

"All of you must be clean," he added.

Did he intend her to bathe before those present?

As if reading her expression, he shook his head. "When we are gone."

Theta snickered.

"Quiet thyself!" Christophe ordered and thrust a basin and washcloth into the woman's hands. "Cool your lord."

Her face lightened, and she smiled at Rhiannyn as she moved to Maxen's side.

Knowing she would make a show of touching her lord, Rhiannyn returned to the foot of the bed.

"If you will raise him, Sir Guy," Christophe said, "I will give him the draught."

The knight lifted his lord, and Christophe put drink to his brother's lips. Initially, Maxen protested, but then he gulped down what was given him.

Next, Christophe turned his efforts to the bedding. He called orders to Mildreth and Lucilla, creating a flurry of activity that had Rhiannyn hugging the bedpost to avoid being swept away with the stagnant floor rushes. New rushes were spread, herbs sprinkled, and surfaces wiped clean. The bedding was changed so completely Maxen had to be lifted to accomplish it.

When it was time to fit him with clean garments, Rhiannyn turned her face aside to avoid seeing him unclothed.

Theta laughed. "Mayhap you would like to finish cooling our lord, Rhiannyn?" She stepped forward and swiped the saturated cloth across Rhiannyn's heated cheek. "Or yourself."

It was always this way between them, though it would surely become worse now that Rhiannyn was of a status beneath Theta's.

"As you seem to enjoy it," Rhiannyn said, "I would not deny you the pleasure."

Theta flashed teeth whose white starkly contrasted with blacker than night hair. "I had hoped you would say that," she drawled.

Wishing herself anywhere but here, Rhiannyn picked up the garments Christophe had brought her and noticed their fine material. They were the ones Thomas had ordered made for her, and which he had presented the day before her escape from Etcheverry. Never worn, both gowns were far from a commoner's clothing.

Though unadorned, the beige chemise was fashioned of linen woven so tightly it had a sheen that would glide smoothly over her skin when she moved. In contrast, the overgown—the bliaut—was of heavier material, its V neckline, flared sleeves, and hemline embroidered with threads that glinted with gold. Shorter than the undergown, the bliaut would fall to mid-calf, leaving a length of chemise to skim the ground. To complete the look, there was a sash of braided gold strands to define the waist.

The garments were not what Maxen would choose for her. Dare she don them, or should she request something more appropriate?

"Rhiannyn."

She saw Christophe had come to stand before her. Beyond, only Sir Guy and Theta remained. "Aye?"

"For now, there is nothing more I can do for Maxen," he said, in that moment seeming more a man than a boy. "He should sleep, but if he awakens, he may wish something to drink. On the table is wine you can give him. I have added herbs for his pain."

The thought of trying to put drink to Maxen's lips unsettling her, she asked, "Where are you going?"

"To tend the wounded."

"The Saxons?" She glanced at Sir Guy and saw from his expression he did not approve.

"Aye."

Though it was difficult to ask the question that had burdened her since she was brought to Maxen on the night past, she said, "What of the hangings your brother ordered?"

Christophe looked to Sir Guy. "They will wait until he is well enough to witness them himself."

The knight's mouth tightened, but he did not oppose the decision.

How long the reprieve? Rhiannyn wondered. For however long Maxen lay abed unable to govern? Or until the fever took him and it was another—Sir Ancel—who carried out the death sentences?

"Do not forget," Christophe said, indicating the basin of water.

She nodded.

For a long time after he and the others left, she stared at the screen around which they had disappeared. Then she set about keeping her promise to Christophe.

14

∽◌∾

"MAXEN!" RHIANNYN CRIED. "I cannot do this alone. You must help me."

He kicked, tossed his head side to side, and called for drink in a voice so hoarse it sounded as if his throat were filled with sharp stones.

"Maxen!"

His arm shot out, nearly knocking the goblet from her hand. "Accursed fire," he growled.

Remembering Christophe's warning against too much movement, Rhiannyn set the goblet on the table, drew her hand back, and slapped him.

His lids flew open. Eyes bright with the illness gone to his head, he snarled, "Witch!"

Were she of wax, she was certain she would melt from the heat of his stare. "I but try to help," she said. "You were throwing yourself about, and I feared the stitches would not hold."

"You feared I might not die."

"That is not true!"

"Is it not?"

Knowing that to argue with him in his present state of mind would be useless, though in his other state it seemed little better, she pressed her lips tight and tucked a tress of freshly washed hair behind her ear.

His gaze moved from her face to her chest that was clothed in the clean chemise she had donned when his thrashing had interrupted her bathing.

Uncomfortably aware of the thin material, she crossed her arms over her breasts.

His lids lowered, and as she watched the slow rise and fall of his chest, she wondered if he had once more lost consciousness.

"Thirsty," he mumbled. "So dry."

"I have drink." She retrieved the goblet.

He narrowly opened his eyes. "Think you I would take it from your hand?"

Bridling at the suggestion she would poison him, Rhiannyn said, "My hand, or not at all."

His eyebrows jerked. "Then it must be." With effort, he levered onto an elbow to receive the goblet's rim against his lips. Eyes fixed on hers, he drained the contents.

Thinking he would settle back to sleep, she was caught unawares when he gripped her arm, pulled her down onto the bed, and leaned over her.

Distantly aware of the goblet's clatter, she stared up at the man who blotted out sight and feel of all but him. And when he took her face between his hands and lowered his head, his mouth upon hers was so unexpected she was too shocked to struggle. But once surprise passed, something stronger than the instinct for survival moved through her. She fought it with a litany of transgressions against her people and her person, but it was stronger than the past, and she heard herself sigh.

It was then she discovered Maxen's motive. He trickled warm wine into her mouth, and though her natural reaction was to expel it, he sealed his mouth over hers, giving her no choice but to swallow or choke. She swallowed.

He lifted his head. "Now if I fall, I do not fall alone."

Assailed by equal parts indignation and humiliation, Rhiannyn snapped, "If you thought I meant to poison you, you had but to ask me to drink ere you."

He smiled faintly. "This held more appeal." Eyes heavily lidded with malaise, he said, "Would you like a proper kiss, Rhiannyn of Etcheverry?"

"I would not!"

He opened his eyes wider, and she saw the predator, though not the one who had chased her through the wood. This one was of want. This one gently slid a hand from her jaw to her neck.

She strained sideways. "Pray, do not—"

"You are not Harwolfson's," he slurred.

Though unfamiliar sensations ran through her, she quelled the urge to struggle for fear she would cause him further injury. "Release me. You are ill and—"

"It has been a long time." He lowered his head and touched his lips beneath her ear.

Rhiannyn knew better than to close her eyes, but she did and felt what no man had made her feel. It was more than a kiss. More than a touch. It was the promise of—

The promise of a Norman! she reminded herself. "Nay, Maxen, you do not want this. You do not want me."

He moved his lips lower to a place between neck and shoulder.

"Remember Thomas!"

His head came up. Out of feverish eyes, he stared at her, then he dropped onto his back.

Struck by an incomprehensible sense of loss, Rhiannyn could not move. It was as if his had been the arms of—

Of what? she silently demanded. *A lover?*

She rejected the thought, reminded herself of the arms of her mother, father, and brothers who were dead. She wanted nothing to do with the arms of the enemy—and Maxen Pendery would ever be that to her.

"Never will I forget Thomas," he said. "And neither shall you."

She lunged off the bed and distanced herself to the full extent of the chain.

Eyes tightly closed, Maxen groaned.

Was he in pain? Had he further injured himself? She prayed not, hoped the herbs Christophe had put in the wine would give him ease.

Lowering her eyes down him, she saw the coverlet was around his bare calves beneath the hem of his undertunic. She knew she should cover him, but feared going near him again.

"Would you have me summon your brother?" she asked.

When he did not answer, she guessed he had returned to sleep.

While she stood there, she tried not to think on what had happened between them. And failed. Why had she felt something only Edwin ought to make her feel? How was it her enemy had such power over her?

She was still pondering it when Sir Guy came around the screen.

His brow wrinkling as he took in her state of dress, he crossed to his lord and drew the coverlet over Maxen. "He rests well?"

Rhiannyn stepped to where the bliaut lay on the chest and pulled it on over her head. As it settled past her knees, leaving the longer chemise to cover her lower legs and drag its hem in the rushes, she said, "He awoke a short while ago. I gave him wine, and he returned to sleeping."

"Was he in pain?"

She looked up from knotting the sash around her waist. "He did not speak of any, but I believe so."

He inclined his head. "What did he speak of?"

She was taken aback by his question. "Little, though he suspected I had poisoned his wine."

"Understandable."

She put her chin up. "Because I am Saxon?"

"Because one Pendery has already died because of you."

Though she accepted the blame, she was sick of hearing it spoken so often by murdering Normans. "How many of my people died because of him?" She jerked her chin at Maxen. "How many innocents did your liege slay in the name of the usurper?"

The knight's eyes hardened further. "In battle, many were the Saxons who fell to his sword, for which he spent the past two years in repentance."

"Repentance! All he knows of that is his mockery of it when he donned monk's clothing and pretended holiness to deceive Edwin and his followers. He does not know God, and never will he."

"You are wrong. The monk is the truth of him. Since Hastings, and prior to his being summoned to Etcheverry, he served in a monastery. If not for Thomas's death, he would yet be there."

Rhiannyn nearly gaped. Upon discovering the identity of the monk who had saved her life, never had she considered he was truly of the brotherhood. She had thought it pretense, the tonsuring of his head an act of sacrifice in the name of revenge.

Reflecting on the night he had preached at the camp, and later when he had stood before the horde and pronounced them sinners for what they meant to do to her, it seemed possible Sir Guy spoke the truth.

Maxen—Brother Justus—had swept away her suspicions by presenting himself as a monk worthy of his station. She had felt God in his words, drawn strength from them, and known a kind of peace before Dora had shattered it with her accusations. Still, the man Rhiannyn had come to know these past days did not fit the monk Sir Guy said he had been.

But as if to push her nearer the truth, she recalled the words Maxen had spoken when he had kissed her.

It has been a long time.

Surely only a man long without the company of a woman would desire one he hated.

She shook her head. "His anger is too great, his manner too vengeful."

"You are surprised?" Sir Guy raised his eyebrows. "A second brother has been killed, forcing Maxen to renounce his chosen life to hold safe what belongs to his family. *Non*, Rhiannyn, he is not a saint. No man truly of this earth is. He is but a man who, in one day, lost two things precious to him. And both because of you."

Yet another lost life upon her conscience. Maxen was not dead—at least, not yet—but the man he had chosen to become after Hastings was no more, and all because she had refused to be Thomas's wife.

Sorrows multiplying, she looked past the knight to his lord and acknowledged that somewhere there dwelt a human. A man who had given his life to God to atone for the lives he had taken. A man who had risked his life to save hers. But did he yet exist? If so, could he be reached?

"Had I known…" She trailed off, for she did not know what difference it would make had the truth of Maxen Pendery been known.

"You would still be Saxon," Sir Guy said, "and he Norman. You would protect the one you refuse him, and he would seek him."

In one thing the knight was wrong. Regardless of who had killed Thomas, if she knew the name, she would speak it to save the lives of all the others.

"I warn you," Sir Guy said, "If Maxen dies, I will seek your punishment."

"This I know." She moved her gaze to his lord's still form, and heard the knight's booted feet crush rushes as he departed.

Where was the Maxen of mercy? she wondered. Where was the one with the power to bring peace to Etcheverry? And peace this Norman must bring, for to continue believing the Saxons would one day drive out the Normans was a delusion too long fostered. Barring a miracle, Duke William and his barons were here to stay.

Accepting that hurt even more than Rhiannyn would have believed, but it also gave her hope.

"You will not die, Maxen," she whispered. "Where you are, I will find you."

Following a nooning meal accompanied by raucous noise from beyond the screen, Christophe and Theta returned.

Rhiannyn stood and looked to the other woman. "You are not needed," she said.

Theta's smirk flattened as she turned from the table upon which she had emptied her armful of bandages. "What speak you of?"

"I will assist Christophe in tending his brother."

"Truly?" Christophe said.

Theta pushed past him and halted so near Rhiannyn the latter was forced to tip her head back. "As if any would trust you! Is it not enough Thomas is dead because of you? And Maxen may die as well?"

It bothered Rhiannyn that the woman referred to the new lord of Etcheverry with such familiarity, the same as she had done with Thomas even after he had made it clear he would not wed her.

Though Rhiannyn longed to step back so she would not have to crane her neck, she knew it would appear as if she backed down. "Maxen will live," she said, "and I will assist Christophe to that end."

"Away with you! Take your chain and cower in yon corner."

"'Tis you who must leave," Rhiannyn persisted.

Theta snorted. "She is high and mighty for a prisoner, would you not say, Christophe?"

The young man hesitated, clearly uncertain as to the role he should play in this contest of wills.

"I will not leave," Theta said and shoved Rhiannyn.

Recovering her balance, Rhiannyn said between her teeth, "And I will not tell you again. Go."

There would not be a better time for Christophe to prevent a fray, and as if he sensed it, he stepped between the women and took hold of Theta's arm. Unlike his brother who stood well above him, he came eye to eye with the woman.

"To tend my brother," he said, "I need only one other pair of hands. As Rhiannyn is willing to lend hers, your time is best spent tending your people."

Surprise flashed across Theta's face, but was quickly displaced by anger. "At your side is where I belong, not alone among filthy Saxons."

Had Rhiannyn not been separated from the woman by Christophe's body, she might have set herself upon Theta. It was insult enough to be called names by the Normans, but by one who was also of Saxon birth...

"I have spoken," Christophe said. "Henceforth, Rhiannyn will assist with my brother."

Theta peered around Christophe and gave Rhiannyn a twisted smile. "'Tis good to know you are as much a harlot as I, but when Maxen is done with you, know this—he will come back to me, just as Thomas would have had you not murdered him."

Her belief that Rhiannyn's offer to assist Christophe was an attempt to gain Maxen's bed was almost laughable, but no laughter spilled from Rhiannyn. The intimation that Maxen had already had the woman to bed was too disturbing.

Hips swinging, Theta withdrew.

"I apologize," Christophe said. "I should not have allowed her to say such things to you."

"You are not at fault. Theta says what Theta wants."

"If not that she is so unmoved by the sight of blood, I would not have anything to do with her. But she serves me well."

"I understand, Christophe."

He nibbled his lower lip. "Mayhap you will explain why you have offered to take her place."

"Sir Guy told me the reason your brother is the way he is—what he gave up to succeed Thomas."

"You did not know?"

She shook her head. "I thought it a disguise your brother used to deceive me. Now I better understand, and methinks there must be some compassion in him, some way to reach him and prevent more deaths."

Sorrowfully, Christophe shook his head. "The Maxen I knew of old—years before Hastings—might have been reachable, but this one…I fear not even your goodness and beauty can change who he has become."

But if he could not be changed, why had he committed his life to God following the slaughter at Hastings? Could one truly incapable of change do something so selfless?

"Methinks you are a dreamer, Rhiannyn."

She blinked, offered Christophe a strained smile. "And you are becoming a terrible skeptic."

He shrugged. "Maxen brings that out in others. But come, let me show you what needs to be done."

She followed him to the bed and watched as he raised his brother's undertunic and removed the bandages.

"It is not worsening," he said as he examined the wound, "but neither does it look to be improving."

"The stitches hold?"

"They do." He began to instruct her in how to cleanse the wound, and as he spoke, he performed the task and explained his reason for using the salve he had chosen.

"Now you." He placed fresh bandages in her hands. "When I raise him, pass these beneath."

They quickly accomplished the task, though more for the strain on Christophe's arms than the comfort of his brother who slept through it.

"Secure them," Christophe said and began picking through the items on the table.

Had it been any other whom she passed her hands over, it would have seemed meant for a simpleton. But it was Maxen, and her fingers turned clumsy as they swept smooth muscle.

"Good," Christophe said when she finished. "Now cool him as Theta did."

She placed the basin of water on the floor beside her, wet the cloth, and worked it from Maxen's moist brow down to his neck.

As she raised his undertunic higher, Christophe stoppered the bottle from which he had emptied powder into the wine Theta had brought and said, "When he awakens, have him drink this."

"I will give it to him," she said, silently adding that this time there would be a different outcome to her offering drink to Maxen.

Christophe gathered up his things. "I will return ere dark. Send for me if he worsens."

Though she preferred he remain until she finished swabbing his brother, she knew he was needed elsewhere. "I shall," she said.

He crossed to the screen and paused. "Rhiannyn?"

She looked up.

"I had naught to do with Maxen's plans to follow you to Edwin's camp," he blurted. "You believe me, do you not?"

"Of course I do."

His features relaxed, and he departed.

Rhiannyn rewetted the cloth and drew it down Maxen's chest to his abdomen above the waistband of his braies. Next, she moved to the end of the bed, turned up the coverlet, and cooled his feet and lower legs.

It was strange to willingly touch The Bloodlust Warrior of Hastings, to learn his body in a way few but lovers would ever know it. But it was necessary. So necessary.

Later, when he rose to partial consciousness, she offered the wine, bracing herself should he attempt to test it the same as he had done that morn. But he was too delirious and eagerly drank as she held the rim to his lips.

"I burn," he breathed as he settled back to his pillow.

The water in the basin was no longer chilled, but Rhiannyn wet a cloth and laid it on his brow. "Try to sleep."

As she started to straighten, he reached to her and placed his palm against her cheek. "Angel," he rasped. "Stay."

Though she knew the words were formed by an incoherent mind, her hope was furthered that he might, indeed, be reachable. "I will not leave you," she said. "Now, sleep."

He closed his eyes, trailed his fingers down her neck to the V of her bliaut, and dropped his arm to his side.

Rhiannyn stepped back and rubbed her hands over her arms.

Cold is what I am, she told herself. *Only cold.*

15

THE DAYS FELL one over the other, Maxen's illness taking him into an unconsciousness so deep he could not know who assisted Christophe in the cleansing and bandaging of his wound; who cooled his body and wet his parched mouth; who slept lightly beside his bed during the long nights; who coaxed him from dreams in which he called out to Nils; who by sight and touch became familiar with nearly every span of his battle-battered flesh.

He did not know, but others knew it was Rhiannyn who refused him the peace of death, though it often seemed the best end for him. Those who came and went—Christophe, Sir Guy, servants bearing viands, and occasionally Sir Ancel—cast their curiosity upon her. And the eyes with which Sir Guy watched her lost much of their condemnation.

On the fifth day, as night began to give unto morn, Rhiannyn awakened, though what had roused her she could not have said.

"Maxen?" She rose from her pallet alongside the bed and touched his arm. His skin was frighteningly cold.

"Ah, nay," she whispered, but before the cry rising up her throat passed her lips, his body shook and he groaned.

It was not death come for him. Not yet.

Praying his chill was caused by the sudden breaking of his fever, she looked near upon his shadowed face. "Maxen?"

"Cold," he said and threw out a hand to retrieve the coverlet he had earlier kicked off.

"I have it." She reached to the foot of the bed, untangled it from his legs, and pulled it up over him. As she tucked it around him, he shook again, and with more violence.

She snatched up her own blanket and spread it over him, but it was not enough, and there were no more covers to provide the warmth he needed.

There is you, whispered a voice that roused childhood memories of the bitingly cold nights she and her brothers had crept off their pallets to share their mother and father's bed. The warmth of body cradling body had been unequalled by fire or blanket.

Of course, she could call for more covering, but it would awaken many. And was there not a better solution at hand? Though she would not begin to consider such intimacy were Maxen not so ill, she lifted the covers and, chain rattling, slid in beside him.

With an answering rattle, he turned onto his side, curved an arm around her waist, and drew her back against him.

She held her breath as the manacle on his wrist pressed into her abdomen and he fit his muscled contours to her softer ones. It was almost too much, this embrace made for lovers, but she would give him what he needed.

Slowly emptying her lungs, she tried to relax, but it was impossible with chills continuing to rack him.

When he finally stilled, the only movement his breath stirring the hair at her crown and the thump of his heart against her back, she told her fingers to unclench, her jaw to loosen, her back to unbind. As much as possible, they complied, and she closed her eyes and prayed for sleep to take her far from the disturbing feel of him.

But not the grave of my dreams, she silently beseeched. *Not that far.*

"I thank you," Maxen murmured.

His gratitude surprised her as much as his wakefulness. Though she told herself he spoke out of muddled thoughts, without knowledge of the one to whom he directed his words, she was warmed by the gesture. And as she felt herself drift into sleep, it felt strangely right to be here with him. In the arms of her enemy.

The last time Maxen had been with a woman, she had smelled of smoke from tending kitchen fires and sweat from too many hours spent there— far different from the one whose scent now wafted to him.

The kitchen servant had been soft, but not soft like this woman. She'd had dark, straight hair bearing no resemblance to the gilded tresses curling around his fingers. And she had slipped away afterwards, unlike this one who had clearly spent the night with him. A night he could not recall.

Nor did he feel satiated. Indeed, it felt years since—

It has been years, he told himself as the last of sleep slipped away.

It was not a dream he had given his life to God, nor that he had been forced to renounce that life. He was Maxen Pendery, reluctant lord of Etcheverry, and this woman was Rhiannyn—she who would have been lady of Etcheverry through marriage to Harwolfson had the Saxons not been defeated, and again through marriage to Thomas when the con-quering was done. Twice, she could have been a lady, and now she was a prisoner.

Why had she come into his bed? And had he truly not taken what she offered?

Searching backward, he recalled hands coaxing the heat from his body and brushing damp hair off his brow; a soft voice beseeching him one moment, reassuring him the next; a lap upon which his head had been raised to put drink to his lips.

Had it been Rhiannyn? Nay, not one who hated him as she did. More likely, Theta. But last eve…

That had been Rhiannyn, for the one who had given her warmth to him still lay beside him. And warmth was all she had offered. Not the use of her body for carnal pleasure, but something he had needed more.

Why? The woman he believed she was should have left him to the chill that was more of the grave than anything he had known.

He pushed up onto an elbow. The movement causing daggers to stab the backs of his eyes, he pulled deep, calming breaths. And prevailed against the darkness seeking to drag him back.

Focusing on Rhiannyn, he swept aside the hair falling over her face. She looked so beautifully innocent, as if she could harm no one. But therein lay deceit, did it not? Or did it?

He rolled onto his back and stared at the ceiling.

Was it yesterday he had awakened to the slap of her hand? He remembered naming her *witch*, more vividly recalled the kiss he had stolen from her under the pretense of fearing she meant to poison him. What had possessed him? Why did he so desire her?

Her low moan swept aside his pondering, and with a rattle of chain, she twisted around, laid her head on his upper arm, and settled a knee atop his thigh.

Maxen clenched his teeth. He could push her away, and he should, but he was loath to do so. Thus, as during the first year at the monastery when his thoughts had turned to women, he determined he would calm his body as he had done then.

Although he had doubted he could maintain more than a bare semblance of faith after all the ill that had befallen his family, he closed his eyes and turned to prayers used in times of carnal weakness. To a degree, they had served him well, though sometimes merely as a result of fatigue from hours spent on his knees.

Unfortunately, they had little effect this day, unlike those other days when he had not had a warm, desirable body at his side.

She longed to keep her eyes sealed against the light of day, to ignore the feeling of being watched, to regain the hours of sleep lost to...

Lifting her lids, she focused on her hand and saw it lay on Maxen Pendery's shoulder, the flesh being neither hot nor cold.

She raised her gaze to eyes she had not seen the color of for days. In the morning light, they shone blue upon her.

"You are awake," she said and offered a tentative smile.

His eyebrows rose.

"The fever has passed."

His mouth twisted. "Disappointed?"

She felt her smile slide away. Having put so much of her heart into his care, it hurt to be confronted by the Maxen with whom she had left off.

Did you truly expect a changed man? she silently chastised. *Believe he would let your people go and make no more war upon them? All because you did what Theta could more easily have done?*

Feeling tears, she blinked them back, and determinedly picked up her hope and brushed it off.

It is a beginning, she told herself, *and that is better than no beginning at all.* It was still possible to get to the other side of him. Unfortunately, there was much to do and not much time in which to do it.

Sitting up, taking the cover with her and pressing it to her chemise-clothed chest, she said, "I am not disappointed. I am relieved."

"Then there must have been a greater threat to your person did I die rather than live. Sir Guy, am I right?"

Though it was as she had been warned, it alone did not fuel her relief. She'd had an ulterior motive in wanting Maxen to live, but it went beyond her people. With each passing day, it had become more personal. She wanted him to live simply that he might live—so the man who had gently set his hand upon her and called her *angel,* and had thanked her for her warmth, might someday show a similar kindness to others.

"You are wrong," she said.

"And you lie." He sat up, grimacing as his swaying body testified to his weakness.

She laid a hand on his arm. "'Tis too soon to rise. You have lain ill five days—"

"Five days!"

"Aye."

He considered her hand on him, pushed it off. "I prefer your fear to concern. It is more trustworthy."

The same Maxen—unchanged and ungiving. "You have much to be thankful for," she forced past stiff lips. "By God's will you live, and to him you must give thanks."

"God," he scoffed. "It is Christophe who should be given credit." He tossed back the coverlet, and with a clattering of chain, swung his legs over the opposite side of the bed and stood. For a moment.

"Accursed weakness," he murmured. Face ashen, he dropped back down upon the bed.

"If you are not to undo your healing," Rhiannyn said, "you need food and rest, Maxen."

Gaze cold as steel, he said, "Do not pretend to know what I need, and do not make me tell you again the proper way to address me."

She swallowed the retort that had no place in helping him become human. "Aye, my lord." She lowered her feet to the floor. "Christophe will be here soon. He will wish to examine you."

Maxen made no reply, though she felt his gaze follow her around the bed.

She lifted her bliaut from atop the chest, shook it out, and pulled it on.

"Fine clothes for a prisoner," he said.

She looked up from knotting the sash. "They are what were brought to me. If you prefer otherwise—"

"I do."

"Then I am sure you will see to it as soon as possible."

"Indeed."

Rhiannyn was grateful for Christophe's appearance that gave her respite from the battle Maxen was attempting to draw her into.

"Give praise," Christophe exclaimed as he hurried to the bed. "It was feared you might not awaken."

"You have much to learn about self-confidence, little brother." Maxen gave him a smile Rhiannyn wished were for her. "It is by your hand I live."

"And in good spirits," Christophe added.

"You can thank Rhiannyn for that."

She stiffened, from the glint in Maxen's eyes feared he would reveal he had awakened to find her in his bed.

Christophe glanced at her. "You refer to her tending you these past days?"

"*Non*, I am sure it is Theta I have to thank for that."

Christophe shook his head. "Rhiannyn cared for you when I could not. She insisted. Did she not tell you?"

The glint fled Maxen's eyes, but instead of giving answer, he asked, "How do I fare, Brother?"

With a twitch of his lips, Christophe granted him the change of topic. "It seems well, but I will know better after I have examined the wound."

While he did so, Maxen brooded on Christophe's revelation. Though under different circumstances he would have been grateful for the care given him, he was suspicious—even angry—for Rhiannyn eluded him at every turn, refusing to stay in the role in which he cast her.

Shortly, Christophe proclaimed Maxen on his way to being completely healed, but was adamant a few days of rest were in order. "I will tell the others," he said.

And end the speculation over who would succeed him, Maxen mused. "I am hungry."

Christophe nodded and was gone.

Maxen propped himself against the headboard and asked, "Why did you do it, Rhiannyn?"

Avoiding his gaze, she raked fingers through her tangled curls. "We may be enemies, but it does not mean I am without heart when one is in need."

"Theta could have tended me just as well."

"She could not have. I was here, she was not."

"She could have been here."

Rhiannyn settled her eyes upon him. "I wanted you to live, for it to be me who helped you back to life."

"So I would be owing to you?"

"You could not be owing to me after having saved my life. Nay, not owing. Knowing."

"What?"

She swept her hair back and stepped to the bed. "That all Saxons are not as you believe them to be. That we feel compassion, know pain and hurt, and have only fought for what is rightfully ours."

Maxen knew it. He had grown up amongst these people, been befriended by them and friendly toward them before Duke William had called him and his brothers to prove their fealty by taking up swords against them.

Caught up in the passion of a battle he had trained for since childhood, he had forsaken those he could more easily have called his own than the Normans. It was something he knew too well, one of two reasons he had been sickened by the carnage of which he had been so great a part. The other reason was Nils, whose dying had opened Maxen's eyes to the unpardonable thing he had done, the atrocity for which he had spent two years in repentance. However, since learning of Thomas's death, he had repeatedly fought off memories, anger and revenge guiding him to the point at which he now found himself.

But which way to go from here? Toward the pleading in Rhiannyn's eyes, or the taking of Saxon lives in payment for Thomas's?

He felt almost torn. Though he did not know which was stronger in him—the good or the bad—he turned the way of compromise. "I want only the one who killed Thomas, Rhiannyn."

Tears ran into her eyes, and the flare of her small nose attested to her struggle to control her emotions. "If I knew, do you not think I would tell? Give one life for so many?"

It made little sense she would not, but he found it difficult to believe she had not seen the one behind the dagger. Even had she not, surely the Saxon who had defeated the Norman lord would have made himself known to his countrymen by way of bragging.

"Nevertheless," Maxen said, "there must be punishment, else there is naught to prevent such from happening again."

"Hanging innocents will not prevent it," she exclaimed. "It will drive the Saxons to further warring, bringing more death upon Etcheverry."

Maxen knew he ought to waste no more time on the matter, but he said, "Who will bring this war upon Etcheverry? Harwolfson is gone, his rebels under my control."

"He will return. This I promise."

"I am to fear that?"

She shook her head. "Not if you act upon it."

"How so?"

"Give the rebels a reason to make peace with you. If Etcheverry is to prosper again, you will need them for planting and harvesting, tending cattle and—"

"Need men more inclined to plant scythes in my back than in the harvest?"

"Aye, they may be more inclined to do that, but if you are fair with them, in time they could serve you well."

He laughed. "Your sense of reality is as poor as Christophe's. Never could Harwolfson's men be trusted."

"You do not know that."

"I do, just as I know I am done with this conversation." Past done. So much that the thought of sleep held more appeal than the need for food.

Though he could see Rhiannyn wished to continue the discussion, she sighed. "I suppose you will return me to the tower."

He had not thought that far ahead. Even when he had sent her back there after bringing the vanquished Saxons into the castle walls, he had not known what he would do with her. And he still did not. "Eventually, perhaps."

"Why not now?"

"I am not done with you."

Done with me, Rhiannyn silently mulled the words. Maxen had touched her, kissed her with wine, and made her feel things of which she had heretofore been innocent. Did he now intend to violate her?

Fearing she fooled herself by questioning the possibility, she acknowledged he meant to take what no man had, possessing her as she had once happened upon Thomas possessing Theta.

She tried to convince herself it did not matter. After all, the loss of her virtue would not impact her future since she had accepted Thomas's curse to never wed. But what of children? That she would never know the joy of them had also been his curse, but she still might grow round with a misbegotten child.

Sir Guy's appearance, along with Lucilla bearing viands, was welcome.

Rhiannyn crossed to the one chair she could reach by the length of chain, and sank into it.

"You are well," Sir Guy said as he drew alongside the bed.

"And hungry." Maxen smiled wryly. "Been brawling?"

Sir Guy rubbed the bruise yet visible along his jaw. "With you. It seems you do not care to be moved once you are abed."

Understanding transformed Maxen's face, then he grimaced and glanced at Rhiannyn before setting himself at the food.

She clenched her hands. Would he have her this night? Or would he wait until he was fully recovered?

Pray, not until he recovers, she silently pleaded, then considered it might be better to have it over with.

"Rhiannyn?"

She peered up at Lucilla who surprised her with a small smile. "Aye?"

"I've food for ye. Where would you have me set it?"

"I am not hungry."

"I will put it on the clothes chest for later." The woman turned away.

Drawing her knees to her chest, Rhiannyn winced at the noise made by the links. How she hated it—more, these past two years that had brought her to this cruel conquering.

Pressing her teeth into her lower lip, she trained her gaze on the floor and blocked out Maxen's and Sir Guy's voices, and all those who came after.

16

BLOOD.

Staring at the dagger, Rhiannyn wondered why she was only now beginning to feel pain. When she had scooped up the napkin, she had not known a blade was hidden beneath it and had felt only mild discomfort as it sliced through her grasping fingers. But now there was pain that paralleled the brilliant red soaking through the napkin's weave.

She opened her fingers and swept her gaze down the blade nestled in the napkin, the edges of which shone more red than silver, then lifted the weapon from her injured hand and fisted her bloody fingers in the napkin to stem the flow down her palm and wrist.

Not since her return to Etcheverry had she been given a meat knife with her meals, let alone a dagger of deadly intent. Who had placed it on her tray? And for what?

Her first thought was Lucilla. Had there been a message in the woman's smile? If so, what was it? That she kill Maxen? Herself? Might Sir Ancel be responsible? He had also come into the chamber and was more likely to have slipped the dagger beneath the napkin when he thought none were looking. In fact, she had seen him nibbling at the foodstuffs on her tray while conversing with his lord.

There had been others during the two hours Maxen had received them, but most were a blur, and none so likely to have left the dagger as Sir Ancel. Still, there was the question of who it was intended for. Was she being given the mercy of taking her own life before another did? Or was the hunger for power so great the lord of Etcheverry was the quarry?

"Almighty!" Maxen's bellow broke through her speculation.

She startled and looked to where he sat up, having arisen from the sleep he had fallen into an hour ago.

Imagining the picture she presented standing at the foot of his bed, a dagger in one hand, the other red from knuckles to wrist, she said, "It was not…I did not…"

As if he had never been ill, he sprang off the mattress and gained her side. "Why?" he demanded, something like concern grooving his face and turning his eyes a deeper blue.

She shook her head. "Why?"

He grabbed her arm, snatched the balled napkin from her hand, and began winding it around her wrist. "Naught is so bad you must take your life!"

He thought she had cut her wrist? To escape from this world into another she was not sure would receive her?

"I was not trying to kill myself," she said and opened her hand to show her slashed fingers.

The color in his face ebbed, and he unwound the napkin and peered at her wrist. "Then you mistakenly cut yourself ere you could use the dagger on me."

Rhiannyn gasped. "How can you believe that if you do not believe I put a dagger through Thomas?"

Maxen shifted his gaze to the bloody weapon. "Do you intend to do something with that?"

As if burnt, she released it to the floor. "You have not answered me," she said. "You refuse to believe I killed Thomas, but think me capable of killing you?"

"You could not have hated him as much as you do me," he said and began wrapping her hand in the bloodied linen.

But she did not hate him as a Saxon ought to, nor could she now that she knew what drove him to revenge—that he was not the devil, but a man with years of hurt and regret behind him that had seeped into his present. He was touchable. How, she did not know, but she would not give up hope.

"I do not hate you," she said.

He released her bandaged hand. "You should."

"Why? Because of anger that is your due? Another brother dead, your calling stolen from you, your prayers unanswered?"

"You dare go where you ought not, Rhiannyn," he warned.

"I know."

"Then know this as well. I do not need nor welcome your understanding. Try as you might, no bearing will it have on the fate of the Saxon rebels. I will do with them what I will."

"You will not kill them," she said, praying she was right. "This I know."

A muscle in his jaw spasmed. "You know nothing." He pressed her down onto the wooden chest, strode to the screen, and with the chain taut between them, called for Christophe.

"Where did you get it?" he asked when he returned to where she sat cradling her hand.

She followed his gaze to the dagger at her feet. Something about the weapon was peculiar. Nay, not peculiar. Familiar. The hilt with its intricately carved leaves...

"Answer me, Rhiannyn."

She nearly told the truth, but fear for what he might do to Lucilla if he believed she had delivered the dagger birthed a lie. "I found it on the floor. One of your knights must have lost it."

"How did you cut yourself?"

"I saw its glint among the rushes, but did not know what it was until I picked it up—by its blade."

His eyebrows rose. "I thought the dagger might have come to you on your meal tray."

Trying to keep her face impassive, she wondered how he had he known. Because she had been standing over the tray when he awakened? Or might he be responsible for the dagger? Was this a test?

"I found it on the floor," she repeated.

He lowered to his haunches and lifted the dagger covered in blood and rushes. "For one who lies as often as you do"—he turned the weapon over—"I would expect you to be much better at it."

Her gaze also drawn to the dagger—specifically, its unusual hilt—Rhiannyn reflected it was true she lied, and often, but she did it to protect her people. Of course, what good was a lie not believed?

Of a sudden, she placed where she had seen the dagger before. "Thomas," she said.

Maxen's gaze landed hard upon her. "What about him?"

The urgency in his eyes propelled her past caution. Heart beating hard, she said, "The dagger. It is the one."

"That killed him?"

She nodded.

"How do you know this?"

She saw it again the day of Thomas's death, his blood in the recesses of the carved hilt when she had retrieved the dagger from the muddy ground to prove she had done the deed.

"I remember it," she whispered. "Too well."

Maxen felt her fear in the air between them, and found himself drawn to offer comfort. But he would not, for it would show heart he did not have—rather, could not afford to have.

He returned his attention to the instrument of death. Although he knew his brother had been murdered with a dagger, he had not learned what had become of it, nor thought to ask. Now he had it, though not in the way whoever had passed it to Rhiannyn wished.

"Was it Sir Ancel who pulled it from Thomas's body?" he asked, thinking the aggrieved knight likely responsible for its appearance this day.

Rhiannyn lowered her head into her hands. "It was Thomas," she said, her voice muffled.

Meaning he had not died immediately. There were other questions Maxen wished to ask, but he determined to stay the present course. "Sir Ancel picked it up?"

She shook her head. "I did, but he knocked it from my hand."

Patience thinning, Maxen lifted her chin and peered into her moist eyes. "*Then* he picked it up?"

"Nay, it was Sir Guy."

Maxen could not have been more surprised, but he refused to believe his friend sought his death. This must be another lie Rhiannyn told, an attempt to take from his side the only one among his men whom he trusted.

"You do not believe me," she said softly.

Refusing to be pulled into her eyes, he stood and called for Guy.

Christophe arrived first, disheveled from whatever task he had been pulled from. Fear widening his eyes, he looked from the dagger his brother held to the bloody napkin Rhiannyn grasped, and hurried forward.

Kneeling before her, he uncurled her fingers. "How did this happen?"

"An accident. I turned my hand around the blade ere I knew what it was."

He looked over his shoulder at his brother as if seeking confirmation it had, indeed, been a mishap.

"It is the truth," Rhiannyn assured him. "Will it require the needle?"

He gently probed the injury. "Bandages only."

While he tended her, Guy entered. "My lord?"

Maxen raised the dagger. "This was left for Rhiannyn—by you, she would have me believe."

"I did not say it was he!" she protested.

Maxen gave her a silencing look. "She claims she does not know who left it for her, but she says it was you who last possessed it."

The knight's face incredulous, he said, "As God is my witness, Maxen, I did not give her the dagger."

"Did you take it from the place Thomas died?"

"I did, but—"

"Then it was last in your keeping."

"It was, but obviously no longer."

At least Rhiannyn had told the truth, Maxen reflected. "You say it was stolen from you and given her by another."

"There can be no other explanation but that it was taken from my belongings." Guy's eyes implored Maxen to believe him. "Never would I betray you. Have I not proven my fealty many times over?"

After a lengthy pause, Maxen said, "You have, but I must know who seeks my death."

"Not I, my lord."

Maxen cast his thoughts back to each of those who had come and gone this morn and settled on two—the serving woman, Lucilla, and Sir Ancel. Though it could be the servant, he thought it more likely the knight was responsible.

"Have you the key, Guy?" Maxen asked. "I would be free of this chain."

With uncertain relief, his friend drew it from his pouch and fit it in the iron. "It could have been one of the Saxons," he said as the iron clattered to the floor.

"I have thought of that, and of another—a Norman."

Guy nodded. "*Oui*, him."

"Regardless, the punishment will be the same."

"And the punishment of Harwolfson's rebels? Does the sentence you pronounced on them hold?"

Maxen met Rhiannyn's pleading eyes. "It holds. And will be done on the morrow."

She stared, unable to believe he would execute the Saxons. Or was it that she did not wish to believe it?

Christophe rose and faced Maxen. "You are not my brother," he punctuated each word and limped past him and out of the chamber.

Something resembling pain crossed Maxen's face, but it was too fleeting to be certain.

Shortly, Rhiannyn found herself no longer chained to a man, but to the frame of the bed and left to herself as Maxen joined his men in the hall for the evening meal. Her own meal pushed aside, she curled up in the chair with a blanket and waited for what the night would bring.

It brought hours of tortured thought, and nearing the middle of night, it returned Maxen to her.

He strode across the rushes to her.

When he did not speak, nor touch her, she asked, "Did you discover who left the dagger?"

"I did not, but I shall."

She nodded, then the question she had tossed around her mind these last hours burst from her. "What will it take to free the Saxons from your vengeance?"

Eyes glimmering in the muted light, he said, "Start telling the truth, and I will start showing mercy."

Knowing he referred to not only the one who had provided the dagger, but who had murdered Thomas, she said, "I do not know. I give you my word."

"I almost believe you."

She gasped. "You do?"

"Almost."

It was more than she'd had. "Maxen," she said, belatedly remembering she was forbidden to call him by his given name, "show your mercy."

As if he did not notice her impropriety, he said, "The decision has been made," and turned toward the bed.

His callousness was like casting oil on the fire burning in her—a fire Thomas had been singed by many times, but which had not vented from her with such intensity since his death. She threw off the blanket, shot to her feet, and amid the chain's clatter, followed him.

At the bed, he came back around. "I warn you, Rhiannyn. I have had too much drink and too little food with which to soak it up. Take your misplaced anger back to your chair."

She halted before him. "Misplaced?" she said, uncaring that she might awaken those who slept in the hall. "You can be angry and I cannot? You lost two brothers and your life of repentance for the atrocities you committed, and for that I am to feel owing to you?"

She scoffed. "Still you have your parents, a brother, a sister, even a country that does not belong to you. What have I? All dear to me is gone—two brothers, a father, a mother, and my country. I have less than naught since I have not even myself now that I am your prisoner."

Ignoring the darkness moving across his face, she continued, "What vengeance mine? Should I have used the dagger as intended? Taken your life as you shall take the lives of innocents on the morrow?"

"I will hear no more!"

"I am not finished."

"Aye, you are." He took her arm, propelled her to the chair, and pushed her into it. "Do not rise or speak another word."

She started to stand, but he gripped her shoulder and pressed her down. "Think on it, Rhiannyn," he warned, his face so near hers their noses nearly touched.

Teeth clenched to hold back words she longed to loose, she held his gaze. For what seemed minutes, they remained thus. Then, as if the wind that fanned the flames of her anger had stilled, she slumped.

Maxen released her, crossed the chamber, and extinguished the torch. Then his dark figure moved to the bed and he lowered to it.

Alone, but not alone, she peered into the darkness and waited for morn.

17

Where Rhiannyn stood on the wall-walk that spanned the top edge of the outer wall, the Saxons assembled below looked like a peasant's patch cloth mantle. There was no uniformity to them, no organization, and no hope against the scores of soldiers prepared to carry out Maxen Pendery's punishment. By nightfall, they would all be dead, their only victory escaping Norman rule.

Tearless, though her eyes burned with her refusal to be otherwise, she shifted her gaze to the gallows, and away. It was cruel of Maxen to force her to witness the execution of her people—to stand in full sight of them at this highest point in the bailey where none could miss her, and alongside the new lord of Etcheverry himself. Now, in the most terrible way, she had proof of how wrong she was about him. He was too broken to be reachable. And, she feared, soon she would be as well.

She was so caught up in her emotions, she did not realize Maxen leaned near until he said in her ear, "You are a foolishly brave woman, Rhiannyn."

She turned her face to him, acknowledged he still looked unwell. "And you are a devil."

He straightened. "That is the least of the things I have been called."

As she had nothing to lose, she said, "Very well, something stronger—The Bloodlust Warrior of Etcheverry." Pretending pride in her choice, she nodded. "Far more appropriate."

If the daggers in his eyes could have leapt from them, they would have killed her where she stood.

Drawing a deep breath, he clasped his hands behind his back and returned his attention to the Saxons. "Bloodlust Warrior," he murmured. "Not in this instance. This is different."

Was it? His choice of words ignited a spark of hope, but she extinguished it. Maxen surely meant he was more justified in what he was about to do, than in what he had done at Hastings. And perhaps he was in the eyes of man, but he forgot the eyes of God were also upon him. Once, perhaps, he could be forgiven for the blood upon his blade, but surely not twice.

When all quieted, the Saxons having fully turned their attention to where Maxen and Rhiannyn stood, Maxen called in the Anglo-Saxon language, "For two years, many are the Normans you have killed, and yet the battle of Hastings has been done for as long, England defeated, and King William crowned its ruler. You have left your families, your homes, and your crops, all for something that can never be—for Edwin Harwolfson, a man who has selfishly spent your lives to achieve his own end."

A murmur of dissent rose, but it died with Maxen's next words. "I offer you something different."

Aethel stepped forward, raised a fist. "What be that, Norman devil? Dangling at the end of a rope?"

"It is your choice whether or not death figures into it," Maxen answered.

Rhiannyn's knees nearly buckled. Had she heard right? She could not have—unless he played with words.

"Do you go the way of Harwolfson, your fate is sealed. Do you pledge fealty to me, rebuild your homes, and put plough to the land, I will give you back your lives."

As disbelief rippled through the Saxons, Rhiannyn silently beckoned Maxen's gaze so she might see if what was there matched his words.

Keeping his profile to her, he said, "But first, those who accept me as their lord must prove themselves. There are walls to be raised." He swept a hand to the vulnerable, unfinished stone rampart enclosing the outer bailey. "And buildings to erect ere winter."

Rhiannyn swayed, remembering to breathe only when her lungs began to ache.

"Those who stay the side of Harwolfson," Maxen continued, "remain where you are. Those wishing to live under the House of Pendery, gather left." At their hesitation, he commanded, "Make your choice. Now."

More hesitation and glances at the nooses dangling from the gallows, then a handful of Saxons, heads down, separated from the others. Some of the men tried to block them, but they pushed past and formed their small group.

More, Rhiannyn silently beseeched. *Lord, show them the way.*

A dozen more, and all the women, stepped left. Then more followed until only five remained loyal to Edwin, Aethel among them.

Maxen motioned for the men-at-arms to remove those who chose to stand with their absent leader and turned to Rhiannyn.

"I do not understand," she said, trying to glimpse his soul in his eyes. "Why have you done this?"

"Be assured, it has naught to do with you," he said and walked around her.

Of course it had nothing to do with her, but what? Had he done it for Christophe? "And the others?" she called. "What of them?"

He halted, but did not turn back. "They have made their choice," he said, anger evident in his stiff posture, cutting voice, and hands curled into fists. "They are Harwolfson's men and will be treated accordingly." He resumed his stride.

Though Rhiannyn told herself to be grateful most of the Saxons would live, she was pained by the five who would die. But when? Why had Maxen not put them to the gallows straightaway as he had led her to believe he meant to do with all the Saxons?

She recalled this morn when she had awakened to the feel of his hand on her ankle as he removed the iron and chain. He had told her she was to accompany him to witness the reckoning herself, and during the long walk had said nothing of his true intentions, allowing her to believe the worst.

Anger swept aside relief. How dare he subject her to such pain! How dare he make pretense of a slaughter he'd had no intention of carrying out!

Though the voice trailing her thoughts insisted she not question him but be thankful for what he had *not* done, she snatched up her skirts, traversed the wall-walk, and descended to the bailey. Behind, she heard a Saxon woman call her a vile name, but she did not falter in her bid to gain the causeway leading up to the motte. There was much she had to say to Maxen Pendery.

18

Upon entering the hall, Rhiannyn located Maxen where he stood behind a trestle table, head bent, arms outstretched, palms flat on the table. Before him were a great number of his knights, and beside him sat the steward who was ardently explaining something.

Forgetting her station, forgetting propriety, forgetting all that would have served her well to remember, she advanced on Maxen. When she was halfway across the hall, he straightened and narrowed his lids at her—doubtless, calculating what she intended. And what that was, she did not know until she ascended the dais.

She grasped the cloth covering the table and yanked, catapulting goblets, tankards, and the books the steward guarded with his every breath. Harmless missiles, except the one that struck Sir Ancel in the temple and staggered him back.

Despite the knight's expletives, when all settled, Rhiannyn remained untouched. Holding the cloth, eyes fastened on Maxen's blue gaze, she said, "You are the lowliest of curs."

He splayed his hands on the bare tabletop and leaned forward again. "You think?"

So cool, as if unmoved by what she had done. But he was not unmoved. His eyes and the bunching of muscles beneath his tunic mirrored her own anger, and she was so fascinated with the control he exercised that the realization of the mistake she had made was slow to dawn. But when it did, she did not heed it.

She dropped the cloth, stepped nearer, and swung her palm across the table.

He caught it, denying her the stinging contact she sought. "I cannot allow you to do that—again," he growled and glanced from her bandaged hand to her flushed face.

Aye, twice before she had struck him. Once out of anger, once to awaken him, and now again in anger—of which he was more than deserving.

"I have not asked for permission," she tossed back.

He arched an eyebrow, then ordered his men and the steward to take their leave.

Muffled laughter and crude comments accompanied the men from the hall.

"This is not what I expected," Maxen said when he and Rhiannyn were alone.

"What did you expect? I would fall to my knees? Embrace you? Worship you?" She jerked her hand to free it, but he held firm.

"I had thought you would at least be grateful."

"Grateful! You let me believe you intended to hang the Saxons, but all along planned otherwise."

"Would you prefer I had taken their lives?"

"Of course not! But neither did you need to be so cruel to allow me to think you meant to slay them all."

Maxen considered her. It would be easy to quell her anger—and his—or at least lessen it by explaining what appeared to be cruelty had really been his final test of her story that she did not know who had murdered Thomas. Now he believed her, for she had not broken when faced with the nooses waiting to embrace the necks of her people.

But let her think him cruel. After all, was he not? Too, it would afford him more control over her, something needed with one such as she.

"You were told," he said, "in my time, not yours."

Fire leapt higher in her eyes. Odd, he thought, but there was something appealing about her daring. Something that went beyond a desire to know her intimately.

"Though I tried to hate Thomas for who he was and what he had done," she said, "I could not. But you…I do not even have to try."

Maxen was truly amused. "You do not hate me, Rhiannyn. You told me so yourself."

"I lied!"

"Then at least I can console myself with one thing." He leaned nearer across the table, liking the way his breath stirred the hair upon her brow. "That which you refused Thomas."

She frowned.

"You desire me. Hate me…Very well, but you are not averse to my touch."

She gasped. "You suffer from the same delusions your brother did."

"I recall a kiss you did not object to days ago. You denied yourself the surrender, but you enjoyed it as much as I."

Color that could not be mistaken for anger flamed her cheeks, evidencing she well remembered his wine-filled kiss. "You dream," she said.

"Should I prove it to you?"

"Try, oh mighty Norman!"

Maxen knew they were words spoken in anger, not an invitation, but he released her hand, gripped her beneath the arms, and lifted her slight figure across the table. Amid her protests, he set her on the table's edge before him.

She jerked her chin up. "What are you doing?"

"Seeking the truth," he said and cupped a hand to the back of her head and lowered his own. Had she evaded him, he would have stopped, but she caught her breath—*his* breath—when he touched his mouth to hers. He slanted his head, pressed his lips to hers, and she allowed it still. He deepened the kiss, and she brought her hands up to his chest, but not to push him away. To hold onto him.

As time reeled out, he took as he could not remember ever taking, drank as he had never drunk, and tasted as he had not once tasted. And true to his seeking, Rhiannyn flowered in his hands and beneath his mouth, revealing her passion alongside her Saxon anger and pride. Not for Harwolfson. Not for Thomas. For *him*.

He did not understand why he wanted that, only that he did. Thus, when the monk yet beneath his skin warned against falling prey to what his brethren had called a *Daughter of Eve,* he reminded the monk he was no longer of the Church—that he was willing, as was this woman.

You think that makes it right? challenged his much too recent past.

He breathed in Rhiannyn, deepened the kiss, slid his hand from her nape to the small of her back, drew her off the table and against him.

All of her bright and awhirl, Rhiannyn did not want to think. She wanted only to sink into these sensations and forget losses that made her feel things she wished to never again so much as touch the hem of her gown. *This* she wanted to feel. Maxen Pendery.

"Too long," he groaned.

Those words—barely heard—had the power to remind her of who she was. A captive. And who he was. Her captor. She was a spoil of war, not even of such value as his brother had placed upon her. Maxen might not forcibly take her virtue, but he would use her sinful willingness to ease his desire as Saxon women before her had satisfied the lust of Normans.

All that had been bright and awhirl going dark and still, she silently beseeched, *Dear Lord, forgive me. I do not understand what possessed me to act the harlot Theta accused me of being. But perhaps I am the same as she.*

"Rhiannyn?" Maxen said.

She opened her eyes, and when she saw his face above hers, realized he had ended their kiss.

"What is it?" he asked.

Almost faint with shame, she said, "I cannot do this."

His lips curved. "It is but a kiss."

She jerked her head side to side. "It is more." Indeed, it went all the way through her, and though she had little experience with men, Maxen's kiss was unlike Edwin's and Thomas's. Thus, perhaps it went all the way through him as well.

He brushed his mouth across hers. "Not yet," he said, "but it could be more."

She tried to pull away, but came up against the table. "I will not fall into your bed."

His eyebrows rose. "Shall I seek that truth as well? Tempt you as Eve tempted Adam?"

If he did, would her body once more betray her? Would she fall?

She swallowed hard. "Pray, do not."

As his eyes held hers that had begun to sting with tears, his struggle was momentarily visible.

Hoping to push him over the line he seemed to teeter upon, she said, "Though you are no longer of the Church, it does not give you leave to reject teachings you yourself preached to my people. So, nay, I would not have you tempt either of us." She drew a deep breath and waited to see which of him would win—the man who had become the monk, or the one who had earned the title of The Bloodlust Warrior of Hastings.

The man she had vowed she would find beneath the warrior released her and looked down between them. "If you speak true in not wishing to tempt either of us," he said gruffly, "you had best loosen your hold."

She released the handfuls of tunic she could not recall having grasped and snatched her arms to her chest.

He stepped back.

Shame deepening the heat in her face, she turned aside, but had put two strides between them when he said, "Rhiannyn."

She turned.

"Henceforth, you will serve in the hall. You will attend me and my men at meal and assist Mildreth with whatever she assigns you."

She knew she should be grateful, for such tasks were less dangerous than those she had undertaken these past days while chained to him, but still there would be contact with him. "And when night is come?"

"You will make your bed here with the others."

As she had when Thomas lived, though that was where the similarity ended. Now she was servant to a man who would have her be his leman, not his wife as Thomas would have if she had accepted him. In which case, he would be alive.

"And your clothes," Maxen continued. "As you play the part, so shall you dress it."

"Aye," she said, though how she was to obtain less fine garments she did not know.

He walked to where one of the steward's books lay open on the floor, retrieved it, and returned to the table. "You may go," he said.

When Rhiannyn went from sight and her footsteps faded amid the commotion of the courtyard, Maxen gave up his pretense of study. He slammed the book closed and sank into his shoulders.

He did not wish her to be right, but she was. As angry as he had been, as certain he could abandon these past years of seeking God and bending to Him, it was not easily done. Still there was right and wrong. Still there was good and bad. Still there was Rhiannyn who, by his own devices, would tempt him day in and day out.

"Lord," he rasped, "what fool am I not to send her away?"

"I've a bliaut I will give you."

Rhiannyn and Mildreth turned together to stare at the woman they had not realized listened in on their conversation.

Rhiannyn had been on her way to the kitchen, a short walk from the donjon, when she had run into Mildreth and revealed her clothing problem.

"Give me?" she asked, knowing Theta might be generous with words, but not her belongings.

Theta stepped from the kitchen doorway. "You are a bit scrawny and short, but my gown will serve you fine."

"What price your generosity?" Mildreth asked.

"That." Theta swept her gaze down the fine bliaut and chemise Rhiannyn wore.

"A peasant's garments for a lady's?" Rhiannyn said. "I think not." Besides, for the bliaut and chemise to fit, Theta would have to let out the seams and walk with bent knees. Though she was of good figure, her breasts were larger than Rhiannyn's, and she was taller by a good hand. Of course, if she used one of her own chemises beneath the bliaut, it would improve the look.

"Pity." Theta sighed. "It seems you will have to serve at table dressed as you are, and further displease our lord."

That last convinced Rhiannyn to surrender the bliaut, though not without concessions. "Very well, but I will require two of your bliauts for this one."

"Two?" Theta laughed. "I will give you one."

"And the chemise stays with me."

"Then methinks you will have to look elsewhere. But do not forget the nooning meal is served an hour hence."

Rhiannyn sighed. "I suppose I will have to make this one less fine."

"How?" Theta asked sharply.

"A bit of dirt and grease, and a few rips will serve the same purpose."

Horror rose in the woman's eyes. "Two bliauts," she said. "I can manage it."

Rhiannyn put her head to the side. "You are sure? I would not wish to leave you needful."

"Two." Theta turned away. "I will return shortly."

"You can be a sly one," Mildreth said when she and Rhiannyn were alone again.

"When I have to be."

Though the smile Mildreth offered was tentative and lacking the warmth it had once held, it was welcome. "That is good," she said. "You will need it with the new lord."

Deciding it best not to discuss Maxen with her, Rhiannyn asked after her duties in the hall.

"He wishes you to serve, eh?"

"And assist you in whatever else is needed."

"Ain't that kind of him," Mildreth mused, "though 'tis probably more for his benefit than mine."

Rhiannyn silently agreed. Having her serve him and his men would appease some of his need to avenge his brother's death.

Mildreth sighed. "'Tis good, for I certainly could use help."

"How?"

"Ere the meals, you will assist in the kitchen. During them, you can serve wine and ale."

Although Thomas would have considered it beneath the woman he had wished to make his wife, Rhiannyn did not. She had been raised modestly, helping her mother with household chores, which had included cooking and serving her father and brothers. But waiting on Normans was not something she looked forward to.

"Ah, me!" Mildreth gasped. "I forgot about the lord's bath. When he returned from the bailey, he ordered hot water to be brought to his tub." She looked across the yard to cauldrons that fogged the air with heat. "And 'tis well and boiling." She considered her armload of laundry. "You could help carry water."

Rhiannyn blinked. Carry water to Maxen's chamber so she might suffer further humiliation from what she had so recently allowed him?

"Of course, with your hand injured," Mildreth continued, "it will be difficult."

Rhiannyn longed to avail herself of the excuse, but she said, "I will do it."

Theta's reappearance halted Rhiannyn and Mildreth's progress to the kitchen. She thrust two well-worn bliauts into Rhiannyn's arms. "Now out of my bliaut."

Rhiannyn would have preferred a more private place to make the exchange, but there were few about to prevent her from stepping into the shadows and changing. Too, she would have the cover of her chemise.

She went into the shadow of the donjon, removed the bliaut, and replaced it with the least offensive of Theta's gowns. It was too large, too coarse, smelled, and was woven of dun-colored thread, but she told herself she did not care. It hung too long, and the sash was so badly frayed she doubted it would stay tied, but again, she told herself she did not care. It would serve her better than the other she traded, making her appear without shape and less likely to catch a man's eye.

When she exited the shadows, Theta snatched the fine bliaut from her, turned, and hastened toward the donjon. As she ascended the steps, Sir Guy intercepted her and spoke something that did not carry past Theta's ears. But it made the woman smile and more quickly delivered her into the hall.

Wondering what news she had been borne, Rhiannyn frowned at her companion.

Mildreth shrugged and grimaced at the picture Rhiannyn presented. "A shame," she said. "Now even I look better than you." She swung toward the kitchen. "Come, I will show you where the buckets are."

Wishing Mildreth had not said anything, Rhiannyn followed.

19

Perhaps he would have been tempted if she had not pranced into his chamber wearing the bliaut he had last seen on Rhiannyn, reminding him of what he had given up by not seeking further truths from the woman he should not want. But Maxen could not take what Theta offered, and not only because she was not Rhiannyn, but for the recent reminder that the act of repentance stolen from him did not give him leave to reject the teachings of the Church.

He reached up, pulled Theta's arms from around his neck, and set her back from him.

She opened her eyes wide. "Milord?"

As he peered into her face, he wondered again what hold Rhiannyn had over him. In a dark way, Theta was more beautiful, her woman's body more voluptuous, yet she left him unmoved.

"Not now," he said and turned away.

Behind, he heard the crackle of rushes as she followed. "But milord"—she slid her arms around his waist—"Sir Guy thought you might like company."

He was not surprised the knight had sent her. Guy knew the appetites of the Maxen of old, and when he had returned to the hall following Rhiannyn's exit and his lord had barked at him, he had surely believed he knew the cure for Maxen's mood. But it was not Theta.

He turned. "Leave. Now."

He glimpsed resentment a moment before she covered it with a seductive smile. "Later, then." She smoothed her hands down the bliaut that was too snug, though it emphasized her breasts and plentiful hips to good advantage. Doubtless, it had been traded for the clothing he had ordered Rhiannyn to wear for her new duties.

The bliaut off one shoulder, she fluttered her lashes. "Do not be too long in sending for me, milord. If 'tis not you, it will be another."

Which was among the reasons he did not desire her. The leavings of other men she had lain with, including Thomas, held no appeal, though before he had taken his monk's vows, he had enjoyed the pleasures of experienced women who sought his attentions.

"So be it," he said.

Resentment once more rising in her eyes, though this time she did not turn it into a smile, she pivoted and stepped around the screen.

Blowing breath up his face, Maxen turned to the bed, tugged off his tunic, and tossed it on the mattress. As he reached to his braies, he glanced at the tub that had been delivered earlier. And wondered at the water missing from it.

Water sloshed over Rhiannyn's bandaged hand. Thankfully, it was no longer boiling as when she had first taken up the buckets. Barely noticing the heat, she stared at the woman coming from Maxen's chamber with one shoulder of her new bliaut askew.

Theta looked angry, but upon noticing Rhiannyn, her tongue darted out to taste her lower lip and she changed course and halted before Rhiannyn.

"As eager as Thomas," she purred. "Ah, but how would you know, hmm? Thomas wanted you as his wife only. It was me he wanted in his bed."

And her he'd had.

Unwanted emotions gripped Rhiannyn—hurt, sorrow, even jealousy that Maxen might have lain with Theta. Nay he *had* lain with her, she forced herself to acknowledge. Sir Guy his messenger, he had sent for the woman for no other purpose than to bed her.

But why did she care? She had not cared when Thomas continued to take Theta into his bed after proclaiming Rhiannyn would be his wife. In fact, she had been grateful he had channeled his desire into another. But she was not grateful Maxen had done so.

A movement past Theta drew Rhiannyn's gaze. Maxen came around the screen, chest bare, braies all that covered him hips to calves—further confirmation he had done with Theta what he would have done with her had she not stopped him.

Though it seemed his intent to advance farther into the hall, he halted when he saw the two women.

His stare sent her emotions soaring where they had no right to spread their wings, and she determinedly told herself it was not hurt she felt but relief, not sorrow but joy, and certainly not jealousy.

Theta followed her gaze around and whispered, "Fear not. He has no need of you now."

Rhiannyn squared her shoulders and stepped past her. Staring at a point beyond Maxen, she continued forward. Blessedly, she was allowed to pass without comment. But after she emptied her buckets into the tub, Maxen stepped into her path.

"What is this?" He flicked the sleeve of her ill-fitting bliaut.

She pinned her eyes to his chin. "More appropriate, my lord. Exactly as ordered."

"Not exactly, but I suppose it will do."

"It does just fine. Now do you step aside, I will bring more water for your bath."

He inclined his head and let her pass.

The buckets swinging from her hands, she contained the expression of her relief until she exited the hall and once more gained the shadows of the donjon. Assuring herself she needed only a few moments to compose herself, she dropped the buckets and leaned back against the wall. But the moments grew long as she fought anger and hurt. She swallowed hard, but the lump in her throat lodged itself again. She unclenched her hands, but the tension remained. All because Maxen Pendery had pulled back when she had asked it of him—and, instead, turned to Theta.

"Rhiannyn?"

She opened her eyes.

Christophe stood before her. "Something is wrong?" he asked.

She shook her head. "I am not feeling well. That is all."

"Your hand?"

It pained her some to carry water, but it was insignificant compared to this other thing she felt. "My hand is fine. It is my head that fares poorly."

"Perhaps I have something that will help."

"It will pass," she said and stooped to retrieve her buckets.

"With the injury to your hand, you should not be hauling water," he said as she stepped around him.

She continued to the kitchen, and five more times came and went, in silence emptying the water while Maxen watched from the chair in which he reclined. However, the last time she rounded the screen, she stuttered to a halt. He sat in the tub, head back against the rim, eyes closed.

Lest she suffer further humiliation, she nearly retreated, but another part of her would not allow it.

Arms aching, the cut fingers of her hand burning, she carried the buckets to the tub. She set one down, lifted the other, and stared ahead as she poured the water. She did the same with the second and turned away.

"You are not going to assist with my bath?" Maxen asked.

Her back to him, she said, "It is not among my duties, but if you would like, I shall send a squire."

"Or Theta."

She nearly startled. "Or Theta."

"Of course, I could make it one of your duties."

She glanced over her shoulder, but quickly looked forward again. "I ask that you do not."

"I see no harm in it."

Certainly not for him. "I prefer not to, my lord."

"Rhiannyn."

Something in his voice tugged at her, but she refused to answer it.

"Rhiannyn," he said again, and his wet hand encircled her wrist, pulled her around, and tugged her forward.

Given the choice of joining him in the tub or dropping to her knees beside it, she chose the latter.

He released her wrist and moved his hand to her jaw. "Do not believe everything you see—or are told."

Struggling to suppress the stirring within, she said, "I know not what you speak of."

Maxen searched her face, and despite the warning voices in his head, said, "Then I will show you," and leaned forward and crossed his mouth over hers. With the first touch of their lips, longing once more sprang through him—as it had not with Theta. He desired one woman. But she refused him, and his point had yet to be made.

When he released her, she sprang back onto her heels, overturning the buckets. Upon gaining her feet, she dragged a hand across her mouth as if to wipe away all traces of him—or, perhaps, Theta.

He settled back in the tub. "As I said, do not believe everything you see or are told. It was not Theta who last knew my touch. It was you."

"You think it matters to me with whom you lie?" she snapped. "As long as it is not me, I care not."

Maxen closed his eyes in an attempt to savor the warmth of a bath he had long been denied. "I warned you about that lying of yours, Rhiannyn. Either better it, or be done with it."

He felt her silence, then heard her footsteps.

Wondering at the mess he had made of things, he pushed a hand through his hair and settled it at the back of his tonsured head that was hardly tonsured anymore. In place of the smooth scalp he had often shaved at the monastery was hair—short, but before long it would wipe away the last vestiges of the monk, leaving him no more a man of God and, instead, the lord he had not wanted to become. The lord Rhiannyn had made him.

20

IT WAS WORSE than expected, especially where Maxen was concerned. There was no hiding from him, nowhere in the hall to retreat from the weight of his stare. And to worsen matters, many looked at her with open speculation as to what had occurred between her and their lord when they had been ordered from the hall this morn.

Let them speculate, she told herself. While Thomas lived, his claim on her had prevented the knights from bothering her as they did other Saxon women. If they believed Maxen also claimed her, mayhap it would serve the same purpose—unless they thought her the same as Theta. Praying otherwise, Rhiannyn lifted one of two vessels she carried and poured ale into the tankard thrust at her.

"Ale!" another called from farther down the table.

Feeling pulled in too many directions, she hurried forward and discovered it was Sir Ancel who summoned her—needlessly so. She shifted her gaze from his full tankard to his satisfied expression and started to move opposite, but he grabbed her arm.

"Where are you going, wench?"

"There are others awaiting drink, whose needs are real."

"And mine is not?" He raised his tankard to his mouth, pulled long on it, and set it on the table. "My tankard is not full."

Biting back a retort, she filled his tankard to the brim.

He did not release her, but drank down half the ale and once more presented the tankard.

She poured and tugged to free herself.

Tightening his grip, he eyed her bandaged hand. "You cut yourself?"

"A mishap."

"With a dagger, I presume?"

A chill swept her. It had to be he who had placed the instrument of Maxen's death beneath her napkin.

Grateful for the unanswered calls for more drink, she said, "It is not only you I serve, Sir Ancel."

"Not yet, but it shall be."

"More wine!" Maxen shouted from the high seat.

Grin grotesque, the knight released her.

Heart beating so hard she thought it might burst, Rhiannyn whirled around. But in the time it took to cross to the dais, she collected enough of herself to pour Maxen's drink without spill.

"You are slow," he said as she drew back.

"Forgive me. I was detained."

"Sir Ancel?"

She was surprised he had noticed. "It was."

"For what reason?"

Believing it would be petty to complain against the knight for taunting her, she said, "He was quite thirsty."

"For?"

"Ale."

Maxen leaned forward. "You will tell me if he ever grows thirsty for anything other than drink?"

Heat rushing to her face, she nodded.

He sat back. "Resume your duties."

Moving down the table, she filled tankards and goblets as she went, and when she had emptied her last drop, she hastened to the barrels against the wall to replenish her supply. There she crossed paths with

Lucilla, with whom she had not had an opportunity to speak since the day before when the dagger had appeared on her tray.

"I must needs discuss something with you," she said.

A frown rising on her pretty face, Lucilla shifted her tray of viands to the opposite hand. "Now?"

"When the meal is finished."

The woman nodded and continued on her way.

Rhiannyn refilled both vessels and turned to find Maxen's gaze upon her. She looked away.

Unfortunately, the nooning meal stretched into the evening meal without break, and expanded further into a night of drinking that left her feeling haggard.

Although it took her a while to catch on, she realized what motivated Maxen to allow and even encourage such indolence. Drinking little himself, he watched and listened as those around him relaxed under the effects of alcohol, their tongues loosening, their manners careless.

He studied them, measuring them for loyalty and integrity while he searched for the betrayer or one who could tell him the name of the betrayer. And yet it seemed he knew, for his gaze often returned to Sir Ancel.

Finally, he rose and pronounced the night at an end. There was grumbling, but all began preparing to bed down.

Using the opportunity created by the commotion of tables and benches being pushed against walls in readiness for the night's sleep, Rhiannyn slipped out of the hall, crossed the courtyard, and entered the kitchen. There she found Lucilla. Sitting on a stool, head on the table, the woman slept in the solitude and quiet offered by this place far removed from the hall.

Rhiannyn nearly retreated. As certain as she was it was Sir Ancel who had placed the dagger, the question she had wanted to put to the woman seemed hardly worth awakening her for. But she shook Lucilla's shoulder.

Groaning, the woman lifted her head and looked bleary-eyed at her. "'Tis finished with?"

"Aye, they gain their beds."

"Too drunk to bother with me, I hope."

"I think so."

Lucilla sat back. "So when I finally have a chance for a night's unin-terrupted sleep, ye awaken me to talk?"

"I am sorry, but there is something I need to know."

"About the dagger?"

Rhiannyn felt as if punched in the stomach. Was it possible this woman was responsible? "How did you know?"

Lucilla cleared sleep from her eyes. "I've been questioned by the lord who wished to know if I was responsible."

Of course. "You did not put it on my tray?"

Lucilla smiled wryly. "Two years ago, I would have done it while I was yet abrew with foolish pride and hate for the Normans. Now…" She shook her head. "Such a risk I would not take. Though it has not been easy, I have come to accept these new masters, just as I accepted Edwin's father when he held these lands."

When all of Etcheverry belonged to the Harwolfsons, Rhiannyn reflected. When the fields had run with the water of irrigation, rather than the blood of men.

Lucilla clasped her hand over Rhiannyn's. "They are not leaving. Accept it."

Rhiannyn turned her palm up into the woman's, squeezed, then pulled free and stepped back from the table. "Thank you. I am owing to you."

Lucilla shrugged. "'Tis the way of friends."

Rhiannyn's sagging heart took notice. Was she no longer suspected of betraying her people? "Truly?" she asked.

"Truly."

One shining star to light the night of this miserable day, Rhiannyn smiled and turned to leave.

"What is it between ye two?" Lucilla asked.

The question pulled Rhiannyn back around. "Between us?"

"You and Maxen Pendery. What is between ye that was not with Thomas?"

Rhiannyn nearly startled. "I know not what you speak of."

Lucilla fanned a yawn from her mouth. "I felt the air between you when I came to the lord's chamber. I saw how ye watched each other this night. And now, at mention of his name, you flush like a girl about to know her first lover."

Rhiannyn gasped. "You are wrong!"

"Am I?"

"What would I want with him? And he with me? He has Theta."

"Has he?"

"He took her to his bed this day."

Lucilla frowned. "Ye are certain?"

"He denied it, but I saw her come from his chamber with her clothes mussed, and he in naught but braies."

Lucilla stood. "He denied it?" she asked, suspicion crossing her sleepy-eyed countenance.

Rhiannyn felt cornered, as if her next words could determine whether or not she became a meal for Lucilla. "Aye, but I know different. As Thomas took Theta to his bed, so does his brother."

"Does it bother ye?"

"Not at all! Why do you ask such questions?"

"We are friends, are we not?"

"I begin to wonder."

Lucilla laid a hand on Rhiannyn's arm. "We are friends, which is why I ask these things. If only to yourself, ye must admit what you feel for our lord. Then perhaps it can be used to your advantage."

Rhiannyn scoffed. "I want naught from him."

"Then in time, you will become his leman when 'tis his wife ye should seek to be."

"I would more be Thomas's wife than his brother's," Rhiannyn exclaimed, "and that I certainly did not want. I detest Maxen Pendery."

Lucilla shrugged. "Part of you does, but part of ye aches at the thought of him taking pleasure with another."

Rhiannyn nearly continued her protest, but in that moment, she acknowledged it for what it was—a lie. She sighed. "I do not understand it. How can I feel this when it mattered not that Thomas did the same?"

"The body is a strange thing. In most matters, it serves the mind, but not so when it is taken with desire. That is when it rules."

What Lucilla said was true. Rhiannyn was attracted to Maxen, her insides stirring at remembrance of his kisses, but there was something more to it than desire.

"Listen to me." Lucilla's voice became urgent. "Do you give yourself to Pendery without benefit of vows, ye will be lost, your destiny that of a leman, and the children you bear him misbegotten. But deny him—give a little and pull back—and methinks he will wed ye to gain your favors."

She, wed? What of the vow she had made to belong to none—no husband, no children, only the emptiness to which Thomas had banished her? More, what of Maxen? Never would he wed her. And if he gave her a child, it would not bear his name.

She shook her head. "I cannot do what you suggest. I will deny him, but not so I might become his wife."

Lucilla dropped her hand from Rhiannyn, and the sigh she heaved became a yawn. "Then I pray ye are strong."

"I am."

Looking doubtful, Lucilla walked past her. "Good eve," she called over her shoulder.

If not for Rhiannyn's rumbling belly, she would have gone to the hall as well.

She carried a stool across the kitchen, stepped onto it, and located the key hidden atop the pantry—the same place it was kept while Thomas lived. When she was first brought to the castle, many were the nights she had ventured to the kitchens to eat. In her anger, she had refused to partake of anything put before her in the company of Normans. Eventually, that had changed, but the hiding place for the key had not.

Trying not to think on her conversation with Lucilla, she cut a chunk of hard cheese, several pieces of dried meat, and a crust of bread. Then she locked the pantry, replaced the key, and turned with her filched viands to the table where Lucilla had slept.

And there stood Maxen.

She nearly dropped the platter. "You frightened me!"

"I apologize. I thought you heard me."

"I did not." When had he come? Hopefully, after Lucilla's departure.

He leaned against the table, jutted his chin at the platter. "Do you intend to eat or merely stand there looking as if you wish to?"

Only then did it occur to her she had been caught sneaking food—a terrible offense for one no longer a lady.

"I..." She glanced at the viands. Assuring herself it would be easy to forget hunger in sleep, she crossed to the table and set the platter down. "For you, my lord," she said and started for the door.

He stepped into her path. "I have eaten."

She moistened her lips. "I would like to take myself to bed."

"While still hungry?"

"If needs be."

"It need not be." He motioned to the tall stool. "Eat."

What mood was he in? she wondered. What did he want with her? Nothing he was yet willing to make known, it seemed.

Warily, she seated herself, pulled the food before her, and asked what was heavy on her mind. "What is to become of the Saxons who refused you?"

Once more, he leaned against the table. "They have chosen death over life."

"Why did you not have done with them this morn?"

"In my time, Rhiannyn. Always my time."

His words more deeply unsettled her, but she pressed on. "I ask you to allow me to speak with them." Hopefully, she would find a way to convince Aethel and the four others to stay upon Etcheverry.

"You may not speak with them," Maxen said. "Now eat."

She did so quickly, and when she finished, nearly jumped off the stool.

"So," he said, "another of your lies uprooted."

Dear Lord, which one? she wondered. Was it possible he had heard her tell Lucilla she had found the dagger on her tray, rather than on the floor as she had told him? Perhaps he had heard her admission that it mattered to her if he made love to Theta. Or was it another lie to which he referred?

"I know not what you speak of."

"Why did you lie about the dagger? What gain in telling me you picked it off the floor when it was upon your tray?"

She caught her breath. If he had overheard that, he had heard the last of her conversation with Lucilla. Everything in her groaning, she said, "I feared for Lucilla."

His expression hardened. "As you fear for her now?"

"She did not do it, my lord. I give you my word she is blameless."

His eyebrows shot high, silently mocking what he thought of her word. "If not her, who?"

"Methinks it may have been Sir Ancel."

"Why?"

"He partook of the food upon my tray yestermorn when he and the others came to your chamber. Too, he…"

"What?"

"This eve, he inquired about my hand—asked if it was a dagger with which I cut myself."

Maxen appeared unmoved. "Mayhap you lie to put Lucilla's punishment on a Norman."

She shook her head. "I speak the truth—as I know it."

He straightened from the table, leaned near. "As you spoke the truth when you told you killed Thomas? When you said you found the dagger on the floor? When this noon you said it mattered not who I lie with so long as it is not you? Those truths, Rhiannyn?"

Steeped in humiliation, she said, "Believe what you will," and started for the door.

"Rhiannyn!"

She looked over her shoulder.

"If you think to play games with me, you will discover how wrong Lucilla is."

Of course he would not wed her, no matter how tempted he might be to bed the one he held responsible for his brother's death. "I need none to tell me how wrong she is, especially you," she said and hastened from the kitchen.

Maxen momentarily closed his eyes. Then, deeply feeling the fatigue of a body yet struggling to heal itself and emotions wearing themselves thin, he dropped onto the stool and kneaded the back of his neck.

Just as Rhiannyn believed Sir Ancel had left the dagger for her, Maxen had concluded the same long before he had followed her to the kitchen and happened upon a conversation he had felt little remorse with listening in upon. Trifling as it was to learn where the dagger was placed, he had been angered to have it confirmed Rhiannyn lied again.

But there had been little chance for his anger to deepen, the shift in their conversation to her feelings for him a dangerous distraction. Her claim she detested him and would rather be wife to Thomas, whom she had not wanted, had made something sharp turn in him. And begin to loosen when, despite those words, she admitted to an attraction for him she seemed not to have felt for Thomas. Might she be more willing to wed the new lord of Etcheverry?

Not that he would marry her, but it was good to know how she might attempt to bring about a union—one that should never be, that would be ill-fated. Would it not?

21

◈

RUBBING HIS UNSHAVEN jaw, Maxen stood atop the wall-walk, scanning the donjon, stables, granary, smithy, chapel, and beyond the rising walls, land as far as the eye ventured.

He returned his gaze to the chapel, a small whitewashed building. Not since his arrival at Etcheverry had he attended mass, nor gone down on his knees to speak prayers that for nearly two years had been more familiar to him than his own name. The closest he had come was prayers in passing, their primary purpose to douse desire for one he should not want.

Pushing aside imaginings of Rhiannyn, he once more considered all that was his. And wished Etcheverry were something he wanted. If only he could take it all in with the pride of a landed noble. If there were someone at his side with whom he could share it and father a son to pass it to. But it hung about his neck like the weight of the dead.

A shout brought his head around and moved his hand to the dagger of Thomas's death.

Narrowing his eyes against the risen sun, he picked out the dust-billowed fight of two Saxons who, until a sennight past, had been loyal to Edwin Harwolfson. Now they struggled to give up the spent past and accept Norman rule. Knowing whether or not they succeeded would likely determine the fate of Pendery lands, he allowed them their quarrels, but not much more.

By day, the Saxons toiled under the weight of stone they raised to the walls and beneath eyes that marked their every passing. By night, they slept under the close watch of men-at-arms given license to strike before asking questions. Fortunately, there had been no incidents of consequence.

Of course, there was Rhiannyn, an incident unto herself. Ever elusive, she ran a fine chase. The closest he had come to her since that night in the kitchen was during meals when she put her pitcher to his drinking vessel. A good thing, every day bringing more responsibilities from which he needed no further distraction.

As Etcheverry's harvest had been paltry, there was the issue of food for the winter, the matter of wood for fires needed to ward off the cold, and clothing, blankets, and shelter for Saxons who numbered too many for their cramped quarters within the castle's walls. And now there was Blackspur Castle.

Maxen descended the steps, and when he set foot in the inner bailey, the clash between the Saxons had ended. Amid grunting and cursing, the task of raising the walls was resumed.

As Maxen turned toward the stables and those preparing to ride with him, he came face to face with his brother. "Christophe."

The youth shifted foot to foot before bearing the greater of his weight on his lame leg. "I have not had the opportunity to thank you," he said.

"For what?"

"The Saxons."

"Ah." Uncomfortable himself, Maxen started to step around his brother.

Christophe caught his arm. "It was good of you."

Maxen raised his eyebrows.

As if no longer able to bear weight on his impaired leg, Christophe leaned into the solid one. "I owe you an apology for believing the worst of you."

For some reason, it irritated Maxen to have good thought of him.

Weak, the resurrected warrior denounced.

Not so, the monk-laid-to-rest countered.

"Do not be so quick to apologize," Maxen said gruffly. "It is yet to be seen whether the Saxons are true to their new-found loyalty."

Christophe inclined his head. "If you would allow it, I shall accompany you to Blackspur."

"For what purpose?"

"It is long since we talked as brothers. Methinks it would be a good opportunity."

Then they were brothers again, Maxen reflected, and grudgingly acknowledged how much Christophe's wariness—even rejection—bothered him. "I would like your company," he said.

"Then I will make ready." Christophe hurried toward the stables.

When he disappeared within, Maxen settled his attention on the others. Squires scurried to meet the demands of their masters—among them, Sir Ancel, whom Maxen would be a fool to leave behind. Thus, the knight had been ordered to join the party, and it was Sir Guy to whom Etcheverry was entrusted.

As the latter was not yet among those gathered, and it would be a while before all were ready to ride, Maxen determined to seek out his friend and have final words with him in private. Though he had not intended to return to the donjon, he pivoted and strode to the causeway.

Thinking herself fortunate in devising all manner of ways to avoid Maxen, Rhiannyn knelt on his stripped bed and grasped the far edge of the mattress that required shaking and turning. Throwing her weight backward, she pulled the mattress free, searched a foot to the floor to balance herself, and heaved again.

When the seam beneath her fingers tore, she stumbled and tried to right herself—and failed.

The mattress and sprung feathers followed her to the floor, and she screeched in surprise and pain as she landed on her rear. Then, darkness.

Grateful no one was near to make her feel more the fool, she rose onto her hands and knees and crawled out from beneath the mattress. As her head emerged, she swiped at the feathers tickling her face and spat out the one in her mouth.

Deep laughter preceded the booted legs that appeared before her.

Dear Lord, she silently beseeched, *why now?* Though tempted to duck back under the mattress, she pushed it off and lurched to her feet.

A man she hardly knew stood before her. His eyes sparkled, teeth flashed, and mouth forsook its usual downward turn for the very human smile of laughter.

In this moment, he was younger, more handsome, and reachable. Here was the Maxen Pendery she sought, the one she had hoped to find beneath anger and vengeance.

As she savored this glimpse of him, his laughter subsided, but the light in his eyes did not.

"You are quite the sight, Rhiannyn of Etcheverry."

She peered down her figure and was dismayed by the extent of her feathering. But it was a small price to pay. Indeed, a thousand times over she would pay it to gaze upon this Maxen.

"I thought you had gone," she said.

He reached forward and picked a half dozen feathers from her hair, the gesture more intimate than she would have believed possible.

"As I also thought, but something called me back."

She frowned. "What?"

"Sir Guy, but I cannot say I am disappointed I found you instead. Forsooth, I am pleased."

"I do not understand," she said. But it was not exactly true.

He trailed a feather down her jaw to the thrilling place where neck met shoulder. "Though I fear the time might be better spent plucking you, I am thinking a kiss to speed my journey would not be amiss."

Something warm and hopeful moved through Rhiannyn, something she named foolish. Still, she reached up and set a hand to his jaw. "I like this Maxen."

His eyes flickered, and like the shifting of day into night, began to darken. "As opposed to?"

She lowered her hand. "As opposed to the one who cruelly allowed me to believe it was a hanging to which I accompanied him a sennight past."

Maxen could not have said what was responsible for the admission that rose to his lips, but he knew it was more than desire—a need to reassure her he was not the beast he had let her believe he was. "It was a test, Rhiannyn."

She frowned.

"I thought, faced with the deaths of your people, you might finally give me what I need. Thomas's murderer."

She drew a sharp breath. "What you need, I do not possess."

"I know this now."

Upon her face, he glimpsed relief a moment ahead of anger, but as he readied to intercept the hand she would let fly, relief returned.

"It seems I owe you thanks," she said.

"For?"

"The truth. More, for allowing my people to live."

"A decision I fear I shall regret."

Her lips turned into a slight smile. "I pray you do not."

As he considered her mouth, he remembered their last kiss. He knew better than to want another, but he did. And it was not all he wanted.

Maxen did not believe he was of an impulsive nature, and yet he barely acknowledged his thoughts were in opposition to his determination he would not sin with her, nor provide her a means to tempt him to marriage. Instead, he spoke what he should not. "If I asked it, would you yield to me—*this* Maxen?"

Her eyes widened. "I would not."

Raggedly spending his breath—part frustration, part relief—he touched a thumb to the corner of her mouth. "Not even a kiss?"

Her lips parted, and as she said barely above a whisper, "I must return to my chores," he drew her close.

The kiss was well explored by both, and it was Rhiannyn who ended it. Dropping her chin, she said, "I will not yield. Pray, release me."

He lowered his arms to his sides.

She brushed trembling fingers across her lips, curled them into her palm, and lifted her face to his. "Why do you persist?"

He also wished to know the answer. Or, perhaps, not. Feigning nonchalance, he said, "It was but a kiss to speed my journey. Do not make more of it."

Her anger rising between them, she narrowed her lids. "Then God speed it, my lord—in one direction only."

In that moment, he felt almost a youth again, one chastised for his foolishness. And he could not say it was not deserved.

He inclined his head and strode opposite.

When he arrived at the stables, his men were ready to ride and Sir Guy stood alongside the destrier that would deliver the lord of Etcheverry to Blackspur.

"What of Rhiannyn, my lord?" Guy asked as Maxen accepted the reins from his squire. "Should she continue in her duties, or would you have me secure her in the tower whilst you are away?"

He was tempted by the tower, but only to ensure she was here when he returned. "Nay," he said, trying not to think on the kiss *this* Maxen, the one she liked, had given her. "Unless she proves difficult, allow her the reach of the castle, but keep a good watch on her."

The knight inclined his head.

"I leave Etcheverry in your hands," Maxen said, then added, "and Rhiannyn. Keep both for me."

A question leapt in the knight's eyes, but it need not be answered. All that was required was for Guy to understand the importance of not disappointing his lord. Even if Maxen did not wish to understand it himself.

Rhiannyn's heart moved in remembrance of Maxen's eyes and the light dancing in them, beat harder at the revelation it was not cruelty he had shown in allowing her to believe he meant to execute her people. A test, he had said. Also deserving of anger, but anger she had been unable to express against the Maxen who had stood before her.

Somehow, she had reached that other side of him, and found hope in it—until he asked if she would yield to him, as if theirs was a battle of life and death such that if she did not, she might suffer the same as a knight who refused the one whose blade was against his neck. In her case, she would know suffering if she did yield, for she was not unmoved by his touch. And his kiss, particularly this last one, had fit her too well.

Determinedly, she pulled herself back to this moment when there was no one to prevent her from doing what she must to once more become one with her people—if it was possible.

Though she had not previously ventured out among them, certain Maxen would forbid it, she had watched from a distance as the Saxons built his wall. Long were the hours and strenuous their work, and with only his promise of reward to carry them.

As she descended the causeway, a bucket in each hand, the three kitchen servants who followed her bearing equal burdens, Rhiannyn reflected on Aethel and the four others still imprisoned beneath the donjon. Twice she had attempted to slip past the guard, but had been forced to retreat to avoid discovery. Perhaps with Maxen gone, the guard would ease his watch.

Despite the number of men Maxen had taken with him, he had left behind a great many to ensure the Saxons did not try to take advantage of his absence. And all of those men seemed to be following her progress across the bailey. However, it was not they who roused a shiver of apprehension as she neared the workers. It was fear of her reception.

She wondered if she should have heeded Lucilla's warning. The woman regularly carried food and drink to the Saxons, and when Rhiannyn had asked to take her place, she had protested. But Rhiannyn had persisted, and it was too late to turn back.

"See who has come down off her fine perch," called a Saxon man atop the wall.

Rhiannyn recognized him as Peter who, with Aethel, had come upon her in Andredeswald after she had fled Etcheverry. He had not liked her then, and clearly less so now.

The men on the scaffolding, those on the ramps up which the stone was conveyed, the handful working the hoists and pulleys, and the women whose job it was to mix mortar, paused to search out who had caught Peter's attention. And none appeared any more welcoming.

Rhiannyn set her buckets on the ground. Behind, the three serving women noisily lowered theirs, then came the sound of retreating footsteps, portending she would stand alone.

"I have brought drink," she said, "and midday bread and cheese."

A woman named Meghan stepped forward and wiped a forearm across her sweaty brow. "What be a Norman harlot doing among lowly Saxons?"

"A Saxon among Saxons," Rhiannyn said. "And as I am not Norman, neither am I the harlot you make me to be."

"Ha!" Peter laughed. "Even were you not, still ye are a betrayer."

"I did not betray you."

"Aye?" snapped another Saxon. "Then why do we build a wall against our own when 'tis on the other side we ought to be?"

"It is true I led Pendery to Edwin's camp," she said, "but I vow I did so unknowingly. As you were deceived, so was I."

"We are to believe ye?" Peter asked.

"No doubt, you will believe what you like, but still I would have you hear the truth."

"A traitor's truth," another woman slung at her.

Rhiannyn moistened her lips. "I grew up amongst many of you. You know me, and if you search your hearts, you will see that never would I betray you."

"I would not see that," Meghan said. "For the bed of the handsome monk, methinks many a harlot would turn."

Rhiannyn sighed. Having outworn the argument of her innocence, knowing it would take time and patience for these people to come around, she said, "There is food and drink aplenty."

Meghan tossed aside her mortar hoe, crossed to Rhiannyn, and looked bucket to bucket. "By the hand of the enemy we are fed."

"An enemy you have accepted so you might know peace again."

"Ye think so?"

Fear uncoiled within Rhiannyn. Had they lied to Maxen? Did they plan to rebel? Hoping it was but anger this woman spoke, Rhiannyn said, "I pray so."

Meghan propped her fists on her hips and lowered her gaze down Rhiannyn's gown. "The lord be a bit stingy. Of course, he is only concerned with what is beneath."

The Saxons snickered, as did their Norman guard.

Rhiannyn longed to tell these people she was less than they, that when the wall was completed and they were released to the land, she would still be a captive, but she could not. Even were they capable of pitying her, she wanted none of it.

"The bliaut suits me fine," she said.

"Easy in, easy out, hmm?"

The snickering grew louder, stirring resentment similar to what Rhiannyn felt during her encounters with Maxen, but she said, "Do you intend to eat?"

Meghan snorted, then knocked Rhiannyn off her feet and slammed her to the ground alongside the great tub of mortar.

Before Rhiannyn could recover her breath, the woman sat upon her and delivered a fist to the left eye. Amidst glaring pain, Rhiannyn knocked aside the next blow and countered with a punch. It was poorly executed, for she had never come to fists, but she caught Meghan hard on the nose and mouth.

The woman yelped, and when she toppled onto her back, Rhiannyn shoved onto her knees and straddled her. "Do you wish more?" she demanded.

Removing the hand clapped over her face, Meghan revealed bloodied teeth and said, "Aye, much more," and snatched hold of Rhiannyn's hair and flung her to the side.

Once more on her back, Rhiannyn saw Meghan gain her feet.

"Get up!" the woman said, fight in her stance.

Rhiannyn swept her gaze over the Saxons who had left their work to more closely follow the contest, and their Norman guards who seemed more interested in bettering their view than ending the confrontation.

Reassuring herself Meghan and she were well matched—neither taller or heavier—Rhiannyn said, "Let us end this."

The Saxon woman breached the space between them and fell on her with flailing fists.

Numerous times over the course of what could have been no more than the spit of an hour, Rhiannyn was the recipient of painful blows, but she gave back much of what she was given.

It was the tub of mortar that decided the contest. Slammed back against its rim, she evaded the next attack by jumping to the side. Meghan, unable to check her headlong rush, doubled over the tub. As she wheezed, struggling to return air to her lungs, Rhiannyn twisted one of her arms up behind her back.

Meghan shrieked. Saxon and Norman voices rising around them, Rhiannyn pressed the woman down toward the mortar. "Would you care for a closer look?"

"I give!" Meghan cried. "Bless it, I give!"

Feeling as if outside herself, Rhiannyn bent to the woman's ear. "I require more."

"Speak!"

"No longer will you name me *harlot*. Nor will you seek to engage me in further scraps."

At the woman's hesitation, Rhiannyn pressed her arm farther up her back. "What is your answer?"

Meghan groaned. "Agreed!"

Hardly had Rhiannyn released her than John, the master mason, strode forward. "What goes?" he demanded in poor Anglo-Saxon.

Knowing she appeared a mess in her begrimed clothing and with an eye swelling closed, Rhiannyn stepped before the Norman whose job it was to supervise work on the wall. "A disagreement now settled."

"Is that right?" He looked from her to Meghan. "I have no need of more trouble than already I am given by this lot of griping Saxons. Return to your kitchen duties and vex me no more, woman."

Rhiannyn shook her head. "I would stay and work alongside my own."

"Be gone!"

"But I——"

"Surely you could use one more pair of hands, Master John?" a voice called in her language.

All turned and shaded their eyes to see who stood atop the wall. Looking the lord but for the droll smile curving his mouth, Sir Guy crossed his arms over his chest.

Rhiannyn was surprised he spoke Anglo-Saxon, never having heard him utter a word of it.

"But Sir Guy," John protested, "see what this one has wrought." He jerked a thumb toward Rhiannyn. "She will be more hindrance than help."

"Has she not said the dispute is settled?"

"Aye, but——"

"Put her to work."

"I do not think Lord Pendery would approve."

"If there is question upon his return, I will answer to him."

The man tossed up his hands. "Upon your head." He turned back to the Saxons. "Be quick about your bread and drink. There is much to do before dark falls."

As the others moved away, Rhiannyn continued to stare at Sir Guy, who should have been the first to send her back to the kitchen. Why had he not?

His own gaze fixed on her, he swept a hand before him in silent invitation for her to join the others.

She nodded her thanks and turned to the simple meal that would have to sustain her throughout what would be a taxing day for body and mind.

22

"You will not name Sir Ancel lord of Blackspur as Thomas intended?"

Pleased with all he had seen, though it was less than expected considering the construction on Blackspur Castle had commenced shortly after Etcheverry Castle was raised, Maxen turned to his brother. "*Non,* it is to be Sir Guy's reward—unless you would like it for yourself."

Christophe shook his head. "You know such is not for me."

"I would have it be otherwise."

"And I would not."

Maxen inclined his head. "Then Guy it is."

"What of Sir Ancel?"

Maxen looked down into the bailey and located the man where he lay stretched out to receive the uncommon warmth of an autumn sun come out from behind the clouds. "As I have said, he cannot be trusted. For certain, he left the dagger for Rhiannyn, and he will continue to seek my death."

"Then you will have done with him?"

Maxen eyed Christophe, trying again to assess who was beneath the young man's awkward exterior. "You do not sound averse to his passing."

"If that is required to rid you of him, I am not."

"For one as gentle of heart as you, Brother, it surprises you would approve of such means of ridding one's self of an adversary."

Christophe's mouth twitched. "More and more, I fear there are some of whom one can be free only by way of their death."

"And you believe Sir Ancel is one of those?"

"He beat Rhiannyn and tried to murder you. I know I should not wish the taking of life, but I fear the shedding of the blood of those I care about, far more than the shedding of his."

"Understandable."

Christophe stepped nearer. "Knowing what you do about him, why have you not acted?"

Again Maxen considered his brother. Was it only Christophe's lameness that had shaped him this way? Or did it go deeper? Nils's death? The horror of Hastings, which he had surely heard much about? Thomas?

"If death it must be," Maxen said, "the time must be right."

"When will it be right?"

"I wait for Sir Ancel to decide."

Christophe's eyes widened. "Explain."

Maxen rolled his shoulders to break up the tension that had settled there during the journey from Etcheverry. "If naught else, a dying man ought to be able to choose when he dies."

"Then you will allow him to draw nearer? To try again?"

"That is the plan."

"The next time he may succeed."

"Perhaps, but tell me, would it trouble you much?"

Christophe's expression turned outraged. "I have lost two brothers. You cannot think I care to lose another!"

"Consider who this brother is," Maxen said. "Cold-hearted, merciless, brutal—but a few of the words used to describe me, and all deserved. It would be half-truth to defend what I did at Hastings by calling it duty to my liege. Though not alone in what I became, the need to prove myself a man and a warrior well-earned me the name The Bloodlust Warrior of Hastings. I am despicable, so much that two years with God did not cleanse me of those sins."

Sorrow replacing ire, Christophe laid a hand on his brother's arm. "You are wrong. No longer are you that man. You proved it with the Saxons when you gave them back their lives."

"Did I? Or was it but the needs of the flesh I proved?" As soon as the words were out, he wished he could drag them back. What had possessed him to speak them? To open to his brother what he could hardly open to himself?

"Rhiannyn," Christophe said, and it was not a question.

Maxen shook off his hand and stepped away. "*Oui,* she haunts me."

"For her you were lenient with the Saxons."

"Not entirely for her, but I am not certain I would have been so lenient had she not asked me to show mercy and put them back to the land." He heard the bitterness in his voice. "It will serve me right if they all turn on me."

"You think they will?"

"I do not trust them, especially while Harwolfson prowls the wood."

"Likely, he has gone."

"*Non,* he is still there. He wants what is his."

"The land."

"And Rhiannyn."

"To end this, would you give him either?"

Maxen nearly barked with scorn. "As the land is Pendery through King William, even for peace, I could not confer it upon the Saxon rebel."

"But you could give him Rhiannyn."

Maxen hated that he recoiled at the thought. If it meant peace, of course he ought to hand over Rhiannyn. And happily. But he could not imagine doing so, and not just because it could mean the death of her if Harwolfson still kept the old crone who had nearly succeeded in murdering her. Something about Rhiannyn appealed to him as no other woman had. Thus, had she yielded, he feared that would not be the end of it—of them.

"Maxen, do you have feelings for her? Love, perhaps?"

He narrowed his gaze on Christophe. "As Thomas wanted her, so do I. That is all."

A lie, said a voice within. *If she follows Lucilla's advice, you could lose yourself to her.*

"It is true she did not return Thomas's affections," Christophe said, "but still he loved her—in his own selfish way."

"And it got him killed."

"*Oui*, but you err in believing Rhiannyn is responsible."

"As you have already told."

"And will continue to tell until you concede."

Maxen heaved a sigh. "Is it not enough there is finally peace between you and me, Christophe? Content yourself with that and do not ask me to hold Rhiannyn blameless. She played no small part in Thomas's death."

"A similar role to the one I played for you in assisting with her escape, yet am I not innocent of betraying her?"

Maxen backhanded the air. "Enough. I like this peace of ours too much to destroy it with petty arguments."

"Very well, but there is much unsaid that should be spoken."

And would be eventually. Without further word, Maxen pivoted and descended the steps.

23

ONLY IN HER untimely grave had Rhiannyn been so filthy. Now, though, it was not dirt that clung to her, but the mortar of a wall raised against Saxons.

The accumulation of five days' fatigue causing her feet to drag, she leaned against the stable fence to study the wall she had worked upon. Side by side with people determined to keep her out, she had mixed mortar, lugged buckets to the ramps, and assisted in hoisting rubble up the scaffolds. Never had she worked so hard, not even when Edwin had forced her to learn the sword. But it was worth what it cost her.

She had made enough progress with her people to reward the aches and pains. No longer were her ears filled with the malicious words the first three days had heaped upon her. Though now generally ignored, there were moments when she was almost one with the Saxons, such as on the previous day when she had gone for water to thin the mortar and lost her footing. Doused, she had joined in their laughter.

Then there was the pulley that had let go in the midst of hauling a ladened basket up the wall. She had seen it coming and jumped aside, but had been struck by an errant stone. Several Saxons had rushed to aid her, concern upon their faces until they saw she was only bruised. They had grumbled all the way back to their labors. Although she knew the mishap may not have been an accident, she had been comforted by the knowledge some cared—even if they did not wish to.

"Pray, Maxen, stay away a while longer," she whispered into the coming night that had cleared the bailey of nearly all but the guards stationed atop the walls. Why Sir Guy allowed her to work amongst the others she still did not know, but she did not believe Maxen would permit it once he returned. And if he returned too soon, all she had toiled for could be lost. "A few more days…"

"My lady is saddened?" one of hoarse voice asked.

She swung around and opened her mouth to voice her displeasure at being sneaked upon. But something familiar amid the shadow of the man's hood held her tongue. Warily, she reached to push it back from his face, but his voice froze her hand midair.

"Do not!"

"Edwin?" she whispered.

He lifted his head just enough to raise the shadow from his face. "You expected another? Maxen Pendery?"

She shot her gaze to the men-at-arms within sight and saw none looked her way. "Certainly not you. How did you come within?"

"As there was no portal open to welcome the true lord of Etcheverry," he dripped sarcasm, "I had to make my passage by wall. But come." He slipped a hand from beneath his tattered mantle and grasped her arm. "We have much to discuss."

Knowing to refuse him would draw attention, she yielded to his pull and, shortly, faced him in the deserted stables.

"You are looking poorly, Rhiannyn." He brushed a thumb beneath her eye that was yellowed from the bruise Meghan had given her. "Far from the fair maiden I remember."

She drew back. "I have been helping build the wall."

"And brawling."

"When I must. But tell, why are you here?"

He pushed back the hood, revealing a face so harsh, it was hardly familiar. "What a strange question."

It was, she silently agreed, and said, "You have come for your rebels."

"And?"

She shook her head. "Nay, Edwin, do not ask them to challenge the Normans. No good will come of it. More will die."

"You do not believe in the superiority of our people over Normans?"

"There are more of them than Saxons, and heavily armed. Pray, leave your people be so they might live and rear children and raise crops upon which to feed them. Maxen Pendery has promised them this. Do not take it from them."

"The promise of a Norman," Edwin spat. "They are my people. I trained them, and they will join with me against the Norman dog with whom you fornicate."

"I have not lain with him!"

"You think me a fool? You left with him—betrayed me."

"I did not. It was from Dora I ran. Maxen Pendery saved me from the death she tried to work upon me."

"What lie do you tell?"

"No lie, Edwin. You saw Dora that night. She wanted me dead. When all slept, she and three others took me from my tent and tried to bury me alive. It is the truth!"

He was silent some moments, then said, "The only truth I know is Pendery murdered three of my men before you left with him, not to mention those lives he took when he attacked our camp."

"Three?" Rhiannyn gasped. "There were two dead when I came to consciousness. The third was wounded and ran with Dora."

"I do not understand your part in this, Rhiannyn, but it was three who died—three I buried."

She could think of no reason Maxen would lie when he had readily admitted to taking two lives. "Mayhap Dora killed the third," she said, knowing it was true the moment she spoke it. "Aye, so he could not be made to tell the truth of what she tried to do to me."

"Dora is a healer, not a murderer."

"Are you so blind, Edwin? Did you not see the grave she put me into?"

"Grave?"

Rhiannyn sighed. "She must have moved the bodies to hide the truth. She is evil, Edwin. If only for your soul, you must send her from you."

Contempt further lined his face. "It is as she foretold—you would betray your own people and take another to your bed. What she said has come to pass, and yet you wish me to believe lies that fall from your mouth like venom?"

"They are not lies. Believe me in this!"

"As you would have me believe you did not lead Pendery to us?"

"I know now that in fleeing Etcheverry, I led him to the camp, but I did not know it then. And upon my soul, I have not lain with him."

He grasped her chin and lifted her face toward his. "Even were it true, you *will* lie with him."

Which she could not vow she would not do, Rhiannyn realized as she was flushed with memories of their last encounter—Maxen's laughter, his smile, his hand gently picking feathers from her hair. And their kiss...

"What? You do not deny it?" Edwin said. "Tell me you will not give yourself to him—swear it upon your soul—and mayhap I will believe your other untruths."

On the verge of tears, she whispered, "I cannot."

Edwin shoved her back and strode away. "You may give yourself to the Norman dog," he said over his shoulder, "but you will not give away my people." He pulled the hood over his head, eased the stable door open, and slipped into the night.

As the door whined closed, Rhiannyn leaned against the stall wall and looked heavenward. "What am I to do? How to end this?"

The door whined again.

"Edwin?" She peered through the shadows. He was not there, but as she watched, the door closed a second time.

"Ah, nay," she breathed. Someone else had been in the stables with Edwin and her, someone who might alert the Normans to the Saxon leader's presence.

Rhiannyn ran from the stables to the outbuildings where her people were quartered. In her flight, she nearly tripped over two of the men Maxen had set to watch over the Saxons. She paused to verify they lived, and finding them unconscious—a wonder, considering Edwin's hatred of Normans—she ran to the larger of the buildings where the Saxons took their evening meal.

"Do we stand together?" Edwin asked from atop a table. "Take the castle and all who defend it?"

"Edwin!" Rhiannyn called as she pushed her way through the crowd. "You must leave. Now!"

"You are not welcome here," he said. "Go."

"Heed me," she pleaded. "Methinks the Normans may be coming."

His lids narrowed. "You told them?"

A path opening to the table upon which he stood, she hastened forward and strained her neck to meet his gaze. "I did not, but another may have."

"How would you know?"

Desperate for the moments being lost to argument, she cried, "There is not much time. Leave!"

The Saxons began muttering, looking from Edwin to Rhiannyn, no doubt weighing the wisdom of what their leader asked of them.

"What is your answer?" Edwin demanded.

An older Saxon stepped forward. "Were I not forty-three summers aged, I would, Edwin. Were I still willing to die no matter the cost, indeed I would. But I cannot." He stepped back.

"Pendery has promised to return us to the land," said another of significantly less years. "I am a simple man, and would like to sow the seed of children and crops ere I die."

"You believe Pendery?" Edwin asked, fists at his sides.

"Since the coming of the Normans, there has been less to believe in, but his promise is the best we have."

"Aye," agreed a Saxon not much more than a boy. "He provides well. There is food aplenty, clothing, and fuel for warming fires."

Rhiannyn stared, stunned by their response.

"And when winter comes and this ravished land has provided only enough for the Normans?" Edwin asked. "You will either starve or meet your death of cold."

The murmuring increased, and Rhiannyn also wondered what winter would bring, for it was true what Edwin spoke. The harvest after another year of Saxon rebellion was insufficient, and Thomas had hardly managed to feed his own during the winter past, leaving many of the Saxons who had taken him as their new master to fend for themselves. And there had been deaths.

"Are there none who will follow me?" Edwin asked. "None who will take back what is ours?"

"What is yours," Meghan said. "Aye, we are all of us Saxons, Edwin, but we are simple folk, whereas ye are noble. Be it Norman or Saxon who possesses the land, still we answer to a master. For what should we give our lives in exchanging one for the other?"

Agreement stirred among the others.

"I will follow ye," Peter said and jumped onto the table alongside Edwin. "Who stands with the betrayer"—he pointed at Rhiannyn—"and who remains loyal to the rightful lord of Etcheverry?"

Rhiannyn held her breath, but her prayers were quickly answered—or nearly so—when only two more took up places alongside Edwin.

"Is Aethel not among you?" Edwin called out, eyes searching for the height and breadth of a man who would have been conspicuous among those present.

"He and four others are imprisoned 'neath the donjon for loyalty to you," Peter said. "Though they do not yet hang, they shall."

From the look in Edwin's eyes, it was obvious he had set himself to devising a way to release them.

But it was not to be. Moments later, all was thrown into chaos as Normans swelled into the building with weapons drawn and Sir Guy at the fore.

Much of what followed was a blur. Edwin passed a dagger to Peter, and with sword in hand, leapt from the table and hurled himself at the Normans. The air was filled with shouts, curses, the meeting of weapons, and the cries of Saxons who feared for their lives.

Though those who had decided against Edwin dropped to the ground in surrender, Rhiannyn remained standing.

"Your neck if they escape!" Sir Guy shouted.

Rhiannyn looked around and saw Edwin and two others fight their way to the door and out, a dozen men-at-arms following close behind. But where was the third who had joined Edwin? Dead?

"If you wish to live," Sir Guy shouted, "remain where you are. Any who rise up will taste the edge of a sword." He shifted his gaze to Rhiannyn.

The fury in his eyes chilling her, she looked away and began praying. And did not stop until the men-at-arms who had pursued Edwin returned.

"Regrets, Sir Guy," one said, "two escaped."

"The other?"

"Wounded, but death is nigh."

"Tell me it is Harwolfson."

The man shook his head. "He and the Saxon named Peter went over the wall. We followed, but could find nothing of them before Andredeswald."

Sir Guy's shoulders bunched, but he did not strike the man. After a long moment, he turned to Rhiannyn. He did not have to speak his summons, for it was in his eyes.

Feet feeling as if encased in stone, she wove her way between the ones who had laid themselves at the mercy of the Normans, faltering when she came upon one of the three Saxons who had chosen Edwin. He was dead, his tunic bloodied neck to hips.

She continued to where Sir Guy awaited her and beseeched, "Will you allow me to speak?"

He jerked his head and said between clamped teeth, "Speak and be done with it so we might begin the fettering."

Then he had come to his own conclusions that all the Saxons had joined the uprising. Thus, their punishment would be bondage until Maxen returned to pronounce judgment.

"It is not what it looks," she said. "Edwin asked these people to join with him, but they chose to remain under the house of Pendery, as was their promise to your lord—now their lord. Only three joined with Edwin."

Sir Guy stared.

"She speaks true," Meghan said, rising to her knees.

From the ground came murmurs of agreement.

"She speaks lies!"

Rhiannyn gasped, sped her gaze to Theta.

The woman skirted the men-at-arms, sidled up to Sir Guy, and put an arm through his. "With my own ears did I hear Rhiannyn and Edwin make plans with these people to take the castle while our lord is absent. Had I not brought word to you, they would be overrunning Etcheverry and slaughtering us all."

It had been Theta in the stables with her and Edwin, Rhiannyn realized. She who had alerted Sir Guy to what was barely a half-truth, she who this moment renounced her own people.

"Theta lies," Rhiannyn said. "None of these people plotted with Edwin. They are innocents."

"Aye, 'tis the Norman harlot who lies," Meghan concurred.

"If you wish to live, woman," Sir Guy snarled, "lie down."

Meghan complied.

Sir Guy returned his attention to Rhiannyn. "I trusted you. Though your place is in the hall, I allowed you to work upon the wall so you might know your people again."

"Listen to me. I—"

"I have listened enough, and now you will lie down, too."

"But they have done naught wrong. Theta—"

"Down, Rhiannyn!"

Feeling as if the bones had gone out of her, she lowered to the ground between two Saxons.

"You tried," whispered the man on her left, his sad smile welcoming her back.

If only such were not the circumstances under which she gained acceptance, she silently bemoaned and squeezed her eyes closed.

"You, you, and you," Sir Guy called to his men. "Carry word to our lord of what has transpired. He must return at once."

Calm, Rhiannyn silently urged. Within a day and night, Maxen would return. If she was to reach him again past the fury that would be like a wall around him, she must be calm—and prepared to sacrifice whatever was required to keep the noose from her people.

The missive was delivered, but Maxen asked no questions, uttered no word, before sending the messengers away.

"It cannot be," Christophe said as soon as the men departed the hall.

Maxen closed his eyes and felt pain behind his anger. Time and again, he had thought on Rhiannyn these past days. Time and again, he had moved nearer a place he had told himself he would not go. Time and again, he had resisted stepping over that line—until upon awakening this morn when he had been the one to yield, though he had excused his decision to wed Rhiannyn as but a means of strengthening his hold on Etcheverry by joining their two peoples. But she had deceived him again, plotting with her Saxons to take Etcheverry.

Lord, he silently called to the heavens, *why did she have to be at the center of this?*

"Wait until you have spoken with her," Christophe said.

Maxen set his jaw. "I warned you about being quick with your apologies. As Rhiannyn and her people have not fulfilled their end of the bargain, I need not fulfill mine. I am done with them all."

Ignoring Christophe's outburst, he strode from the hall. Within the half hour, he and his men rode out from Blackspur Castle.

24

I AM READY, Rhiannyn told herself when Maxen returned the following day.

From the clamor outside, she and the others knew when he rode beneath the portcullis. Yet he did not immediately come to the outbuilding that had become their prison. For some, it might have seemed reprieve. For her, it made his return that much more terrible.

They were bound one to another at the ankles, but now that the silence of waiting was upon them, the chains were eerily silent.

Finally, footsteps.

Though Rhiannyn felt Meghan's gaze, she did not look her way. She stared straight ahead, and when Maxen threw open the door and strode into the midst of those he believed had betrayed him, reminded herself she was ready.

She was not.

The moment his gaze picked her from beneath the layer of dust and mortar she had worn since the day before, a part of her folded. Never would she be ready for one such as Maxen Pendery, but neither did it mean she would throw up her hands in surrender.

Anger was visible all about him—the set of his shoulders, the hard line of his mouth, the flare of his nostrils, and those eyes.

With a generous measure of docility and a rattle of chain, she stood. "My lord, will you hear us?"

He walked forward, his gaze growing heavier with each footfall. "No more, Rhiannyn." He halted before her. "I have had enough of your lies."

A retort sprang to her lips, but she swallowed it and said, "They are not lies. What I would tell you, what you need to hear, is the truth."

He put his face near hers. "I said *no more*."

She moistened her lips. "But there is more. What you have been told is not true. These people rejected Edwin for their new master. Pray, do not punish them for gifting you their loyalty."

Near to bursting with all the brooding he had done since learning of Rhiannyn's treachery, Maxen stepped back and swept his gaze over the expectant faces of men and women whose only champion was a small, filthy, infuriating woman whom the weak part of him—the Maxen she liked—wanted to believe.

Could it be Theta who lied? It could, but as easily, it could be Rhiannyn.

"Only three joined with Edwin," she further defied him, "two of them now dead. The others stood down. You must believe me."

He returned his gaze to her. "You plotted with them, though why Sir Guy allowed you to work on the wall is beyond me."

"You are wrong. Does it not tell you something that these people immediately surrendered? Ask Sir Guy." She looked to where the knight stood at the door—and beside him, Christophe.

"Did they not go to the ground when you and the others came in?" she demanded. "Was there one among them who resisted?"

Before Sir Guy could answer, Maxen said, "Fearing for their lives, no doubt."

"Nay, keeping their word to you."

It further angered him how much he wanted to believe her, but still he held to the single, taut thread of control. "You will not convince me, Rhiannyn, so waste no more words." What was done was done, and he must do what he should have in the beginning. He headed for the door.

"What do you intend?" she called.

"You know the answer," he said over his shoulder.

Silence, then she cried, "I yield!"

He halted, turned. Though he knew to what she referred, he waited.

She lowered her gaze and, so softly he more imagined than heard it, repeated, "I yield."

Then if he wished it, if he rejected the teachings of the Church she had reminded him he did not have the right to do, without benefit of marriage she would give herself to him. For her people, she would sacrifice the only thing she believed he desired of her.

As he stared at her, much too aware that beneath her begrimed, pitiful figure was a woman who moved him more than any other, he told himself to throw her yielding back at her and do what needed to be done to ensure Etcheverry's future, to forget it might be Theta who lied and be done with these Saxons. But he could not.

He motioned to a man-at-arms. "Bring her to my chamber," he said and stalked from the building.

Sir Guy followed, his silence more irritating than the scratch of claws on a door.

Past the stables, Maxen swung around. "I want every one of them questioned. Separately."

Guy frowned. "I thought…Rhiannyn…"

"If punishment is due, it will be given, regardless of what she offers in exchange for her people."

Relief lightened the man's face. "Wise, my lord," he said and turned back to the outbuilding.

Wise. Fortunately, not all of him was trapped in Rhiannyn's web. He would discover for certain, or reasonably certain, if the Saxons had rebelled. If so, this time he would deliver punishment.

Rhiannyn stared ahead—beyond the guard who stepped around the Saxons to gain her side, past Christophe to a point of emptiness.

She was about to become what Lucilla had warned against—Maxen's leman. Blessedly, she had not succumbed to him earlier, for she would have nothing with which to bargain. But what if a child was born of their union?

No children, Lord, she silently beseeched. *I would be barren as Thomas wished it ere I deliver into this world a child branded by illegitimacy.*

She looked out over the Saxons, nearly all of whom gazed at her with some degree of pity. They knew what she had surrendered, and those who had thought it already given to Maxen Pendery—having been most vocal in naming her a harlot—appeared contrite.

Rhiannyn offered Meghan a tight smile and looked to the guard at her feet. He was rough in the removal of the manacle, but she knew it only from watching him. She hardly felt the scrape of the iron on her skin as, over and again, she heard the shrill voice of one who had foretold this day.

'Tis another she will fornicate with, old Dora had said. *Another she will fornicate with.*

Agitation dragged the minutes into hours they were not. He was restless, not merely with waiting, but irritation at Christophe's plea that he behave the godly man and leave Rhiannyn untouched—that he return her yielding to her and have faith in her word the Saxons were innocent.

Maxen had withheld his reproach and sent his brother away. However, it was the youth who had the last word, declaring Maxen's future with Rhiannyn doomed if he took advantage of her attempt to save her people.

Future. Though Maxen spurned the thought, Christophe's words continued to press in upon him, and he groaned. The young man had declined a lordship of his own, certain he would make a weak master, but he was gifted with wisdom.

As Maxen further contemplated his brother, his mind wandered so far from the one he waited upon that he nearly startled when Rhiannyn came around the screen.

He considered the waif she presented—hair wild and unclean, face smudged and unsmiling, mortar-streaked clothes more destined for the burn pile than the wash.

"You may leave us," he told the guard, and a moment later was alone with Rhiannyn—as he had longed to be since she had come out from beneath his mattress a sennight past with feathers in her hair.

He raised his ride-weary body from the chair, crossed to her, and lifted her chin. It was then he saw the remains of a bruise beneath her eye. Thinking he must have been too angry and the outbuilding too dim to have not noticed it before, he rasped, "Someone struck you?"

She lifted a hand toward her face, but quickly returned it to her side. "A disagreement only."

"Who?" he barked.

Clearly, she contemplated another lie, but she said, "The Saxon woman, Meghan. I fought—and bettered—her. It is done."

A woman. And Rhiannyn had prevailed. A strange swell of pride for her victory pushed through him, but he determinedly turned his thoughts to the pact they had made.

Staring into eyes that at first appeared vacant, but upon closer examination revealed a spark in their depth, he said, "The Saxons are being questioned."

Confusion rose to her face, next suspicion. "Why when our arrangement precludes such?"

"I must know what they have to tell."

She pulled her chin out of his hand. "And if you determine they are culpable?"

"It will be as it should have been. Those who betrayed will be punished."

The spark in her eyes flamed, and he felt the weight of her loathing. But she raised no hand against him, nor gave further retort. Instead, she spun and headed from the chamber.

With one stride, he caught her. "Where are you going?"

She glared up at him, and he thought how lovely she was even amid filth and deception.

"It is beyond me why you wasted your time in bringing me here."

"You have changed your mind?"

She gasped. "For what should I yield to you?"

"Your Saxons."

Her laughter was scornful. "As they have gained naught, you are owed naught."

"But they have gained."

Confusion returned to her face. "You speak in riddles, Maxen Pendery. I yielded so my people would not suffer undue punishment, and you are not keeping your end of the bargain."

"If the Saxons are shown to be guilty, their fate is the same as it would have been when I came to the outbuilding. If they are innocent, all will be as it was when I rode to Blackspur. I give them an ear, Rhiannyn, a chance to convince me of their loyalty a second time, a chance they had not ere you made a sacrifice of yourself."

The flicker in her eyes evidenced she understood. "It is not what you agreed to," she said.

"Do you recall, I did not say what I would give in return for your yielding."

"You knew exactly for what I offered myself—absolution, not trial."

"Only a fool imperils his life for naught but the pleasures of the body, Rhiannyn. But come, do you have so little faith in your people you fear their answers to my questions?"

She drew herself up to her full height, which was not much. "The Normans believe what they wish to believe, not the truth."

Deciding he was done with an argument of which neither could convince the other, Maxen asked, "Do you accept these conditions?"

He saw refusal in her eyes, and she drew breath as if to speak it, but when she breathed out, it was on the words, "I accept."

He lowered his head and touched his lips to hers. He was not surprised by resentment he could almost taste, but he regretted it. He longed for the woman with feathers in her hair and a hopeful smile on her lips, the woman who had said she liked him—Maxen

Pendery who, for those blessed minutes, had been free of what he had become at Hastings.

And could be again. *If* he heeded Christophe. More, if he heeded what he knew to be right regardless of whether or not he wore the robes of a monk.

He raised his head, and as he silently battled the two sides of him, considered the upper bow of her mouth, its lower curve, her neat white teeth. Then he released her. "Forgive me."

She frowned.

"The Saxons will be questioned, for I cannot blindly grant them absolution, but I decline your yielding."

Her lids fluttered. "Why?"

Though tempted to leave it be, he said, "Since receiving news of the Saxon betrayal, I have been moved by anger, to which one entrusted with the fate of others should not succumb. Since the day you and I were last here, I have been further moved by desire, to which your friend, Lucilla, would have me fall victim that I might wed you. Thus, I decline. You will not share my bed."

A soft breath fell from her, and the extra bit of height she had gained slid from her shoulders. "I thank you."

"It is your champion, Christophe, you ought to thank." He hated the resentment in his voice. "Now, I leave you to remove those filthy garments."

She startled, and though he disliked how quickly he tried to put her at ease, he said, "I ordered a bath for you. But, as told, it is not for my benefit—other than to make you presentable enough to once more serve in my hall."

As the distress eased from her face, he said, "You may use my robe for cover until the water arrives." He nodded at the garment on his iron-banded chest, turned, and called for ale as he strode around the screen into the hall.

Too confused to indulge in the relief begging to be felt, Rhiannyn stared at where Maxen no longer stood. When several minutes had passed and he did not reappear, she crossed to the chest and fingered the fine material of his robe.

"I am reaching him, Lord," she whispered. "Am I not?"

More minutes passed, during which she caught the sound of his voice as he conversed with others in the hall.

Finally, she untied her bliaut's sash, removed her garments, and wrapped herself in a robe too large and too suggestive of the one who had last worn it.

The water for her bath arrived, and she sat on the edge of the chest as the Saxon serving women carried pail after pail to the waiting tub. They knew—or *had* known—the purpose of their task, as evidenced by the way their eyes darted at her. But though tempted to tell them that whatever tales they had heard, Maxen would not dishonor her by claiming her as his leman, she feared she would not be believed. After all, she was in his chamber, wore his robe, and would soon be in his tub.

When she was once more alone, Rhiannyn removed the robe and stepped into the warm water. A gasp of pleasure fled her. Not since before she had escaped Etcheverry with Thomas in pursuit had she enjoyed a proper bath. She sank back and sighed as boiling water cooled by the many steps from the kitchens seeped its warmth into her, and only then realized how cold she had been.

After all of her was warmed, she washed her hair and began removing the dirt that gave her skin a gray cast. She scrubbed until she shone more pink than pale, until her flesh stung with raw awareness, and the water lost its clarity. Then she stepped from the tub, dried herself with a towel delivered with the bath water, and once more donned Maxen's robe.

She waited, hoping he would send someone with clean garments so she could leave, but only a tray of food was delivered amid the rising din of those who came to the hall to feast.

And feast they did, while she picked at her viands and waited.

When she heard Maxen call for silence, she guessed two hours had passed since he had left her.

Fearing the announcement he was about to make concerned the questioning of the Saxons—that already their fate was decided and it was not a good one—she crept to the far side of the screen. Peering around it, she could see most of the hall.

When all quieted, Maxen rose from the high seat. "As I have this day returned from Blackspur Castle and found it to be in a state near ready for settlement," he said, "it is time to announce the one I have chosen to install as its castellan."

Most eyes turned to Sir Ancel, who sat a half dozen men down from Maxen. Wearing a smug smile, he raised his goblet toward his mouth.

"Sir Guy Torquay," Maxen said, "stand."

Stunned silence reflected Sir Guy's bewilderment as he rose at the right hand of his lord.

"For serving me faithfully," Maxen said, "your reward is Blackspur Castle. At its completion, I shall bestow it and its lands upon you to protect and lord in my name."

Before Sir Guy could answer, Sir Ancel slammed his goblet to the table, stood, and reached for his dagger.

Rhiannyn's heart leapt, but before she could call out a warning, Maxen said, "Think on it carefully, Ancel."

The knight gripped the hilt, and across the distance, Rhiannyn saw his hand flex as if he measured risk against gain. Risk prevailed. Leaving the dagger sheathed, he opened his hand, spread his fingers wide to show they were empty, and said, "Blackspur is mine."

"Blackspur is Pendery," Maxen corrected. "And I am Pendery."

"Thomas promised it to me."

"Thomas is dead."

Ancel's hand moved to the dagger again, hovered, and lowered to his side. "You will not honor your dead brother's wishes?"

"I will not."

The knight gave a curt nod, stepped over the bench, and traversed the hall to the doors that stood open to the night.

Rhiannyn returned her gaze to the high table and caught the look Maxen exchanged with Sir Guy as he lifted his goblet in salute. There followed a murmur of agreement, and others raised their vessels to join their lord in receiving Sir Guy as castellan of Blackspur.

Rhiannyn crossed to the chest, once more made a seat of it, and clasped her hands between her knees. If Maxen had not been convinced it was Sir Ancel who had placed the dagger for her to slay him, surely he must believe now. But why did he do nothing? Did he believe the knight was made merely of threats? Or did he wait? And for what?

As night lengthened, the din in the hall lulled to the quiet of sleep, and still she remained alone and unable to leave. Even had she been willing to don her filthy garments, she could not, the women who had delivered her bath water having taken the bliaut and chemise with them.

Where was Maxen? Why did he not come?

She dropped her feet to the floor and paced the chamber several times before returning to the chest. She lowered to it and scooted back until she came up against the mattress. Exhaustion pulled at her, and after a time, she closed her lids for just a moment.

He would not awaken her, Maxen decided as he considered the angel who lay half on his bed, half on the chest holding his clothes, her hair golden even in the dim light.

He regretted not sooner returning or sending clothes so she could leave. However, his preparations to announce Sir Guy as castellan of Blackspur had pushed Rhiannyn not to the back of his mind—never that—but to the side of him where he had ever felt her presence though he tried to ignore it.

Doubtless, with nearly all abed, it would be believed she had, indeed, yielded to him. But there was naught for it.

He slid his arms beneath her and lifted her.

She stirred, pushed her face into his shoulder, and resumed her deep breathing as he carried her into the hall. He laid her on the bench he had discovered she had claimed for herself when, in the days before his journey to Blackspur Castle, he had arisen before dawn. Then he had not touched her—had only stood a time and looked upon her—but now he laid a hand to her cheek.

She murmured, turned onto her side, and curled in on herself. Since the robe was not as thick as the layers of clothing in which she usually slept, he bent to a snoring knight and took the blanket from atop him. The man grumbled but did not awaken.

As Maxen draped the ragged blanket over Rhiannyn, one who had come unannounced to his back murmured, "My lord?"

Maxen turned. Only Rhiannyn was capable of rendering his instincts and senses useless such that he had not heard Sir Guy's approach. Had it been Sir Ancel, the knight would be gloating over Maxen's body, the rushes turned red.

I must do something about him, he told himself. *And soon.*

"What is it?" he asked in a harsh whisper.

"May we speak in your chamber, my lord?"

"Can it not wait until the morn?"

"It can, and would have had I not seen you here."

Maxen motioned him to follow.

As they crossed the hall, movement drew his gaze to the right, and torchlight revealed Christophe sat up on his pallet against the wall. There was a crooked smile about his mouth, and Maxen did not doubt he had seen his older brother enter his chamber and too soon return—that he approved of Rhiannyn being delivered to the hall and guessed the pact made with her had been, at least, postponed.

Dismissing him, Maxen continued forward. "All the Saxons have been questioned?" he asked once Guy and he gained his chamber.

"They have, and all tell the same. As Rhiannyn told, they denied Harwolfson for you."

"Why?"

"In this it seems most were honest, my lord. They stayed your side for what you can provide. They are tired of fighting, tired of cold, and most tired of hunger."

"A beginning," Maxen muttered. "What of Rhiannyn's role?"

The knight shook his head. "There is not one among them who does not say she also stood down. They tell she pleaded with Harwolfson to leave."

Pleaded, though she had done nothing to alert the Normans of the enemy within. But it was too much to expect. After all, she was still a Saxon no matter who made himself her master.

Pushing a hand through the hair on his scalp that had grown long enough to allow the gesture, Maxen dropped into the chair. Could he believe the Saxons? Of course, the real question was whether he could believe Rhiannyn.

"What do you think, Guy?"

"Though the Saxons are not to be trusted, I now believe it more likely they did choose to stay."

"And Rhiannyn?"

Guy shook his head. "I thought she had betrayed, but perhaps not."

As Maxen wished to believe. "Theta?"

"She has much to gain by lying—at least, thinks she does."

"Such as?"

"You, my lord."

Maxen scoffed. "Is that so?"

Guy shrugged a shoulder. "You asked what I thought, and that is my answer now that more is known of what transpired."

Maxen nodded. "On the morrow, return the Saxons to their work upon the wall."

Guy did not appear surprised. "What of punishment? A reminder of what will be if they turn on you?"

There was merit in the suggestion, and would have appealed to the Maxen of Hastings. This Maxen, wound up as he was with Rhiannyn, spoke from another side of his mouth. "No further punishment."

"And of their guard?"

"Double it."

"As you will." The knight turned away.

"Guy."

"My lord?"

"We have not spoken of your reason for allowing Rhiannyn to work on the wall."

He shifted his weight, though not self-consciously. "As she wished it, it seemed the easiest way to keep watch over her, and there looked to be little threat to her in the mixing of mortar."

"That was your only reason—keeping watch over her?"

This time, the shifting of the man's body showed unease. "I pitied her longing to regain her people's acceptance."

"Did she regain it?"

"I believe so, though methinks more because of the stand she took for them following Harwolfson's flight."

Whether or not Rhiannyn's return to her people was of benefit to Maxen had yet to be determined, but he nodded his approval. "You have served me well."

"As is my desire."

"Is it also your desire to lord Blackspur?"

Guy strode the distance between them, went down on a knee before Maxen, and bowed his head. "I am pleased and honored you have chosen me. Upon my vow, you will not regret it."

Maxen grasped his arm and raised him to standing. "We will speak more of it on the morrow."

Guy's face solemn, though behind it there surely clamored a multitude of emotions, he took his leave.

25

RHIANNYN WAS NOT where she had feared she would be when she had told Maxen she yielded. Nor was she on the chest where she had fallen asleep. She was not even in his chamber.

In the dull light of a new morn, she sat up, causing the blanket up around her shoulders to slip to her waist and reveal she still wore Maxen's robe. It was as disconcerting as knowing he had carried her to the hall, laid her on the bench where many a night she had gained her sleep, and covered her with a blanket. Unfortunately, her deliverance from his chamber had been too late to save her from the belief she had become his leman.

She frowned. Had he intended that? This the reason he had been so long in returning to her?

Immediately, she chastised herself for worrying over what others thought of her when there was the greater concern of what was to become of her people. Was the questioning done? If so, what had Maxen decided?

She stood, drew the blanket around her shoulders, and carefully stepped over and around sleeping figures. Knowing they would soon rise, and seeing from random vacant pallets some already had, she hurried across the hall in the hope Maxen was in his chamber.

He was yet abed, she saw when she came around the screen. She faltered, but seeing he was fully clothed atop the coverlet, crossed to the foot of the bed.

He opened his eyes. "I had not expected yours would be the first face I saw this morn," he said, voice deep with the sleep out of which she had pulled him. He sighed, sat up against the headboard, and motioned her forward. At her hesitation, he said, "As I did not claim your yielding on the night past, surely you can trust I will not force myself on you."

Feeling foolish, she stepped near.

"Speak," he prompted.

"What of my people?" It came out in a rush. "Are you satisfied with their answers?"

He raised his eyebrows. "Hardly."

She caught her breath. "Then——"

"They are safe, Rhiannyn. Sir Guy has questioned them, and it seems to be as you claim."

Her knees softened so suddenly she had to brace her feet apart to remain upright. "I thank you for sparing their lives—for believing them and not Theta."

"For the moment, it is as I believe," he qualified, "and only for as long as your Saxons give me no further cause to question their place at Etcheverry."

"They will not. They are loyal to you."

He swung his legs over the edge of the mattress and rose before her in the bit of dawn slipping through the window. "Then all will go well for them," he said, gazing into the face she turned up to him.

She smiled as she had thought she might never again do, and a door within her swung open. In that moment, it was as if Maxen Pendery strode inside and crossed to the other side of her.

She felt a twinge of fear at letting in one she had thought her enemy, but before it could send roots down through her, he asked, "What of you, Rhiannyn? Are you also mine?"

His.

"Loyal to me?" he added.

Though in the dungeon, bound and blindfolded, she had insisted never would she accept him as her lord, she said, "As my people take you for their lord, I take you."

He slowly nodded. "A good beginning."

"Beginning?"

His gaze lowered to her mouth. "Would you permit me a taste of what I denied myself last eve?"

Though disquiet removed the last of her smile, his own mouth curved, softening his face. "A kiss only, Rhiannyn."

As if it were no more than a touching of hands. But though she knew she ought to take her cue from memories of their past encounters, he asked little considering she would now be spoiled had he not released her from her yielding.

Silently vowing she would keep control of this encounter—one kiss, then parting—she moved nearer and rose to her toes. "You will have to bend your head to me," she whispered.

He did, and their mouths met. That should have been all, but he was on this side of her now, and she longed for him to linger. She gripped his forearms, distantly acknowledged the blanket falling from her shoulders, and deepened the kiss.

It was heady, and she noted that always she had been more the recipient, giving only when given to, and best intentions went awry. Now, seeking beyond the limits a small voice told her she ought not trespass upon, she glided her hands over sinewed arms, across thick shoulders, curved one around his neck, and pushed the other into his hair.

Maxen set her back from him. "You would not wish it to go further, would you?" he said, the color of his eyes eclipsed by the dark of his pupils.

"Of course not," she gasped and gripped the lapels of the robe closed.

He glanced at her white-knuckled hand. "As told on the night past, I will not ruin you."

Had he not corrected her course, might she have allowed him to progress well beyond a kiss? she wondered, further shamed that the question so easily rose to mind.

Lord, what is happening to me? What do I feel for this man?

He stepped past her to his clothes chest. "Most unfortunate," he said as he raised the lid, "it will surely be believed I ruined you on the night past, and I apologize. I should have seen you away from my chamber as quickly as possible."

Then it was not intentional.

"But there may be some good in it—for both of us." He began rummaging through his clothing.

"Good?" she asked.

He met her gaze. "My men will not think me weak for making concessions without gaining something of value in return."

Something of value, she reflected, but though the reference embarrassed her, she could not be truly offended that he made it sound as if she were of greater worth than a harlot.

"What gain for me?" she asked.

"You may more easily move about without worry of unwanted attentions. My men will not cross me."

They would believe she belonged to Maxen Pendery, just as when she had been Thomas's intended. Nay, that was not exactly true, but the perception was the same—she was the property of one with the authority to punish.

"I see," she said.

As he resumed his search of the garments, she remembered what needed to be told of the night Edwin had breached the castle walls.

"Maxen, about the third man—the one who escaped with Dora after she tried to bury me alive."

He looked sharply at her. "He lives?"

"Nay. Edwin accuses you of killing him as well, though it was surely Dora who did not wish him to know what she tried to do to me."

"Did you tell him?"

"I did, but he would not believe me. He knew naught of the grave."

"She moved the bodies," Maxen concluded. "Unfortunately for Harwolfson, his ignorance may prove his undoing." After more tossing about of clothes, he asked, "How fare you with a needle?"

"I…am proficient."

"Good. I am short of garments."

The thought of sewing for him settled like lead in her stomach, though it was not the stitching she minded. It was the measurements and fittings it would take to produce his clothing.

"And clippers?" he asked.

"Clippers?"

He scissored his fingers across his brow. "I am in need of a cut."

"I fear I am not good at that." It was a half-lie, for many times she had trimmed her father's wild beard and evened the ends of his long hair and that of her brothers. What was not a lie was that she had no experience with the Norman hairstyle of the crown cropped close and the back of the head shaven down to the base of the neck.

"You will do," Maxen said.

Only if he preferred jagged-shorn hair to the severity of his monk's tonsure. "I shall do my best."

He withdrew a well-worn tunic of coarse woolen, further proving he had not spoken false in telling he needed new garments.

When he began to remove the tunic he had slept in, Rhiannyn turned her back to him. And almost laughed. She, of whom it would be said had given her virtue to this man, feared looking upon his bared chest.

"It is done," he said, and she heard the smile in his voice.

She turned back and saw he sat on the clothes chest.

"There is much to be done this day," he said, pulling on his boots. "I will send a servant with proper attire so you may return to your duties."

"I thank you."

He stood. "No more will you work upon the wall. Understood?"

He meant to keep her from her people? To seclude her? "But—"

"I have spoken."

Anger returning, she said tightly, "And I have heard, my lord."

He strode to the screen, paused. "I have not said you cannot see them, Rhiannyn. Simply that you are not to assist them. Your duties are in the hall."

Indignation draining, she nodded. "Once more, I thank you."

His gaze momentarily fixed on her mouth, then he was gone.

Hoping she would not cross Maxen's path, Rhiannyn followed the food being conveyed from the inner to the outer bailey where the Saxons labored on a wall nearing completion. If the weather held, another sennight would likely see it finished. But what then for the Saxons? Of what use would they be come another winter of less than adequate food? Would Maxen turn them out as Thomas had done with the others the year before, only then granting the freedom denied them in forcing them to work upon Etcheverry?

Determined to set aside her worry—for now—she returned her attention to the path in time to avoid tripping over a dog who had claimed what seemed the only ray of sunshine cast over the entire castle.

Wishing she wore a mantle to keep out the chill, she rubbed her arms and quickened her step to keep up with the women ahead.

Although she had offered to help carry food and drink, Mildreth had forbidden it, saying the lord of Etcheverry would look ill upon it. Thus, it was an awkward thing to go amongst her people with empty hands and without offer of easing their burden.

When she came to their notice, she saw their surprise, then guilt, and knew they believed she had sacrificed her virtue on the night past.

Meghan was the first to approach—hesitantly, then with a brisk stride. "How fare ye?" she asked, voice pitched low so no others might hear the delicate question.

"I am well."

"Did the knave hurt you?"

"Not at all."

Suspicion narrowed the woman's lids, and she glanced over her shoulder at the wall. "I saw his anger on the night past. Ye need not lie."

It was no easy thing to discuss, especially with so many onlookers, but Rhiannyn had to set her straight. And a double purpose it would serve, for all would be apprised by Meghan's penchant for gossip, and their guilt eased. "I did not lie with him, Meghan. He…decided otherwise, and I slept in the hall."

Her head jerked. "Ye do not say!"

"I do."

She shook her head. "Imagine!"

Though Rhiannyn knew Meghan would eventually tell all, she was dismayed at the prospect of her doing so at this moment. "Pray, Meghan, speak not so loud."

She glanced around, said more quietly, "It certainly explains why he is workin' so hard."

"Who?"

She jerked her head and darted her eyes upward.

Rhiannyn looked to the scaffolding against the wall upon which a half dozen men were held aloft. And there was Maxen. The clouded sky the backdrop against which his large figure was painted, he looked down at her, his tunic dark with the perspiration of a common man's work.

Though they were separated by many feet, it felt as if he stood as near her as he had this morn. Blessedly, he did not look displeased that she had left the donjon.

"And here we were plottin' how we might make him a permanent part of the wall," Meghan muttered.

Rhiannyn shot her gaze to the woman.

"'Course that was when we thought…eh, he did you wrong." Meghan chuckled. "I suppose we will have to let him live a while longer."

Passing over the woman's attempt at humor, Rhiannyn said, "I do not understand what he is doing here."

"Workin'."

Rhiannyn grimaced. "Aye. But what is his reason when 'tis not his place?"

Meghan gave a one-shoulder shrug. "Impatient. Says he wants the wall done so buildin' can start on living quarters here in the bailey."

"For whom?"

"Us, though I will not believe it 'til I see it."

Movement returned Rhiannyn's gaze to Maxen. He motioned others to precede him and began his descent of the ramp to the bailey where food and drink were being set out.

A fluttering in her chest, Rhiannyn almost wished he would remain the cur. Then she would be safe.

"And if that ain't doubtful enough," Meghan continued, "he says come spring he will lay out a village before the castle where we might dwell and from which we can work the land."

Would he truly provide for them? Rhiannyn wondered. Or would he fold as Thomas had done? He seemed of stronger resolve than his brother, but again there was the question of who would be sacrificed when food supplies ran low. Certainly not his Normans.

"Aye, he said it," Meghan continued, "but winter will tell."

Rhiannyn watched Maxen pause to take drink, and when he continued toward her, warned, "He comes this way."

Meghan looked around, grinned. "For all the Norman in him, he's a fine-lookin' man.

Rhiannyn frowned. For as little time as Maxen had spent among the Saxons, it did not seem possible he could have earned even the grudging admiration of a woman who still considered him the enemy.

"I must needs get my share of food ere the gluttons take it all," Meghan said and hurried away.

Discomfited by the Saxons' furtive glances and Maxen's unswerving stare, Rhiannyn clasped her hands before her.

"Meghan?" he asked, halting before her. "The one who darkened your eye?"

"Aye, but we have become friends."

He nodded and swept his gaze down her. "These garments fit better than those you had from Theta."

She smoothed the skirts. Though the material was also worn and faded, it was not as threadbare or snagged. "I thank you for sending them to me."

He inclined his head. "You waste no time."

It took her a moment to catch up to his thoughts, but she realized he referred to her presence in the bailey. "I did not come to work, but to assure them all is well."

He raised his eyebrows. "And is it?"

She let a smile lift her mouth. "You have made it so, my lord. But tell, for what do you labor on the walls when such is not the work of a lord?"

"To know these Saxons of yours better."

"Is it not enough to know them from the high seat?"

"Not if I am to gain their loyalty." He raised a hand to stop the denial she had been about to speak. "They may not have betrayed me with Harwolfson, but it is not by loyalty I hold them. It is by fear."

He was right. "It is the way of the Normans," she reminded him.

"If this land is to know lasting peace, that will have to change."

"You think it will?"

"Once Edwin Harwolfson is brought to heel."

His honesty hurt, but at least he had not lied. Seeking another direction for their talk, she asked, "What of Sir Ancel?"

His eyes narrowed. "What of him?"

Though he must know she had heard what had happened in the hall on the night past, she said, "I looked around the screen. Why do you naught about him when it was surely he who placed the dagger on my tray? When yestereve he threatened to put a blade through you?"

Maxen's sudden smile was charmingly lopsided. "Are you concerned for my welfare, Rhiannyn, or for your Saxons should Ancel accomplish what he has twice failed to attain?"

Though weeks ago she would have denied concern for him, she said, "Both."

"I am gladdened." His smile widened. "And hungry." He swung away.

"But what will you do?" she called after him.

"Wait," he said over his shoulder.

Wondering what he meant, she turned toward the donjon. As she approached the causeway, a feeling of ill drew her eyes to the wall-walk. There stood Sir Ancel.

Rhiannyn's feet forgot the simplicity of walking, and in the righting of her footing, she was forced to break eye contact with him. But when she looked up again, his gaze had traveled beyond her to where the Saxons and Maxen filled their bellies.

Shivering with a chill not of the wind, she continued up the causeway.

26

Ten days passed before Maxen paid Rhiannyn more attention beyond probing glances and the brushing of sleeves in passing. With the completion of the wall five days past, he now spent daylight hours in the hall with the ledgers, the steward, and one or another of his knights—usually Sir Guy.

Rhiannyn told herself she was grateful for his disregard. It allowed her time with her people and an easing of spirit she had long been without. But those days were not without difficulty. Theta took every opportunity to belittle her and boast of the attention the lord of Etcheverry paid her and the favors she cast his way. Rhiannyn tried not to believe that last, seeing no evidence of Maxen's interest in the woman, but she was nagged with reminders of his loss of interest in herself.

"Fine, fine," she muttered as she lifted a pry bar from its hook and crossed to the nearest ale barrel. "I do not care. Truly, I do not."

She worked the flat end of the bar beneath the lid and pressed her weight on it, but it gave only slightly. She tried again, and with the same result.

She glowered at the man whose job it was to dispense drink to the castle's occupants. Aldwin sat propped in a corner, oblivious after a night of too much ale—no different from the night before, or the night before that.

Excusing the sorrowful old man for his fondness for brew, she repositioned the bar and pressed harder.

"Rhiannyn," Lucilla called down the cellar steps.

Rhiannyn peered up at her. "Aye?"

"Lord Pendery asks for ye. He said to say 'tis time."

Time? Rhiannyn turned the word over and caught her breath at the thought he wished her in his bed. But he had freed her from their bargain. Of course, he might have changed his mind.

"Did he say what it is time for?"

"He said ye would know, but dally not. He seems impatient."

Rhiannyn set the bar atop the barrel, ascended the steps, and hastened to the hall.

Maxen stood alone behind the lord's table. To the right of him sat the ledgers in which all transactions regarding Etcheverry were recorded, to the left, bolts of cloth ranging from white to a green so rich and deep it reminded her of grass after a spring rain.

He looked up when she halted opposite him.

"Time, my lord?" she asked.

"You have forgotten."

She frowned.

He reached for the scissors beside the ledgers and extended them.

She breathed easier. He meant her to cut his hair, which also meant the cloth was for his new garments. "I thought you might have decided against it," she said.

"Nay, there simply has not been time to attend to it."

"Now there is?"

He lowered into his chair. "There is not, but the hair is nearly in my eyes."

She walked around the table. "A bench would be better," she suggested, certain the high-backed chair would hinder her.

He moved onto the bench beside his chair and pulled a ledger in front of him. "Shorten the fringe to the same length as the crown," he referred to the halo of hair that remained of his tonsure, "and the sides a bit, but leave the back long. I wish it to grow out."

"You do not intend to adopt the Norman hairstyle?"

"I have ever preferred the style of the Saxons—rather, their lack of one—but as I have no choice in the matter of the hair atop my head, I will compromise."

As she had seen when his men were Thomas's, many of the Normans had begun to embrace the less severe Saxon hairstyle, but Thomas had not. Though he had allowed his men to do so, he had said a baron of King William's must maintain the face of Norman dominance. It seemed Maxen was of a different mind—and in more ways than this.

Rhiannyn lifted the scissors, parted off a section of hair, and began cutting—at first with indecision, then vision. The blades flashed, their meeting a hiss in the silence of her task and Maxen's attention upon his ledger.

"A curiosity," she mused. "A Saxon holding over a Norman what could easily be made a weapon. Are you not worried I might do you harm?"

"I am not," he said without looking up.

She paused mid-snip and awaited his gaze. But though he surely sensed it, he remained focused on his figures. "How is it you trust me in this, but not other things?" she asked.

He sighed, looked up. "You lie, Rhiannyn—granted, more for others than yourself. You are more willful than any woman I have known, and you test my patience so I must constantly adjust the bounds. But you are not capable of murder."

"Yet you hold me responsible for Thomas's death," she unthinkingly reminded him. And silently chastised herself lest the peace between them exploded into renewed hostility.

But his eyes grew just a bit hard, his mouth a pinch tight, and when he spoke his voice was beset with only a trace of ire. "Responsibility and murder are two different things. We have already established it was another who killed him—your faceless hider in the wood."

Leave the subject be, she told herself. She could not. "But I am as guilty, am I not?"

He raised his eyebrows. "Are you?"

She blinked. Should he not readily agree? Why did he offer her room to defend herself? Though part of her pressed her to turn from further talk of Thomas's death, another longed for him to understand. "I but wanted to escape. No harm did I wish your brother."

Maxen absorbed her pitiful defense, said, "But Harwolfson wished him harm."

Set further off-center by his seeming lack of enmity, she was slow to respond. "They fought, but I give you my word, Edwin did not kill him. You must believe me."

"I do," he said, and in the midst of her wide-eyed surprise asked, "Why did you not flee with Harwolfson?"

Trying not to see that fateful day awash in crimson and gray, she said, "I could not leave Thomas to die alone."

"Why?"

How had her comment of scissors being made into a weapon come to this? And why this need for Maxen to accept her accounting? "I did not love him as he wished me to, but I was not entirely without feelings for him. Your brother was a good man."

"And foolish. He should have let you go." His words were bitter, but of a sudden, he laughed. "I am the same fool, for neither will I let you go. And if you flee me as you did Thomas, methinks I would also ride after you." He lifted a hand and touched her cheek. "I wonder, Rhiannyn, will you be the death of me?"

She shook her head. "Though I thought once to escape you, I have accepted my lot."

"And if Harwolfson comes for you again?"

"Do you not understand?" she said. "As I did not go with him when last he was here, neither will I go with him if he returns."

"Will he return?"

She frowned. "I do not know. There is only Aethel now, and the four others who would join Edwin were he able to release them from the dungeons. It seems too great a risk to add so few to his ranks."

Maxen dropped his hand from her. "Saxons are wont to great risks," he said, and sank into reflections he did not share with her.

Fearing what he contemplated, Rhiannyn said, "Maxen, pray do not use Aethel and the others to your own end. They have not chosen your way, but still they are good men." At least Aethel was. Of the four others, there was not one she knew well enough to vouch for.

"What would you have me do? Release them?"

"I would," she said, though she knew she asked too much.

He rubbed a hand across his shaven jaw. "It is the gallows to which they ought to go."

"Why have they not?"

He looked as if he might disregard her question, but he said, "Part of me admires them. Though it would serve me well to ensure I need never again engage them in battle, it is not easy to fault a man who stands firm in his beliefs."

A day of revelations, Rhiannyn realized. Never would she have guessed Maxen capable of such feeling. Yet surely here was the reason he had not yet dealt with his prisoners. "What will you do?"

"They ought to have had plenty of time for thought. Mayhap now they will be willing to accept me as the others have."

"If they do not?"

He pushed a hand through the hair she had clipped. "I cannot say one thing and do another, Rhiannyn."

Her heart sank, though not as deep as it would have had he not offered hope. "This I know," she said, for it was the way of things for those who dared step into the path of might over right.

"Finish your task," he said, ending the discussion.

While her mind turned front to back all they had spoken of, Rhiannyn took up the scissors again. Why Maxen had discussed such things with her was a mystery, for she would more have expected him to refuse talk beyond the complication of what lay unresolved between them. But somehow they had avoided that.

Clipping by clipping, his hair fell away until all that was left to cut was above his brow. "If you come around," she said, "I will soon be done."

He turned on the bench and faced her.

Rhiannyn was not prepared to stand between his legs. It was enough that she had spent so long in his immediate presence—sliding fingers over his scalp and pulling them through his hair—but this?

Avoiding his gaze, she stepped to the side, but he drew her back in front of him.

"It is easier this way," he said when her startled eyes met his.

Easier for him, she thought and lifted the scissors.

It took but a few minutes to complete the cut, then she stepped back to survey her work. "It is done."

"Better?"

"Indeed." She was more pleased than expected. The monk was entirely gone, the last of the man of the Church scattered upon Maxen's shoulders, the bench, and the rushes. Before her was one more handsome for it.

He stood and brushed the hair from his tunic, stomped his legs to shake it from his hose, and swept it from the bench. As he regained the high seat, he motioned to the cloth. "For my garments."

She stepped alongside him, lifted the beautiful green, and rubbed it between her fingers. "It will make a fine tunic. And the others." She touched each bolt in turn.

"The green is for you."

She returned her gaze to his. "Whatever for?"

He flicked the skirt of her old bliaut. "I tire of seeing you clothed in such."

"But it is as you ordered."

"And this is as I order now. I will not have you further debased."

It was true she was the most poorly clothed of the women servants, but it drew less attention to her. Still, if Maxen wished her in finer clothes, there were those Thomas had provided. Immediately, she rejected the thought. Their material was of the same quality as the green, but heavily embroidered, and one was set with gems about the neck.

"The green is not suitable for a serving woman," she said and pulled forth another bolt. "Brown is better."

He dragged the green back over the brown. "This one," he said. "And if enough remains when your gown is completed, you may fashion a tunic for me."

Seeing he would not be moved, she said, "Very well," and began gathering the bolts together.

"Leave them, Rhiannyn. I will have them delivered to my chamber."

"Your chamber?"

"A quiet place to make stitches."

A dangerous place to make stitches, her presence there furthering the belief she was his leman. "I can sew just as well before the hearth."

He shrugged. "As you wish. The cloth will be stored in my chest."

She stepped away. "I will begin this eve after supper."

"Rhiannyn."

She looked around.

"First, your bliaut. My need is not as great as yours."

Before she could protest, someone called, "My lord!"

"Sir Guy?" Maxen asked of the one who entered the hall.

The knight lifted a thinly rolled parchment. "A reply from Trionne Castle."

Home of Maxen and Christophe's parents. "I will take my leave," Rhiannyn said and stepped away.

Maxen allowed her departure, his attention on the missive passed into his hand.

As she crossed the hall, she heard him say, "It is good. The supplies are being amassed and should arrive before the new month."

Then the stores needed to tide Etcheverry through the winter were on their way—from Trionne? During the winter past, Thomas's father had been able to assist little, his own harvests scant, but they must be more abundantly blessed this year. That worry easing, Rhiannyn quickened her steps with the thought she must tell Mildreth, the woman's fretting greater than her own.

"So, it will not be such a chill winter after all," Guy's voice drifted to her.

The parchment crackled. "Only if the others—Sir Jeremy of Bronton and Darik of Westering—also provide."

Rhiannyn's steps faltered. Trionne could not render all they needed?

"Think you they will?" Guy asked.

"If they are able to, for they owe me their lives."

Norman lives saved at Hastings, Rhiannyn guessed.

Once around the corner, she leaned against the wall and listened. It was not good of her, but she had to know what might be said once it was believed she was no longer present.

"The Saxons will be a great burden upon the foodstuffs if there are no more stores forthcoming," Sir Guy said.

"All will be a great burden, but none will be treated differently. If more of an effort must be made with winter hunting, it shall be done."

Struck by the force of Maxen moving through her, burrowing a place just beneath her heart, Rhiannyn slumped. He did care, would provide for the Saxons even as he provided for his Normans.

"It will not be easy," Sir Guy said.

"*Non,* it will not."

Rhiannyn pushed off the wall and hurried down the corridor and out into a cold day that seemed tenfold warmer than when she had earlier passed beneath the same overcast sky.

A fortnight later, in the wake of news of Edwin Harwolfson's plundering to the west, three missives arrived—two expected, one not.

Maxen stared at the third. Dispatched by King William, it likely concerned his rival for Etcheverry.

Though few were the details gathered about the rebel leader, much was the talk of the growing number of Saxons joining Harwolfson to form a stronger rebellion than that which he had accumulated in the wood of Andredeswald. No doubt, he gathered into his fold many already bitten by the coming winter—Saxons without much hope of surviving the season unless they joined their countrymen and took what they were not given.

Deciding it best to open the missives in private, away from talk of the rebels that seemed to fill every corner of the hall, Maxen rose from the nooning meal. Gesturing for the others to continue filling their bellies, he strode to his chamber. As he dropped into the chair, he broke the first missive's wax seal.

Darik of Westering would not fail him. The supplies would soon arrive. Unfortunately, such was not the case with Jeremy of Bronton. The knight offered sincere regrets, his anger over the loss of a vast amount of winter supplies to the "wolf"—Harwolfson—evident in every stroke of the quill.

Maxen set the two missives aside and ground the heels of his hands into his eyes. He knew what must be done to curb the voracious Harwolfson, and it was he whom King William would call upon. Fortunately, he had all of winter in which to plan the Saxon's downfall, for it would be spring before he was ordered to take up his sword and slay the conquered.

Rather, it was his hope. And should have been his prayer all these days.

He closed his eyes, cracked open the door to heaven, and silently sent through the narrow seam, *You do not want me back yet, Lord. All is still too dark within me, and I would make promises unkept.*

He eased the door closed, lifted his lids, and considered the third missive before breaking the seal.

It did concern Harwolfson. Blessedly, it did not call Maxen to arms in this chill season. But there the blessing ended. The king was aware of

Harwolfson's grievance in losing his betrothed to Thomas, having granted Maxen's brother permission to wed Rhiannyn. Now he instructed the new lord of Etcheverry to keep close watch over the Saxon woman, regardless of whether or not she warmed his bed, lest she slipped away and an opportunity to bring Harwolfson to heel was lost.

There was no elaboration as to what that opportunity might be, but one was not needed. Whether it was threat of harm to Rhiannyn, an offer to return her to her betrothed, or some other means of controlling the Saxon rebel, her fate would be out of Maxen's hands if King William found a good use for her.

And it did not sit well with Maxen who let in the thought that had long been stealing around the edges of him.

I should have wed her.

It would not have been remiss of him since the king had given all that was Thomas's to his older brother, and Maxen could hardly be faulted for also taking Rhiannyn to wife, but...

With William's ploy revealed, it would likely be regarded as an act of defiance if Maxen claimed Rhiannyn, thereby thwarting the king's plans. Though he had been grateful these past weeks had so teemed with preparations for winter that there had been no time to pursue her, now he begrudged their every distraction.

Too late.

He stood, crossed to his chest, and thrust the king's missive to the bottom. He would think more on it later. Now, he would join his men for the meal and, as instructed, keep close watch over the woman he should not have denied himself.

27

"The wolf!" Elan Pendery spat into the wind she rode against.

So much talk of a mere man. Others might fear him, but she did not. Though he surely reveled in exaggerated tales of his prowess, he was a mortal like all—and destined to be cut down by a Norman. Or trampled beneath her horse, she entertained and smiled at the vision born of a mind her mother said was too fertile.

It amused her to think such things, though she knew better than to own to them. And she had good reason to indulge—to resent Edwin Harwolfson and those of his ilk. Not until Duke William had crossed the channel two years ago to claim his throne, had she been so confined within the castle.

At ten and five, she had tolerated it well enough, especially as there had been Christophe with whom to pass the hours. But her brother had gone to Etcheverry, taking with him all the fun they had made together. Now she was forced to look for amusement elsewhere—or, considering the day's turn of events, a place to more fully worry over her father's announcement. Remembrance of it stole her smile and caused the scenery to blur.

Six months past, she had been too indifferent to propriety to be concerned for the future, but now those days were upon her and promised to be terrible.

This morn, she had swallowed dismay with her bread when her father announced he had made a suitable match for her. She would wed one Sir Arthur, a man of no less than fifty years, three wives passed on, four children, and a demesne equal to Trionne. The prospect turned her stomach, but not as much as that other thing which would be discovered on her wedding night.

She had made a mistake, driven by the recklessness it was said came too easily to her, but there was no way to change the past. Nor wipe away traces of it.

She heaved a breath up her face, shook her head. There would be time aplenty to dwell on it. For now, she would enjoy the hours before last light.

He saw her long before she saw him, which was as it should be. But who was this fair young woman who, from the top of her head to her fine woolen mantle, down to the toes of her slippers, looked a lady? And why was she without escort?

For all the anger that had become as much a part of him as breathing, Edwin could not help smiling. She was lovely, her ashen hair visible beneath the veil the stirred air lifted. And as she drew near the bordering wood, he saw she was not as dainty as she had appeared from a distance. She was of average form, but it was the only thing average about her. Though he could not determine the color of her eyes, they sparkled as she scanned the trees. Then from her pretty mouth came laughter.

She spurred her horse into the wood, slowing when fully hidden from sight of the castle walls—not fifty feet from where Edwin had set himself to watching the stronghold of Trionne.

She reined in and patted her horse's neck. "Once again," she said in clear Anglo-Saxon, "we have done it—escaped them one and all." She grimaced, an expression which might have turned another's face unattractive but not hers. "Not that our absence will be noted."

A curious creature, Edwin mused. More, the lady could prove useful.

He peered over his shoulder and motioned for those hidden behind and to the sides to hold their positions.

The men nodded and sank more deeply into their hiding places.

When the lady prodded her horse deeper into the wood, Edwin moved, using the sounds of her movement to mask his. In this way, he overtook her and gained ground ahead that would arouse less suspicion than if he had revealed himself at the edge of the wood.

Then the act began. "Testra!" he called as he worked his way back over ground he had just tread, and called twice more for a horse nowhere near.

Blue eyes wide, the lady halted her mount and stared at Edwin, who feigned his own surprise. "Who are you?" she demanded.

Guessing she had passed into her twentieth year, he said, "I fear I have lost my horse. Rather, he has lost me."

Her lids narrowed. "Who are you to come upon my father's lands?"

Father's? A smile being difficult to suppress, Edwin used it as a sign of friendliness and stepped forward. "Your father's lands?"

"Aye, Baron Pendery, possessor of all you have no doubt tramped this day."

Maxen and Christophe's sister, though had he not heard she was ten and seven? Regardless, a better pawn he could not have hoped for. But how to convince her to come down from her horse so he might steal her away?

"I am Bacus," he said, using the name of his brother who had fallen at Hastings, "come from across the wood to seek winter shelter in yon castle."

Something measured showed in her eyes. "Of what village are you, Saxon?"

"Of no village. Thus, I seek to enter Trionne."

"You and hundreds of others. Have you something to offer they have not?"

With steps made to appear casual, Edwin began to close the distance between them. "I have good knowledge of the training and care of horses. But tell me, by what name are you called, daughter of Pendery?"

She smiled faintly. "I am Lady Elan."

"I should have known, for much is told of your beauty." Much he had not heard, though there had been mention she was lovely.

This time, she smiled with her teeth.

Edwin used her moment of vain unguardedness to draw half a dozen steps nearer. And halted, certain a single lunge would have her off her horse.

"Aye, my lady, you make a man's eyes ache to look upon you," he fed her more.

She fluttered her lashes, slowly moved her gaze down him. Returning to his eyes, she asked, "What do you hope to gain with such flattery? Is it truly winter shelter you seek?" She leaned forward, and in a conspiratorial tone, added. "Or a tumble up my skirts, *Bacus*?"

Edwin could not hide his surprise over her unladylike daring, nor how astute she was. Might she have guessed who he was? Instantly, he rejected the possibility. She was suspicious, but she could not know—unless this was a trap laid for the *wolf*. It seemed hardly possible, for he had advanced on Trionne with the tightest control of his forces, and those he had left a short space behind had not called out a warning.

"What do you think I seek, my lady?" he asked.

She shifted in the saddle. "I think you are neither Bacus, nor come to beg shelter at Trionne. And Testra—your horse's name, eh?—is likely tethered nearby."

If a trap, she played her part poorly by voicing her suspicions, but still he was wary. He arched an eyebrow. "Then who might I be, and what think you I do in your wood?"

He nearly startled when she put out a hand, beckoning him to assist in her dismounting.

Now the trap would be sprung if it was indeed a trap, he thought. Eyes watchful, ears alert, sword and dagger a hand away, he strode forward. When he raised his arms to her, she came into them.

No whisper of a breeze begot by advancing soldiers, no vibration of their coming beneath his thin-soled boots. Not a trap. Merely a woman filled with foolishness.

When he released her, she did not step back as a lady ought to, but tipped her face up, frowned, and touched a finger to her lower lip. "I think..." she played at thoughts he did not doubt she knew well.

Something he had long ago pushed down rose in Edwin as he looked upon her comeliness and felt the warmth of her body across the small space. In her face were eyes of blue framed by long lashes; beneath, a fine nose; and below, a mouth full and red. It was by no artifice she was lovely. God had made her so.

Affecting revelation, the lady gasped. "I think you are one of those Saxons who does not accept his Norman master."

Perceptive, he allowed, but not in the safeguarding of her person. In this, she was unwise. "If you believe that, why are you unafraid?"

She stepped nearer, causing him to be filled with a longing distant from revenge. "Because, Bacus of no lord, I like what fills my eyes."

It was Edwin who stepped back. The woman had set herself to seducing him! Might it be a lie that she was Elan Pendery? No lady he had known was so brash and provocative. Certainly, Rhiannyn had not acted in this manner, and she had been a lady only by Thomas Pendery's decree. Indeed, the only women Edwin had known to behave in this manner were those who took coin for favors upon the sheets.

"Have I put you off?" she said.

"It surprises me to hear a lady speak so. Indeed, it makes me question if you are, indeed, a lady."

"There is a time to be a lady and a time to be a woman," she said. "This day I deign to be the latter."

Whoever she was, he did not doubt he would enjoy knowing her better, but he remained too taken aback to do more than stare.

"How much more invitation would you like, Saxon?" She unfastened the brooch from her mantle and let the garment slide from her shoulders to her feet, revealing a bliaut of finely woven material and a figure as lovely as her face.

He hated that he must seem like an untried boy, but though his pride was in danger of being ground beneath her pretty slippers, it was she who came into his arms. Lady or not, Elan Pendery or pretender, he claimed her mouth—or perhaps she claimed his.

She was no more Elan Pendery than he was Bacus, Edwin determined, certain the elder Pendery would not tolerate such behavior from his daughter who must wed with her virtue intact. But whatever the name of this woman who was surely several years older than Pendery's daughter, of three things he was certain—she was of the nobility, was not inexperienced, and was a pretender through and through.

She scooped up a handful of water, sipped it, and let the rest trickle between her fingers as she straightened. When she turned back, she smiled prettily.

And thus, they regarded each other.

"Methinks you are a brooder, Bacus." She closed the distance between them, leaned up, and lightly kissed him. "Still, I may be in danger of falling in love with you."

Liar, he wanted to name her. Instead, he forced a smile.

She *tsked,* set herself back on her heels. "You could at least lie and tell me you feel the same."

Not for the first time, he wished he had not taken what she had given. The little bird might have pretty feathers, but he sensed the beak and claws of a hawk.

"How is it you came alone to the wood?" he asked, determined he would speak no more of what had transpired between them. "I would not think your *father* would allow it."

"He would not," she said with such pleasure it allowed a glimpse of the child beneath the woman.

Might he have been wrong in believing she was a score of years aged? "Who allowed it?" he asked.

"The guard at the postern gate. We have an understanding."

Lovers, then. "I am sure," he said derisively.

She wagged a finger. "Not that kind of understanding, Bacus."

"Then?"

She adjusted her veil. "As I am fond of freedom, so he is fond of fine drink. One for the other, you see."

Norman greed, Edwin labeled the man's conduct. No lady ought to be allowed to leave the castle without escort. "The man should be flogged and clapped into irons for making such a bargain. No Saxon would allow what he did."

She laughed. "He is Saxon," she said, reminding him the Penderys had resided on English soil when it was still English, their association with the Saxons going back more than twenty years.

"A Saxon turned Norman," he said.

"One or the other, it is no concern of yours. Unless…" She touched a finger to his flesh above the V of his tunic. "…you are in danger of falling in love with me."

Though Edwin knew she could prove a useful pawn regardless of who she was to the Penderys, in that moment, there was nothing he wanted more than to send her away. Of course, when he held all of Trionne come the morrow, they would meet again.

"You are back to Trionne?" he asked, turning toward her horse.

She drew alongside him. "Unless you would like my aid in locating your mount."

There was teasing in her eyes. Certes, she knew there was no horse that needed finding, that he lied the same as she, but still she showed no fear.

He halted alongside her mount. "Nay, the beast cannot be far off."

"As you will." She offered her arm. "Do you hand me up, I will be on my way."

He lifted her into the saddle with nearly as much ease as when he had lifted her down. "Fare thee well," he said and stepped back to allow her to turn her horse.

She did so. However, when some distance separated them, she reined around and smiled. "I know who you are, Edwin Harwolfson."

He stared.

"I knew the moment I happened upon you."

He jerked free of his stupor. "What is your game?" he demanded, knowing he stood little chance of reaching her before she put heels to her horse.

"Farewell, *wolf!*" With a snap of her wrist and a nudge of her heels, she spurred her horse away.

Knowing if he was to salvage his plans for Trionne he must apprehend her, Edwin bolted after her. Over thicket, muddy ground, and stream he bounded, around trees and beneath low-hanging branches he raced. But though twice his prize was nearly within reach, he was forced to surrender the chase.

Breath heaving, he stood at the edge of the wood staring out upon the meadow, into the midst of which sped horse and rider. Gradually, the two diminished in size until they were a speck against the castle walls.

Edwin berated himself for his stupidity in allowing the vixen her freedom. There had been little danger in her thinking it was but a discontented Saxon to whom she had given herself, but that she knew he was Edwin Harwolfson...

He cursed loudly. Though it was possible the lady who was not a lady in the truest sense might not inform Pendery of the one who watched outside his walls, he could not risk trying to obtain what was to have been his greatest triumph to date and the cornerstone of the Saxon uprising.

He slammed a fist into a tree trunk and felt the pain of bloodied knuckles, but it did not compare to his rage and desire for revenge. He drew his arm back to strike again, but Dora came to mind.

She would know what to do. She always knew, just as she had known Rhiannyn would betray him with another.

28

THERE WAS GREAT cause to celebrate. This day, the promised supplies had arrived from Trionne. But though wine and ale flowed freely, the platters of viands were only slightly more generous than in previous weeks.

Many grumbled that they were allowed little taste of the windfall, but the lord of Etcheverry refused to diminish foodstuffs that must sustain them through what could be a harsh winter.

Avoiding his gaze that she felt often upon her, especially this night when she first wore the green bliaut made of his cloth, Rhiannyn moved down the table filling tankards and goblets. When the last of the ale dripped from her pitcher, she returned to the barrel against the far wall. It proved as empty as her vessel.

Had the last one who dipped into it called for another barrel to be carried up from the cellar? If so, was the butler too deep in his cups to do so?

She crossed the hall and descended the steps to the cellar. Aldwin was where he was often found—in a corner slumped on a stool.

"Aldwin," she groaned, "what am I to do?" His answer a stuttering snore, she retrieved the pry bar with which she had been unsuccessful the last time she had tried to use it and crossed to the nearest ale barrel.

She had just slid the tool beneath the lip when a sound carried to her from the dungeons where Aethel and the others remained imprisoned. She stilled, wanting to go to them, but certain she would not make it past the guard. Though she listened to discover the source of the noise, it did not come again and she returned to the barrel. This time, the lid gave, and she triumphantly laid it aside and dipped her pitcher in the ale.

The sound came again, followed by a throaty laugh. Theta?

Rhiannyn set her pitcher atop an unopened barrel and crossed to the dungeon's entrance. She peered around the doorframe into the dim corridor where shadows moved on the walls across from the guard's station.

More laughter, murmurings, and other noises that could be mistaken for pain. Not pain, she knew, for she had heard such sounds when Thomas summoned Theta to his bed and knights took women servants to their pallets.

Rhiannyn wavered between returning to the hall and taking advantage of an opportunity that might not come her way again. With all that stood between her and Maxen—lies, deceit, accusations, misunderstandings—and twice now his mercy upon the Saxons, she knew she should not tempt fate. She really should not.

Fixing her gaze on the moving shadows, she stepped lightly into the corridor and slowly advanced.

In the alcove of the guard's station, she glimpsed the lovers. As thought, it was Theta whom the guard had lured to his dreary world beneath the castle.

Rhiannyn slipped past the station and headed for the cells around the bend. But upon turning the corner, she halted in this cold, dark place and shivered as memories swelled—days and nights when a vengeful Sir Ancel had asked questions of her whose answers had earned her the abuse of his hands, and sitting bound and blindfolded before a faceless Maxen whose anger and condemnation had made of him a beast. It was as she had imagined hell must be. It must be the same for Aethel and the others.

She retraced her steps, retrieved a torch, and ventured forth again. When she drew near the open cell in which Maxen had first presented himself to her, she kept her eyes trained ahead. Upon rounding the next bend, the silence from the cells ahead made her falter.

The possibility Aethel and the others might no longer be here, and the implications therefrom, too horrible to think on, she told herself they slumbered. It was, after all, near on night.

Not that they would know the moon from the sun in this place, she reminded herself.

"Who goes?" a voice hissed.

Thanking the Lord, she hastened forward. "'Tis Rhiannyn, Aethel," she said in a high whisper.

"The harlot," said another.

"I am here." Aethel pushed his large fingers through the grate of the door in the end cell where she had passed day after night after day.

Ignoring the faces pressed to the other grates she passed, Rhiannyn lifted the torch and shined it on the small opening to reveal a portion of Aethel's bearded visage.

"Have you a key?" he asked.

"Nay, I—"

"Why have you come? Did he send you?"

Maxen. "Nay, I am here without his knowledge."

"Come to pay your last respects ere he hoists us to our deaths?" one of the others sneered.

Rhiannyn wanted to deny it, but she did not know Maxen's plans. Not since their discussion while she had cut his hair weeks past had he spoken of them. "Has he come to you?" she asked.

"He has," Aethel said, "bringing lies of food, shelter, and land for all who settle peacefully beneath his rule."

And they had declined. "Would you rather suffer death than the chance he speaks true?" she asked.

"A Norman speak true?" scorned the Saxon in the cell beside Aethel's. "Because he beds you well does not mean God speaks through him."

"He does not bed me," Rhiannyn protested.

"'Tis what Theta tells," another hissed.

"Keep your mouths about you," Aethel snarled.

She was not surprised Theta came here to work her worst upon Rhiannyn's name. "Theta lies."

Aethel grunted. "Aye? Is it also a lie you alerted the Normans when Edwin came to free us?"

"Theta revealed them, not I."

"We are to believe you, the same who led Maxen Pendery to our camp?" Aethel said. "Do you think us fools?"

Heart sinking faster, she said, "'Tis true he followed me, but I did not knowingly lead him to you."

"Nor knowingly follow him back to Etcheverry after he murdered three of ours, eh?"

His sarcasm cut deep. "I will defend myself no more," she said, wishing Aethel's gaze were the gentle one she had often beheld before the Normans. "But I would ask you not to sacrifice yourself for a cause long lost."

"You are weak," he rebuked. "Keep your Norman company, but do not think to press us into the service of that devil. We stand with Edwin."

Though the agreement of the others sounded around her like the closing of a door, she said, "Pray, Aethel—"

A voice raised in anger—Maxen's—rumbled down the corridor, and was answered by the anxious voices of Theta and the guard.

"He is come," Rhiannyn gasped.

"Then go to him," Aethel said.

"Aye, and tell yer lover there be no more Saxons bowin' to him," spat another.

Rhiannyn turned and hurried down the corridor. Around the first bend, she realized she still carried the torch. She thrust it into the nearest sconce, then crept along the wall toward the voices coming from the guard's station.

"Just having a little fun, milord," Theta drawled. "No harm."

"No harm?" Maxen said. "What of your duties, guard?"

"I-I have kept them, my lord. There is none come or gone this eve. All is secure."

Believe him, Rhiannyn silently beseeched. Later she would find a way past the man.

"What of Rhiannyn?" Maxen demanded.

"*Non,*" the guard said. "Had she come, I would have seen her."

"Mayhap milord is jealous?" Theta's words were softly vibrant like the purr of a cat. "I did warn if 'twas not you, it would be another. So it be your fault I sought elsewhere."

"As I do not wish you in my bed," Maxen said, "I care not with whom you carry on so long as it does not take my men from their duties. Now be gone."

Rhiannyn caught her breath. Maxen had not lied when he denied having Theta in his bed.

"When you grow tired of Rhiannyn," the woman said, "you have but to call me to you."

Maxen gave no answer, and as Rhiannyn listened to the patter of Theta's retreat, she imagined his glower.

"The consequences will be dire if I find one here who does not belong," Maxen warned.

The guard cleared his throat. "Upon my word, you will not, my lord."

Heavier footfalls sounded. And they moved toward the cells.

Rhiannyn swept her gaze around, searching for a place in which to conceal herself. The nearest refuge was no refuge, but the open cell where first she had encountered Maxen. Resigned to it, she hastened down the corridor and entered it just as she heard him round the corner.

Heart beating hard, she slipped into the farthest corner, slid down the wall, and huddled on the floor. Over the arms she wrapped around her knees, she peered at the corridor that was coming to light with the torch Maxen carried before him. Then he was there, rolling back the shadows.

Blessedly, hers held, though only because he had not fully brought the torch within. If he did, he would see her.

He stood unmoving, perhaps also remembering the past—seeing her upon the stool with her hands bound, hearing her declaration she had murdered Thomas, feeling the rage he had not turned upon her.

"Show yourself, Rhiannyn," he commanded.

She released her breath, pushed to standing, and walked into the light.

His expression was grim, but she did not falter. Halting before him, she said, "I know what you think."

"What do I think?" he asked tightly.

"That I deceived you again, and though you will not believe me, I tell you it is not so."

He narrowed his lids. "What was your purpose in coming here?"

"To speak with Aethel."

"Which I forbade you to do."

"You did."

He lowered his eyes over her. "Did you speak with him?"

"I did."

"What result?"

"The same as yours. He and the others stand with Edwin."

He nodded slowly. "A pity."

So the end was near for men who were of no use to him locked away and who could not be trusted outside the cells. "What will you do?" she asked.

"What would you have me do?"

Certain he baited her, she said, "It hardly matters what I wish."

"Does it not?"

She blinked. "Why do you ask me this?"

After a long moment, he said, "I am not sure myself."

Might that be good?

He shifted his gaze, and as he slid it over the walls and floors, his face darkened further, and she guessed he remembered the cell as she remembered it—rather, as the predator to her prey.

Eager to be away, she said, "I am ready to return to the hall."

His eyes swung back to her. "I am not," he said and took her arm and turned her back into the cell.

As more of it came to light, she saw it was barren but for the stool in the center and chains fastened to the far wall.

"*Non*, Maxen," she beseeched as he secured the torch in a sconce. "Let us leave this place."

Wordlessly, he drew her across the cell.

"Maxen—"

He pulled her around to face him. "Sit."

She glanced at the stool behind. "I do not wish to."

"Trust me."

How could she when it seemed he meant her to relive that day? Might this be punishment for seeking Aethel?

"It is not what you think," he said so solemnly she looked nearer upon him. She could find no anger in his face. Something else was there, but it did not fit the Maxen Pendery who had last been here with her.

Slowly, she lowered herself.

"Close your eyes."

She startled. "Why?"

"Trust me," he repeated.

Gripping the stool on either side of her, she let her lids fall. But the memories rushed at her—the foul guard who had brought her here, the figure of a man in deepest shadow, the rope and cloth with which her hands and eyes were bound, the tread of boots.

She threw her eyes open. "I do not like it here. If you must punish me, do it another way."

"Punishment is not what I intend." His reassurance was edged with impatience.

"But I did what you forbade."

He bent close. Face inches above hers, breath warm on her chill cheeks, he said, "I understand your reason. Now close your eyes."

She blinked several times, and the last time did not raise her lids.

"Do not think, Rhiannyn," he murmured. "Just feel."

She did. Too much. "Maxen——"

He touched his mouth to hers, and in a deeply soft voice far different from the one that had demanded Edwin's whereabouts, said, "I am going to erase that memory. For both of us."

He also felt the ill of this place? Regretted the fear he had put through her?

She opened her eyes and saw he had lowered to a knee before her. "How?" she asked, heart straining against her ribs.

He pushed a tress out of her eyes, the brush of his fingers around the back of her ear making her tremble. "By putting another in its place. Are you willing?"

What did he ask of her? Kisses? Caresses? More? That which she had bargained away, but he had returned to her? "I do not understand."

He set his hands to her arms, slid them downward and uncurled her fingers from the seat, placed her hands on his shoulders.

Hardly able to breathe, she looked into the eyes of the man she feared might tempt her to do what she should not.

And when next he spoke, it was in her language, here in this place where he had said he did not embrace her vulgar tongue and had commanded her to speak Norman French. "Hold to me, *leof*."

Leof. Was she truly dear to him? Surely he would not speak it unless there was some truth to it, for sweet words were not needed to deliver her to his bed when he had but to collect on their bargain.

"*Leof?*" she said.

He leaned close, his mouth so near she tasted wine on his breath. "*Leof*."

In that moment, she knew what she felt for him. The door that had swung open to him when he had once more pardoned her people, allowing him to cross to the other side of her, was the one to her heart. This was love—not the love of a child for its parent, a sister for a brother, a friend for a friend. It was the love of a woman for a man who was not the enemy she had believed.

I love him, she silently acknowledged, and met her hands at the back of his neck and held to him. "Love me," she whispered.

She felt his hesitation over words she had not meant to speak, but he closed the space between them.

Rhiannyn thrilled to his mouth covering hers, fingers gripping her waist, hands moving to the small of her back, arms drawing her off the stool.

You go too far, entreated the voice of all that was good and right.

I love him, she excused herself.

As he does not love you, who will ever remind him of his brother's death. If you are truly dear, 'tis because he desires you the same as Thomas. That is not love.

Perhaps in time, she ventured.

You are weak, Rhiannyn of Etcheverry who deserves not the name. Better Rhiannyn the obsession of Thomas, Rhiannyn the betrayer of Edwin, Rhiannyn the downfall of Aethel, Rhiannyn the harlot of Maxen.

"Ah, nay," she breathed and pulled her hands from around Maxen's neck.

He lifted his head, and when she met his questioning gaze, it was through tears.

"I am weak," she whispered.

Desire-darkened eyes yielding to fiery blue, he said, "Weak?"

She gave her head a shake. "I do not wish to be, but…Perhaps it is because I am so tired."

"Of what?"

Words she had not known were in her tumbled forth. "Of paying for goods I did not purchase nor receive. Bearing guilt for things I can no more control than night can become day at dusk. Being pulled between two peoples such that I hardly know who I am."

He stared at her, and when her tears brimmed over, brushed them away. "I know these past years have been difficult for you."

"Difficult?" She laughed sharply. "Terrible is what they have been. I know life cannot be as it was, that Saxon rule is over despite all to which

Edwin aspires, but it seems we cannot even begin anew——that we who are innocent of all but being Saxon, shall ever by constrained by our defeat and never again be who we were." A small sob escaped her. "I want to be Rhiannyn. Just Rhiannyn——daughter, sister, friend."

Emotions shifting across Maxen's face, he asked, "Betrothed as well?"

She frowned.

"Could you, would you be betrothed again, Rhiannyn? To Harwolfson?"

Edwin, whom she had cared for, but not loved. She nearly rejected the thought, but it was selfishness. "I would, providing all those lost to me were also restored and it could be the way it was before the Normans."

"Then could you have only Harwolfson, you would not wish it? You would remain here with me?"

Wife to Edwin. Or this...

Silently, she asked the Lord to forgive her the sinful thing her answer would tell of her. "Here I would remain."

Tension easing, Maxen said, "I give you my word I will make it better for your people when I put them back to the land and under my protection."

She tried to smile, but the expression would not fit her lips. "I thank you."

He lowered his gaze to her mouth as if he meant to continue what was begun, and perhaps he did, but he said, "I thank *you,* Rhiannyn."

Before she could ask his meaning, he drew a hand up her back, pushed his fingers into her hair, and pressed her head under his chin. And held *her.*

She stiffly accepted his embrace until she became aware of his heart beneath her ear. Closing her eyes, she thrilled to the thought she was somewhere there in its beat.

One moment passed into another, lengthening like soft wool gently twisted and wound around a spindle. For the first time in what seemed never, she felt safe and dear, as if the years of heartbreak and hardship were at an end, as if something good and blessed might come of her love for this man.

"This is how we should have started," he said.

If only they could have. But that did not mean they could not now. And was that not his intent—to replace memories of this place with better ones?

Rhiannyn drew back. "We can begin anew. At least, in this."

He grazed a thumb across her lower lip. "So we can."

When he did not kiss her again, she slid her hands up his chest, over his shoulders, and pushed them into the hair at his nape. It was she who put her mouth to his so she might feel what no other made her feel.

He gathered her closer, deepened the kiss, explored the curves of her neck and back.

Rhiannyn the harlot, the voice once more condemned her.

She pushed it behind, sighed when his hands moved to her waist and up her sides.

Rhiannyn the wanton.

She thrust the voice away, marveled that Maxen made her feel more than she had ever felt.

Rhiannyn the whore.

The ugliest of those things she was in his arms made her drop her chin to her chest. "I long to," she said, "but though I would remain here with you, this is wrong."

Her words returning Maxen to the prison cell out of which he had ascended, he stared at the golden hair atop Rhiannyn's head, felt the silken strands he had wound around a hand. And knew what must be done—even though his brother's obsession with her had been the death of him, even though Maxen had said he never would, even though it meant defying a king.

"We will make it right," he said, "for your soul and mine."

She lifted her face, and the confusion there seemed genuine—as if she had not maneuvered him as Lucilla had advised her to do. "How?" she asked.

"Speak vows with me."

Her lashes fluttered. "What?"

"Unite our two peoples, *fricwebba*."

Peace-weaver, a Saxon woman wed to an enemy in the hope of establishing peace between two tribes.

Rhiannyn frowned. "You wish to marry me?"

"What say you?"

She searched his face, and her quivering mouth curved. "I will wed thee, Maxen."

From some place grown distant these past weeks, he caught a whisper of dissent that sought to draw him back to the monastery and the anger and resentment bred by tidings of Thomas's death. But he would not go there, certain where he dwelt now was more pleasing to God. As it was to him.

He eased back, took up her hands, and enclosed them in his. Having witnessed informal wedding ceremonies amongst the Saxons of his father's lands—much like the one he and Rhiannyn had observed the night in Andredeswald when he had played monk to her soul—he began, "I, Maxen of the Penderys, lord of Etcheverry, take thee—"

She startled. "You would wed me here? This moment?"

He inclined his head. "We will make what is wrong right, and no more will any name you what you are not."

Though she did not appear convinced, he said, "I take thee, Rhiannyn, to be my chosen one. Without sin or shame, I shall desire only thee that I might be desired by only thee. I shall possess only thee that I might be possessed by only thee."

Her wary eyes moistened, inviting torchlight to dance across them.

"From this day forth, the first name upon my lips shall be thine, the first eyes I behold come morn shall be thine, the first sip of my wine shall be thine."

A soft sob escaping her, she pressed her teeth into her lower lip.

Feeling his chest tighten with emotions that alarmed him for how vulnerable they made him feel, he stared into her lovely, hopeful face before continuing. "This day and all days to come, my sword and shield shall bear thy name above all others. I shall honor and cherish you through life, respecting thee, thy ways, and thy people." He drew her hands to his mouth, kissed her fingers. "Hence, I take thee, Rhiannyn of Etcheverry, in sacred marriage, in the sight of God, to be my wife."

She shuddered, whispered, "Maxen."

"Your husband, do you wish it," he said.

Smile uncertain, she began, "I take thee, Maxen Pendery, to be my one." She raised her eyebrows, and he nodded his approval.

"Without sin, without shame, only thee shall I desire, only thee shall I possess that thee might desire and possess only me."

Reassuringly, he drew his thumbs across the backs of her hands.

"Through day and night, through all of life, thine name shall be first upon my lips, thine eyes first upon mine. Ever shall I honor and cherish thee, ever shall I respect thee, thy ways, and..."

It did not offend when she faltered over her vow to respect his people. If in this she was truthful, it gave credence to the vows that had not struggled off her tongue. Too, after all she had endured, only a fool would believe respect for the Norman she wed should extend to all his countrymen.

"Hence," Maxen prompted her to forego what need not be spoken.

"Hence, I take thee, Maxen Pendery, in sacred marriage, in the sight of God, to be my husband."

Her voice trailed away, and he drew her near and sealed their vows with a kiss.

Now they were one. Or nearly so, for consummation would fully validate their marriage. But ere the middling of night, in all ways they would join. No sin, no shame, no taint upon children born of their union.

Maxen lifted his head, and the smile Rhiannyn shone upon him was more beautiful than any he had seen.

"Hold to me," he said, and this time when she put her arms around his neck, he rose and swung her into his arms. As he did so, he swept his gaze over the cell that, for a brief time, had known the light of this memory supplanting the dark one.

Pressing Rhiannyn's face into his chest so she would not look upon it, her last memory of it being of his face above hers as they knelt before each other exchanging vows, he carried her into the corridor.

The guard's mouth went agape when Maxen appeared with the one who did not belong here. The man and the drunken one in the cellar would be dealt with on the morrow. They could wait. Maxen could not.

He ascended from the cellar into the hall. Not wishing Rhiannyn to suffer the curiosity of his men, he continued to hold her face against him. But there was nothing he could do to shield her from the sudden lowering of voices that rose again with coarse mutterings only a drunken man would speak in the presence of his lord.

Maxen felt Rhiannyn stiffen, but she did not attempt to lift her head, nor to clamber down from him.

He nearly ordered his men to their pallets, but the revelry would provide his bride and him with privacy that could not be had in a chamber separated from a silent hall by a screen.

It was Christophe who made Maxen falter. The youth stood quickly from before the hearth, and when he caught his brother's regard, his eyes shone with condemnation. Of course he thought the worst of The Bloodlust Warrior of Hastings—believed his brother had decided to make Rhiannyn his leman after all. And Maxen could not fault him. But there would be time aplenty to set Christophe and the others right.

Though the hall was well illuminated, only a glimmer of light filtered through to the chamber he entered, no torches having been lit this side of the screen.

It would do for now, he decided. Beyond this night, there would be days in which to look well upon his wife's every curve and hollow.

He set her on her feet alongside the bed, and she immediately released him.

"What they all think of me…" she breathed.

When she did not look up, he raised her chin and regretted the uncertainty in her eyes. "The night is ours," he said. "The morrow is soon enough for them to know it is the lady of Etcheverry who shares my bed."

She slowly nodded.

"Now, Wife"—he lifted the sash tied around her waist—"I would do this right."

She frowned. "Is there a wrong way to do it?"

He did not think her innocence feigned, and it made him all the more determined he would not too soon yield to desires suppressed since he had committed his life to the Church.

"Indeed there is, but I vow you will not know it." He untied the sash, dropped it to the rushes, and turned her back to his front. Drawing aside her hair, he pressed his mouth to the soft place between neck and shoulder.

Rhiannyn set her head back against his shoulder and whispered, "Is this the right way?"

He raised his head and met her gaze that, despite what she asked of him, was no longer uncertain. "But one of many," he murmured and drew one hand up her hip to her waist and began loosening her bliaut's laces, with the other hand, turned her face up to his.

He set his mouth upon hers.

She sighed into him.

And kiss by kiss, touch by touch, lace by lace, they gained the bed. And became one.

29

Hɪs ᴘʀᴏᴍɪsᴇ ᴋᴇᴘᴛ, Maxen held her against his side, and once again she listened to the beat of his heart beneath her ear. It had eased and become so steady she thought it might put her to sleep if she could but still her mind.

But no matter that silence had finally fallen over the hall, no matter that she closed her eyes and slowed her breath, her thoughts went hither and thither—from that night in the cell to this, from these past years to the years before them, from terrible loss to blessed gain.

"Blessed," she whispered, not realizing she spoke the word until it slipped into her own ear.

She had thought him awake, but when he did not react in any way to indicate he had heard, she lightly drew her fingers over his chest.

Not for the first time this night, she recalled her mother's warning of two years past when marriage to Edwin was imminent. She had revealed what a woman must endure on her wedding night, reassuring Rhiannyn each time thereafter would be easier and offering hope that, eventually, there would be some pleasure.

She had been wrong—at least, where her daughter was concerned. And Rhiannyn guessed it had more to do with Maxen than herself, for with what seemed great patience, he had kept his vow to know her the right way, awakening her to things heretofore a mystery. But more sweetly, he had made her feel cherished—almost loved, though he could not possibly feel such for her.

But how I love thee, she silently spoke what she dared not say lest she scatter all that now was. Though she could admit to desiring Maxen, to reveal a love he might never return would make her ache to the point of pain. Of which Thomas would approve, for he had wished her to never again know the love of a man.

Thus, she must resolve to be content with what she had. And grateful, for it was much. Rhiannyn of Etcheverry was Maxen's wife.

A Pendery, she silently acknowledged the part of Thomas's curse that if she would not belong to a Pendery, she would belong to no man. Surely this was not what he had meant, but for those who believed in such things, they would think the curse come true this night. Even so, what had happened between Maxen and her was no more a curse than white was black.

Even if I am never more to him than fricwebba, she consoled, recalling when he had given her the name of one who weaves peace by wedding the enemy, one whose duty it was to bear children to blend the bloodlines of the two peoples.

Will I bear children? she wondered and recalled the other part of Thomas's curse—never would she hold a child at her breast, the pain of which would be second only to the possibility of never knowing the love of a man. The love of Maxen…

She recalled his words in Andredeswald when, in the guise of the monk he no longer was, he had said God did not serve man—that a person wishing ill upon another had no power over the one they cursed, and they were but words spoken in anger. Regardless, tears sprang to her eyes, and she closed her lids and pressed her teeth into her lower lip.

"Why do you cry?" Maxen's voice rumbled from his chest.

She lifted her face toward his, and against her cheek felt the moisture she had spilled upon him.

"Regret?" he asked, and when he glided a thumb beneath one eye, then the other, she knew the bit of light played upon the tears fallen from her lashes.

"No regret," she said. "Memories only."

"Of your family?"

Of the family I might not make with you, she silently corrected. *Of the love you may never return.*

But as she could not tell him that, and the loss of her parents and brothers were ever near, she said, "I still feel adrift without them."

"Speak to me of them."

"Why?" she asked warily.

"Though I have heard of their deaths at the hands of Normans, I ought to know more about who and what shaped the woman I have taken to wife."

Though it was not an unreasonable request, it made her uncomfortable.

"Unless you are not ready."

After further hesitation, she once more settled her head on his chest. "The conquering haunts me. As, methinks, it haunts you."

Maxen tensed. It was true. That past was rarely far from this present, especially Hastings—the screams of life yet lingering in those hunted by death, the smell of blood tenfold worse than the mass slaughter of pigs, the desperate mutterings to God who seemed to have turned away, the eyes of the dead wide with disbelief, and Nils...

Set upon by his own people.

"Forgive me," Rhiannyn broke through memories that tempted him to more blood upon hands so thoroughly soaked no amount of prayer had made them white.

Tempted only, he told himself and, finger by finger, unclenched the fist at his side and called his body back from the edge that made his muscles ache. "Perhaps one day I will tell you what haunts me, but this eve, let it be your telling."

He felt her draw breath. "'Twas a one-room wattle and daub hut in which I was born and raised, and though all I had of my own was a pallet, it was enough. While my father and brothers worked the land under Edwin's father, my mother and I kept the home and sewed for Lord and Lady Harwolfson. I quarreled often with my older brother, Claye, who was even more protective of me than my father, but Mother knew how to soothe hurt feelings, and Father how to turn anger into laughter. We were happy."

She gave a little gasp. "I know it must sound dismal, but they were wonderful times. Often hard, but never short of love."

Far different from Maxen's upbringing. He had been raised in the comfort of a great hall, his training for knighthood of paramount importance to a father whose contact with his sons was nearly exclusive to that end. Her life did not sound dismal. In some ways, it was enviable.

"And Harwolfson?" he asked, his thoughts having earlier ceased their circling around the Saxon rebel when tears had followed her whispered *blessed*. "How did you come to be betrothed?"

"Though he was not the eldest son, his gain was to be great in wedding a noblewoman who was her father's only child. Thus, he rode from King Edward's court for the wedding, but when he arrived at Etcheverry, he learned his intended had been taken by fever. Until that day, I had known him only by sight, but shortly thereafter, we talked."

"How is that?"

"He happened upon me while I gathered rushes at the river, and though I begged leave of him so he could be alone to mourn, he insisted I finish my task. After a time, he spoke of his betrothed. Though he had not met her, he was saddened by her loss, and more so when he told of the son he had hoped a year would bring him. He so wished to be a father."

Idly, for Maxen did not believe Rhiannyn yet knew the power of her touch, she drew her fingers over his sternum, causing his heart to accelerate. "When I had bundled the rushes, I asked for my leave-taking, but he bid me sit beside him. Though unseemly, I could not refuse the lord's son. Hours later and after much talk, it was as if we had known each other for years." She laughed softly. "Great friends, I thought. Wife, he decided, and told me so. I did not believe him, but his father came to mine the following morn and the betrothal was made."

Maxen told himself he had no cause to feel jealous. She had said she preferred to remain here with him than be betrothed to Harwolfson again. Too, there could be no doubt neither the Saxon rebel nor Thomas had known her as Maxen had this eve. Even so, he asked, "Did you wish to wed Harwolfson?"

"I did." Her fingers upon his chest stilled. "He was a good man, Maxen. The Edwin of Andredeswald is not the one beside whom I sat at the river. But even as changed as he is, I believe the man I knew remains, albeit dug down deep beneath these years. Norman or Saxon, such loss—especially of loved ones—cannot be erased."

Nils once more rose to mind. "It cannot." Reminding himself of the reason he pressed her about Harwolfson, Maxen asked, "Did he love you?"

She was silent so long, he thought she might not answer, but she said, "Though I know not how to read love in a man, I do not believe he felt that for me."

"You were not dear to him?"

"Methinks only insomuch as being pleasant to look upon, of good health to bear children, and of enough wit to converse well outside of bed, which is as my mother told me when I asked why our lord's son wished to marry one far beneath him."

Maxen reconsidered the king's missive. Alongside Harwolfson, it had occupied his thoughts since he and Rhiannyn had consummated their marriage. From what he had gleaned of her relationship with the Saxon rebel while in Andredeswald, and from what she told, it seemed unlikely she would be a means of bringing the rebel to heel. Too, just as she had not fled with Harwolfson following Thomas's death, and again when he had stolen inside the castle walls, the man did not seem of a mind to force her to leave with him. Thus, not dear to him.

"Why did you not wed immediately?" Maxen asked.

"We meant to, but hardly had our families agreed upon the betrothal than King Edward died and Edwin was called back to London. Then King Harold ascended the throne."

Maxen needed no further explanation. Harold Godwinson's reign had lasted less than ten months. Rife with conflict, it had culminated in his defeat at Hastings. "Your menfolk stood with Harold."

"It was Edwin's father with whom they stood, and he with Harold. Wynter—my younger brother—was barely fifteen summers old when he marched to Hastings..." Her voice trailed off.

For some minutes, Maxen allowed her to take refuge in silence, and it was with reluctance he pressed onward. "What of your mother and you?"

She stiffened. "We remained behind."

He stroked her head. "What happened?"

Breath shuddering across his chest, she said, "Days before the great battle, the Normans rode on our village. We resisted, but there were so many, and we were mostly women, children, and men of too great an age to stop them. They ravished our womenfolk, pillaged our homes, and set nearly every building afire."

"How did you escape?"

"When we could no longer hold them off, my mother and I hid in the stables, but they set fire to it as well. As we fled, the roof collapsed. It burned my skirts, but my mother..." She swallowed convulsively. "Though I tried to pull her from beneath the timbers, the fire burned too hot, then the Normans came for me. I fled to the trees, and all the way there I heard my mother's screams."

Rhiannyn was crying again, her tears wetting his skin.

"They did not capture you."

She shook her head. "In that, God was with me. Day and night, I prayed for my father and brothers' return, but they never came. Hastings stole them away."

It struck Maxen he might have slain one or more of her menfolk, but before he could step into his own hell, Rhiannyn's storm rolled out. Though she turned her face into his chest and shook with the effort to hold all inside, a sob escaped.

Maxen held her and murmured comforting words he had not believed himself capable of. When she finally lay slack in his arms, softly hiccoughing, he smoothed tear-dampened hair off her face and murmured, "What I can make right, I shall. I give you my word."

Impulsive.

Staring into darkness, the woman pressed to his side holding to him in sleep, Maxen discarded the word.

Imprudent fit better. Though aware of the danger in taking Rhiannyn to wife, he had not shown due care for the consequences of willfully defying a king. In his bid to replace memories of that place where first Rhiannyn and he met, he had offered a solution to their mutual attraction. A godly one to overcome her objections—and his own, though he would not have stood as firm as she.

Wedding her had been the right thing to do. Even now, unable to sleep for what his actions portended, he would do it again to ensure she was not taken from him, for it was not mere desire he felt for her. But here imprudence must end.

Had he immediately answered the king's missive, informing him he had wed Rhiannyn and correcting the assumption she could be no more to him than a leman, William would not have liked it. However, allowances would more easily have been made for not seeking permission to take to wife the woman his brother had also wanted.

Thus, a way must be found to keep hold of Rhiannyn should the king persist in the belief she was dear enough to Harwolfson to be used against the rebel, something Maxen was certain William would not hesitate to do should the opportunity arise—even were it known she was now wed to another.

"I will find a way," he promised himself, just as he had promised Rhiannyn that what could be made right would be made right.

Hours later, when stirrings in the hall scattered the silence and the somnolent dawn peeled back its lids to gaze upon Etcheverry, Maxen stared at Rhiannyn's hand that had remained pressed to his chest throughout the night—as if she found the beat of his heart reassuring. Next, he peered into her trusting, upturned face.

So wrong about her, he lamented. In so many ways.

But of those things about her of which he was most certain, it was that she would not like what must be done to keep King William from descending upon Etcheverry and undoing what had been done. But, hopefully, the woman with whom Maxen had vowed to spend his life could be made to understand. And play the game for as long as necessary.

30

Rhiannyn awoke in a tangle—not of blankets, but of limbs not all her own. She did not move or open her eyes, but lingered over the warmth of her husband's body at every place they touched, savored the slow rise and fall of his chest, counted the beats of his heart, and silently thanked the Lord the night past had been real.

"Wife," she whispered and opened eyes that no longer ached from crying.

She had known it was morn from the light prying at her lids, but was surprised the day had reached so far beyond the dawn. Not only had she slept through the rising of those who made their beds in the hall, but so had Maxen who ever rose with or before all others.

She tilted her head back and considered his face. It was too troubled for one who slept, and she wondered how long he had lain awake after sleep had taken her.

Carefully, she extricated herself and lowered her feet to the floor. Her garments lay amid the rushes where they had fallen on the night past, and were more tangled with Maxen's clothes than her limbs had been with his. Cheeks warming in remembrance of how they had touched, she scooped up the clothes, crossed to the chest, and laid them on the lid.

As she donned her chemise, she heard the approach of one whose footsteps were set apart from others'. Hurriedly, she crossed to the screen and peered around it.

Christophe faltered when he saw her, sloshing water from the basin he carried onto the towel draped over an arm. Continuing forward, he offered a smile amid concern.

Like the others, he assumed the worst. Thus, eager to assure him all was well and there being no others present in the hall, she hugged her arms around her chemise-clad body and stepped around the screen.

When he halted before her, she saw rose petals floated on the water in the basin. "For you," he said.

His consideration pleasing and embarrassing in equal parts, she said low, "I thank you," and dipped a finger in the water. "Oh, it is lovely warm."

"I sent all from the hall earlier, having arranged for them to break their fast in the bailey outside the kitchen so you would not have to..."

Face them. Though what he had done was not necessary—or soon would not be—Rhiannyn felt a surge of love for this young man who had become her brother. Though he could not replace those lost to her, it was a balm to add to the family she had begun on the night past when she had taken Maxen as her husband.

"Are you well?" Christophe asked in a rush.

She smiled. "Quite well."

"You are sure? After what—"

"It is not what you think."

"But I heard weeping. Did Maxen harm you? If he did..." He shook his head.

She laid a hand on his arm. "I vow, your brother did not hurt me. 'Twas for another reason I wept. I cried out the past. That is much, Christophe, but it is all over which I lamented."

"Your family?"

Though she had never spoken at length of them, he knew she had lost all to the Norman invasion. "Aye, my parents and brothers."

His eyebrows rose into the hair on his brow. "You told Maxen?"

"I did, and he offered comfort."

His face twitched. "I find that hard to believe."

"As I would have ere last eve, but much has changed."

He passed the basin to her. "As my brother will offer no apology for what he has done, I can but offer mine." He lifted the damp towel from his arm and draped it over hers. "What happened should not have."

"Christophe," she said, "no apology is necessary. Maxen did not take what was not given him. He and I—"

"You love him?"

It was her turn to slosh water, wetting the front of her chemise. "I…" She did not wish to lie, but neither was she willing to admit this deepest emotion. Determinedly returning to what would ease his concern, she said, "'Tis true I freely gave myself to your brother, just as it is true we are wed."

He stared wide as if playing again her words to verify he had heard right, then he startled. "You spoke vows last eve?"

"We did."

"In the cellar."

He did not need to know it had been the prison cell. "Aye."

"Without witnesses."

His concern was the same as hers had been, and she hated the uncertainty that returned to her. "We are husband and wife," she said firmly.

His jaw shifted. "After last eve, all those who questioned if you are, indeed, my brother's leman, question it no more."

"This day, Maxen will set them right by announcing he has taken me to wife."

"Will he?"

She inclined her head. "Until he does, I ask you not to speak of it so he may himself correct the misunderstanding."

Christophe jerked his chin. "I pray my brother is as changed as you believe, for your sake as well as mine, for I would call you sister."

Were her arms not full, she would have embraced him. "I thank you." She glanced at the water, breathed in the scent of roses. "Now I shall enjoy your gift."

He inclined his head and turned away.

Rhiannyn watched him until he went from sight, then slipped back around the screen, confirmed Maxen slept, and set to bathing.

A scent—like the roses of summer when he had walked the monastery gardens and tried to replace dark memories with the smell of unfolding petals. Instead, their crimson color had reminded him of the blood on his hands.

Arising from a dream whose images eagerly fled, Maxen lifted his lids and slid his gaze down his body and over the coverlet to the foot of the bed. Rhiannyn sat on the clothes chest with her back to him, fair hair curtaining her shoulders.

Why had he not awakened when she had left his side? He did not sleep deep—nor could he afford to if he was to live to a good age.

Though tempted to call her back to bed, he watched as she pushed aside the sleeve of her chemise and dipped a towel in a basin of water beside her—no doubt scattered with rose petals, the scent of which had drifted into his dream.

Slowly, as if with a mind divided between the task and great thought, she rubbed the cloth up her arm, beneath it, and down to her fingers. In this fashion, returning often to the basin, she bathed. When she finished, she peered over her shoulder. And blinked wide.

He smiled. And wished the smile she returned was not destined to gutter out—that she would understand what he must ask of her.

"Good morn, Wife."

"Good morn, Husband." She stood, clasped her hands at her waist, and nodded at the basin. "I have bathed."

"And I have watched."

Her lashes fluttered. "I did not know."

"As I wished it."

Pink spotting her cheeks, she said, "Your brother was kind enough to deliver me bath water."

"Ah, Christophe." Maxen felt his smile falter. "Come to rescue the fair maiden his depraved brother ruined."

Rhiannyn came around the bed and lowered beside him. "He was concerned. We are friends, you know."

"Great friends, as evidenced by the betrayal of his own brother to aid in your escape into Andredeswald." Even before fire brightened her eyes, he regretted the reminder that spoke even worse of the one who had used their friendship to his own end. Too, what must yet be revealed would be more poorly received cast upon ground already sown with ill will.

"Forgive me," he said. "That is best left in the past." He pulled her down onto the mattress, rolled to his side, and bent over her.

She did not kiss him back, but when he lifted his head, a smile approached her mouth.

"I want it to be better between Christophe and you," she said. "As he is now my brother, he is more dear to me."

"It will be better," he said. Of course, after last night and what had shone from the youth's eyes when Maxen had carried Rhiannyn through the hall, it could be a long while before they reached a better place in their relationship.

"I had to tell him," she said.

Maxen drew back. "What?"

"I said we are wed. Though I know you would have preferred to reveal it, he was so worried I thought you would not mind."

Anger began to knot in his chest, but it was not Rhiannyn in the fibers bending and coiling and pushing in and around themselves. She had but tried to reconcile the brothers, and though he did not doubt it would soon be worse between Christophe and him, he had only himself to blame.

"I told him to speak naught of it," she added. "That you would tell all."

He closed his eyes and lowered to his back.

"Maxen?" This time it was she who turned onto her side and bent over him. "What is it?"

He knew he should be done with it, but he wanted a few more minutes alone with her before all gained on the night past shuddered beneath the force of King William.

He opened his eyes and laid a hand to her cheek. "*Faeger*," he named her *beautiful* in her language.

She smiled, leaned down, and said against his lips, "*Leof.*"

That he was dear to her made what he must tell ten-fold more difficult. Further delaying, he asked, "How do you feel?"

Her smile flexed as if uncertain it belonged on her mouth. "I am well, though sorry I burdened you with my woe and weeping."

"I asked you to unburden yourself."

"So you did. And I am glad." She drew back, studied his face. "Something is amiss."

He slid his hand down her jaw to the hollow of her throat, felt the pulse there. "I made a mistake. And yet not, for I would do it again."

He was not surprised by the wariness rising on her face and realized it had been just beneath the surface.

She swallowed. "Now you shall tell me something better not told."

"Nay, better told. But with much regret."

"Ah." She caught her lower lip between her teeth and pushed herself to sitting. "It was not real. For you."

"Rhiannyn…" He rose and turned her to face him. "It was real—*is* real. It just cannot be told. Not yet."

Her eyes moistened. "You think I played Lucilla's game—giving just enough so you would wed me to have me—and this is you with the winning piece, me with no witnesses." She shook her head. "He knew."

She surely spoke of Christophe who had not believed Maxen honorable enough to do the godly thing.

"I know you played no game," he said, "and though the dark past out of which I stepped to become lord of Etcheverry gives my brother good reason to doubt my honor, in this he is wrong."

Her nostrils flared. "Tell, you who said you would make known that the one who shares your bed is the lady of Etcheverry, why must our marriage be kept secret?"

"I did not first seek the king's permission, a grievous offense."

"You did not consider that on the night past?"

"I did. But only afterward, while you slept, did I allow myself to think fully on the consequences."

"Most convenient." The color in her cheeks rising higher, she gave a short, sharp laugh. "*Fricwebba!*"

Maxen could not remember a time he had felt so splayed open, and it further vexed him.

Calm, he counseled. "When the truth is told," he said, "a peace weaver you will be."

Her eyes searched his, and he was relieved to glimpse in them what seemed hope. Still, she said, "*If* ever it is revealed."

"I vow it shall be."

"In this I ought to believe you?"

"As told, I would wed you again—"

"You would deceive me again!"

He ground his teeth. "Could I relive the night past, I would not carry you through the hall to my bed—would not allow impatience to expose you to the derision of others."

She lowered her chin. "But you cannot relive it. Thus, in the eyes of all, I am your leman in truth. Not a *fricwebba*. A harlot."

That word spoken against her—so coarse, so crude, so vulgar—was a foul blow. But she was right. Though he would allow none to say it of her, many would be the whispers behind his back and the sly comments fast upon her ears.

He lifted her face and set his forehead to hers. "In the eyes of God, you are my wife, and I am your husband."

"*Only* in His eyes."

"Nay, in mine and yours as well. Is that not what matters?" When she did not answer, he said, "The night we watched a couple pledge their lives to each other in Andredeswald, having invited only God as their witness, you said it was a beautiful thing."

"It was. But they were Saxons, and though you pretended to be, you are not. And do not forget, that same night you questioned the legitimacy of such vows, cautioning against nobles speaking them."

So he had. "I can but ask you to trust me in this."

She drew back and, mouth trembling, said, "How long must our marriage remain untold?"

He hoped her question meant she would allow him the time needed. "Until I can ensure you will not be taken from me."

Her eyebrows pinched. "Taken from you?"

Maxen had been undecided about showing her the king's missive, for though she claimed not to feel for Harwolfson, still her roots remained entwined with those of the rebel. But if it gained him her trust...

He turned, lowered his feet to the floor on the opposite side of the bed, and retrieved his robe from the end post. He pushed his arms into the sleeves, belted the garment, and stepped to the clothes chest.

The missive was at the bottom where he had buried it. "Nearly a month gone, I received this from King William." He unrolled it as he came around the bed. "Can you read Norman French?"

She glanced at it. "Not well."

"Well enough, I hope." He extended it. "As I have given you cause to distrust me, it is best you read it yourself."

She took it from him. When she bent her head to it, her struggle to translate the written words was obvious, but finally she looked up.

"Your king wishes to use me to gain leverage over Edwin. That is what it says, does it not? That whether or not you have me to bed, you are to ensure I do not escape."

Maxen inclined his head. "Should news of our marriage reach him, and he remains set on using you, he could try to remove you from Etcheverry. And if he does not, what I have done, fully aware of his intentions all these weeks, would be seen as defiance."

She set the missive beside her. "Such he will not tolerate from The Bloodlust Warrior, one to whom he owes much?"

There was hope in that, but Maxen was not certain it was enough. "The Penderys have long been on Norman soil, too long and too well rewarded for some who have the king's ear and oft question the strength of our ties with the Saxons. Thus, when my brothers and I were called to take up arms against your people, it was upon us to prove our allegiance to our overlord. And so we did on the battlefield." He thrust aside the memory of Nils. "But though Thomas and I earned the king's favor for our family, it is not merely unwed conception which gained him the name, William the Bastard. It is as much the temperament behind what appears a composed face. Thus, in addition to losing you, my defiance puts Etcheverry at risk—indeed, all of my family's holdings since I am heir."

She pulled a deep breath. "I see. But tell, if the king does determine I am best used against Edwin, whether by relinquishing me to him or threat of harm, what then?"

"I will find a way around him, another way to bring Harwolfson to heel. I give you my word."

Her laugh was as weary as it was bitter. "Forgive me if I wrong you in questioning the word you give." She pushed off the bed, stepped past him, and retrieved the green bliaut that bore some of the blame for his imprudence on the night past. As she had served at table, he had envied the way the garment clasped her curves and imagined he was the soft, woven threads that told the tale of her body.

"I must make ready for my day," she said and lowered the gown over her head and pushed her hands into its sleeves.

Maxen stepped to her side. Before she could undertake the tightening of her laces, he caught their trailing ends, tugged them snug, and secured them.

She considered the bow that was too long in its loops, murmured, "I thank you."

"Remain in our chamber until I summon you," he intentionally named the room hers as well as his.

She looked up, and though light flickered in her eyes at his attempt to reassure her of their relationship, she frowned. "I have duties to which I must attend."

"No more." He returned to the chest, lifted the lid, and withdrew a clean tunic. "Set your hands to sewing if it pleases you, but no longer will you wait upon my men."

Rhiannyn stared at her husband to whom she could not yet—and might never—lay claim as he donned the tunic and reached for hose. She knew she should be grateful for his consideration, for it was no pleasant task to tote drink for men who grew callous when their cups had been filled one too many times. Or not enough. But in the guise of Maxen's leman, she resented it.

She squared her shoulders and waited for him to look up from the belt he secured about his waist. When he did, she said, "Sewing, rather than serving at table, is as a wife would do, Maxen, not a leman."

"This day is not the same as yesterday. You *are* my wife, and though our two peoples do not know it, I will not suffer you to wait upon them."

But he would suffer her to appear a harlot. He would suffer her to move among those whose eyes defiled her with their knowing. He would—

Enough! she silently commanded her hurt. *I will make peace with this.*

She must, for though she detested the corner into which she was pressed, she was more inclined to believe Maxen than not—that what had happened between them in the cell was true, that he had intended to announce their marriage, that neither did he want this, that he would make all right. But when?

"Rhiannyn?"

She opened eyes she had not realized she had closed and found him standing over her. Of what had they been speaking?

Placing herself, she said in a rush, "If I do not resume my duties, others will believe you favor me."

He brushed his lips across hers. "So they will, but it is not unseemly for a man to be so taken with a woman that he affords her greater consideration and protection."

Heat rose so thick to her face she felt near to perspiring, and before she could think better of her words, she said, "Such speaks well of a wife. What it speaks of a leman is that she brings much to the bed."

He straightened, and though she expected him to meet anger with anger, he said, "Bear with me, Rhiannyn. If I cannot find a way through this, I will *make* a way through it."

Those words and his seemingly sincere regret eased her hurt. "I want to believe you."

"Do. Now I must speak with my brother." He retrieved his boots, shoved his feet into them, and crossed to the screen. "You will remain here until I send for you?"

"I shall."

He stared at her as if to determine whether or not to trust her, and once more hurt put words in her mouth. "If you doubt me, mayhap you ought to chain me again."

His jaw tightened, and he strode around the screen.

"Ah, Rhiannyn," she murmured, "this day you are more a woman than ever, yet you let the girl speak for you. Make your peace with this."

She turned toward the bed. As it was much in need of straightening, she saw to it first and once more found King William's missive in her possession. Before returning it to the chest, she again struggled through the Norman French and was glad Maxen had entrusted the missive to her. Though fear of pain caused doubt to persist, she was nearly convinced he had taken her to wife as sincerely as she had taken him to husband.

She closed the lid on the missive and busied herself with ordering the rest of the chamber. When she was done, she paced the room. How many times, she could not have said, but when she sank into the chair, her mind flew to the cell where Maxen had replaced memories of their first meeting with their second.

I take thee, Rhiannyn, to be my chosen one, he had vowed.

Her nose tingled.

From this day forth, the first name upon my lips shall be thine.

Her eyes ached.

I shall honor and cherish you through life, respecting thee, thy ways, and thy people.

Her throat tightened.

I take thee, Rhiannyn of Etcheverry, in sacred marriage, in the sight of God, to be my wife.

Her sob went around the room, and she dropped her head back and beseeched, "Let him be true, Lord. Let every breath upon which we spoke vows be as proper in the sight of men as it is in Yours. Even if he can never feel for me as I begin to feel for him, let him not slip through my fingers. Strengthen my grip and his so we might hold to the one we became on the night past—"

Another sob.

"Let him find—or make—a way through the conqueror."

There had been none of the usual difficulty in locating Christophe. He was outside the hall in the donjon's shadow. The moment Maxen appeared, he hastened forward.

Though the youth clearly intended to deliver his accusations and arguments in sight of all, he quieted when Maxen asserted the necessity of conversing where none could overhear. Thus, they rode to the wood beyond the castle and dismounted alongside a stream rippling with sunlight.

While their horses took water, Maxen began to explain to his indignant brother all he cared to explain about his marriage.

But the Christophe he thought he knew quickly proved there was more beneath his reserve than believed. As if not slight of figure, lame of limb, and shy of tongue, he stepped near and, eyes afire, demanded, "Do you love Rhiannyn?"

That one word among the others made Maxen feel like he was the youth. Unsettled that four letters ordered such had the power to unman him, he scoffed, "Love?"

Christophe grunted. "Do you desire her as much above the waist as below?"

Though part of him was tempted to look near upon the extent of his feelings for her, it made him feel further unmanned. "I do not."

Disappointment flickered in Christophe's eyes, and with further accusation, he said, "Have you any idea of that emotion—if not by way of your experiences, then observation of those who are moved more by love than blood?"

Hastings. Rivers of red. Nils.

Maxen yanked himself from the place where he had become someone he had not known he was.

Etcheverry. Clear, sparkling streams. Christophe.

Relieved to return here, in spite of the condemnation of one who had once held him in high regard, he said, "One day, I will tell you about the blood. For now, all you need know is that though it can be washed from one's hands, leaving no visible stain, it sinks through one's pores and warps and hardens the soul such that even God is repelled."

Christophe's lids fluttered, and when next he spoke, his voice was more familiar. "Such that you can never love?"

Maxen stared. Could he? Were feelings that pure beyond him? Though this talk of love was distant from what he had intended to discuss, he answered honestly, "I do not know, Christophe."

His brother's eyebrows nearly met. "That does not inspire confidence in your intentions toward Rhiannyn. Thus, I will make it easier. Do you desire her in *any* measure above as you do below?"

It would have been easier to claim he felt nothing at all *above*, but this was his brother, not an enemy—unless he continued to treat Christophe as the child Rhiannyn had warned he should not when he had first returned her to Etcheverry.

Recalling her beseeching to show the youth respect and not beat down his voice, he said, "I would not have wed her did I not feel more for her than desire."

Christophe's shoulders relaxed. "Then you did not speak secret vows to get her in your bed and more easily discard her should you weary of her?"

"I did not. In the sight of God, we are wed evermore."

Maxen almost regretted the relief shining from his brother's face, for what had yet to be told would give ear to more accusation and argument.

He stepped around Christophe to the stream and lowered to his haunches. After drinking deep and clapping handfuls of water on his face and neck, he looked over his shoulder. "There is more, and it will make you think no better of me than when I carried Rhiannyn through the hall last eve. Worse, even."

Christophe's slight smile lowered. "Tell."

Maxen stood and revealed the contents of the king's missive. As expected, Christophe was outraged by William's plan to use Rhiannyn to end the threat of Harwolfson.

"It is even better you have wed her, then," he said.

"Indeed, and I would speak vows with her again, regardless of how imprudent it is."

Christophe opened his mouth as if to question that, then he closed it and his eyes twitched with thought. "The king will not like it," he said, and there was more the man about him than Maxen had ever seen. "You risk making an enemy of one whom others have caused to question our family's loyalty, one who can take all from the Penderys with the lift of an eyebrow. A dangerous thing."

Maxen was grateful he had drawn the conclusion on his own. "You understand that though I had intended to correct the belief Rhiannyn is my leman, it must wait."

Christophe's mouth pinched. "You have told her this?"

"I have, and as you surely know, she does not like it any better than you or I."

"How long must she suffer the belief she is a harlot?"

Maxen tensed, for even in this he took offense at hearing the word applied to her. "Only as long as necessary, but I cannot say if it will be days, weeks, or months before our marriage is revealed."

Christophe nodded slowly. "I shall try to trust you—believe Rhiannyn is safe in your care."

It was something, and more than Maxen had known he wanted from his somewhat estranged brother. "Tell, Christophe, why do you care so much about her?"

The youth's eyes went soft, and he jerked his chin to his chest.

Maxen gripped his shoulder. "Christophe?"

In a choked voice, he said, "I love her."

Though Maxen had suspected as much, the admission jolted him, but before he could respond, Christophe's wide-eyed gaze returned to his. "*Non,* not as she should be loved by you. She is the sister who does not treat me as a pet, the mother who does not hide me behind her skirts, the brother who does not look upon me with long-suffering tolerance."

A tear fell to Christophe's cheek. "Rhiannyn believes in me as no other has. Even if she stood me alongside my brothers, she would not find me wanting, might even think me worthier than one who wields a sword. To her, I am Christophe the friend and healer, not the imperfect, impaired Pendery." He swallowed. "For that, I love her and will do all I can to ensure no harm is done her. And if I fail, I will die having tried."

As Maxen stared into his brother's earnest face, he heard the drag and push of his own breath and felt movement around his heart. Though different from what he experienced with Rhiannyn, it was there all the same. "I am with you," he said. "If naught else, trust me in this."

Christophe took a faltering step forward.

The warrior who had been trained into Maxen from an early age commanded him to draw back. But the one whose quest to avenge Thomas's murder grew distant in the light of Rhiannyn, moved him forward. He released his brother's shoulder, put his hand to the back of the youth's head, and pulled him into an embrace.

Christophe's stiff surprise melted, and they remained thus until he himself pulled back. "I am glad you are returned from Hastings."

Maxen inclined his head. "The journey is not yet done, but it is good to be on the road home."

Christophe turned and limped to where his mount nibbled at the patchy grass. Once both were astride, he said, "Methinks you do love her. You just do not know it yet." Then he put heels to his mount and left his brother to ponder what he had told, reject it, and ponder it again.

31

It was Sir Guy who came for Rhiannyn following the nooning meal.

She pushed away the platter of viands Lucilla had brought her and followed him into the hall where Maxen stood before the dais with two dozen knights flanking him. And before the hearth stood Christophe, watchful but not as wary as he often presented. Indeed, he seemed a bit taller, perhaps wider.

Though Rhiannyn was in little better spirits than when Maxen had left her hours earlier, curiosity over this strange gathering took the edge off her emotions and her mind off the knowing glances.

When she met Maxen's gaze, he said, "Come stand beside me."

As if the wife she could not own to being. Lest her hope be dashed that he had already found a way through King William, she pressed it down and, chin high, stepped alongside him. "My lord?"

"A moment." He fixed his gaze on the entrance to the cellar.

It was a long moment, but five Saxons came into the light, each led by a man-at-arms.

Rhiannyn lost her breath. Was it time to carry out their death sentences? If it was what Maxen intended, surely he would not bring her countrymen before her. After all, though he had forced her to accompany him to the hanging that had not happened, her presence had been but a means of discovering whether or not she lied.

Feeling Aethel's stare, made all the more palpable by the bond forged between them long ago—even if he now deemed it broken—she looked to him. His weeks below ground had paled him and grown his hair and beard wild, but his eyes were sharp with accusation.

The Saxons halted ten feet distant from their Norman captor, and as their clattering chains fell silent, Maxen considered them. "Aethel of Etcheverry," he said in Anglo-Saxon, "what is your decision?"

The big man flexed his shoulders. "The same as when last we spoke, Norman."

Rhiannyn's heart trembled. If they would not stand with Maxen, they could not be allowed to take up arms against him.

Fearing his pronouncement, she closed her eyes.

But it was to her Maxen turned and said, "My gift to you."

She raised her lids. "What do you mean?"

"They are yours, to do with however you wish."

The few of his men who understood Anglo-Saxon began translating for the others, and the prisoners shed their shock and added their voices to the din.

Maxen put his mouth to her ear. "Your *morgengifu*, Rhiannyn Pendery."

Morning gift, that which a Saxon bestowed upon his bride, and which was often a considerable amount of land or coin over which she was given control.

Tears blurred her vision. She had not expected a *morgengifu* from her Norman husband, and that he gave her one swelled her heart past the hurt there—more so since of all things he might bestow upon her, it was these men…her people…his enemy. And in that moment, she did not care if any thought this her reward for becoming his leman.

She glanced at Christophe, and on his face was something hopeful, surely akin to what she felt in her breast. "'Tis well received, Maxen," she whispered. "I thank you."

He turned his attention to his men. One look at his reproving face quieted them.

"What is to be the fate of your countrymen, Rhiannyn?" Maxen asked.

She eyed the Normans, lingering longest upon Sir Ancel. He was the most provoked, as told by his rigid stance, high color, and wide-eyed hatred.

"Name it," Maxen prompted.

Would it be acceptable? she wondered and ventured, "They will not serve you well at Etcheverry."

"This I know."

"Neither will they be of benefit at Blackspur."

He inclined his head.

"Then I would redeem your generous gift by requesting their release."

"To Harwolfson," Maxen said, and though she did not sense disapproval in his tone, she feared it was asking too much to allow the Saxons to strengthen the ranks of an enemy he might later face in battle.

"If that is what they choose," she said.

"They shall," he murmured and said loud, "They will be released on the morrow." He motioned the guards to remove them.

Rhiannyn looked to Aethel and caught his slight smile before he was prodded toward the underground.

"Return to your duties," Maxen ordered his men. "It is done."

As they began to disperse, Sir Ancel stepped forward. "For her"—he jabbed a finger in Rhiannyn's direction—"you unleash the very Saxons who aspire to murder our king? For this *whore*?"

One moment the fractious knight was upright. The next, he was on his back, cupping a hand over his gushing nose and staring up at his lord whose fists appeared ready to strike again.

"Shall we end this now?" Maxen's voice was large in the silence once more fallen over his men.

Showing his teeth in a blood-colored snarl, Sir Ancel started to rise.

Maxen slammed a booted foot to his chest, pinning him to the floor. "Shall we end it?" he asked again, the hand with which he had struck the knight turning around his sword hilt.

Sir Ancel's inner struggle raged for what seemed minutes, but he said, "I am at your feet, my lord. What else is there to end?"

"Much, and I do not think you will keep me waiting long." Maxen lifted his foot and ordered him to stand.

Sir Ancel did so slowly, as if fearing the draw of a sword, then dragged his bloodied palm down his tunic and bowed curtly. "I ask your leave, my lord."

"Granted."

With a red-rimmed grin and a swagger that belied his disgrace, he departed.

Talking amongst themselves, the others also withdrew from the hall, leaving only Maxen, Rhiannyn, Sir Guy, and Christophe.

"Why?" Sir Guy asked.

Maxen studied knuckles flecked with easily won blood. "Why the Saxons, or why Sir Ancel?"

"Both."

"As the Saxons are only five, the power to determine if King William keeps the crown lies not with them. Thus, I gifted them to Rhiannyn."

The knight glanced at her, and she saw nothing in his gaze that judged her for the manner in which he might believe she had gained the gift. Had Maxen confided the truth to this one who seemed more a friend than a vassal? If not, did Sir Guy suspect the Saxons were her *morgengifu*?

"As for Ancel," Maxen continued, "The time is not right."

Guy threw his hands high. "When?"

"Soon."

"Mayhap not soon enough," Christophe said, the strength in his voice rarely heard. "Do you not do something now, we could see your death before his."

Maxen turned to where his brother remained before the hearth. "Such confidence," he said, though not with anger—indeed, he seemed almost amused. "You do me great honor."

"And you underestimate Sir Ancel."

"You believe I ought to spill his blood though he refuses to meet me at swords?"

Rhiannyn glanced between the brothers and wondered at their exchange that, if the two had spoken this morn, ought to be strained by the decision to keep the wedding vows secret. Despite the seriousness of what they discussed, there was an air between them that was almost...

Brotherly, she realized, harking back to the brothers she had lost to the conquest. If this was the result of Maxen's talk with Christophe, surely it meant the latter was confident of his brother's intentions toward her?

Christophe stepped forward. "As you must know, Sir Ancel declined to raise his sword against you because he was at great disadvantage. Such he will not be if it is your back he steals upon. Thus, at the very least, you ought to expel him from Etcheverry."

"I agree," Sir Guy said.

"Your concern is noted," Maxen said, "but unless he leaves of his own will, what is between us will be finished here where I am best prepared to know which direction to face."

"But—"

Maxen held up a hand, halting his brother's advance. "It is decided. Now, there is much that requires our attention, Sir Guy." He nodded at Rhiannyn and strode to the great doors with his knight.

Alone with Christophe, Rhiannyn determined to ask what had transpired between him and Maxen, but as she stepped toward him, a Saxon woman ran into the hall.

"You are needed, healer," she called. "One of ours fell from the scaffolding and appears to have broken his arm."

Christophe threw Rhiannyn a look of apology and hurried after her.

Though Rhiannyn knew Maxen would wish her to return to their chamber, she'd had enough of solitude.

Shortly, she entered the kitchen where Mildreth and Lucilla wielded sharp knives against unsuspecting vegetables while several other servants worked mounds of dough.

When Mildreth caught sight of Rhiannyn, she beckoned. "You look a mite pale."

Rhiannyn halted before the immense table and lifted a hand to her cheek. "Do I?"

Lucilla bobbed her head, but though she held words behind her lips, her eyes were expectant, and Rhiannyn silently bemoaned the questions there.

Mildreth swept her gaze over Rhiannyn. "Are you well, child?"

Even were it known it was as Maxen's wife she had lain with him, still Rhiannyn would not have been comfortable answering. "I am fine."

Lucilla's teeth broke through her suppressed smile. "Certes, she is much tired."

Heat rising to Rhiannyn's cheeks, she repeated, "I am fine," and hastened to turn the conversation with good tidings. "The Saxons held below ground are to be released on the morrow."

Mildreth frowned. "To work on the wall?"

"Nay, to leave Etcheverry."

"Go on with ye!" Lucilla exclaimed. "The lord wouldna let them go."

"He has said he will."

"Why?" Mildreth asked.

Rhiannyn hesitated. "As a gift to me."

"Generous!" Lucilla crowed. "For but a night with him, five lives. Makes one wonder what manner of gifts ye'll be receivin' after a full sennight."

Mildreth gasped. "Lucilla!"

"'Course now he's had ye, he'll not wed ye, and any babes will be fatherless little souls." She sighed. "I did warn you 'bout that."

"Hush," Mildreth hissed.

Rhiannyn pushed her fingers into her palms to keep from touching her abdomen. Might Maxen's child grow there? Not if Thomas—

I do not believe his curse, she reminded herself. If she never grew round with child, it would be because God chose not to gift her with children, not because a dying man demanded it of the Lord.

Lucilla chuckled. "But at least it will be a fine brood of bastards Pendery makes on ye."

Rhiannyn caught her breath. Though any child she conceived would be legitimate, the thought of others naming it so cruel a thing for however long it took Maxen to find or make a way through the king made her hurt anew.

Bastard.

What if something—namely, Sir Ancel—happened to Maxen before he could reveal they had wed? Their child might forever bear that name.

Bastard.

What if the king took her from Maxen and returned her to Edwin? Her former betrothed would not accept the child of his Norman enemy.

Bastard.

And what if Maxen did deny their vows and set her aside—

Nay, she told herself, *not that.*

"Rhiannyn!"

She whipped up her head, wondered when she had lowered it, and braced her hands on the table.

"Are you ill?" Mildreth asked.

Feeling a hand on her back, Rhiannyn looked to where the woman had come to stand alongside her.

"As Lucilla said, I am tired." She tried to smile, but could not for what she must ask of the woman. "Mildreth, know you what will keep a child from growing in me?"

The woman shot her gaze to Lucilla, glowered.

Rhiannyn pushed off the table. "Do you know?" she asked again.

It was Lucilla who gushed advice, Mildreth who more often asserted some means were ineffective, others dangerous. However, the latter gave

Rhiannyn hope by reluctantly revealing such aid was provided to the smithy's wife who had birthed five children, one a year, and nearly died in delivering the last two.

But the one who had given her the means to prevent conception was not easily approached for who he was to Maxen. Still, Rhiannyn went in search of Christophe.

"How fares the worker?"

Christophe looked up from the dried plants he had spread on a table. "Blessedly, his arm was merely out of joint. I have fit it back in place, and he will have to wear a sling, but he should fully recover."

"I am glad." Rhiannyn drew a deep breath, stepped inside. "Maxen spoke with you this morn?"

As if to be certain they were alone, he glanced around the one-room hut where he prepared his medicinals and motioned her forward.

She closed the door behind her.

"Aye, we spoke—and well." That last was said with wonder, but then he frowned. "I do not like what must be thought of you until he deems it safe to reveal you are wed."

She pulled her lower lip between her teeth. "Do you believe him? That our marriage is as valid in his eyes as it is in God's and mine?"

Do not hesitate, she silently beseeched.

He hesitated. "I am inclined to believe him. You?"

Her shoulder jerked, and she hastened to allay the unbidden expression of doubt with, "I am."

"But only inclined."

Pain in her palms alerting her to the dig of her nails, she splayed her fingers on her skirts. "Too much is unknown, too much could happen, and too much is in the hands of one who would use me to bring down Edwin."

The name Christophe spoke against his king was not one she had ever heard pass his lips, but he apologized.

"Though I pray I shall remain wed to your brother," Rhiannyn said, "we cannot be certain all we hope for will come to pass. Until it does, I would make no children with Maxen. Thus, I am in need of a means of preventing conception."

Though the stunned expression on his face made her wince, she continued, "I understand you provide one to the smithy's wife."

Distress deepened the lines in his face. "I prepare it just as Josa put down." He jerked his head toward a small table in the corner upon which sat dozens of rolled parchments. "Though were it known," he added, "the Church would look ill upon it."

Rhiannyn had not considered that. "Is the herb effective?"

"It is a root," he corrected, "and it is mostly safe and effective in making a woman barren for as long as she uses it."

"Mostly?"

"On occasion, a child takes, though it could be more the result of consuming insufficient doses."

"And when one stops taking it?"

"If ever a woman was fertile, she is fertile again. Had not Thomas—" He snapped his teeth closed.

Rhiannyn stepped nearer. "What of Thomas?"

He was some time in answering. "Theta also uses the preparation— of her own making, not mine. During her time with Thomas, I noted she ceased preparing it. As I suspected she hoped my brother would get her with child so he would wed her instead of you, I warned Thomas. He told me he would take precautions, and she did not conceive though he continued to have her to bed."

"Is the root safe, Christophe?"

"For the woman." His eyes flicked to her abdomen. "But if she is already pregnant, she should not take it lest it harm her unborn babe."

Rhiannyn touched her belly. Regardless of what was thought and said of her if she and Maxen had made a child on the night past, such a risk she would not take—at least, not until the arrival of her menses proved her womb was empty.

She sighed. "In this, I will not ask for your help."

"I am glad." Christophe smiled. "You love my brother. Am I right?"

It was the same question he had put to her this morn, and to which she had not responded.

"I have seen how you look at him, Rhiannyn. I would but know if I am right in believing it is love that shines from your eyes."

What harm? she decided and said, "I tell only you this, Christophe. I do love Maxen, and if he never returns my affections, methinks I shall ever love him."

The length and depth of his smile widened. "He is not as easy to read as you, but he is changed in a way which makes me think he will return your affections if he does not yet."

Though wary of embracing what he told, Rhiannyn said, "I hope 'tis so."

"And I hope, Sister, when all comes right, you and Maxen will give me a nephew or niece—better, several of each."

His words made love fill her so full, it felt as if it might burst from her. "If God wills it, dearest Christophe," she said softly and left him to sort his plants.

Outside, she looked heavenward.

Lord, she silently prayed, *forgive me any wrongs I dealt Thomas, and if you did lend an ear to his curse, let it pass so all comes right for Maxen and me and we are blessed with little ones.*

The day dragged toward its close, as if the night was its enemy and it would not willingly go into that darkness.

But it went, and Rhiannyn's hands that pushed needle and thread pushed no more. However, her expectation of being allowed to take the evening meal in the lord's chamber proved false.

Maxen insisted she sit at his side upon the dais, the same as she had done as Thomas's unwilling betrothed. She had reminded him that in the eyes of all she was but a leman, but he said their suspicion did not concern him, and when their marriage was made known, such consideration would give credence to the vows they had exchanged.

Thus, Rhiannyn sat beside her husband, picked at her food, and as she tried to ignore the curiosity on all sides of her, mulled the possibility that even now she was with child. And were she not, this night her husband would be granted another opportunity to make it so.

Could she resist him? Not feel what he had made her feel last eve? If so, would he allow her to turn from him?

The trencher into which she had been staring blurred, and she longed for her mother who would surely have better prepared her for what to expect in being intimate with a man.

Fearing Maxen would notice her tears, she drew a long breath through her nose.

"It is over," he said near her ear.

She turned her face to him, and he offered a crooked smile, the charm of which she would not have guessed he possessed. It made her smile in return, and the longing for her mother recede.

He pushed his chair back and stood. "An early night for all," he announced.

There was grunting and grumbling from those who wished to linger over tankards of ale, but it was accompanied by the scrape and screech of benches, the thump and rasp of booted feet.

Maxen reached. "Come, Rhiannyn."

As he raised her, she was tempted to teasing—at least, the appearance of it—and said low, "Then I will not be bedding down in the hall this eve, my lord?"

Regret flickered in his eyes and he rumbled, "Your place is with me."

But would it remain with him?

She pushed down doubt, told herself she must be patient and understanding and all things that did not come easily to a conquered people.

When they were on the other side of the screen, Maxen pulled her before him. His kiss was light and brief, then he released her and said, "The day has been long, and there is naught I want more than to lie down with you."

She wished it too, but not another opportunity to get her with child.

As he stepped past her and began unfastening his belt, she peered down her bliaut and grew warm at the thought of removing it. Though she had given all of herself on the night past, her modesty remained intact.

Maxen's did not. He removed his boots and pulled off his tunic and undertunic. Back bared, he glanced around. "Would you like me to assist?" he asked.

She shook her head, reached for her sash, and eager to turn the conversation, said, "Did you tell Sir Guy the truth of us?"

Clad in long braies, Maxen crossed the chamber and lifted her sewing from the chair arm. "I did not, but like you, methinks he suspects there is more to us than what we allow all to believe. But worry not. He will not speak of it."

As she began loosening her laces, he said, "I fear you should have taken my measure before you began sewing for me."

She looked up and was grateful he kept his back to her. "I used another of your tunics to determine the size."

"Unfortunately, nearly all the tunics I possess belonged to Thomas, and they are ill fitting."

Rhiannyn suppressed a groan. She had been so pleased at her solution to busying her hands in the absence of his measurements that she had not considered how much larger he was than his brother. "I can make the seams smaller," she suggested. Hoping she had left enough room to do so, she padded across the floor and reached around Maxen to take the pieced tunic from him.

He relinquished it, turned, and slid his gaze down her. "It seems you do require assistance." He settled a hand to her waist and urged her closer.

"Let me hold the tunic to your back so I might know whether or not it can be made to fit," she said.

He plucked it from her, tossed it on the chair behind, and began raising her bliaut.

What am I to do? she wondered as the skim of his hands caused her body to start answering questions she would rather it did not in the absence of a means to prevent a child.

Her bliaut joined his tunic on the chair, and it was she who moved nearer when his warm hands made themselves felt through her chemise. And when he kissed her, she pressed nearer yet.

He swept her into his arms, carried her to their bed, and laid her down. "A moment," he said and moved away.

As he extinguished the torch and candles that provided most of the chamber's light, Rhiannyn came back to herself.

"Maxen," she said when he lowered beside her, "I do want this, to be with you in this way."

The fingers he had pushed into her hair settled at the back of her head, and she felt more than saw his frown. "But?"

"This night, can you not just hold me?"

With his eyes, Maxen tried to part the shadows around Rhiannyn's face, but he could make out little more than the glitter of her gaze, the curve of her nose, and her full lower lip that he longed to taste. From the night past, he knew she was not averse to making love. Thus, she must be telling him her body needed time, and he counted himself a swine for not considering one so recently virtuous might suffer discomfort.

"Aye, *leof*, to hold you will be enough." He turned her, and as he pulled her back into the curve of his body, felt her surprise. Doubtless, she had expected it to be difficult to stop a man from claiming his husband's rights.

"Cold?" he asked and reached behind to retrieve the coverlet.

Beginning to relax into him, she said, "Not with your arms around me."

Drawing his hand back empty, he attempted to fill it with the soft curve of her belly. There was too little of it, but in time, their child would more than fill his hand—both his hands, then his arms. He was warmed by anticipation, but almost immediately cooled. What kind of father would The Bloodlust Warrior of Hastings make?

"I thank you for my *morgengifu*," Rhiannyn whispered him back to this moment. "You could not have gifted me with anything of greater value."

And that is why I feel for her as I do, he thought, then added, *however it is I feel for her.* As Christophe had long known, and perhaps even Thomas, Rhiannyn was no Theta—indeed, like no woman he had encountered.

"I am glad to have pleased you," he said. "Now, sleep. On the morrow, your Saxons go free."

32

IN THE OUTER bailey before the portcullis being raised inch by creaking inch, Aethel stood tall and proud at the head of the four who were to accompany him away from Etcheverry. Though by presence alone, the great man was menacing, he was more so with his wild hair and beard that he made no attempt to put to order. He looked like a bear Rhiannyn had seen skirting her village when she had been a child with only dreams to cloud her eyes.

When the portcullis made its last protest, a quiet fell over the bailey as knights and men-at-arms looked on, and those Saxons who had given their fealty to Maxen watched from the sidelines. The prisoners remained unmoving, though their eyes seemed everywhere as if suspecting Norman trickery.

Maxen stepped before Aethel. "Do you reach Harwolfson, I would have you deliver him a message."

"*Do* I reach him?" Aethel boomed. "You think I will not?"

Ignoring the belligerence, Maxen said, "Tell him I will see him come spring, and we will end this."

"I will tell him." Aethel looked past Maxen to Rhiannyn. "Have you also word for Edwin?"

"Naught," she said, almost wishing she had been less effective in persuading Maxen to allow her to attend this leave-taking.

Aethel took a step toward her.

In an instant, Maxen's dagger was unsheathed, its blade pressed to the Saxon's throat. "Leave now, else you will leave not at all!"

Rhiannyn stared at the dagger that had been placed on her tray so it might be the instrument of death for Maxen as it had been for Thomas.

"I mean her no harm," Aethel said.

"Good, else I would have to disembowel you."

As Rhiannyn stared at her old friend, she was certain she had nothing to fear. He was not the same Aethel of her childhood, but neither was he the one who had frightened her during her visit to his cell. Though his eyes were hard, there was a softness at their centers.

"My hands are empty," he said. "Surely a word with Rhiannyn will hurt naught."

Before Maxen could refuse, she stepped forward. "What is it, Aethel?"

With Maxen's blade continuing to threaten the large vein in his neck, he could barely bend his head to look down upon her. "I would ask your pardon."

Then he no longer believed the lies told of her? Did not think her a betrayer? She swallowed to keep control of her emotions. "You need not."

"I do. I misjudged you. Thus, I beg your forgiveness."

Because she had asked for and been granted his release? It mattered not. "You are more than forgiven."

Aethel's smile was slight. "God be with you, Rhiannyn of Etcheverry." He shifted his regard to the man who held his life on the edge of a blade. "And God be with you, Pendery. You will need Him."

Accepting the threat without expression, Maxen lowered the dagger and jutted his chin toward the freedom beyond the walls. "Deliver my message."

Aethel grunted and motioned the others to follow him beneath the portcullis. With only the clothes on their backs, a pouch of food and a skin of drink each, the five passed out of the bailey to begin a journey that could see them traipsing all of England in pursuit of their leader.

"I would like to go up to the wall-walk to watch them away," Rhiannyn said, nodding at Christophe who had already gained that advantage.

"I will take you." Maxen led her to the steps and reached a hand behind.

She twined her fingers with his, raised her skirts, and followed.

At the top, he drew her to the notch in the wall past the one before which Christophe was positioned, and pulled her in front of him. "They are in little hurry to quit Etcheverry," he mused as he stared over her head.

Aethel and those coming behind crossed the land at a pace which seemed almost leisurely. Still, Rhiannyn was certain if it were not Aethel leading, the four would run for the wood.

She smiled. No matter the outcome of Edwin's battle and what role the Saxon played, Aethel would ever be in her heart.

The shrill sound of a loosed arrow ran the air, and an instant later, the Saxon at the rear of the party dropped to his knees. A darkly feathered shaft protruding from his upper back, he fell on his face amid the scrubby grass.

Though Rhiannyn could make little sense of what she witnessed, the horror of it made her cry out.

But Maxen was quick to make sense of it, pushing her down on the wall-walk and spreading himself atop her as an arrow meant for one or both of them struck the wall and clattered to the stones.

"Ancel has decided it is time," he growled. Then he was on his feet, sword in hand, running toward the watchtower where the knight stood atop its roof.

"Christophe!" he called. "See Rhiannyn to the donjon."

Past anguish over the Saxon's death and worry over whether the others had met the same fate in the seconds since the first had laid down his life, Rhiannyn heard the clamor arising from the bailey. She lifted her head and saw Sir Ancel nock another arrow.

"Maxen!" she cried.

But her husband moved too fast, and once again the knight's arrow fell unbloodied to the walk.

Christophe dropped down beside Rhiannyn and gripped her arm. "Make haste!"

"But Maxen——"

"He is a warrior. Come."

She watched as her husband began mounting the steps to the tower roof. Christophe was right. She had to believe he would prevail. But what of Aethel and the others?

"The other Saxons?" she asked as Christophe assisted her to her feet.

"I do not know, but we must——"

She pulled free, swung around, and leaned into the embrasure to search the land.

The Saxon who had taken the arrow in the back lay motionless, and running toward the wood were the four who had abandoned their leisurely departure to save their lives.

Rhiannyn could not be certain, but from Aethel's peculiar gait, it appeared he had been struck.

"You have seen," Christophe said. "Delay no more."

As she turned to him, Sir Ancel shouted, "The time has come to choose!"

Rhiannyn shifted her gaze to the man on the roof's edge, bow flung aside, sword raised above his head as he looked down on those in the bailey who had paused in their flight to aid their lord. Maxen also paused upon reaching the rooftop opposite Sir Ancel.

"Now we draw the lines!" the traitorous man called to the knights and men-at-arms. "Those who stand with King William and me, there." He pointed left. "Those who stand with the Saxons and Pendery, there." He pointed right.

Voices rose as Maxen's men pondered aloud the knight's words, for none wished to stand against their king.

Sir Guy moved first, pushing through the gathering to the place where he would stand with Maxen. "The side of right is King William *and* Maxen Pendery!" He jabbed a finger in Sir Ancel's direction. "Not the side of the traitor!"

"It is Pendery who betrays the crown!" Sir Ancel turned sideways and leveled his sword at Maxen who remained unmoving as he waited to see with whom his men would stand. "He has released the enemy to make war upon our own."

"War?" Sir Guy scoffed. "What is a handful of untrained Saxons to the greater Norman army? Are you so weak to fear five men who know more of ploughs and scythes than ever they will know of swords and horses? Are you so short of memory you have forgotten our victory at Hastings?"

There was a stirring among the multitude as eyes swept from Sir Guy to Sir Ancel to the lord of Etcheverry.

"You will die with Pendery if you do not come to my side," Sir Ancel warned, this time with a note of desperation. Doubtless, his belief there would be enough division among Maxen's men-at-arms to support his cause floundered.

"Mine is the only way," he persisted.

The mass continued to hold.

"Decide!" Maxen bellowed.

They began moving right to stand with Sir Guy.

Rhiannyn had not realized she held her breath until its release nearly folded her over.

"It is between you and me," Maxen said and strode toward Sir Ancel. "Defend yourself!"

"Fools!" The knight ran toward the rooftop opening that led into the tower's bowels.

In the bailey below, the men who had cast their lot with Maxen pressed back as one great body to better follow a contest destined for blood.

Maxen leapt after Sir Ancel and overtook him before he could escape down the opening. "To me!" He beckoned with his sword.

Having no choice but to fight, Sir Ancel lunged.

The first meeting of steel on steel knelled in the expectant silence, and grew more deafening, as did curses, grunts, and groans.

That the opponents were not well matched soon became apparent as all watched their lord transform into the celebrated Bloodlust Warrior. He seemed completely ungiving, allowing neither his opponent nor himself a moment's rest. With each thrust of the blade, his great body bunched and strained and terrible sounds tore from him. And when he took first blood, he loosed such a shout it caused knights well-tried in battle to flinch. As if more beast than man, he drove Sir Ancel back until the knight stood only by the grace of God who seemed close to abandoning him.

As Rhiannyn fearfully watched the macabre contest, Christophe said, "We must go."

"I will stay."

He stepped in front of her, blocking her view. "You should not see this."

She skirted him. "I need to."

"You do not. This is not the Maxen you love. Pray, do not taint your feelings for him with this."

Would her love for him wither after witnessing Sir Ancel's slaughter? she wondered as the conqueror and the defeated continued a battle clearly decided. Regardless, she could not turn away, for this was Maxen's demon, and to understand it, she must know it all.

"I beseech thee," Christophe continued, "come away."

She shook her head.

Showing signs his arm had grown heavy and pained, Sir Ancel clasped his other hand atop the first in a two-handed grip that allowed him to lift his sword to counter Maxen's next blow. It was not enough. Maxen's blade knocked the other aside and slashed through the knight's chest.

Sir Ancel cried out, dropped his sword, and slapped a hand to the wound.

Although Maxen did not immediately finish the knight as Rhiannyn imagined The Bloodlust Warrior would have done, he appeared ready to end what the other had started.

"Devil's seed!" The knight thrust his stained palm before Maxen's face. "My blood!"

Whatever Maxen's response, it could not be made out by those who watched.

With a shout, Sir Ancel snatched his dagger from his belt and lurched forward.

So swift Rhiannyn thought she might have imagined it, Maxen thrust his sword through the faithless knight, laying him down as cleanly as the piteous Saxon who had been felled by Sir Ancel's arrow.

Victorious shouts rose from those of Maxen's men farthest back who saw all that transpired atop the watchtower, and other voices joined theirs as word of their lord's triumph spread. They had chosen well the one with whom to side.

"Have you seen enough?" Christophe demanded.

Rhiannyn turned to him. Though grateful her husband was not the one lying in a pool of blood, something in her sought to counter the good of what had happened. She had witnessed many horrors these past years, but this touched her with fingers nearly as chill as when Dora had laid her in a grave.

Why? Maxen was not in the wrong to defend himself. Sir Ancel had initiated the confrontation by murdering a Saxon, wounding another, and attempting to put an arrow through the lord of Etcheverry. Surely there was no other course Maxen could have taken. Why, then, this tumult of feelings?

She returned her gaze to her husband who remained unmoving before the dead knight, head bent, broad shoulders bowed.

Realizing the terrible feeling inside her was his anguish, she said, "I must go to him."

"You must not!" Christophe cried, and when his bad leg prevented him from catching hold of her, shouted, "Maxen! Rhiannyn comes!"

Hardly had she set foot on the first step up to the roof than her husband appeared at the top.

Rhiannyn stepped back, and as he descended, looked from the splatters on his tunic to the hem where parallel streaks evidenced he had wiped his blade on it. Though she tried to keep her face impassive, she knew she failed when he stepped down to the wall-walk and she saw the guardedness in his eyes.

"You were to have returned to the donjon," he said and took hold of her arm and pulled her after him.

"Maxen, I know you must feel—"

"Speak no more!"

Closing her mouth, she told herself she could wait until they gained their chamber.

He led her to Christophe and said, "Your Josa is avenged."

Rhiannyn caught her breath. He spoke of the Saxon healer who, two years past, had been murdered by Sir Ancel, his one crime being compassion and care for the dying.

Christophe nodded.

"I ask you again to deliver Rhiannyn to the donjon." Maxen pushed her toward his brother.

"He is not to blame," she protested, but he did not linger to allow her to defend Christophe.

He descended to the bailey where a mass of men clamored to his side. His sharp words turning them aside, they opened a path for him to walk the bailey alone.

His destination—the chapel.

33

"IT IS GOOD," Christophe said as he watched his brother enter the building.

"He goes to pray?" Rhiannyn asked.

"I believe so. Let us go now."

All the way down the steps, she fought the impulse to be with Maxen. But upon reaching the bailey, she lifted her skirts and ran. Ignoring Christophe's shouts, she made for the chapel and paused at the great doors long enough to compose herself to quietly enter the sanctuary.

She halted inside the dim interior and located Maxen where he stood before the linen-covered altar, head pressed to the forearm he propped on it.

"What do you here, Rhiannyn?" he asked without looking around, his voice more weary than angry.

Wondering how he knew she was the one who trespassed, she said, "I did not think you should be alone."

"Is God not here?"

"He is."

"Then I am not alone, am I?"

Denying him an answer he surely did not expect, she started forward. Halfway down the aisle, she stepped on something. Having been too intent on Maxen to notice he had cast off his belt upon which his sword was fastened, she stared at it.

"Leave it!" he commanded.

She stepped over the sword and closed the distance between them. "It had to be done," she said and set a hand on his shoulder.

The muscles beneath her fingers were taut. "You know naught, Rhiannyn. Now go."

"I know you are greatly burdened."

"I said go!"

"I know there is much blood on your hands you wish away."

He pushed off the altar, swung around. "Wish away? *Pray* away!" His face darkened further. "Though God knows I have done enough—and to no end. Hardly am I out of the monastery and already I have killed several men. And do not forget the Saxon who lies dead this day, shot through because I did not do with Sir Ancel what should have been done long ago. Now tell me how God could be with me."

She longed to put her arms around him as he had held her when she had spilled her misery two nights past, but his pain was of guilt and self-condemnation, whereas hers had been of loss. "You cannot change Hastings," she said, "but you can change what happens now in this place. And you have."

He stepped around her as if in distancing himself he might gain control of his emotions. "Did you not yourself just witness a killing?"

"What choice had you? For that matter, what choice did you have at Hastings? 'Twas for your liege you fought—to him you answered."

He faced her again. "You truly believe that?"

The derision in his tone frightened her. "Is it not true?"

Though his eyes remained hard, regret and disgust and other dark emotions crossed his face. "It is not."

Her insides twisted. "What is the truth?"

He looked past her as if searching for it there. "The truth is that I well earned the name given me at Hastings. As a man who has been long without food, I longed for the blood of those against whom I took up arms."

Rhiannyn swallowed hard. Though never would she have believed she would defend a Norman over a Saxon, she said, "Hastings was a battle between two peoples. You are Norman, your opponents Saxon. What else were you to do?"

"There is the lie, Rhiannyn. By birth I am Norman, but as I was reared in England among Saxons, I am as much one of them as I am one of King William's."

"But as your family's liege, it was your duty to fight at his side."

"With such atrocity?"

So much he bore a name that conjured visions of mass slaughter. Though she feared asking him to speak further of it would take back whatever ground she had gained, she said, "Why did you do it?"

He stared through her. "It was what I had trained for all my life. Nils, Thomas, and I had ever to prove ourselves such that there was not a day I can remember having been without a weapon in hand. All I learned, I learned from my father—not at his knee, but against the swing of his sword." His hands closed into fists. "Though I had killed before Hastings, it was always with just cause. But William's battle was different. As already told, it was for me and my brothers to prove our family's allegiance to our Norman liege. But I was also eager—not to gain land as many sought to do, but to prove myself a warrior in every sense. To prove it to myself, my father, and William. And I did."

It was difficult to hear such things, especially with the faces of her father and brother rising before her, but the Maxen he spoke of was not the one she had come to know. Nor the one she loved.

"You repented." She took a step forward. "To atone, you entered the monastery and gave your life to God."

"And took it back."

"Not by choice. With Thomas dead..." She shook her head, repeated, "Not by choice."

His eyes flashed, and he strode toward her, but she was not his destination. He stepped around her and slammed a fist on the altar. "If you think that is excuse enough, why does God not take this haunting from me? Day and night it is before my eyes when they are open, behind them when they are closed." He shook his head. "You wished to know why

I released the Saxons, and I told you. What I did not tell is I did it for myself as well."

His pain piercing her, she drew alongside. "You must forgive yourself."

"How? Only after so many lay dead did my sword no longer run with blood. After I saw…"

"What?"

"Nils!"

"What did you see?"

Though Maxen tried to push down the vision, it came. He did not wish to speak of it, did not want any of it to touch her, but she needed to know. And so he would tell her, even if it meant losing her.

"I was wet through," he began, "as much with blood as perspiration, and though William's victory was assured, I raged on."

She sank her teeth into her lower lip, nodded for him to continue.

"As I searched out the next to slay, I heard Nils and found that the powerful, invincible man he had been that morn, was a man barely alive. Sprawled atop Saxons three deep, his chain mail was being torn from him as he writhed and groaned."

Rhiannyn shuddered.

"His own were stripping him of everything of value." At her gasp, he smiled grimly. "Aye, the very ones alongside whom he had fought robbed him. No honor. No respect."

When she swayed, he demanded, "Have you heard enough?"

"Are you finished?" she breathed.

"Would that I were."

"Then I am not finished."

He shifted his jaw. "I smelled it, saw it, tasted it—the blood of William's conquering. Rivers of it. And when the Saxon women came upon the field to search for their dead, the hems of their skirts grew so dark with blood they seemed weighed down by it. All those lives—lost for naught but greed."

She closed her eyes. "I am sorry."

"*You* are sorry? You who lost your entire family to Normans? Has it not occurred to you I might have slain your father? Your brothers?"

She lifted her lids. "No more of my life will I squander pondering their deaths, nor the deaths of the others. And neither should you. You must forgive yourself. The battle, one not of your making, is done."

"I assure you, by the end of it, I had made the battle mine."

"It is done," she repeated.

He turned his body toward her. "Who do you think the king will summon to put an end to Edwin Harwolfson come spring?"

She looked away.

"Aye. For my liege, blood will again stain all of me."

"You will find a way to stop it," she said with pleading. "You are no longer the…"

"Bloodlust Warrior of Hastings," he said what she could not, and strode to his sword, belted it on, and spread his hands to display it. "You are certain?"

Rhiannyn hated how menacing he looked—how ready to take life.

"Certes," he broke her silence, "we will know soon enough."

She put up her chin. "I already know."

"So innocent," he scoffed.

She stepped from the altar and crossed to his side. "Nay, forgiving."

His eyes moved sharply over her face as if to catch the lie there before it slipped away.

Confident he would find no trace of it, she held.

What seemed minutes passed, then he sighed and caught a lock of her hair between thumb and forefinger. "Have you truly forgiven?"

"I try."

"Then you have not forgiven."

"Every day a bit more. And so, too, must you."

He searched her face. "You give me hope."

And love, she silently added.

He pulled her close, and his muscles began to relax. When finally he drew back a space, his face had softened as if the terrible memories waned. "I am glad you are in my life."

She laid a hand to his jaw. "As I am glad you are in mine."

He turned his mouth into her palm and kissed it.

Rhiannyn's heart swelled so large it hurt, and she nearly told him what filled it so full. Curling her fingers into his kiss, she lowered her hand and said, "Let us wash away this day, aye?"

He looked down his crimson-stained tunic and immediately released her. "Forgive me. 'Tis wrong for me to touch you when I am like this."

"Then let us have done with it so you might all the sooner touch me again." The moment she spoke the bold words, she regretted them. She who feared conceiving should not issue such an invitation. And yet, it gladdened her to see the upward tilt of his lips and to fit her hand into the one he held out to her.

Side by side, they exited the chapel, and as they passed a group of Saxons, several men and women offered him respectful nods.

Even if Aethel and the others believed Maxen had ordered the killing of one of their own, the Etcheverry Saxons knew the truth. And if any good came of the bloodletting beyond removing the threat of Sir Ancel, it would be that Maxen had secured the loyalty of Rhiannyn's people by delivering justice to the Norman who had killed one of them without cause.

"Methinks you have won them over," she said when they were past the Saxons.

Without reply, he led her up the causeway. When they reached the donjon steps, a voice called to him.

He turned Rhiannyn toward the youth whose lopsided gait carried him forward.

Eyes dancing with light, Christophe said, "The Saxon lives. Though badly wounded, methinks he will heal."

The relief rising on Maxen's face made Rhiannyn's heart ache all the more for him. "I thank you, Christophe," he said.

His brother nodded and hurried away.

"And you say God is not with you," Rhiannyn mused.

Maxen sighed. "Certes, He is with your Saxon."

"*Our* Saxon."

He appeared to think on it a moment, then led her up the steps.

A half hour later, fresh towels and basins of hot water having been delivered to their chamber and a stool set before the brazier whose coals Maxen had coaxed to life, Rhiannyn lifted her husband's tunic and undertunic.

He captured her wrists. "You are certain?"

She raised her eyebrows. "Am I not your wife?" *Lord,* she silently sent to the heavens, *let me remain so.*

"You are."

"Then I shall do for my husband as he would do for me."

When he released her, Rhiannyn drew the tunics off over his head. She knew there would be splotches of blood on his skin, but had not considered some of it would be his own and not all of it dried. Though his injuries seemed minor enough that Christophe's needle and thread would not be required, they yet seeped.

She motioned him to the stool, and as he lowered to it, wet a towel. She started with his flecked face, swabbing away the battle that had granted Sir Ancel the grave. When she moved to his neck and shoulders, he closed his eyes, and the bones seemed to go out of him. Back bowing, forearms settling on his thighs, he let his head hang.

Rhiannyn returned to the wash basin, wrung out the pink-tinged evidence of the battle fought, and rewet the towel from the basin of clear, unsullied water. Back to front she worked, and upon finishing with his torso, replaced the towel with a clean one, wet it, and lowered to her knees before him.

Seeing Maxen's lids remained closed and wondering if he dozed, she worked the towel over his arms. Upon reaching his wrists, she lifted one of his hands hanging slack between his thighs, turned it up, and rubbed the blood from the thick pads and deep creases. Shortly, his other hand came as clean as the first.

"There," she whispered, "it is washed away." On impulse, she pressed her lips to his palm as he had done hers a short while ago.

Maxen stopped breathing, and when she looked up, his eyes awaited hers. "Would that you had been there for me after Hastings," he said. "Better, would that I had given one such as you cause to be there for me."

She leaned in, and when he lifted his face toward hers, touched her mouth to his. "I am here this day," she said, "as I will be here on the morrow and the morrow after."

"I thank you."

Struck by the realization they had been here before—or nearly so—she almost laughed. "Now you are the one on a stool, though it can hardly be said you are at my mercy."

"Am I not?" he murmured.

Hoping his words meant he felt more for her than desire, she breathed in the moment. As she breathed it out, he pulled her to him and made far more of the meeting of their mouths than she had done. And the clean hands moving over her foretold that soon they would love again.

Trying not to question him or his motives or the future that his consideration of the king made so uncertain—to but feel as he had made her feel on their wedding night—she kissed him back.

Do not do this, warned two years of fear and distrust. *Find a way to turn him aside. And yourself.*

Her mind having joined forces with her body that too much liked his embrace, she silently argued it was too late to turn either of them aside.

Only until your menses, cried the sliver of her that tried hard not to feel. Blessedly, its voice was shrill.

"Maxen," she said when his mouth moved to her ear. "We must stop."

He lifted his head. "Your body is not yet ready?" he asked in a voice so tight it seemed one more turn might break it.

She understood then why he had, without question, let her deny him on the night past. And it would have been easy to allow him to continue to believe as he did, but she wanted truth between them.

"It is ready, but I fear the timing."

He frowned.

"Until our future is certain, I would not chance a babe." Though his met eyebrows and lined brow eased with realization, she continued, "It will be difficult, perhaps even impossible, to gain acceptance and respect as your leman, but more so if I grow round with child. Worse, any babe I bear will be thought—and named—illegitimate, a belief that may persist even after our marriage is revealed. Thus, I would wait."

"You are right," he said and hooked an arm around her waist and lifted her onto his lap. "I am sorry I did not consider it."

"Then you understand?"

"That it would be folly to get you with child now? I do."

Once more, his easy acceptance surprised her. And bothered her, raking nails across the worry he might set her aside, a thing done with the least amount of resistance without a child to hold him to her.

"What is it, Rhiannyn?"

Seeing concern upon his face, she told herself she did him ill in thinking such thoughts. "We have but to wait on my menses. When it is certain we have not already made a child, it will be safe to take a medicine to prevent pregnancy."

"What medicine?"

"A root. I asked Christophe about it, and he said it is mostly safe and effective—"

"Mostly?"

She had questioned that word as well. "A babe can take, though it is rare. Of more concern is that the medicine can harm an unborn child, which is why I would not take it until my monthly time is upon me."

"Nay, Rhiannyn." His voice turned harsh. "You will not take it at all."

"But—"

"If it can harm an unborn babe, do you not think it can harm you as well?"

"It is believed to be safe for the woman."

"That does not mean it is."

His concern for her caused tears to prick her eyes.

In turn, those tears smoothed his face and softened his voice. "There are other ways to make it nearly impossible to conceive."

There was only one other way she knew, and there was nothing *near* about it. "I do not think you speak of abstinence," she said.

"I do not. With this other way, it is not likely we will make a child. But if we do, I vow it will bear my name the same as you, that I will be its father as you are its mother and my wife."

At her hesitation, he prompted, "Trust me, Rhiannyn."

Tentatively, she closed the small space between them. And softly, sweetly, hopefully, she accepted his embrace.

He had come to see the fallen Saxon, but more out of need than courtesy.

As Rhiannyn had gently—was it possible, lovingly?—washed away the blood, he had been freed of the vision of the Saxons setting off in search of Harwolfson, the one at the rear taking an arrow to the back. But it had returned when he had parted from his dozing wife.

Now he stood alongside the sleeping Saxon who lay on his belly with his face turned to the wall, back wrapped in bandages that evidenced they had earlier bled through. And he knew as he had known when the arrow dropped the man that he, Maxen Pendery, was responsible.

But had he truly done wrong in keeping Sir Ancel near? Whether this day or another, the same or worse would have happened had he sent the knight from Etcheverry. In Sir Ancel's air and eyes and words had dwelt one not merely driven by revenge, nor one who, in a passion, lost control. There had been too much purpose about the man, villainy either bred or beaten into him. Now, he would never again harm another, and God willing, the Saxon would recover.

"He is called Hob," said Christophe whose face had shone with delight when Maxen had appeared.

"Still you think he will recover?"

"Providing the arrow hit nothing vital, as I am fair certain it did not, and infection does not set in. If he still wishes it, I believe he will be able to depart Etcheverry within a month."

He surely would wish it. After all, he had taken an arrow in the name of Maxen Pendery.

Maxen started to turn away, but Christophe said, "Would you have me examine your wounds?"

"I thank you, but Rhiannyn tended them."

The youth smiled, said low, "You have chosen well."

But had Rhiannyn chosen well? "This I know." Once more, Maxen moved to leave.

"Hold!" Christophe stepped to the table alongside the Saxon and retrieved a small pot. "Have Rhiannyn rub this salve into your wounds so they do not go bad."

Maxen took it. "I thank you." He strode across the room, and at the door, looked around at his brother who had followed. "I need you to promise me something."

"Aye?"

Maxen hated the wariness in Christophe's voice. "Rhiannyn revealed her concern of conceiving a child whilst it is not known we are wed, and told of a medicine that makes it less likely a babe will take."

The wariness spread to Christophe's brow. "You wish me to prepare some?"

"I do not."

"You would not also wait on children?" Now there was something hopeful about Christophe, as if Maxen's desire to soon begin a family proved his intentions were as claimed.

Though inclined to brush aside his brother's question and let him believe what he would, Maxen had too much felt and needed—perhaps more than Christophe—their brotherly embrace in the wood. For nothing would he undo what good was being done between them.

"I would not wait on children," he began.

But perhaps The Bloodlust Warrior of Hastings should, the thought once more inserted itself.

"As told," he continued, "Rhiannyn is and shall ever be my wife. Ere she shared her concern, it occurred to me that though William would feel no compunction in bargaining away my leman, were Rhiannyn to become pregnant, it would strengthen my claim upon her. The king would not like it, but he would be more amenable to allowing one of his nobles to assert his right to the mother of a child he wished to name his own—and, thus, more easily forgive me for wedding her without permission."

"Indeed," Christophe said, and Maxen nearly laughed at the wonder on his face. Christophe saw the merit of it. But now...

"However," Maxen said, "Rhiannyn's concerns are real, and I would not have her or our child suffer for what would be thought and spoken against them while our marriage remains hidden."

The wonder slipped away. "But you say you do not wish her to take the preparation."

"As it can harm an unborn child, I do not trust it. Thus, I want your word that if she asks for it, you will deny her."

"I would prefer to, Maxen, but unless you intend to abstain—"

"There are other ways, and likely as effective as your medication. Of this I have assured her."

Christophe blushed. "Ah."

"I have your word?"

He inclined his head.

Maxen gripped his shoulder. "I did not think I would ever be grateful you called me out of the Church, but I am. And I pray that if you wish it, you shall remain at Etcheverry with Rhiannyn and me."

Throat convulsing, the youth bobbed his chin. "I thank you. Truly."

Maxen was prepared to embrace him, but the Saxon groaned, and Christophe hurried to him.

For a time, Maxen watched his brother tend Hob, and when he stepped outside and smelled the coming winter, the cold did not worry him as much as it had.

34

THE PARCHMENT FELL from Maxen's hand. Before it hit the floor, it had rolled back on itself.

Sensing the gravity of the missive, Rhiannyn motioned for the scattered knights and servants to clear the hall. She did it with little thought, realizing only after they began withdrawing that they had responded as if she were the lady of the castle as she was not yet acknowledged to be. Though with Maxen's prompting, she was growing into the role, it surprised her that his men had complied without hesitation. As if they fully accepted the orders of a leman.

"What is it?" she asked when Maxen and she were alone.

He gave her his gaze where she stood alongside him, but that was all.

With greater foreboding, she bent, retrieved the parchment, and read the Norman French that was all the more difficult to decipher due to the heavy scrawl.

Frustrated, she looked to Maxen. "Tell me."

He sat back in his chair. "It speaks of Edwin Harwolfson."

Fear gripped her. "King William summons you?"

"He does not," he said, and she saw the color of wrath crawl up his neck.

"What, then?"

"Over a fortnight past, my sister, Elan, was caught outside the castle walls and set upon by a Saxon."

"I am sorry," she gasped. "Was she badly hurt?"

The color ran into Maxen's face and hair. "She was ravished."

Rhiannyn clamped her teeth onto her lower lip. Much she knew of ravishment from when the Normans had attacked her village, though she had been spared personal knowledge of it. Hence, hearing Maxen's sister had suffered violation stirred the pain of her past.

"I am sorry," she said again.

"You are also blind!" He leapt from his chair and began pacing the dais.

"What say you?"

He swung around. "I told the missive speaks of the one to whom you were betrothed, revealed my sister's ravishment, and yet you see no connection."

In that moment she did, and it nearly stole her breath. "It cannot be. I vow it cannot!"

Suddenly, Maxen was before her, the savage in him lifting its head. "Harwolfson was in the area, he is as Elan described, and she tells that when she guessed it was he, he did not deny it."

Rhiannyn stepped back. "Either someone posing as Edwin did the deed and she is mistaken, or she lies."

"You said Hastings changed Harwolfson."

"Not in that way!"

Fury visible in every line of his body, heard in his every breath, Maxen stared at her. But as the moment stretched, something else rose through him and forced the savage down.

Though still a menacing figure, there was control in his voice when he asked, "How can you be certain?"

"I know the good of Edwin, and enough of the bad to assure you that, at his worst, he would do no such thing."

He leaned nearer. "If she lies, for what gain?"

"I do not know, but whatever happened to her, I vow Edwin did not ravish her."

"And I vow, if he did, come spring he will pay with his life."

Finding some comfort in his concession Edwin might not be responsible, she asked, "What of Elan? Was she not to wed soon?"

He swung away, dropped into his chair, and retrieved the missive. He read the remainder of it. And cursed beneath his breath. "Here is the reason only now I am told what befell her. The man to whom she was recently promised has broken the betrothal."

"I do not understand."

"Because you do not understand my father. He does not tell it, but I see it. My sister's ruin was not to have been known lest it threaten what was to have been an advantageous marriage. I would guess her betrothed learned of her loss of virtue either by way of loose tongues or suspicion over my father's attempt to move up the wedding the easier to pass off an ill-gotten child as legitimate."

"I see." And she did not like it for what it said of his sire.

Maxen was silent a long while, then said, "I think it wrong to wed her to a man who could be her father thrice over. Thus, though never would I wish upon her the ill that befell her, mayhap it will make a better future for her once all is known." He looked up. "And so my father waits."

On whether or not a child had been made on Elan. A child who would be named a *bastard,* just as one born of Rhiannyn might have been had she missed her menses. She had not, and hopefully, would not until it was known she was the rightful lady of Etcheverry.

"If she is with child," Rhiannyn ventured, "what will your father do?"

"Send her away until it is born."

To a convent, where the illegitimate children of nobles were often left behind so the mothers could return to their lives, however changed they might be after so evident an indiscretion.

"Then," Maxen continued, "he will find her another marriage that benefits our family."

"Will he seek revenge against Edwin?"

Maxen's smile was caustic. "There is no greater sport he enjoys than vengeance, no better thrill than blood on his blade." The muscles in his jaw worked. "As told, he taught me well."

Though she was certain he and his father were not of the same ilk, the man Maxen had become at Hastings and nearly again upon his brother's death, was better explained.

"What will he do?" she asked.

"Bide his time."

"He will not try to gain William's ear?"

"You misunderstand. Likely, the king received news of Elan's spoiling before I. With the betrothal broken, my father will think naught of casting further dishonor upon her by making known what happened. He will have his revenge, and it will be sweeter with others cheering him on."

She shuddered. "I do not think I would like to meet your father."

"If I can keep him from our walls, you will not."

It seemed always there was something new to worry over. "Will you make me a promise, Maxen?"

His lids narrowed. "Ask it."

"I would have you work no revenge on Edwin until you know the truth of what was done to your sister."

"Rhiannyn, I know it pains you to hear this, but whether or not Harwolfson did what is told, his death will be sought. The only question is the manner in which his life is forfeit."

True, for hardly a day passed without word of his raids and pillaging. Three days past, a messenger from the north had stopped at Etcheverry to rest his horse and replenish his food and drink. While at Maxen's table, he had spoken of his lord's wooden castle set afire by Edwin and his growing army of Saxons. It was this news he was to deliver to King William, and a pleading for aid to fight the ruthless Saxon *wolf*. And yesterday, news had come that the king had raised the reward for the one who brought him Edwin's head. It was a staggering amount.

Aye, Edwin's death would be sought even were he innocent of ravishment, but Rhiannyn was not certain his death would be gained—providing she could prevent Maxen from being the one to confront him.

"Promise me," she pressed.

"Do I meet him again, I will give him a chance to prove he did not do what is said of him."

She leaned down and put her lips to his cheek. "I know you do it for me." Just as he had set free Aethel and the others, just as he had several times visited the bedside of Hob and assured him he could leave Etcheverry whenever he wished. That last made Rhiannyn smile. Having believed himself dead by way of a Pendery, Hob acknowledged the scar he would ever bear was not of Maxen's doing and had begun to hint he might remain here.

Maxen sighed. "Do I do it for you, Rhiannyn?"

She pulled back. "Do you not?"

His smile showed few teeth, but it was real. "Anything for you."

Soul reaching toward his, she also smiled.

35

~~~

ANOTHER MONTH PASSED, and fall fell into winter with the arrival of one who came without warning.

Upon a chill wind, a dozen riders descended upon Etcheverry and were allowed within its walls. Though the demeanor of the pretty young woman at the center of her escort suggested shame, often she lifted downcast eyes and peered around with childlike excitement.

"You are welcome at Etcheverry," Maxen said, lifting his sister from her mount.

As she settled on her feet, she peeked up at him. "I fear it is not good tidings I bring."

"I guessed as much. We shall speak of it later."

"Elan!" Christophe pushed his way toward his sister and embraced her. "Years," he said.

"Too many," she agreed.

He looked at her head to toe. "You have grown!"

A smile leapt to her lips, but she put it away as if remembering it was not fitting. "As have you," she said in a soft voice that did not agree with the glimpses thus far afforded of her.

Mayhap I look too hard, Rhiannyn thought. *Mayhap I want too much to find something that is not here, something to prove she speaks false about Edwin.*

Unfortunately, it was hard to be fair to one she had come to resent these past weeks. As Maxen had predicted, his father had dishonored his daughter by making public what had befallen her. Now word was among knights, men-at-arms, and servants that Edwin Harwolfson had defiled Elan Pendery.

Maxen motioned his father's knights to dismount. "Wine and mead await you in the hall. Come warm yourselves."

It was a quiet procession that ascended to the donjon, Rhiannyn walking behind Elan who was flanked by her brothers, the others following farther back. But once inside the hall, voices rose and became a clamor as drink commenced flowing.

While warmed wine was served at the high table, those seated around Maxen watched the young woman in their midst.

"Elan," Maxen said, "I present Rhiannyn of Etcheverry."

Rolling the goblet between her hands, his sister moved her gaze to the woman beside her brother. "Of Etcheverry?"

"*Oui,* she was of this place before it was Pendery."

"She is Saxon."

"I am," Rhiannyn answered for herself.

Interest lit the young woman's eyes, but she veiled it by fluttering her lashes down. When she lifted her lids, her eyes were still. "What does she here at your side, Brother?"

"Rhiannyn serves as lady of the castle."

Elan glanced at Rhiannyn's left hand. "Yet she possesses not your name. To share a bed with a man does not make one a lady. It makes one a…" She gave what sounded a nervous laugh, though discomfort did not reach her eyes.

Rhiannyn let the spark in her rise to flame. "Ah," she said, "but I also share his bath."

From Maxen's stiffening, she knew he was as angered by her bold claim as his sister's malice.

But there was one who found humor in Rhiannyn's frankness, she who had little to gladden her since Christophe had wearied of her lack of dependability and replaced her with Meghan. Reduced to cleaning and serving at table, Theta was more spiteful than ever, looks more slaying, words more cutting. Now she snickered, sloshing ale over a knight's hand as she poured, but whatever angry words he unleashed upon her were lost beneath Maxen's.

"Rhiannyn is the lady, Elan," he said, "and while you reside at Etcheverry, you will show her the respect accorded to one in her position."

His sister opened her mouth, but Christophe said, "Elan, allow me to introduce Sir Guy Torquay." He gestured at the knight beside him.

Elan snapped her teeth closed and turned to her younger brother.

Refusing to meet Maxen's gaze, Rhiannyn looked past him to his favored knight who, for once, appeared interested in something other than duty to his liege.

"Sir Guy," Elan said. "I..." Her voice trailed off, and she swung her gaze back to Rhiannyn. "I know your name! You are the one Thomas wished to wed." She sucked a breath. "The one who led him to his death."

Feeling Maxen's tension rise, Rhiannyn said, "It is true Thomas wished to wed me."

"That is all you have to say? No apology for being the cause of his death?"

"As she is not responsible," Maxen said, "she can hardly accept the burden of it."

His words rooted Rhiannyn to the bench. Elan, however, shot up from hers, causing heads to turn. Eyes losing their studied demureness, she spat, "You, Thomas's brother, defend her?"

"Seat yourself," Maxen ordered.

She drew a whistling breath, teetered, and dropped back onto the bench.

"When you have finished your drink," Maxen said, "you and I will talk of the reason you have come to Etcheverry."

She huffed. "Surely you already know."

"Later," he growled.

Touched by his open defense of her, Rhiannyn hardly noticed what followed.

But Maxen was beyond aware of the next hour. Ignoring the pull of the woman at his side, he watched his little sister and assessed all she had come to be since last he had seen her more than two years past. She had been reckless then, quick and sharp of tongue, but the woman she was fast becoming—or perhaps not so fast becoming—seemed to have magnified every one of her undesirable traits.

She was well acted, he conceded as he attended to her conversation with Sir Guy and Christophe. Of greater concern, she was overly adept at drawing men's notice. Though Guy was mostly immune to the advances of women, deciding for himself when and where he would better know one who caught his eye, his usually set face reflected rapt interest in Elan's smiles, fluttering lashes, and husky voice.

It caused Maxen to entertain the possibility Rhiannyn was correct in defending Harwolfson against the charge of ravishment. But why would his sister claim such?

"You are finished," he said when Elan emptied the last of her drink.

"One more," she implored and raised her goblet to be refilled.

"You have had enough." He took the vessel from her, set it on the table, and stood.

She looked as if she might protest, but when he took her arm and raised her beside him, she lowered her eyes. "As you will, Brother."

Within the privacy of his chamber, Maxen held out a hand. "The missive."

Elan removed it from the pouch at her waist and, grimacing, placed it in his palm.

"The seal is broken," he said.

She shrugged. "As it concerns me, I saw no reason why I should not read it."

Maxen raised an eyebrow. "What does it say?"

She lowered her gaze. "Why do you not read it yourself?"

"I shall, but for now, save me the trouble."

When next she met his gaze, it was with long-suffering eyes. "As you know, I was..." She squeezed her eyes closed, drew a breath, lifted her lids. "I was ravished."

Though he suspected her pain was not as deeply felt as she would have him believe, his compassion stirred. "I have heard."

Tears forming, she launched herself into his arms. "It was terrible. The most awful thing!"

Inwardly, Maxen groaned. Despite his doubts, this was his sister, and if she was truly hurting, he had no right to deny her comfort. He wrapped his arms around her. "No more can he harm you."

She angled her head back to peer at him. "Is it a promise you make?"

"It is. Whoever did this will not go unpunished."

"Whoever?" She shook her head. "It was Harwolfson. Did Father not write it to you?"

"He did."

"Then why do you not acknowledge it was he? I do not lie in this, Maxen."

He hoped not—or did he? Was it better his sister was truthful, or Rhiannyn was right about Harwolfson?

"I have not said you lie, Elan. It is just that Rhiannyn does not believe him capable of such an offense. She submits it must have been another who disguised himself as Harwolfson."

"Rhiannyn!" She jumped away and strode across the chamber and back. "She who was betrothed to the Saxon rebel. Of course she defends him."

"I also met Harwolfson," Maxen said, "and neither did he seem to me one who would behave in that manner."

Elan swung around. "You do not know him as I do," she snapped, then her face fell and she pressed a hand to her belly. "Of course you do not."

"Are you with child, Elan?" Maxen asked, though he knew it was so by way of her—

What? he asked himself.

Performance, he silently named it, recalling the girl who had darted about the castle while her brothers swung swords. With exaggerated emotions and behavior, she had vied for attention, and it appeared the years had not matured that out of her.

She dropped her hand from her belly. "*Oui,* your ravished sister is pregnant."

Maxen considered her. "You seem not as disturbed as I would expect."

She gasped. "What would you have me do? Put a dagger to my wrist? Throw myself from a cliff? Never! I will bear this misbegotten child and..."

"What?"

He saw struggle in her eyes, and he hoped it was evidence of a conscience. But the indulgence of youth so firmly a part of her trampled the responsibility of an adult when she said, "I will give the babe to the Church to raise as God wills it."

"As easy as that?"

She laughed derisively. "Surely you do not suggest I keep the child of a man who violated me?"

"I suggest naught. I simply ask. But tell, why come to Etcheverry rather than enter a convent?"

She nodded at the missive. "Read it."

Maxen tapped the parchment against his thigh, but did not unroll it.

She sighed. "Father would have sent me to a convent, but I begged him to send me to you for the duration."

"Why?"

She rolled her eyes. "Me in a convent? I would die of boredom or be mercilessly berated—perhaps flogged—for some little thing I said."

"You think I will not do the same?"

She sharpened her eyes upon him, attempted to draw a smile from him with her own, but when he remained unmoved, she said softly, "Would you?"

"Do not test me, Elan. You are welcome here, but if you wreak havoc on my household, I will send you to the nearest convent. Understood?"

Though resentment flared in her eyes, she inclined her head.

Still, he was certain she would unsettle his household, but after chastising himself for the chance he took in allowing her to pass her pregnancy beneath his roof, he said, "Now the rules."

She groaned.

And he began listing the things he would not allow, and what would be expected of her.

She had barely considered she might become pregnant. After all, she had more than once lain with Royden, her father's man-at-arms, before duping Edwin Harwolfson into taking the blame for her loss of virtue.

Feeling sick down to her toes for all that had gone awry, Elan turned on the pallet which had been overstuffed to accommodate her condition and stared at the shadowed ceiling.

Ah, the lie of it, she silently lamented as she thought back to the day she had begun this ruse. Following her tryst with Harwolfson, she had ridden back to the castle with well-placed rips in her gown, tangled hair, and scratched face and limbs. She had thrown herself at her father's feet, and between his shouts that ascended to the beams above and the heavens beyond, blubbered all of what had befallen her.

But though she had done well to make herself look ravished, she had not thought to stain her skirts with blood. Thus, harboring hope her chastity remained intact enough to give her the appearance of purity so her betrothed would not question it, her father had summoned a physician. In the presence of Elan's mother, the man had made his examination.

Recalling when he had straightened and looked into her eyes, Elan shuddered. In his own eyes had shone suspicion that the one accused of ravishing her had not been the first to have her. But perhaps because he was so staunchly Norman, he had not revealed her. Rather, he had muttered about the necessity of cleansing England of the barbarian Saxons.

When her sire was told she was no longer a maiden, his raging against Edwin Harwolfson had resounded around the hall. Then his wrath had turned from the Saxon rebel to her. And her mother against whom she huddled—a woman of pitifully weak disposition—had spoken not a word in defense of her daughter.

As the lord of Trionne whipped Elan with his tongue for riding une-scorted outside the walls, his wife had simply patted and stroked and hushed her. There had been nothing affected about Elan's tears then, for never had she been so harshly spoken to, nor so near to being struck. When her father's fury eased, he had set in motion plans to see her wed earlier than what had been negotiated lest a child grew in her. Providing her betrothed had agreed, a hidden vial of blood on their wedding night would have proved she had come to him a maiden. He had not agreed.

Elan's father had counted on the man's old age to make him ripe for deception. But his years made him wise, and his suspicions caused him to break the betrothal.

She had been secretly relieved, for though her ploy had been a means of absolving her of responsibility for her loss of virtue, she had dared to dream she would also be absolved of being bound to a withered old man whose bones creaked beneath flaccid skin and muscle and whose hands upon her would surely make her heave.

Thereafter, the wait began to see if the handsome Saxon rebel she had invited to put his hands on her had gotten her with child.

A sob escaped Elan. If her belly had not swelled, she might have persuaded her father to make a better match for her, might even now be wed to one befitting her youth and beauty. But even when this babe was out of her and out of sight, it would not be easy to wed well, for though talk of her ruin might be overcome, there would be other whispers that reached ears she would rather they did not.

She swiped moisture from her cheeks, hating what tears wreaked upon her face—flushing it an unbecoming color, puffing her eyes red and sore until she could barely see past narrow slits.

No need to cry, she told herself. Once she birthed Harwolfson's brat, she could begin anew—providing she survived the birthing. She slid her hands down her hips and wished them a bit wider. She was not such a small thing, but the physician had warned birthing would be difficult.

Another sob escaped, and she silently cursed the Saxon rebel for being so virile it took but one encounter to impregnate her. Next, she cursed him for being so tall and broad that his child would likely be of a size that further endangered her life.

"Lady Elan, are you well?" asked one whose voice vibrated through her.

She swung her head around and found the attractive face of Sir Guy before her where he crouched beside her pallet. Had her sobs awakened him, causing him to rise from his own pallet in the hall?

She breathed in, liked the smell of him. "I am well."

"I heard you crying."

She shrugged. "I am sad."

"To have left Trionne?"

"That is some of it." Not truly, for she did not miss her father's glower, air of disgust, and harsh words.

"What is the rest of it?" Sir Guy asked.

Something inside her shifted, took a peek, and began to blossom beneath his concern. Opening her throat a bit, the better to answer on a husky breath men found so appealing, she said, "Has my brother not told you?"

"*Non,* lady."

He would know soon enough, she thought, her hand drifting to her belly that would not long remain flat. She sat up. "We should speak elsewhere." Away from those with whom they shared the hall's sleeping quarters.

Sir Guy held out a hand. "I know a place."

The moment his fingers closed over hers, she was certain of one thing—she liked his touch.

When they gained an alcove across the hall, he released her.

Wishing he had not, for she might better gauge his reaction with his hand upon her, she said, "I am…" She caught her breath. "…with child."

Though her words must have shocked him, it was too dark in the alcove to catch his expression. "I see."

She sniffed. "*Non,* Sir Knight, you do not." She let a long moment pass. "It is not any misbegotten child I carry. It is…" This time, her pause was not planned, her pending revelation flushing her with shame she had previously experienced in small measure. "It is the *wolf's* child."

"As expected."

Elan felt a sinking in her center. Though she was aware her father had made it known Harwolfson had ravished her, she had not expected the news to spread so soon so far. Nor had she expected to regret it as much as she now did. Why? How could this man make her feel vile when she should not care what he thought of her? He was just another man, no different from Royden.

"I understand your loathing, Sir Guy," she said, unable to keep resentment from her voice. "I shall return to my sleep."

He pulled her back. "I do not loathe you, for surely you are not to blame for the babe."

No other, she silently admitted. "*Non,* I am not," she spoke perhaps her hundredth lie on the subject of her violation.

He nodded. "Harwolfson will pay for what he did. This I vow."

Though she shrugged off guilt as she had many times, it always left enough residue to easily return. Doubtless, either by her father's hand, her brother's, or this knight's, her lover would pay a debt he did not owe. And all because she had needed to explain her lack of virtue. Still, Edwin Harwolfson had been a dead man long before she had named him a ravisher. Regardless of her accusation, he would die for his rebellion against the Normans. Thus, she was not to blame.

Conscience easing again, she asked, "Why would you take up my cause, Sir Guy?"

"If you wish it, lady, I would be your friend."

Friend? That was all?

For shame, Elan Pendery, she silently chastised. *You carry a misbegotten child and already your mind turns to taking another man into your bed.*

She summoned her prettiest smile, hoped some of it would be seen. "Then friends we shall be."

"Friends," he affirmed.

Oddly moved by his offer, she walked beside him to her pallet. "Good eve," she said as she settled beneath her blanket.

He reached down and pushed the hair off her brow, a stirring gesture for all its seeming innocence. "Good eve, lady."

For a long time, she stared at where he bedded down. Then, smiling, she gave over to sleep and its lovely dreams.

36

"SHE IS GONE," Maxen said.

Rhiannyn turned from Lucilla to her husband who entered the hall. Leaving the vapor of his warm breath in the cold morning air outside, he pushed the door closed and continued toward her.

"You speak of Theta?" she said, thinking he must have heard her ask Lucilla about the woman's whereabouts.

"I do." He halted before her.

Lucilla murmured something and hurried away.

"Where has Theta gone?" Rhiannyn asked.

"I have sent her with my father's men. On their journey to Trionne, they will deliver her to Blackspur Castle."

"Why?"

"She has plagued you long enough, and I will have no more of her lies filling the corners of Etcheverry."

Rhiannyn smiled. She knew he accepted it was Theta who had lied about the Saxons revolting against him, but it was good to hear it. And better she would no longer suffer the woman's jealousy.

"Does Sir Guy know you have sent her to Blackspur?"

Maxen unfastened the brooch holding his mantle closed. "He knows, though as you have guessed, he is not pleased." He drew the mantle from his shoulders and draped it over an arm. "As tempting as it was to turn Theta out and let her fend for herself, it seemed cruel—even for her."

"I thank you, both for removing her from Etcheverry and giving her another place to go."

"I fear she is not grateful."

"She shall be when the cold of winter is full upon us."

Maxen nodded. "She will be Sir Guy's problem when he takes his place as castellan. Let us hope he deals well with her."

Ravisher!

Edwin had kept his face impassive throughout the telling of his latest atrocity, but now, alone amid trees and lurking woodland creatures, he loosed his fury.

"Jezebel!" he shouted. "Harlot! She-devil!"

Words. Only words. And not one adequately expressed his rage.

There was at least some truth in being named a knave, a miscreant, a pillager, even a savage, but to be branded a ravisher!

He had not and would never take a woman by force, especially the one he now knew was Elan Pendery.

For days after she had given herself to him in the wood, he had knocked his mind senseless pondering her motive for seducing one she had known was an enemy of her people, but the answer had evaded him then as it did now. Worse, the mystery was further clouded by her calling what had happened between them ravishment. Curse her to—

"Hell," Dora said in her grating voice.

Edwin swung around. How did she do it? How was she, of bent and aged body, able to move so quietly over the obstacle-strewn floor of the wood? More, how had she known his thoughts?

She smiled, revealing a new gap in her top teeth. "One day, you will have to accept I am who I am, Edwin."

A sorceress? Nay, she saw and knew things others did not because she was watchful and perceptive. "I do not believe in such things," he said.

"How can you say that when I put breath back into you after it was gone?"

With less patience than the other times he had refuted her claim, Edwin snapped, "There was yet breath in me when you pulled me from beneath the others."

Her pocked nostrils flared. "Did I not foretell you would be the one to free your people and England of Normans?"

He widened his stance. "It has yet to be known if, under my direction, the Normans will be vanquished."

As if he had not refuted that as well, she continued, "It was I who showed you the truth of Rhiannyn. A truth now proven."

Was it? If Aethel and the others were to be believed, she had not abandoned her people, had only yielded when given no choice. Yet what of the one lost to an arrow through the back? Had Rhiannyn known what Maxen Pendery planned?

"She knew," Dora answered.

Edwin shot his gaze to her. "You read me well, Dora, and perhaps you are gifted with seeing and making sense of what others cannot, but that is all."

She advanced and halted before him. "Aye, I have sight, though you know well I possess more. I have the power—"

"Enough!" He would not be drawn further into her web, certain that to do so would be to consort with the devil's own. Not for the first time, he wondered why he did not send her away. He longed to, but something kept him from doing so.

"She will bear you a son, Edwin," Dora said in a conspiratorial tone.

He frowned. "Rhiannyn?"

She grunted with disgust. "'Tis the harlot I speak of—Elan Pendery."

He was too taken aback to remind her she had also named Rhiannyn a harlot. Was it possible his tryst in the wood had made a babe? "A son," he murmured and was disconcerted when the possibility of fathering a child tugged at a part of him he had thought trampled beneath hatred and revenge.

"Heed me well," Dora said. "He cannot be allowed to live."

"What?" Edwin barked. "You suggest I murder my own child?"

"It matters not by whose hand, only that 'tis done."

"You go too far, old woman!" Edwin curled his fingers into fists. "Be gone ere I rid myself of you forever."

Her pink eyes widened. "The child will be Norman!"

"*If* there is one, by my blood, he will be Saxon."

"It takes but one drop of Norman blood to foul the entire child."

Edwin found nothing enjoyable about killing another, but in that moment, the thought of snapping her ugly neck appealed to everything ill in him. "I will not tell you again." He thrust a hand to her chest.

Dora stumbled back, nearly tangling her feet in her trailing mantle. "All I have done for you!" she cried. "I gave you back your life, not only at Hastings, but when Thomas Pendery—" She gurgled on the spit she sucked into her lungs.

All came together then, and Edwin knew he should not be surprised. "'Twas you who threw the dagger."

She eyed him. "I killed him."

He felt chill fingers skim his every limb. Mayhap she was, indeed, a witch, for how else could such a wizened body have the strength to toss a stick ten feet, let alone hurl a weapon twenty or more feet and make its mark?

"Why?" he asked.

Her tongue flicked between her teeth, wet her bottom lip. "He meant to kill you, and I could not allow it—not after all I gave to put life back into you."

It was true that with the injury Thomas Pendery had dealt him, he would likely have died by the man's sword. But now, as then, Edwin found no pleasure or pride in his enemy's death.

"You are owing to me," Dora said.

"I owe you naught! Most especially, I do not owe you the life of my son."

"Such a little thing, Edwin. 'Tis all I ask."

He reached for her.

"You have been warned!" she shrieked and hastened away.

When she was gone, he dropped his chin to his chest. He was weary—of everything that had anything to do with blood and battle, of running, pillaging, and wondering when the usurper would overtake him.

More than anything, he was weary of the evil the old woman breathed into his life.

37

April, 1069

WINTER MELTED INTO spring, and with the passing of Easter, word came of King William's victory at York over the rebel forces that attacked the city and castle there. But of Edwin Harwolfson and his insurgents, it was said they were not present—thus, not among those who had fallen to the king.

Strangely, Edwin had been quiet these past months, and rumors abounded. It was said he amassed weapons not by thievery alone, but through forging; many of his men possessed horses to ride into battle; his followers numbered in excess of a thousand; their training was merciless and patterned after the Normans. But what was true and what was not could only be speculated upon. And worried over.

The king had yet to pull Maxen into his contest to keep England under his control, but the day approached, and each day until then was but temporary reprieve.

Although winter was past, there were still grumbling bellies, but no one at Etcheverry went unfed. The food was rationed for every man, woman, and child, an extra measure allowed for women who carried unborn babes, including Elan. But Maxen's sister partook little of what was set before her, almost as if she hoped to starve the growing child out of her. However, it would not be easily cast aside, pressing forward into the world until all knew by sight of Elan's pregnancy.

The young woman was an enigma, one Rhiannyn steered clear of as much as possible, and not just because she lied about Edwin.

Elan could be pleasant enough when it suited her, but for all her quick wit and childlike charm, she was better known for her bouts of moodiness and ability to be at once fetching and offensive. Thus, she alienated many—though not Sir Guy.

The knight was surprisingly tolerant of her moods, and a humor not apparent before showed itself when Elan needed coaxing out of a particularly low spirit. And if one looked closely, one might even glimpse adoration in his eyes.

As Elan grew rounder, her tirades worsened despite Sir Guy's support. Something festered in her. Still, it was a surprise what passed in the hall on a cool spring day.

As the nooning meal neared its end, she thrust to her feet. "I hear you!" she cried. "All of you whispering behind your hands. And you!" She pointed at Meghan, who stood with pitcher poised above a tankard. "You dare speak ill of me! You who cast your favors about as generously as one casts herbs upon rushes."

"A lie!" Meghan shrilled. Though she had been intimate with a knight here and there, she did not suffer Theta's reputation, especially now that she and Hob—the Saxon felled by Sir Ancel's arrow—were moving toward marriage.

"Lady Elan!" Sir Guy called, stepping from the hearth where he and a handful of knights had gathered.

"Ill fortune upon your heads!" she spat. "A pox on you all!"

"Elan!" Maxen commanded her to silence.

"Think you I require your respect? I do not!" She pressed a hand to her belly. "This babe is misbegotten, but so are many of you. What have I to be ashamed of when my son is of the Saxon who will bring you to your knees?"

Rhiannyn made it to her side before Maxen and Sir Guy and cautiously laid a hand to her arm. "You are tired," she said low. "Come and rest on your brother's bed."

Elan jerked free. "And what of you?" she spat. "You who seem most proud to be my brother's harlot—"

"Enough!" Maxen pulled her away from Rhiannyn.

"I am not finished!"

"My lord," Sir Guy entreated, "if you would allow me, perhaps I can settle your lady sister."

Elan rounded on him. "Think you I am a dog to be patted into submission and set aside? I want no more of your understanding!"

Hurt rose on the knight's face. And was gone. "Fine," he said. "Muck about in your self-pity all you like. I am done with you."

As he strode toward the men he had left in coming to her aid, Elan stared after him with eyes wide and mouth agape.

"I have also had enough," Maxen said and pulled her toward his chamber.

She wrenched free, and in a high, miserable voice, cried, "Sir Guy!"

He did not look back.

"To my chamber," Maxen said, once more taking hold of her, "and from there, the convent."

She strained away, but he pulled her after him.

Moved by the young woman's despairing face as she struggled to keep her champion in sight, Rhiannyn hastened after Maxen. "My lord," she said as she came alongside, "what harm in allowing Lady Elan to talk with Sir Guy?"

"Harm?" he said with unbroken stride. "What good? I ask. He speaks to her every whim, indulges her when a firm hand is more needed, and tries to understand what cannot be understood."

"Mayhap—"

"Mayhap naught! I am sick of all this coddling. It ends this day."

Rhiannyn jumped in front of him. "I beseech thee, let her speak with him. She...needs him."

As he stared at her, she glimpsed softening about his features others might not notice. But it was a face she now knew well.

"Pray, Maxen, allow me," Elan begged.

Sir Guy was before the doors when his lord called him back. With obvious resentment, he returned. "My lord?"

"My sister asks you to lend her an ear. Are you willing?"

"I am not." His jaw shifted. "But for you, my liege, I shall listen."

Maxen looked to his sister. "End this, Elan, else ready yourself for the convent."

"We will speak outside," Sir Guy said and led her toward the great doors.

Rhiannyn watched them go from sight, then turned her regard upon her husband. She was pleased his anger had receded to the point he wore a slight smile.

"Only for you," he said. And it could not be more true, Maxen thought. If not for Rhiannyn, he would have unleashed the words building in him these past months, and which he had nearly shouted when his sister thought to name Rhiannyn a harlot. Without waiting for a full day's light, he might even have sent Elan on to the convent. Only for Rhiannyn.

He stepped near, said low, "Might my wife join me in our chamber?"

He liked her slow smile. It invited kisses. Cupping her elbow, he led her around the screen, and when she slipped into his arms, he accepted her invitation. And more.

Afterward, when she lay with her head on his chest, hair spilled over him, his thoughts went where they were wont to go. As he had assured her, he had not made a babe on her all these months as evidenced by her regular menses. But with each passing day, more and more he loathed the waiting that prevented him from acknowledging her as his wife and seeing their child in her arms.

He was not certain he could have managed it as long as he had if his men, the castle folk, and her people had not quickly accepted she was no ordinary leman. Of course, some had been resistant to showing respect, but a blackened eye or bruised jaw greatly improved their dispositions. More, Rhiannyn made the waiting tolerable. Despite her initial misgivings, she had settled into the role, and he took it as a sign of trust. And she had good cause to trust him.

Regardless of what the king determined, no matter what loss might be suffered, he would not give her up. He wanted his Saxon bride for all the days to come, to make children upon her, and grow old with her. He wanted the waiting done.

"I thank you, Husband," she whispered.

He gently pulled his fingers through the curls turned around them and settled his hand to the small of her back. "For my lady's desire," he murmured.

She lifted her face to his, scowled playfully. "I speak not of that, but of Elan and Guy."

"Elan," he groaned, wishing talk of her had been allowed to lie a bit longer. "What am I to do with her?"

"Methinks much depends on Sir Guy."

"You think he can straighten her crookedness?"

"If anyone can."

"Why do you care so much, Rhiannyn? Why, when she is mostly cool toward you and names you a harlot?"

She pushed up on an elbow and leaned forward, causing her hair to curtain their faces. "Because I know I am not one, as does my husband whose opinion matters most."

He touched her lower lip. "Regardless, she hardly deserves such kindness."

"I know she is difficult, but I feel for her."

"Though you believe she lies about Harwolfson?"

"If Edwin did, indeed, father her child, she *does* lie."

After these past months, Maxen was more inclined to believe his sister was a liar than Harwolfson a ravisher, but he kept it to himself. "Spring is upon us," he said, reminding her he would likely face Harwolfson across a battlefield before long.

She tensed. "So it is."

"There is something I need to ask you—about Harwolfson."

"I shall do my best to answer."

"What would it take to make peace with him?"

She caught her breath. "Even I have heard it is his death William seeks."

"Aye, but methinks I may be able to convince the king otherwise, providing I can also convince Harwolfson."

Rhiannyn sat up. "I thought you also sought his death."

"After all I have told you of Hastings?" He rose to sitting. "If there is a chance to prevent further bloodshed, that is the course I shall seek."

She nodded slowly. "But will William follow your course?"

If the king yet held him in high regard as he had following Hastings, it was possible. "Perhaps, but the first question to be answered is, what will it take to convince Harwolfson peace is the better way?"

Tears brightened Rhiannyn's eyes. "I knew you were worthy of heart."

Was he? Did his hope of peace with Harwolfson prove the savage of Hastings was worthy of being loved? That he was nearer to forgiving himself as she said he must? If he could prevent the battle between William and Harwolfson, might he be able to do so? More, might God finally forgive him his atrocities?

"What price Harwolfson's peace?" he asked again.

"I do not know. I but pray it is not so far gone he has no price."

"I understood he sought to reclaim Etcheverry."

"Aye, his family's lands, but I fear they no longer figure into his rebellion and it may take all of England to satisfy him." She bit her lower lip. "Are you saying you would give him Etcheverry?"

"If it would end his uprising and the king agrees, I would relinquish the lands and castles to him."

Not for the first time, he glimpsed something in Rhiannyn's eyes that should not be possible. Love? Or but deeply felt gratitude?

Love, he told himself, needing to believe it. Rhiannyn loved him.

"I believe you will succeed and bring peace to England," she said.

He shook his head. "Though Harwolfson's following numbers great, there are others who seek to oust the Normans. Thus, even if he can be reconciled to King William, the fighting will lessen, but it will not end. Not yet."

Rhiannyn's smile fell, but returned moments later. "There can be no end without a beginning, and that is what you will have if you convince William and Edwin to set aside their differences."

Maxen nodded. "There is something about Harwolfson I have long pondered. As a royal housecarle, he should have died alongside his king, yet he survived the death of his lord and returned to Etcheverry to mount his rebellion."

"So he did, though it is told he should be among the dead, not the living."

"Dora."

Rhiannyn startled. "You know."

He shrugged. "I know the rumor the old woman brought Harwolfson back to life after death had taken him."

"Perhaps."

"You discount the possibility he was truly dead?"

She fidgeted. "Edwin does not believe it. He always said there must have been life in him when she pulled him from beneath the others."

Then Harwolfson was more God-fearing than pagan, Maxen concluded. "How badly was he wounded?"

"He should have died for all the wounds sustained and blood lost, but Dora would not allow it—even when Edwin prayed for death so he might not suffer the disgrace of one who had survived his king on the battlefield."

"If that is so, why did he not end it himself when he was able?"

"I think he might have, but when he was well enough to walk the village and saw for himself what the Normans had wrought, something came over him."

"Revenge."

She nodded.

Maxen studied her face and the sorrow that had displaced what he hoped was love. "You have answered my questions well. I thank you."

She sighed, scooted down.

He urged her onto her side and pulled her back against him. As her breathing deepened, he found himself brooding over what he had learned. Harwolfson was a man of honor, but also revenge. Loyal to his own, but recklessly so. A Christian, yet one who kept a witch at his side. Stubborn, but able to bend—at least, slightly—when the occasion warranted.

For an hour or more, his mind spun with plotting, but finally he rose, turned the coverlet over Rhiannyn's sleeping figure, and clothed himself to go in search of Elan and Guy.

It was Christophe he found before a game of chess.

"I would call it love," said the youngest Pendery when he caught sight of his brother, and he moved a bishop across the board and captured a piece.

Longing for evidence Rhiannyn did feel love for him, Maxen said, "Of what do you speak?"

Christophe stood, crossed to the other side of the board, and seated himself. Gaze fixed on his game, he said, "Elan and Guy. Whom else would I be speaking of?"

Wily youth, Maxen mused. For certain, his words were not exclusive to Elan and Guy.

Christophe looked up. "Sir Guy and our sister have a great liking for each other."

Maxen dropped into the vacated chair. "What makes you think that?"

Christophe leaned back. "The way they gaze into each other's eyes, the way they hold hands. But what most convinced me was when they kissed."

"Kissed?" Maxen demanded.

"In the garden."

Maxen pushed to his feet, but Christophe stood and stepped into his path. "He is good for Elan. Do not take from her all that is holding her together."

"And let her further suffer the attentions of a man?" Maxen growled, uncaring others might hear.

"I assure you, these attentions she does not mind."

"It is unseemly."

"Only if he does not offer to wed her."

Maxen narrowed his lids. "You think he will?"

"I know he will."

"How?"

"I overheard him ask if she would grant him permission to approach our father and request her hand in marriage."

When Maxen did not respond, Christophe said, "It would be a good match."

For Elan, but Guy? "I do not know that I agree, Christophe."

"Agree or not, our unwed sister is with child, and Sir Guy cares for her though he is not the father. If he is willing, our father would be a fool not to accept him, for it is unlikely another worthy man will offer for her."

"You are right." What Maxen did not say was he would not wish to be the one who spent the remainder of his life with one such as Elan.

"Ah, see!" Christophe exclaimed and, as if his mind had remained half on his game, picked up a piece and moved it. "I have won!"

Maxen grinned. "Who lost?"

"My opponent, of course."

"But were you not your opponent?"

Christophe chuckled. "One must make do with what one has."

Maxen was not unaware of how solitary Christophe was in the absence of his medicines and patients, distanced from others not only by age but a lame body that made him more suited to books than weapons.

Swept by an increasingly familiar longing to be the brother he had not been to Christophe in a long time, he said, "What think you of playing me?"

The youth's eyes widened. "I think well of it!"

Rhiannyn awoke to laughter. She turned to Maxen, but found his warm body had become a cold spot.

More laughter pricked her ears. The indoor games and conversations of winter, though less so of spring, were not without mirth, so why did this laughter seem out of place?

She sat up and listened for the next outburst. This time it was met with the laughter of others, but at its center were the voices of Maxen and Christophe, their united laughter a new sound to her.

Hurriedly, she dressed and stepped into the hall. Before the hearth, a dozen men were gathered, their heads bent toward something.

"Pardon," Rhiannyn said as she eased her way into the group.

"Come see what my brother has done to me," Maxen said.

She glanced from him to the chess game, then to Christophe's exultant face. "I do not understand."

Maxen caught her hand and pulled her to his side. "Look at his cleverness."

He explained Christophe's moves that had cornered Maxen's king, but Rhiannyn heard little of it. She was too filled with joy at seeing these two grow closer, treating each other as brothers rather than the distant acquaintances they had seemed when she had first returned to Etcheverry.

"I am thoroughly beaten," Maxen said.

"Another match?" Christophe asked.

"You would see me on my knees twice in one day?" Maxen shook his head. "Perhaps on the morrow I will try again."

"Anyone else?" Christophe called to the others.

Shaking their heads, they began moving away.

Seeing Christophe's disappointment, Maxen said, "They fear you, 'tis all."

Christophe grinned. "I give them good reason."

"Rhiannyn?" said a soft, almost apologetic voice.

Rhiannyn turned. As it was the first time Elan had addressed her without anger, spite, or impatience, she stared.

"I would speak with you," Elan said.

Rhiannyn glanced at Maxen and Christophe and saw both appeared as surprised as she. "Now?"

Annoyance flashed in Elan's eyes. "If the time is not right, we can speak later."

Wondering what she was up to, for it was unlikely she was amiable for any reason other than personal gain, Rhiannyn said, "Let us speak now."

"Come with me outside?"

Rhiannyn sent Maxen a questioning look before following his sister from the donjon where none could listen in on their conversation.

"I wish to apologize," Elan said.

"For?" Rhiannyn blurted.

"Treating you ill."

Rhiannyn frowned. "Forgive me my confusion, but I had not thought you cared for my feelings."

"I do not much." Quickly, Elan added, "But I begin to."

"How so?"

"You convinced my brother to allow me to speak with Sir Guy. Thus, I owe you."

"That is all?"

Elan shrugged. "Methinks you are not so bad. You perform fairly well the duties of the lady of the castle, lend an ear to the servants when they pick at one another, and seem to make my brother happy, which makes him somewhat tolerable. Nay, you are not so bad."

Though not tactful, at least it was spoken. "I thank you, Elan."

Looking pleased, the young woman said, "That is all," and started to turn away.

Rhiannyn touched her arm. "I hope one day we can be friends."

Elan appeared taken aback, but said, "It is possible," and hurried into the hall.

38

June, 1069

MEGHAN SMELLED OF garlic, the odor so pungent Rhiannyn feared she would retch.

Raising a hand to stop the woman from speaking further, Rhiannyn said, "Tell Mildreth 'tis a good menu," and turned and walked as steadily as she could to the lord's chamber. Once around the screen, she dropped to the floor, crossed an arm over her abdomen, and lowered her head toward her knees.

"Nay," she groaned, "let it not be." But it was. She had feared it yesterday upon realizing a fortnight had passed without her monthly flux. Though part of her was gladdened by this further evidence—of which she had no need, she told herself—that Thomas's curse was only angry words, the part of her waiting to be acknowledged as Maxen's wife was awash in regret.

The nausea was slow to pass, twisting her insides, but finally her belly calmed.

Wiping moisture from her brow, she lifted her head. Here in this chamber was where she would birth the child she should not yet have made with Maxen. A joyous thing it ought to be—and might be if the wait was soon over.

And if he does not set you aside, spoke the voice of distrust that had become mostly a whisper these past months.

She shook her head. Maxen had given his word, and she had no reason to believe he did not speak true.

No reason? distrust argued, this time above a whisper. *Did he object when you told you wished to wait on children? Might he have been a bit too eager to agree—he, a noble who ought to be impatient to make heirs?*

"Cease," she rasped. Maxen might not love her, but he seemed content to have her in his life, made her feel cherished, and felt more for her than desire.

But all might change now you are with child, the voice slid in again.

Attempting the impossible—to think no more about the child growing in her—she stood. Paying her mind no heed, her hand pressed itself to her belly. She would be about a month pregnant, and as it was now June, the child would be born midwinter if it came into the world in a timely manner.

She dropped her hand to her side. Maxen had seemed certain his method of preventing pregnancy was as effective as Christophe's, but it had failed. Or perhaps it had never truly worked, and she was simply not easily impregnated.

Not that it mattered. She was with child, and she could not change that.

Naught that I am willing to do, she silently amended, having caught whispers of how one might terminate a pregnancy. Protectively, she wrapped both arms around her abdomen. The timing was ill, but the babe was Maxen and hers.

An exultant squeal from beyond the screen made her jump.

Elan, she realized when it came again, this time followed by Sir Guy's gruff laughter.

Rhiannyn stepped from behind the screen and located her sister-in-law and the knight where they stood before Maxen who had recently entered the hall and taken his seat at the high table. The others who had been present when Rhiannyn had retreated to the chamber were absent. Dismissed?

"What is it?" she asked as she drew even with Elan.

"He agrees!" Elan pointed to the parchment Maxen held. "My father agrees to the marriage."

Though Rhiannyn and Elan still had difficult moments, their relationship was tempered by understanding and tolerance. Hardly a friendship, but it was an improvement.

"I am happy for you." Rhiannyn moved her gaze from Elan's glowing face to the man who would wed her.

The knight nodded and Elan glowed more.

"We will begin preparation for the ceremony," Maxen said.

"Nay!" Elan squealed. "Not while I am round as a pig."

Maxen lifted an eyebrow. "You would postpone the wedding until after the child is born?"

She scoffed. "I will not be rushed into this. I wish a proper wedding, a proper gown, and a proper figure to display my finery."

Maxen leaned forward. "Your vanity will cast more ill upon this child than has already been." He looked at her swollen belly. "Though it is too late for any to believe the babe is Guy's, the sooner the ceremony is performed, the better."

"I am not keeping the child," Elan reminded him.

"Even though you are to wed?"

"Of course! It was ill-gotten on me, and I will not suffer its upbringing—nor ask Guy to suffer it."

"You are its mother, Elan."

"Not by choice."

Maxen shifted his gaze to his friend. "What think you?"

The knight, visibly uncomfortable with the question, answered stiltedly, "If Elan wished to keep the child, I would make it as good a father as I am capable of, but the decision is hers."

"There, you see," Elan said. "My decision."

Aching for the babe whose mother intended to abandon it, Rhiannyn wondered if it could be reared at Etcheverry with her own child.

"Very well." Maxen's tone was gruff with dislike. "The wedding will be stayed until after the child's birth. Now I have work to do."

Elan and Guy withdrew, but Rhiannyn remained, wanting to tell Maxen their wanted child was wrapped safe and warm inside her body. But the dissenting voice stirred up bile that made her swallow hard.

Maxen pulled a ledger in front of him, dipped a quill in ink, and looked to her.

Struggling against the impulse to once more seek evidence of her babe who might, at least for a time, be named misbegotten the same as Elan's, she curled her fingers into her palms.

"What is it, Rhiannyn?"

She blinked. "Naught. I simply forgot to leave."

While she inwardly sighed over her silly choice of words, he smiled. "Forgot to *leave?*"

She made a face. "Obviously, I am tired."

His eyebrows drew close. "You take too much upon yourself."

"Nay, I am just not sleeping well."

"I had not noticed."

"Worry not, a short lie down and I will be made right." She turned and started toward their chamber.

So fraught were her emotions that she did not hear Maxen move until he was upon her. He clasped her shoulder, pulled her around, and lowered his face near hers. "Are you with child, Rhiannyn?"

That he had so easily guessed the truth nearly undid her, but somehow she ordered her face to reflect disbelief rather than dismay. A good thing, for she was not ready to tell him—not when she must herself come to terms with the pregnancy, especially not with the looming battle between William and Edwin.

"With child?" She laughed. "A woman must miss her time of month for that to be true."

"You have not missed yours?"

How she hated the lie. "I have not."

"You are certain?"

"I am. Though my flow was light this past month, it was present." And he could not denounce it, for he had been absent from Etcheverry, having been called to Blackspur Castle to settle a dispute between the master mason and his workers.

Though she tried to quell a nervous swallow, there being too much suspicion in his eyes, it sounded between them. "As we agreed," she hastened to distract him, "'tis best we wait. Aye?"

Not that she wanted him to agree—not now—but she needed to send the questions from his mind until she was ready to reveal their child.

He did not agree, but neither did he disagree. "Go to your rest, then." He released her, but before she turned away, he said, "Rhiannyn?"

"Aye?"

"Were you to become pregnant in spite of our efforts to wait, you would tell me?"

"I would," she said and silently added, *Eventually.*

She could almost taste his lingering suspicion, but he inclined his head, pivoted, and returned to the high table.

Once behind the screen, Rhiannyn let her shoulders slump. "Lord, what am I to do?" she whispered.

The answer was spoken not to her ears, but to her heart. *Tell the truth. And soon.*

So he might all the sooner send you away, said that other voice.

She drew a deep breath. "On the morrow I will tell him. Aye, the morrow."

Maxen gripped the back of his neck and rubbed at muscles that had tightened during his exchange with his sister and Sir Guy. They had begun to ease when he had believed Rhiannyn might carry his child, but when she said she did not, they had tightened further.

Still, though it would mean she lied, it was possible she was pregnant. He was certain he had glimpsed guilt in her eyes and nervousness in the bob of her throat. Of course, perhaps he had merely seen what he wished to see—evidence she was with child. It was something he should not want, not while he still could not claim her as his wife nor prove the Maxen Pendery of Etcheverry was much changed from the one of Hastings.

"But I do want it," he rasped. He wanted the miraculous place beneath the hand he laid to Rhiannyn's belly at night to hold his child— and not just because the coming battle with Harwolfson breathed down his neck and he believed William would more readily accept his vassal's marriage. He wanted it because, if he was truly capable of love as Christophe believed, it was surely what he felt for his Saxon bride.

He closed his eyes. "I do want it," he said again, this time making it a prayer, then added, "if You deem me worthy."

39

ONCE THE CASTLE had settled into the routine of summer—the ripening of crops and fruit that, God willing, would make Etcheverry self-sufficient the next winter—Rhiannyn found time to take up her loom.

Sitting with Meghan and four other Saxon women she had enlisted to weave new cloth, she found good conversation with them. They talked, laughed, fell silent, and talked again—of crops to be had, the village being raised, and seasons past.

Though the winter and spring had not been easy, there was much for which to be thankful, and it was confirmed to Rhiannyn while she sat with the women that the Saxons had invested all of themselves in their new lord. They were Maxen's now, never again Edwin's.

And there was sorrow in that. With each of William's victories over the rebels, the era which had been the Anglo-Saxons' buried itself deeper in the past and, eventually, it would be no more. Unless Edwin succeeded where no others had...

"I've counted more than a dozen," one of the women said. "A busy winter 'twas."

The others chuckled with her.

"A dozen?" Rhiannyn said, her thoughts having slipped away from their conversation.

"Aye, and there will be more."

Rhiannyn met the woman's gaze. "More of what?"

"Why, women getting with child. Dreamin', are ye?"

Rhiannyn squelched the impulse to touch her abdomen that had yet to grow round, and once more took up her shuttle. The morrow that she had promised herself had not come, for she had still to tell Maxen the truth. Indeed, it was now a fortnight since he had asked if she was pregnant.

Resolving to tell him this eve, she rejoined the women's conversation.

"Think you a crown of flowers would suffice?" Elan's pert voice interrupted a short while later.

None having heard her approach, two shuttles dropped to the floor.

Rhiannyn retrieved hers. "Would it suffice for what, Lady Elan?" she asked.

"My wedding, of course! What else might I speak of?"

Aye, what else? Rhiannyn mused. Leaning near her loom, she traced down the warp thread she had last passed her shuttle over. "A crown of flowers would be lovely," she said and returned to weaving.

Elan stepped near, placing her very pregnant figure alongside the loom so Rhiannyn was forced to look at her. "You are not interested, are you?" she accused.

Rhiannyn stifled a sigh and sat back on her stool. "Of course I am. Now out of which flowers would you like to fashion your crown?"

She beamed. "Violets and columbines."

"Lovely."

"Or roses."

"I like roses."

Elan scowled. "Which do you prefer?"

"For me, violets and columbines, but with your coloring, roses might better suit you. What does your betrothed think?"

She shrugged. "I meant to ask him, but he is nowhere to be found."

"He and Maxen are walking out the village."

"What do you mean *walking out?*"

Meghan snickered.

Rhiannyn shot the woman a warning look and said, "They are laying its bounds."

Elan made a sound of disgust. "Dreary."

"But necessary."

"I do not see as it is."

At rare times, the young woman seemed aged beyond her years, but most often she was the child she presented this day. What made Sir Guy love her? Though Elan behaved better in his presence, did he not notice how she was with others?

Such a strange thing love is, she reflected, forgetting Elan and Guy for the moment and thinking instead of Maxen and their child. Love was indeed strange—and painful.

"I shall need new cloth for my wedding gown," Elan announced and skimmed her fingers over the hand's width of lavender cloth at the bottom of Rhiannyn's loom.

"What color are you thinking?" Rhiannyn asked.

"This is lovely."

More snickering, though this time from one other than Meghan.

Rhiannyn smiled at her sister-in-law. "Surely you know how to weave."

"I do, but I am not very accomplished."

Though Rhiannyn knew it would be easier if she offered what Elan was not so subtly asking, she also knew it would be better if the young woman did it herself. "I will teach you," she said.

Elan appeared dismayed, then affronted. "If you have not noticed, I am pregnant."

"As if one could not notice!" Meghan said.

The other women laughed.

"Why, you…you…" Elan sputtered. "…ungrateful Saxon."

Rhiannyn pushed to her feet, took Elan's elbow, and pressed her down on the stool. "Here"—she placed the shuttle in Elan's hand—"hold it like this."

Elan started to rise.

Rhiannyn eased her back down. "Now draw nearer."

"I do not care to waste my time weaving," Elan protested.

"Do you not wish the most beautiful gown in which to wed your knight?" Rhiannyn asked, hoping to turn Elan's vanity on her.

She opened her mouth as if to speak against it, closed her mouth, and some moments later said, "I *will* have the most beautiful gown."

"Then there is no time to waste." Rhiannyn began instructing her in the art of weaving.

To her surprise, it was not futile. After a time, Elan began to apply herself. And later, when talk among the women resumed, she occasioned to join in, and even laughed with the others. It seemed a miracle, but it was cut short by Christophe's arrival in the hall.

Breathing hard, he gasped, "The king is come!"

Rhiannyn straightened. "Come?" she said, hoping she misunderstood.

Christophe nodded. "With an entourage so great 'tis all you can see from the wall to the wood. Soldiers, Lady Rhiannyn. A thousand or more."

With the passing of spring, Rhiannyn had harbored hope Maxen might not be summoned, but his time had come. Although her short pregnancy had been uneventful, she felt the faintness and nausea Elan had suffered in the early months. With only the loom to steady her, she curled her fingers around it and leaned as much of her weight on it as its frame could bear.

"Nay," she whispered, squeezing her eyes closed.

"You should sit down." Christophe gripped her arm, and she wondered how he had so quickly gained her side.

Opening her eyes, she peered into his anxious face. "I am fine, just a bit…"

"You are frightened." It was Elan who spoke, who lifted her ungainly body from the stool and put a hand on Rhiannyn's shoulder.

The gesture brought tears to Rhiannyn's eyes. "Aye, I fear for Maxen."

"He does not need your fear," Christophe said, though his own fear was visible. "He needs your strength."

Did he? Of that she was not certain, but she released the loom, drew herself to her last hair of height, and looked into the expectant faces of the Saxon women. "There is much to do ere William the——"

She shook her head. It was of no benefit to call the conqueror that other name which acknowledged he was ill-gotten upon a tanner's daughter.

"There is much to do ere our king enters the hall," she corrected and drew a deep breath. "Clear the looms," she ordered two women. "Send word to Mildreth and Lucilla we have visitors," she commanded another. "Instruct the servants to position the tables. Fetch the linens and spread them on the tables." And to a passing servant, she called, "Tell the butler to bring barrels of wine and ale into the hall, and begin filling pitchers."

"What would you have me do?" Elan asked.

Rhiannyn nearly declined her offer, but from the look on the young woman's face, it was the wrong course. "You may scatter herbs over the rushes," she said, wishing she had replaced the floor covering days earlier.

Inwardly, she sighed. If William did not turn up his nose at treading upon the broken and bloodied bodies of men, he could hardly take offense at rushes smelling of mildew and whatever other foul things were trapped in them.

"Can you do that?" she asked Elan.

"Certainly."

An odd creature, Rhiannyn thought, and almost liked her in that moment.

"I would offer to help as well," Christophe said, "but Maxen said I should return as soon as I delivered the message."

Rhiannyn nodded. "You can assure him we will be ready to receive the…king."

Christophe gave her an understanding smile and hastened from the hall.

Rhiannyn turned to the lord's chamber that, this eve, would be occupied by the conqueror if he deigned to pass the night at Etcheverry. The linens must be replaced, the basins emptied, the surfaces dusted, the tub wiped clean…

40

So THIS WAS the one born of the tanner's daughter, Rhiannyn thought.

At the head of those entering the hall alongside Maxen strode the man who had claimed the crown of England, causing vast quantities of Anglo-Saxon blood to soak the ground—so much it was said the water carried up from wells near Hastings yet tasted of blood.

Rhiannyn glanced at Elan, who stood beside her. Noting the young woman's nervousness—twining hands, sharp breaths, flickering lids—she looked closer upon the one who seemed the cause of it.

Odd, she mused, *I did not imagine William would have so human a face.*

Deceptively human, she silently corrected.

The king—she must not forget who he was—halted when he came even with her and appreciatively swept his gaze over her. "I see the reason you have shut yourself up at Etcheverry, Pendery." He took a step nearer, peered so close upon Rhiannyn it was all she could do to keep her feet firm to the floor. "Quite the beauty."

"My liege, I present Lady Rhiannyn of Etcheverry," Maxen attended to the formalities with a chill voice that frightened Rhiannyn more than the king's gaze. Though certain her husband could best his lord, that did not mean he would prevail. A king was not one man but many—indeed, a horde, and all with blades eager for bloodletting.

Blessedly, William seemed not to notice Maxen's tone. "Lady, hmm?"

"Aye," Maxen said, "Lady Rhiannyn manages my household."

A flare of discomfort—that she was mistress of Etcheverry, and yet believed to be a leman—shot through Rhiannyn. But it was what she must be to William, and she was grateful that though his eyes danced with the belief it was all she was, he was not so coarse to voice it.

"I am your king," he said, continuing to regard her from a height equaled by two others in the hall—Maxen and an older man who stood alongside her husband. "Do you speak Norman French?"

Rhiannyn inclined her head.

The usurper's slight smile slipped. "I am your king," he repeated, "King William of England."

The prideful Saxon in Rhiannyn tempted her to argue, but she sealed her lips and stole a glance past the man dominating the space before her. She was comforted by the reassurance in Maxen's eyes. There was something else there, but before she could interpret it, William barked, "Have you no knees, woman?"

That was the other thing in Maxen's eyes. She was to bow to this man who was responsible for the deaths of all in her family. She would much rather spit in his eye, smack the fury from his face, walk upon his grave, see him to the devil—

A jab to her calf yanked her back to the moment, and she saw it was Elan who had struck her, she who had gone to her knees before her king.

For Maxen, Rhiannyn told herself and lifted her skirts clear. For him alone she would bend before this ungodly man. She lowered herself and waited with bowed head for him to order her to stand.

He caught her chin and lifted it. Towering above her, he seemed to have grown twice the size, but she tamped down fear and held his gaze.

"A Saxon through and through," he said.

Holding her breath lest she offend by releasing it on his hand, she peeked at Maxen and regretted that he was so tense. Of her doing, she knew. He feared for her, and rightfully so.

For Maxen, she told herself again and said, "*Oui,* I am Saxon, Your Majesty, *and* a loyal subject. One, I fear, who has much to learn of what is expected of her in this new England you have made." *Desecrated,* was the better word—providing she did not care whether she lived or died.

William's face remained austere, his gaze hard. But then his countenance cracked into a smile. "At leasts she respects one Norman," he said and looked to Maxen. "You must please her mightily."

The king laughed, and the others laughed with him—except Maxen, who managed a tolerant smile.

Shamed to her toes, Rhiannyn struggled to keep from yanking her chin out of the man's grip.

At the end of his laughter, William, said, "You will come to respect me, Rhiannyn of Etcheverry. Perhaps even like me."

How was she to respond? Fortunately, she did not have to, for with his next breath he ordered both women to rise.

Rhiannyn complied, and seeing Elan struggle to lift her bulk, reached to assist her. However, it was Maxen who pulled his sister to standing.

Trying to regain her dignity in spite of a belly so far gone with pregnancy it seemed she might topple, Elan smoothed her skirts and stepped around her brother.

"Father," she addressed the older man who shared height with Maxen and the king.

"Daughter," the man acknowledged her.

Rhiannyn almost laughed at how blind she was not to have noticed the resemblance between father and son. Both broad, both dark haired—though the sire's hair was liberally awash with silver—and both of strong countenance. Remove twenty and more years from the father, and before her would stand a man who might be Maxen's twin.

But there was nothing humorous about finding not only the conqueror in her home, but Maxen's father.

"Bring on the food!" William ordered and turned toward the tables. Shortly, he was settled in the high seat upon the dais.

Though Rhiannyn knew that wherever the king went in his realm, his place was the highest, her resentment flared that he took what was Maxen's. Just as William had taken what had been King Harold's.

"I like this neck," Maxen murmured and lightly trailed a finger to the hollow of her throat. "Pray, do not press the king so hard I will have to go to great lengths to save it."

She looked up at where he had drawn close and nearly yielded to the longing to go into his arms.

Her black mood easing, she managed a smile.

"Good," he said low, "but can you hold onto your smile while I present you to my sire?"

She glanced at the man and had but a moment to study him before he moved his gaze to her. There was no mistaking his dislike, nor the accusation in his eyes. Just as Elan had first regarded her as being responsible for Thomas's death, so did the father who had put the belief in his daughter's head. And he hated her for it.

Maxen surely felt that hatred, but he drew Rhiannyn forward. "Father, I present Rhiannyn of Etcheverry. Rhiannyn, my father, Baron Pendery."

She executed a curtsy, but when she glanced up, his face was as hard as before.

"I am not pleased," he said and shifted his regard to his son.

"Then it is good your pleasure is not sought, Father." Maxen placed Rhiannyn's hand on his arm, turned, and walked her toward where the king sat.

"Your father does not like me," Rhiannyn whispered as they rounded the table.

"No longer does his approval matter. If he takes no liking to you, it changes naught of what is between us, *leof*."

She nearly confessed how much she loved him. Holding it in, she took her place beside him on the bench.

The meal was an ordeal she likened to bare feet on nettles. The odd thing was, what made it such a strain was not what she expected.

Along with the drink William downed, so did he lower his reserve and come fully into good humor. During the two hours, she was often drawn to his wit and charm. Thus, resisting his pull was what made the meal so difficult. But at the end of it, while all was being cleared and the men gathered before their king to hear what he had thus far withheld, William donned the cap of business. No more waggery tumbled from his lips, no more jesting. He was their king, all before him subjects.

As Rhiannyn had feared might happen, she and Elan were sent from the hall. Rhiannyn, her sister-in-law following, was grateful when they gained the lord's chamber unopposed. Although she was not allowed to be in the king's presence when he spoke, she would be able to hear much of what was said and would know first-hand why he had journeyed to Etcheverry with a full army—though she was woefully certain she already knew the reason.

Though it would appear unseemly to Elan for her to stand by the screen eavesdropping, Rhiannyn positioned herself.

"I have word the weasel abides a day's ride north of Etcheverry," the king boomed.

"He speaks of Edwin?" Elan whispered just over her shoulder.

Surprised to find her near, Rhiannyn looked around. "I am certain of it." Though others might name him the *wolf,* a king would not grant the man so menacing a title. Too, it surely made him feel superior to call Edwin a weasel.

"News was also delivered me that he readies for what he calls the final battle," William continued, "and he intends to sneak an attack upon London in a fortnight."

His vassals murmured.

"But 'tis I who will sneak an attack upon him," William said. "On the morrow, we ride, and by the day after, his blood will wet the ground the same as Harold's."

A long pause, then, "Maxen Pendery, are you prepared to ride at my side?"

What choice had he? Rhiannyn wondered.

"I and my men, my liege."

"Guy?" Elan gasped and snatched hold of Rhiannyn's arm. "Surely he cannot mean Guy."

As there was no comfort to be given, Rhiannyn whispered, "It is likely. He is Maxen's first man, and there is no one held in higher regard."

Elan sank, and if Rhiannyn had not caught hold of her, she would have landed amid the rushes. "Elan!" she called low.

The young woman's lashes fluttered and the whites of her eyes showed.

Unable to support her upright, Rhiannyn lowered with her to the floor and pulled her head onto her lap. "Elan," she rasped.

Her eyes opened. "Say 'tis not so," she pleaded.

"I am sorry, but I cannot."

Elan's eyes brimmed. "I never loved before Guy. I cannot lose him."

As Rhiannyn could not lose Maxen. "I know. But we must be strong. And believe."

"How? This child makes me so weak, I hardly have the strength to pass the day." Elan pressed a hand to her belly. "Ah, to be rid of it."

Inwardly, Rhiannyn recoiled. "Do not speak so," she said more harshly than intended. "It is not the babe's fault for being."

Elan stared at her, then slowly sat up. "You are right. It is my fault."

Might she be ready to speak the truth? "Your fault?" Rhiannyn said. "Not Edwin's?"

Emotions worked across the young woman's face, but the last fit itself to her brow and eyes and mouth. "Of course it is his fault. But had I not been so foolish to ride out alone, he would not have laid hands upon me."

Rhiannyn sighed, stood, and reached a hand to her.

Elan took it and staggered upright. "I know it is not what you wish to hear, Rhiannyn, but it is what befell me. Truly."

Without further word, Rhiannyn returned her attention to the voices in the hall. They were not as loud, and when she peeked around the screen, she saw that where there had been a hundred men, little more than a dozen remained.

What had transpired while she had tended to Elan's faint? Had anything of import been said?

She skipped her gaze from Maxen to the king, to Christophe who stood beside his father, then the others who had drawn nearer William. Whatever words they exchanged did not carry far enough to be heard.

"What do they say?" Elan asked.

Rhiannyn drew back. "Naught I can understand. Certes, though, they are planning."

Her belly going well before her, Elan crossed to the bed, set a steadying hand on the mattress, and gingerly lowered to the floor. "I will pray," she said. "And you?"

A praying Elan? She who did not even bow her head during the blessing of meals? Had love done this to her?

Shaking off surprise, Rhiannyn crossed the room and went down beside her sister-in-law. "I shall pray with you."

"We are close to being friends, you know," Elan said and closed her eyes and began moving her lips to silent prayer.

Odd friends, Rhiannyn thought, but it was better than how it had been when first Elan had come.

41

THE BLOODLUST WARRIOR of Hastings, who had raised his head when the king baited Rhiannyn, trailed Maxen as he walked alongside the man who might find himself named The Bloodlust King of England—unless the piety for which William was fairly known could be stirred to life.

Maxen did not have long to await an opportunity to speak in that direction. As they moved toward the wall-walk overlooking the land that was aglow with hundreds of campfires, the king said, "I would know the state of your soul, Pendery."

Maxen was glad he was prepared for such talk, for one's stride ought not falter in the presence of a man whose respect was of greater worth than feeding feelings of superiority. "What was black can never be made white," he said.

"Then after two years at prayer, your soul remains troubled."

"As should the souls of all who take the lives of others."

After a long moment, the king said, "Indeed."

"Still, I am lightened," Maxen said. What he did not tell was that more than the years at prayer, the burden of Hastings had been eased by his return to the world of man—to the England his actions had helped form. What had begun to make him feel human again was making others feel human, valuing them such that their pain was as much his as their joy. And not just the pain and joy of Rhiannyn and Christophe, but all the lives of those for whom he was responsible, Norman and Saxon alike.

The two traversed the turn in the wall-walk, and between the notches in the wall, glimpsed the vast camp outside the castle whose fires aspired to make day of night.

William halted before an embrasure and gazed out at his army whose next task was to bring Harwolfson to ground. "Lightened," he said as Maxen came alongside. "Not so much, I hope, that The Bloodlust Warrior of Hastings will not serve me well in the coming battle."

Maxen shifted his jaw. "*I* shall serve you well, my liege, but I will not be again what I was at Hastings."

William turned a heavy brow upon him, and the fire in his eyes was not merely a reflection of those leaping, crackling things warming his men below. "Will you not?"

Maxen held without flinch. There could be no question he was at the mercy of this all-powerful man, but there was one far more powerful than William—more potent than any. Blessedly, the conqueror also bowed his head to the Lord. And if he did so in this instance, it was possible Hastings would not repeat itself in the confrontation with Harwolfson.

"I mean you no disrespect, my liege," Maxen said, "but I will not become again what offended God such that, regardless of His forgiveness, Hastings will ever be but a glance behind me."

William slowly nodded. "Hastings is farther than a glance behind me, but it is there. Forsooth, were I not so certain of my claim upon England—certain the one who tried to steal it from me gave me no choice but to bloody that field—methinks it might also haunt me." He narrowed his gaze. "Am I right in believing you now have someone to live for?"

The relief beginning to move through Maxen halted its advance. Here was the opening he had been determined to find in requesting a private audience. It was time to make things right with Rhiannyn. "It is true, Your Majesty."

The man grinned. "The Saxon woman," he said and clapped Maxen on the shoulder. "I have had many an occasion to feel the air of one who wishes to put a blade through me, and you, though richly rewarded by your liege, wished it this day."

Then William had been aware of catching the eye of The Bloodlust Warrior of Hastings when he had spoken to Rhiannyn as if she were less than a leman.

"Obviously, she pleases you as much as you please her," the king continued, "And not just in bed, *oui?*"

Maxen jammed his fingers into his palms. "*Oui.*"

"Thus, you do not like that I would use her to bargain with Harwolfson."

Even better than he was known for piety, William was lauded for astuteness.

"I do not like it." Acutely aware of his feet and hands and the dagger upon his belt that was the only weapon the king's personal guard had allowed him for their meeting, and as acutely aware of the king's, Maxen added, "That is among the reasons I wed Rhiannyn."

The fires before the castle showed clearly the color rising up William's neck, as well as the saliva upon which he spat, "Without your king's permission—in defiance of me—you married your leman?"

As a warrior, there was great advantage to being of exceptional stature, and in this instance, as a vassal. Fortunately, Maxen had enough experience with William to know the man was sure enough of his own skill that, rather than being threatened by the steady gaze slightly above his own, he would see it as strength to be used to his advantage—once he descended from his wrath.

"Never was Rhiannyn my leman," Maxen said. "As my wife, she has only ever shared my bed."

Between his teeth, the king said, "Why was I not told of your marriage?"

"Our vows were spoken in private."

William blinked and his color began to recede. "Clandestine—a fairly easy way to lure a resistant woman to bed, and all the easier to set her aside."

"That I will not do, Your Majesty. In the sight of God who witnessed our vows, she is and shall remain Rhiannyn Pendery, the woman who will bear my sons and daughters."

This time when the king showed teeth, it was not in a smile. "What makes you think I will allow this, especially from one who cannot fight for me as he did at Hastings?"

"I will help you achieve your end with Harwolfson but, God willing, this time more honorably."

As the king looked hard upon him, Maxen listened to the man's every breath and, fully aware his life could be forfeit, sensed The Bloodlust Warrior rising behind him. It brushed against him, and as if finding its host receptive, pressed nearer in search of a place to perch.

But Maxen was not receptive. Given good cause—not merely a means of proving himself—he would defend himself and his family, but not with that one's aid. It could raise its head and trail him all the days of its life, but for nothing would it move beneath his skin again.

Of a sudden, William grunted. "Curse all, Pendery! You could have made this easy for me."

Maxen frowned. "My liege?"

"Had you set your mind to getting the woman with child, I could, most benevolently, grant you permission to take her to wife."

Feeling the strain of laughter it would be a mistake to loose, Maxen mused that, as thought, his defiance would be more acceptable had his marriage to Rhiannyn been but a nobleman's desire to legitimize his heir.

"I care deeply for her, my liege," he said. "Thus, I would not have had it be truth she was but my leman, nor would I have our child suffer it being thought he was first misbegotten."

William made a guttural sound that was not quite laughter. "My mother survived that truth—and well."

So the tanner's daughter had. "As did her son," Maxen conceded.

The king's lids narrowed, but not so his mouth. It smiled. "Her son, the duke…the conqueror…the king." He fell silent as if to savor his titles, then once more lowered his lips over his teeth. "Very well, if you want the little Saxon, though she has yet to prove herself capable of providing an heir, I give her to you."

Something loosened in Maxen, not the heart that had been fettered before Rhiannyn, but what might be joy. Seeing no reason to explain that his wife and he had determined to wait on children until their marriage could be revealed, he said, "I am indebted, Your Majesty."

William's eyebrows rose. "You are, so let us be clear as to what I require."

Maxen was not surprised, nor that what had eased in him once more constricted.

"Two things," the king said. "When I reveal on the morrow I secretly granted you leave to wed months past, you and your wife will confirm it."

The better to retain control over others who might take it upon themselves to wed whomever and whenever they wished. "It shall be done, Your Majesty."

William once more turned his face to the camp beyond the walls and moved his gaze over the hundreds of tents quartering soldiers who would kill and be killed for him. "And as a man who now has something to live for, when we face Harwolfson, you will serve me as when you had naught to live for."

This time it was Maxen who ground his teeth. "As told, I will not be what I was at Hastings."

"Providing you yet swing your sword, and the end is the same regardless of how much is written in Saxon blood, it will suffice."

Maxen inclined his head. "I give you my word I will defend your cause, even at the cost of my life, if it be required of me."

"*If?*" the king repeated, then asked, "What do you propose?"

"Much the same as you when you thought to use my wife against Harwolfson—to defeat him in the absence of a battle that, even in victory, will thin our Norman ranks."

"Negotiation."

"*Oui,* though in such a way it brings him and as many of his rebels as possible to your side, thus enlarging your army for battles yet to be fought."

William jerked his head toward his army. "Of course I see the advantage, but there is also benefit in battle. Shed enough Saxon blood, and perhaps the rebels will be discouraged such that they lay down their arms and more willingly accept my rule."

"So they might, but through negotiation, you spare the lives of Normans alongside Saxons, and if you convince one as formidable as Harwolfson to accept your yoke, it may discourage future rebellions."

That caused a crack in William's expression. Though his currency was more often blood, nearly three years of unrest did not portend well for his island kingdom. Thus, the sooner the people accepted him, the more likely he would keep his throne. And the answer could very well be a more peaceful means.

Amid the silence, Maxen prayed William would choose piety and wisdom over bloodlust and pride.

The king's brow smoothed. "What do you believe would persuade Harwolfson to *accept my yoke,* as you say?"

The answer was on Maxen's tongue. "Etcheverry, whose lands were his family's long ere you awarded them to a Pendery."

It seemed William's answer was also on his tongue, for he gave no moment's pause. *"Non.* It is too strategically located to allow one outside my trust to control it."

Though Maxen knew Etcheverry's importance well enough to regret relinquishing it, he had been prepared to do so and settle with Rhiannyn on lands that would be his as heir to Trionne.

"If Harwolfson can be convinced to lay down his arms," he said, "it will not be without great cost, my liege. He will wish lands of his own—substantial enough to settle a great number of his followers on them."

"Not Etcheverry. But if I am of a mood to grant him anything, perhaps Blackspur Castle."

Maxen had not considered that, and with good reason. "Your Majesty, I have promised my man, Sir Guy, the position of castellan of Blackspur."

"Have you?" William's tone almost bored, he lifted his gaze to the night sky. "Your sister carries Harwolfson's child."

Maxen felt his jaws begin to lock. As Rhiannyn could no longer be a puppet, did the king think to use Elan?

"Your father tells she is to wed this Sir Guy."

"An honorable knight who fought admirably for his king at Hastings, Your Majesty."

"So he did, but tell—is the knight set upon your sister?"

"He is. Sir Guy and Lady Elan are much taken with each other."

William nodded. "Since he has served me well, I shall allow him Lady Elan, a noblewoman of high rank. And that is reward enough."

Maxen's teeth ached. "My liege—"

"Should I determine it is in England's best interest to negotiate with the Saxon dog, it is Blackspur I will offer. Of course, much depends on whether or not he makes a good show of force."

Meaning if Harwolfson and his men were more easily returned to the earth, so they would be. Though it would be to Sir Guy's loss if the army of rebels was as great as believed, Maxen prayed it was so the sooner to see peace upon England. There would be other castles raised upon Pendery lands. Guy—and Elan—must only be patient.

"What if Harwolfson will not accept Blackspur?" he asked. "If he cannot be prevented from coming against us on the battlefield?"

William's shrug moved from his mouth to his shoulders. "If Sir Guy survives, you may give Blackspur into his keeping."

Sensing the king had given all he would, telling himself to be content with having made negotiation an option, Maxen said, "I thank you for granting me an audience, Your Majesty. If you would now grant me my leave, I shall return to the donjon to speak with Sir Guy on the matter."

Across the fire-lit night, William said, "Your leave is granted."

Maxen bowed and pivoted, but he was soon called back around. "My liege?"

The king tapped his left hand with his right. "Put a ring on your lady's finger, Pendery. Then make an heir on her."

The first could be done this night, perhaps even the second. "I shall, Your Majesty."

William motioned him away, and though it was Rhiannyn to whom Maxen wished to go, he went in search of Guy.

"What do you think will happen?" Rhiannyn asked Maxen who had stretched out beside her on the pallet she had made for them in an alcove off the hall.

After returning from his walk with the king and conferring with Sir Guy, he had come to her and, amid the rustling and murmuring of the multitude settling in to their rest, quietly revealed what had been discussed regarding the coming confrontation with Edwin.

"What will happen..." he murmured as if to himself and turned his head toward hers on the pillow they shared. "Do you wish the truth?"

The three walls of their makeshift chamber casting deeper shadows than those found in the open hall, she caught the gleam of his eyes before the familiar planes of his face emerged. "Aye, the truth."

"Though, as told, the king was receptive to victory through negotiation—providing the rebel army presents a threat—methinks Harwolfson will not be satisfied with anything less than Etcheverry."

Rhiannyn believed this to be true. If Edwin could be calmed, it would not be by way of what had been promised to Sir Guy.

"Thus," Maxen continued, "'tis more likely we go into battle on the morrow."

Rhiannyn let out the breath she had not realized she held. "Dear Lord."

Maxen turned onto his side and levered onto an elbow. Leaning over her, he slid a hand across her temple into her hair, spread his long fingers, and gently rubbed her scalp as if she, more than he, bore the strain of what was to come—he who refused the most powerful man in England the sword of The Bloodlust Warrior of Hastings.

"I will not be that man again, Rhiannyn," he said as if his wandering thoughts had happened upon the path hers wended. "At least, I shall continue to fight it, for more than once I felt that presence this day."

Rhiannyn nearly shuddered over memories of what he had become in meeting Ancel over swords. Though justified in taking the knight's life, he had seemed little more than a throw from the beasts of the wood. At William's side, would he indiscriminately slaughter as he had done at Hastings?

"With whom did you feel its presence?" she asked.

"William, when he addressed you as if you were my leman."

There was no need to point out the king could not be faulted for his belief, nor did she wish it to weigh on Maxen any more than it already did.

"More than once you felt its presence?" she prompted.

"Again upon the wall when I roused the king's anger."

"By encouraging him to negotiate with Harwolfson."

"Before then."

"Over what matter?"

He drew his fingers from her hair to her shoulder, slid them down her arm, and lifted her left hand. "You again," he said and sat up. "When I revealed we have long been wed."

Rhiannyn's insides leapt—with happiness, disbelief, and fear. In a trembling voice, she said, "Truly?"

"Truly, Rhiannyn mine."

Tears ran to the corners of her eyes, and she said, "He was angered?"

"He was and is, but it is done. Now…" Something warm and smooth touched the tip of her third finger, slid down its length. "…all will know the truth of the woman who shares not only my bed but my life."

Throat so tight it hurt, she drew her thumb across the softly rounded edge she had feared would never be felt upon her hand—visible evidence of their vows that should not matter, but did.

"For months I have carried this ring on my person," Maxen said.

"Months?"

"In anticipation of this day, I had the smithy at Blackspur fashion it for you."

She swallowed hard. "What of William? He will permit this?"

"He has permitted it. We have but to allow him the lie that he secretly granted us permission months past."

It was too easy. "What price?" she asked.

"Rhiannyn—"

"What price, Maxen?"

"I am to prove as worthy against Harwolfson as I was at Hastings."

"Ah, nay!"

He pressed fingers to her lips. "As *worthy*. If peace can be brokered between the king and Harwolfson, I will work it. If peace cannot...With God's aid and the certainty you await my return, I will fight for my liege as is my duty. And only as is my duty."

She stared up at him, wished she could clearly see his face the better to carry this moment with her always, regardless of how long always might be. How she loved this man whom she had once believed impossible to love!

A sob escaped her.

"It is well, Rhiannyn," he rasped.

Another sob.

He put an arm around her, drew her close, and lowered to his back.

Pressing her face into his neck to muffle sounds of misery that were anything but, she felt her heart beat in time with his.

He who had hated her for his brother's death, cared for her.

Impossible.

He who had used her to gain Edwin's camp, had become her shield.

Impossible.

He who had not trusted her, had set her over his household.

Impossible.

He who had wed her in secret, had been true to her.

Impossibly possible.

"Hush, Rhiannyn," he said.

She lifted her face to his. "All that was impossible is made possible."

After a long moment, he said, "A blessing."

"Aye. Do you forgive me, Maxen?"

"What have I to forgive you for?"

"I was frightened when you said…" She steadied her breath. "…we must keep our vows secret. I was afraid you might set me aside."

"This I know. And I gave you cause to feel that way."

"But even after I understood the reason and believed you, I feared I was wrong in doing so. And when you almost eagerly agreed to wait on children, I feared even more." She shook her head. "I suppose it means I never truly believed you."

"Rhiannyn, I understand. As for waiting on children, I did not object because I did not wish you to suffer more stigma than already I had cast upon you by allowing others to believe you were but my leman, and…"

"What?"

"I, too, knew fear—that the man who had become The Bloodlust Warrior would not be a worthy father and the chasm between my sire and me would seem small compared to what there might be between our child and me."

Realizing here, too, was what it meant to become one—feeling the other's pain and uncertainty—Rhiannyn pushed up and kissed his jaw. "Just as you make a wonderful husband, Maxen, you will make a wonderful father." This time, it was she who sought his hand. Taking hold of it, she pressed it to her lower abdomen.

"There," she said, soft and low. "There."

He was still some moments, then his fingers splayed and began moving over what would grow round and full.

"I am sorry I lied when you asked if I was with child," she whispered. "I was…I do not know what I was. Lost?"

The breath went out of him, and her own stuck when he pulled his hand away. But then his fingers were in her hair again, urging her head beneath his chin.

"There will be no more lies between us," he said firmly, but without anger.

She began to smile, only to trip over her love for him and fall back to a time when these feelings had not existed—when he had been beyond angered. Because of Thomas.

On a day of rain and tears, she had accepted the dying man's anger—and curses—as his due. Though she no longer did, it must be told, for like lies, it was between Maxen and her.

Praying he would be as accepting of it, she said, "No more lies—nor hidden things."

He stiffened so slightly, she was certain she only noticed because she expected it. "Hidden things?" he said.

"To which I alluded in Andredeswald when I revealed to Brother Justus I feared for my soul."

"Ah. Thomas's curses."

The irony of them, she thought and said, "Aye, but what you should know is that while he lay dying in my arms, 'twas me he blamed for his death. Had I not run from him—"

"We have already discussed and resolved this, Rhiannyn. You could not have known he would come after you without escort. Thomas's death is upon him, not you."

She did accept that—mostly.

"Now what other hidden things would you have me know?"

She pressed nearer him. "To the heavens he called for his brother to avenge him. I thought he meant Christophe, but when you came to me in the cell, I knew it was you."

"The Bloodlust Warrior."

"Aye, so terribly vengeful."

"Summoned by Christophe," Maxen pointed out, "not Thomas, and not for revenge. You know that, aye?"

"I do."

He stroked her arm. "I am sorry I frightened you. I was angered by my brother's death and certain I was best locked away where I could harm no one. Never would I have guessed I would wish to be here at Etcheverry—with you."

Rhiannyn clasped those words to her before continuing. "A thousand times—to eternity—Thomas cursed me."

"Also as already told, words only, spoken by a man angry with his own death whose passing comes too slowly…" He trailed off, then asked, "Was my brother in much pain?"

Though tempted to deny it, it would be another lie. "He was."

Maxen's hand on her arm stilled and, feeling his dark emotions, she said, "What of your vengeance against the one who murdered him?"

His chest rose with a deep breath. "If I am to know who it was, the answer must come to me. No longer will I seek it."

"You accept his death?"

"As much as I can. Now, tell me the curses he spoke against you."

Under the circumstances, it seemed almost silly. "Thomas said that if I would not belong to a Pendery, I would belong to no man, that never would I hold a child at my breast, and never again would I know the love of a man."

Maxen gave a disbelieving grunt. "Though the first is true, that you will only belong to a Pendery—as I will only belong to you—it is not a curse but a blessing. And further proof that God does not serve man is that our child will be at your breast come the new year." He clasped her nearer. "As for the last, I do not understand how I am capable of feeling as I do, but you have my love, Rhiannyn."

She stopped breathing, then a short, sweet laugh spilled from her as she wrapped her heart around his declaration. Maxen Pendery, once and nevermore her enemy, loved her. But before she could assure him he was not alone in this, he swept aside the silence as if for fear she would not.

"Once more, I must ask you to hold close the truth," he said, "this time that you are with child, though only until the morrow when the king reveals he granted us permission to wed ere you came to my bed."

She frowned. "For what?"

"William would prefer to permit our marriage because I wish to claim the child you carry, the better to maintain it is he who controls his nobles' fates. But I would have the truth known that you were never my leman and our child was legitimately conceived."

"Of course," she whispered, then said, "Surely you know—must know—you are loved as well, Maxen."

She felt his breath in her hair. "I dared hope, *deore.*"

Beloved. Had that word in her language ever sounded so beautiful? "No matter what comes," she said, "on the morrow and every day thereafter, I love you, Maxen Pendery."

"As ever I love you, Rhiannyn Pendery."

42

~⦿~

The baron of Trionne was not pleased, so much that William must know it. But the king seemed unconcerned. His word was law. Thus, having announced he had months past granted Maxen permission to wed Rhiannyn and ordered their vows kept secret to prevent Harwolfson from moving on Etcheverry, the marriage could not be undone.

Unfortunately, Elan's father seemed determined someone should suffer for his son's choice of wife, and that was his daughter.

"I do not wish to go!" she wailed where she came up off her chair before the hearth. "How can you ask me to look again upon the one who did this to me?" She gripped her swollen belly.

"I am not asking," Baron Pendery growled, "I am telling. You will witness the miscreant's death—this your revenge."

"It is enough for me that he dies!"

"It is not enough for me. Make ready to ride!"

On the verge of speaking in defense of her sister-in-law, despite the certainty it would not go well for her, Rhiannyn was grateful when she heard the heavy tread of boots well filled. Halting her advance at the center of the hall, she looked around and offered an apologetic smile when her husband's eyes met hers.

Following the pre-dawn breaking of fast that had ended with acknowledgement of the lord of Etcheverry's marriage, King William had commanded Maxen to accompany him to the camp. In the hour since, she had busied herself with duties which were now truly hers. But though it had been easy to ignore the curious castle folk who were fascinated by the ring upon her hand, Baron Pendery had made his every glower felt. Doubtless, he resented another lost opportunity to make an advantageous marriage for one of his children, and this one his heir.

"My sister—*your* daughter—is too far into her pregnancy to risk the ride," Maxen called to his father as he strode across the room, having surely heard the heated argument through the open doors.

Baron Pendery swung around. "What? You fear she might lose this ill-gotten babe? Hardly a bad thing."

Though Maxen's stride did not falter, Rhiannyn saw him stiffen as if to suppress the desire to loose feet, arms, and fists. He halted before his father. "I do fear she could lose the babe," he said, "as I fear she could also be put at risk. Thus, she remains at Etcheverry."

The baron's face flushed, and he thrust it near his son's. "I say she goes."

Heavenly Father, Rhiannyn silently prayed, *let them not come to blows.*

Maxen did not back down, nor give in to the temptation to make fists of his hands.

"Elan goes with us," the baron repeated.

"She stays," his son hissed.

"I am sorry, Maxen, but I must side with your father," King William's voice boomed across the hall, bringing Rhiannyn's chin around to catch his entrance ahead of a dozen knights.

Maxen turned. "Your Majesty, surely you can see how far gone my sister is with child!"

"I see as well as you," the king said, "and I see Lady Elan could prove useful—"

"Useful!" Maxen bit.

William strode past Rhiannyn and halted before the three Penderys, the smallest and youngest of whom whimpered into her hand.

"*Oui,*" the king said, "if I proceed with what we discussed yestereve."

Though hope was found in his words—that rather than slaughter, he would try to make peace with Edwin—what of Elan?

"My sister is promised to Sir Guy," Maxen reminded him.

"And she will make your man a good wife," William said, "should it be in the best interest of England."

After all Maxen had shared with her on the night past, Rhiannyn would have been confused if not that her husband did not appear to suffer from that state. He was affronted. And he should be, for it sounded as if Sir Guy might not only lose the castle he had been promised, but his betrothed. But surely William would not offer up Elan, for just as Maxen's sister did not want Edwin, Edwin could not possibly want the woman who accused him of a thing of which Rhiannyn was certain he was incapable.

Baron Pendery stepped alongside Maxen. "Your Majesty, may I ask what you discussed with my son—with what you might proceed?"

"As it is not likely to be carried out," the king said, "you need not concern yourself. Eh, Maxen?"

When Maxen answered, his voice was further strained. "Regardless, Elan should remain here."

"She will not, and neither will your Saxon wife."

Rhiannyn stopped breathing, silently called to her husband to carefully descend the precipice from which the king might otherwise fling him.

As Maxen stared at his king, he felt his wife's fear. Though one-on-one he was certain he would be the victor of a match between himself and William, it was not such a contest he faced. As rude as the truth was, with but a nod at those who had accompanied the king into the hall, Maxen's life could be forfeit.

As evenly as he could manage, he asked, "For what would you have Lady Rhiannyn accompany us, Your Majesty?"

The king raised an eyebrow. "Having been betrothed to Harwolfson, she likely knows him well. Thus, should I require insight into the man, your lady wife—a loyal and most grateful subject—will be at the ready."

No mistaking the threat in his words, Maxen eased his clenched teeth. "Then she shall ride with us to meet Harwolfson."

As if there had been no edge over which all could have plummeted, William smiled, stepped forward, and gripped Maxen's shoulder. "You will serve me well again," he said, and turned and exited the hall ahead of his knights.

There followed the silence of Pendery facing Pendery—an air of hostility between father and son.

Elan broke the quiet. "I do not wish to go!"

Her father turned on her. "I give you a quarter hour, then I will drag you out by the hair if need be." He came back around, cast an angry eye upon his son, next Rhiannyn, and strode after the king of England.

"I am sorry, Rhiannyn...Elan," Maxen said, "but it must be as the king commands."

"I will make ready," Rhiannyn said.

"I hope Edwin cuts William's heart out," Elan shrilled. "Disembowels him. Severs his——"

"Elan!" Maxen barked.

"I do," she retorted, tears streaming. "How dare he do this to me! Who does he think he is? God?"

Likely, Maxen thought. "Do as you have been told, Elan," he said, and there being many things to which he must attend before the ride, turned away. And found his beautiful wife moving toward him.

Her face lightened with the meeting of their eyes, and he saw there the love she had proclaimed on the night past. Something to live for.

He reached to her as they drew near, and for a moment, their hands clasped and he felt the ring he had given her. Then their fingers slid past each other's and she said, "I will help you collect your things, Elan, then you can assist with mine."

"I ought to go naked," Maxen's sister mumbled, "then he would see I am in no state to ride a horse."

"Would that not be a sight?" Rhiannyn said. "Had I the courage, methinks I would bare all with you."

Maxen stepped outside into the awakening day and considered the inner bailey and the outer beyond that teemed with preparations for the coming encounter.

"Bend, Edwin Harwolfson," he rasped, "else you will be dead."

As uncomfortable as the long ride had been for Rhiannyn, she knew it must have been miserable for Elan. Whereas Rhiannyn had ridden with Maxen—excepting those times when William commanded him to his side—Elan was too large to ride with Sir Guy. Thus, she had ridden at her betrothed's side, crying and complaining much of the way.

Fortunately, the pace had not been brutal, though it was surely not out of consideration for Elan but merely part of the king's plan.

Dusk dusted the skies before William called a halt to the procession, and on the ridge above a grassy field bordering a wood, a camp was erected. The place was named Darfield, and it was here on the morrow Norman would again meet Saxon in battle.

It was dark before Maxen returned from the king's tent. Throwing back the flap of the tent raised for him and Rhiannyn, he said, "He knows we are here."

She sat up on the pallet. "Edwin?" she asked, though she knew it must be. The tent, lit from without by the torches set about the camp, showed Maxen's shadowed figure as he moved toward her.

"Aye." He dropped down beside her. "He is in the wood, but on the morrow he and his followers will gather at the opposite end of the field to face William."

"You are certain of that?"

"I am—as is the king."

She put a hand on his arm. "Mayhap Edwin will withdraw."

"You think so?"

He did not believe it, and neither did she.

So why do I deceive myself with false hope? she silently chastised. Even if Edwin turned away, the confrontation would simply come a day or so later.

"I do not think so," she said, "but what of the negotiation you proposed?"

"Although King William wearies of these uprisings, his power increases with each victory. Thus, as he likely views the defeat of Harwolfson as a great triumph, I am fairly certain he will negotiate only if Harwolfson makes a fine show. And mayhap not even then."

How she hated it was but a matter of whether Edwin came before the conqueror weak or strong—no concern for what was right and wrong.

"I fear for you," she whispered.

"I would rather you pray for me, Rhiannyn."

"That, too."

Silence, during which too many thoughts leapt to mind—questions whose answers would change naught, reflections that would only fill the silence, and pleadings Maxen had already heard and done his best to answer. But knowing this might be their last night together, that come day he might lay down his life for his king, Rhiannyn pushed all aside and said, "Will you remain with me a while?"

He pulled her into his arms, turned his palm into hers, and wove their fingers together. "How fares Elan?"

"I worry for her. She complains of cramping and pains."

"Christophe is with her?"

"And Sir Guy."

"What does my brother say?"

"Though he knows herbs and healing well, he has had little experience with birthing and is at something of a loss."

Maxen sat up. "The king's physician ought to be summoned."

She stayed him with a hand to his arm. "He has been summoned, and by now he is with her."

"What if the babe should come now?"

"Though Elan tells it is weeks before it is due, it is not uncommon for a child to be delivered ere its nine months have all passed."

"In good health?"

"I have seen it, though rarely with a babe of less age than Elan's."

"You believe it would fare well if it was delivered early?"

"I think it possible, but it is for the physician to say."

"Then let us pray."

43

Bʏ ᴛʜᴇ ᴛɪᴍᴇ night yielded to day, the king and his army stood to arms. As at Hastings, William had positioned his soldiers in three lines—archers at the fore, heavy infantry in the middle, the cavalry of knights at the rear. In the midst of the cavalry, he waited for Edwin Harwolfson to challenge him for the kingdom.

Skirts billowing in the chill morning breeze, mantle flapping against her back, Rhiannyn stood atop the ridge and gazed upon the great formation that might soon be broken if the miracle for which Maxen and she prayed did not come.

How many did they number? she wondered, beginning another count. Again, she lost track, this time when her gaze fell upon the papal banner fluttering high above the king. As it had been flown at Hastings, so it was here, its presence proclaiming William the Bastard the favored son of the Holy Church and bestowing upon him the papal blessing of conquest.

Rhiannyn shifted her gaze to Maxen who was mounted alongside his king. His thoughts surely burdened by the day ahead, he had spoken few words before leaving her earlier. But prior to his departure, he had taken her face between his hands and kissed her long and lingering. And when he had pulled back, his gaze had touched her features as if to memorize them for eternity.

Insides churning, Rhiannyn had watched him withdraw, and only when his shadow melded with the dark had she attempted to confront emotions so at war with one another she had nearly choked. On the one side of her, she wished The Bloodlust Warrior of Hastings to rise again and ensure Maxen survived the battle. On the other side, she prayed this day would prove he had purged the beast. But then she might lose him...

She thrust aside her emotions and put all her prayers into resolution through negotiation. Of course, William did not present the only obstacle to that path. There was yet Maxen's avenging father.

Rhiannyn picked out the man who sat alongside his son. If the king did find Edwin's army to be of sufficient threat, the old man would surely raise an outcry. In which case, it could only be hoped the elder Pendery held no sway over William.

"Rhiannyn." A hand touched her shoulder, and she turned to Christophe.

"Elan calls for you," he said. "She is in labor."

"Since when?"

"The first hours of morn."

"What does the physician say?"

Christophe made a face. "That what will be shall be, since he must make ready to attend the king should injury befall him in battle."

Elan would have her babe in the midst of what might be a war? And without benefit of a physician who would likely but tend the scrapes and scratches of his precious king?

"Will you come?" Christophe asked.

"Of course." She stole a last look at Maxen, fixing the image of his broad-shouldered back in her mind, and nodded for Christophe to lead the way.

The physician was exiting Elan's tent when they reached it. "I have given her a draught for the pain," he said. "There is nothing to do but wait."

"Naught but see her child safely into the world," Rhiannyn said.

He halted, peered at her across his shoulder. "It is only a Saxon."

"You—"

Elan's cry snatched away Rhiannyn's retort, and she ducked beneath the flap Christophe raised for her.

"I am here, Elan," she said, hurrying forward.

Hair in disarray, face contorted, flushed skin beaded with perspiration, she barely resembled the young woman she had been the day before. Only her large belly rising up beneath the blanket evidenced she was the same.

She grabbed Rhiannyn's hand, and squeezing with all her might, whispered, "I am dying."

"You are not. You are simply having a baby."

"Simply!" Fury replaced the pain on Elan's face. "You try it and see how simple it is."

"Mayhap I will. And it will be you holding my hand and me bellowing at you."

Elan struggled as if to keep hold of an anger that, perhaps, was easier to deal with than pain, but it slipped from her face and she laughed weakly. "Then it will be my turn to tell you lies about how simple it is," she said, and added, "Sister."

The acknowledgment they were now kin warmed Rhiannyn. Brushing the damp hair off Elan's brow, she said, "I am sure you shall, Sister."

Suddenly, Elan slackened and sank into her straw mattress. "Ah," she breathed, "it is almost worth the pain to feel its absence."

Christophe moved to his sister's feet and lifted the blanket. "I must look as the physician told me to."

"Think you I care anymore?" she grumbled and grabbed the blanket and tossed it off her nearly naked body.

It was as Rhiannyn's mother had once told her—modesty had no place in the birthing of children.

Though clearly flustered, Christophe completed his examination and hastened the blanket back into place. "The time nears," he said and looked to Rhiannyn. "Once the head shows, I will need you to help me lift her to squatting and support her upright. It will require great effort if the babe is long in coming. Can you do it?"

"I can."

It was not long before another contraction hit Elan. "It is killing me!" she shrieked.

"Find a smooth piece of wood to place between her teeth," Christophe instructed.

One finger at a time, Rhiannyn extracted her hand from Elan's. "I will be back soon," she said, though she doubted she was heard. Slipping out of the tent, her gaze lit first upon the morning sky, next the throng of Saxons advancing on the field where King William sat ready to do battle.

Fear ran through her. Maxen had said Edwin would come, and he had. And it did not appear to be a straggling army marching with him but an impressive array of Saxons come to change what Hastings had wrought.

Dear Lord, she prayed, *let this spectacle be sufficient to turn William to peace. Let him suffer enough doubt about the outcome that he does as Maxen proposed. Let—*

Elan screamed.

Rhiannyn dragged her gaze from the scene and bent to search out a piece of wood.

Maxen stared at the army marching toward William's. Although it could mean his death if he went into battle, he was pleased by what he saw.

In a formation identical to William's—archers, infantry, cavalry— came Harwolfson's soldiers of a number that appeared equal to the Norman army. They might even number more. All were armed with either a spear, a sword, the great two-handed battle-axe of the Saxons, or a bow and arrows. Some were garbed in chain mail.

Though such a show of force Maxen had wished for, he had not thought it possible Harwolfson could muster it. Most admirable.

"Dear Lord, cavalry," William muttered.

Maxen knew what he was thinking. Much of the Norman victory at Hastings was owed to the Normans being accomplished at using horses in battle, whereas the Saxons had fought on foot—something Harwolfson intended to remedy this day.

"Look how he comes," William growled. "See how he configures his army to mine. He mocks me!"

Likely the king had never been better matched. Still, though the Saxon rebels looked the part, it did not mean they could fight the part.

"And weapons aplenty," William continued. "I would not have believed it possible."

Maxen turned his regard upon his liege. "We do battle?"

"Of course we do battle!" Baron Pendery snapped. "I fear not a Saxon dog whose greatest accomplishment is the ravishment of an innocent young woman."

The king's response was quick and crushing. "Do you think to tell me what to do, Pendery?"

Maxen's father hid his surprise well. "I do not, my king. I but voice an opinion."

"Too loudly!"

The baron bent his head in deference. "Pray, forgive me."

William returned his gaze to his adversary, waiting through the clamor and clatter of the Saxons' advance which would be followed by the dead silence that always fell before a clash.

"I die," Elan panted where she hung limp between Rhiannyn and Christophe in the aftermath of a contraction that had brought the baby's head to crown.

Rhiannyn reached to the chest behind and scooped a dripping cloth from the basin there. She squeezed excess water from it and patted the cloth across Elan's brow. "Soon it will be over," she said, trying not to hear the movement of Edwin's army, the sound of which shot up the ridge.

"And I will be dead," was Elan's oft-repeated rejoinder. But this time the eyes she turned to Rhiannyn believed it to be true. "I must confess ere my last breath."

"Nonsense," Christophe said. "You will live to rear this child as it ought to be."

"I must—"

Another contraction, and when it was over, she rolled her head on her neck and dropped it on Rhiannyn's shoulder. "Hear me?" she beseeched. "I must free myself of this burden."

Rhiannyn wiped her brow again. "Do not talk. You waste your strength."

"I must needs…" She swallowed hard. "It might make a difference."

"A difference?" Rhiannyn asked.

Elan nodded. "It was not ravishment."

Rhiannyn slammed her gaze to Christophe whose eyes were as wide as hers felt.

"I knew who Edwin was." Elan whimpered. "Willingly, I gave myself to him."

"Why?" Rhiannyn asked.

A bitter smile rose to her sister-in-law's chapped lips. "With which would you rather present your father—ravishment you were incapable of preventing or…" She moistened her lips. "…discovery on your wedding night you are not a maiden?"

Then Edwin had been a pawn in Elan's desperate plan to absolve herself of the responsibility of lost virtue. "I see," Rhiannyn said.

"My father must be told," Elan said. "He—" In the next instant, she was incapable of words. However, screaming was not beyond her, and she deafened Rhiannyn's ears as the baby tried again to force its way into the world.

This time when Christophe pressed the wood between her teeth, she clamped down on it.

"Push," he commanded, "and do not stop until I say."

And so she did.

As Rhiannyn continued to support her, she longed to think on Elan's confession and find some use in it, but this was not the time. She only prayed it would not be too late when the time came.

44

Underestimated—exactly as planned, Edwin thought as he reined in his mount amid his cavalry. He and his followers had made themselves scarce these past months to ensure the usurper misjudged their numbers and strength.

It was a formidable army the Norman had assembled, but not as immense as it would have been had Edwin revealed the extent of his own. Silence had served him well.

He could only have been more pleased were his men equal in training and skill to his adversary's. He had worked them hard for this day, and though they were no longer simply men of the earth, the land yet resided in their hearts. Also in their hearts was revenge justified by the right to take back what was theirs, and of no better service was it than in this present capacity.

As the remainder of Edwin's forces took position, he looked across the field to where his counterpart was mounted behind the papal banner.

How like Hastings, he mused. Then, as now, William had flaunted the Church's approval of his theft of another people's country, then he had slaughtered nearly all. Would this day end the same?

"Nay," he said, not realizing he spoke aloud until the word was out of him. God owed him this. Today, the Saxons would triumph, and their lands would be returned to them.

"Your mind is heavy," Aethel broke into his thoughts. "You think on that other battle?"

"I almost expect to see King Harold here," Edwin said and looked down at the man who stood alongside him.

Though Aethel was of the infantry, he had marched to the field beside Edwin. "What think you?" the big man asked, jutting his bearded chin toward the enemy.

Once more, Edwin picked out William atop his mount. "Whatever happens this day will secure England's future." He moved his gaze left of the man who named himself king and settled it on a large figure. Though he could not make out the man's features, he was certain it was Maxen Pendery.

Edwin's smile felt bitter. God willing, this day he would have his revenge tenfold. Not only would Normans be purged from English soil, but he would repay the man who had taken not only his lands, but the woman who was to have been his wife. And if he ever got his hands on Elan Pendery...

Something pricked at the edge of Edwin's awareness. He looked to his adversary, and seeing nothing amiss, turned his regard upon his men.

Though silence prevailed, something unspoken coursed through a good many of them. Far too many.

He looked more closely, from one man to another. And knew. The eerie silence before battle had sent unease through their ranks. Not the tense excitement of seasoned warriors about to perform their life's work, but the worry of men about to leap into something they doubted themselves capable of—mayhap were not capable of.

Dear Lord, why? Edwin sent heavenward. After all the times these men had proven themselves capable, why did they now doubt themselves?

The silence, he once more concluded. Though it was nearly as familiar to Edwin as his sword, few of his rebels had faced it.

They would not fail, he assured himself. Once the battle commenced and warfare filled the air, they would wield their weapons more sharply than ever.

Edwin nodded to himself—and stilled when a high-pitched wail split the silence. It was not the sound of trumpets or battle cries. It was...

He frowned. A baby?

Acting as his own herald, Edwin Harwolfson's son told the world he had come. Born early but seemingly in good health, the infant loosed lusty cry after lusty cry.

While Christophe tended Elan, Rhiannyn supported the babe against her chest and cleansed the birthing from his skin—and happened upon what might be needed to prove his parentage.

"Ah, blessed," she whispered, recalling her first encounter with Edwin. He had removed his boots to wade in the river while they talked, and she had noticed the absence of the small toe on his left foot. Unabashedly, he had confided that a hundred years earlier, a witch had cursed his family such that all Harwolfson males would in this way be known for their treachery. When she had asked what treachery he spoke of, he had smiled devilishly and changed the topic.

Once Edwin's son was swaddled in the crook of her arm and had quieted to snuffling and whimpering, Rhiannyn sighed over him. Joyous, as if this were the babe she had made with Maxen, she could almost forget what transpired on the field beyond—rather, what would transpire once the clash sounded.

Lowering to her knees beside the new mother, she said, "Your son, my lady."

Elan kept her eyes tightly closed.

"See here, I have your son, Elan. Pray, look upon him. He is so beautiful—"

She jerked her head opposite. "I do not...want it."

It. Not *him.* As if the babe had not come from her. As if he were something not human.

Rhiannyn glanced at Christophe. Though his head was bent to his work, he had clamped his bottom lip between his teeth.

"Elan," she tried again, "I know you are weary and hurting, but your babe needs its mother's breast. You must—"

"I must do naught!"

Christophe's head came up. "Aye, Elan, you must!" he said, tone so sharp the infant renewed its cries.

"Take it away!" Blindly, she threw out an arm and struck Rhiannyn in the shoulder. "I cannot bear to hear it!"

Having dropped back on her heels lest Elan strike again and hit the babe, Rhiannyn stared at her sister-in-law. Were she not so ill with birthing, a hard shake would be in order, but it could wait for later.

Later…

Rhiannyn peered across her shoulder at the tent opening beyond which a battle might soon be fought that could take from her and hundreds—thousands!—all that was dear to them should Maxen's bid for negotiation fail.

The babe shrieked, loosed an arm from its swaddling, and flailed a tiny fist.

"Ah, precious one." Rhiannyn stroked the hand of this child who could become as fatherless as he seemed to be motherless. "What would you have me do?"

His cries easing, he splayed his fingers and closed them around her finger.

Then Rhiannyn knew. Clasping the babe close, she stood and started toward the tent opening. "Christophe," she said over her shoulder, "I require your horse."

"Where are you going?"

"To end the battle ere it begins." She stepped outside.

Just over the ridge, the two armies faced each other as they waited for the trumpets to sound the commencement of the deadly contest. Determined to reach Edwin before that happened, she loosed the reins of Christophe's horse and stepped to its side to mount—no easy feat while cradling a babe.

"What do you intend?" Christophe demanded.

Grateful he had followed, she looked around. "Edwin must see he has a son."

"But—"

"Trust me in this. Take the babe and hand him up when I am mounted."

He accepted the bundle, and when she was astride in the fashion of men, passed the babe into her arms.

"It will end," she said and urged the horse toward the sloping end of the ridge marking the southernmost edge of William's army.

As much as she longed to set the horse to a gallop, she kept a pace safe for the babe, though still likely to distress him. However, when she glanced down, she saw Edwin's son had drifted to sleep as if the bump and bounce suited him. A good sign for a warrior's son.

Although she had intended to skirt William's army before any could turn her back, she was noticed before she gained the field. Using surprise to her advantage, she made it past the formation. As shouts and the restlessness of horses goaded by their riders disrupted the still of both armies, she guided her mount over the open field between William and Edwin.

Let none fire upon me, she prayed. *Let them see I present no threat.*

Certain Edwin would be among his cavalry, as William was with his own, she searched him out. It was not necessary, for a path opened down the center of his army and he came toward her.

Expression tight, he motioned his men to quiet and commanded her, "Come no nearer!"

She reined in and turned her mount sideways so Edwin could see the one she had brought with her.

"What have you come for?" he asked as he neared. "More trickery?"

She pushed the cloth away from the babe's face. "To present your son, Edwin."

He jerked, would surely have faltered in step had he been on foot. "Son?" He halted his horse several feet from her.

"Aye. Yours."

As he narrowed his gaze on the babe, a change in the air brought Rhiannyn's head around. A single horsemen had broken from King William's formation and galloped across the field. Maxen.

"Edwin, pray let him come!" she entreated. "Surely you cannot fear one man with so many at your side?"

"More Pendery trickery," he growled.

"I vow, he did not know I intended this—I hardly knew myself. He but seeks to protect me."

"What do you intend, Rhiannyn?"

"Peace."

"There can be no such thing between Saxon and Norman."

"But already there is. If you would just—"

The sound of arrows nocked and the hiss of strings being drawn arrested Rhiannyn's voice. Peering past Edwin, she saw his archers had trained their weapons on Maxen. "Edwin," she pleaded, "order them to stand down."

He dropped his gaze to the babe, turned in the saddle, and motioned for his men to lower their weapons.

Rhiannyn nearly slumped with relief.

"The babe is of Elan Pendery?" Edwin said.

"Aye, just born."

She heard his breath, glimpsed something of the past in his eyes, then he said, "He should have been of you and me, Rhiannyn."

It was true. "In a different time and place," she said.

His lids narrowed. "You love Pendery?"

As there seemed no way to make her answer easier to swallow, she said, "I do."

Maxen gained her side a moment later. "Almighty!" He closed a hand around her arm. "What do you, Rhiannyn?"

"The woman who was first mine has presented me with a son," Edwin said derisively.

Maxen looked from his wife's pleading eyes to the one who, if not for Hastings, would have been her husband. Never had he felt such fear as when she had ridden toward the enemy. He had known immediately she carried Elan's babe, and had been fairly certain of what she intended—unlike the king who had roared over what he perceived to be treachery.

Thinking he might go mad before he was heard, but knowing death would be his end if he did not contain himself, Maxen had waited for a break in William's cursing before explaining his wife's behavior. He had told the king he was certain this was her way to peace—that in being shown his child, Harwolfson would more easily submit to Norman domination.

For once, Maxen's father had proven useful. His ravings gave the king the presence of mind to set aside his own anger and ponder the situation. Fortunately, he had quickly granted Maxen permission to cross the field. Though never would Maxen have put Rhiannyn in such jeopardy, he knew what she had done was good, the trumpets having yet to sound. Now there was a chance which the king's pride had seemed inclined to let slip away.

"What think you of your son, Harwolfson?" Maxen asked.

The man flicked his gaze over the child before settling it hard upon the one who asked. "As 'tis told he was born of ravishment, he cannot be mine."

"It is not true he was got in that way," Rhiannyn said, "but it is true he is yours, Edwin."

"How grand of you to believe me incapable of such behavior—believing me over the Pendery harlot."

"Lady Elan recants."

"What?" Maxen and Harwolfson asked in unison.

"As she was giving birth, she revealed the truth to Christophe and me. She said she gave herself to you to hide her loss of virtue from her father."

Maxen had not expected such, having presumed that, regardless of what had brought Elan and Harwolfson together, she had been untouched before their encounter.

"That may be," Harwolfson said, "but do you count the months, you will see the babe comes too early to be mine."

"He was born young by a few weeks." Rhiannyn began to uncover the infant's feet. "But Harwolfson blood gave him life." She lifted the little one's left foot. "Four toes on this one, as have you, Edwin."

Seeing the struggle in the rebel's eyes, Maxen waited.

"This is your peace, Rhiannyn?" Harwolfson demanded, throwing his arms wide. "A son in exchange for all of England?"

"England is William's," Maxen said.

"Not after this day!"

"Even more so after this day if you fight a battle you cannot win." Having seen Harwolfson's men up close, and the uncertainty many tried to hide, he was convinced of it, though he would not tell the king.

The rebel glanced behind. "My army outnumbers the usurper's."

"Numbers only. Of more import is what each man brings to the battle. Can you say half your men are experienced in bloodletting? A quarter? If you stay the course, William will make but another example of you."

This time, Harwolfson sent his gaze to the king's army. "Do we die here or in his prisons, it makes no difference. Here we have a chance to regain what is ours. Your way, we lose all."

"Not if you give the king good reason to keep you and your followers alive and free."

Though Harwolfson tried to hide his interest, enough shone through to hang hope upon, furthered by his glance at the babe.

"What do you propose, Pendery?"

"Submit. Give the king your fealty, and methinks he will award you Blackspur, along with a goodly portion of land upon which to settle your Saxons."

Disbelief erupted from Harwolfson in the form of laughter. "Blackspur, the castle you have raised upon my lands?"

As it was not truly a question, Maxen did not respond.

"Why not Etcheverry Castle, then?" Harwolfson demanded.

"That King William will not consider."

"Convenient for you."

"Are you interested, Harwolfson?"

"How much land with Blackspur?"

"One quarter of the Etcheverry lands."

"One quarter!"

"Are you interested?" Maxen repeated.

Harwolfson's lids lowered to slits. "Were I, for what should I believe you would honor the bargain?"

"If King William agrees, you have my word it will be done."

"Ha! What of your word to Aethel and the others when they were told they could depart Etcheverry without harm? What of the man who died upon the shaft of your arrow?"

"Not my arrow, and neither did he die."

"He was shot in the back!"

"Edwin," Rhiannyn said, "'tis true. It was the knight, Ancel Rogere, who shot Hob. For it, Rogere is dead and, blessedly, Hob lives."

"If that is so, why has he not come to me?"

"He has accepted Maxen as his lord."

"Not the Hob I know."

"A different Hob," she conceded. "Of the same flesh, but of a changed mind, one that has chosen peace."

As the rebel searched her face for a lie, Maxen said, "You, Harwolfson, more than the king, have the power to ensure this day is not covered in blood. I urge you to wield your power well, not just for yourself, but for those who follow you."

Harwolfson considered him, then reined his horse about as if to put heels to it. He did not. Back stiff, he surveyed his men.

Hoping the rebel wisely weighed their lives, Maxen moved nearer Rhiannyn and said low, "Brave, my foolish little Saxon. If I live long enough to have you in my bed again, you will owe me for every worry dealt me this day."

In spite of their circumstances, she managed a small smile.

The minutes stretched, but finally Harwolfson came back around. "I will bargain with the usurper."

The burden that had plagued Maxen's soul for over two years shifted slightly, but something in the man's eyes told him to control the relief rising through him—to creep rather than flood. "Speak, Harwolfson."

"These are my terms. The usurper grants me the entirety of Etcheverry—all of its lands and both castles."

Maxen ignored the small, desperate sound Rhiannyn made and said, "I have told you, he will not give that."

"Further," the rebel continued, "every one of my men, regardless of what they have done to reclaim their country, will be pardoned alongside me."

"I will put it to the king," Maxen said gruffly.

"And I want your sister."

Only the saddle's pommel beneath Maxen's hand kept his fingers from turning into a bone-crushing fist.

"Maxen," Rhiannyn said softly, desperately.

The distress on her face revealing her fear The Bloodlust Warrior moved beneath his skin, he returned his gaze to Harwolfson. "I cannot agree to that. Though my sister has done you ill, she will not suffer your revenge."

One side of the man's mouth hitched. "I make no secret I despise her, but you are wrong about my intentions. As she is the mother of my son, I will take this *fine* example of a Norman noblewoman to wife. And that is not for you to decide. It is for your king."

He was right, and though Maxen was certain William would not bend on Etcheverry, the man would toss his sister Harwolfson's way without so much as a thought for Elan's betrothal to Sir Guy.

"Edwin," Rhiannyn said. "Here is what you want—your son." She nodded at the dozing babe who was years away from the knowledge this day he held sway over the lives of many.

"I do," he said.

As she had known when she had determined to ride out to him. She moistened her lips. "If Lady Elan could be convinced to give over the babe for the sake of peace—and your son's wellbeing so he never suffers what would surely be unending discord between his parents—would it suffice?"

Maxen struggled to keep surprise—and admiration for Rhiannyn—from his face. Unless the birthing had changed Elan's feelings toward her babe, his sister still intended to cast the child upon the Church. Thus, Harwolfson was being offered something of greater value because of the sacrifice required by the woman who had wronged him. And likely, the rebel would find satisfaction in that bit of revenge.

"A child needs its mother," Harwolfson said.

Rhiannyn inclined her head. "But until you wed a woman who will be a good mother to him and a loving wife to you, a wet nurse will serve."

Maxen waited with his wife for Harwolfson's answer, hoping that when dealt William's refusal to give over all of Etcheverry, the man would be so set on gaining possession of his son he would settle for Blackspur.

It was not a man who snapped the ensuing silence, but a babe less than an hour old. He whimpered, wriggled, and once more set to crying.

"He is too long without his mother's milk," Rhiannyn said.

The rebel nudged his horse alongside hers and peered at the howling babe. "My son," he murmured and touched its lower lip.

The babe dropped his chin and sucked at his father's knuckle.

"Indeed, he is hungry," Harwolfson said with what seemed wonder.

"What will you do, Edwin?" Rhiannyn asked.

His nostrils moved with a deep breath. "Though you would have me think it a sacrifice his mother makes in yielding him, I do not believe it—not of the one who, in covering her sin, tried to put greater sin on me. Thus, methinks she intends to give her Saxon-tainted babe to the Church."

More silence, during which Maxen felt Rhiannyn's answering tension.

Harwolfson loosed a hollow laugh. "I can think of naught better for my son than that I bend on taking his mother to wife. But that is all." He drew back his hand and winced as the babe resumed crying. "Deliver him to the one who birthed him," he said. "Pendery and I will finish this."

Rhiannyn looked to Maxen, and at his nod, prodded her mount across the field.

"I did not kill your brother," Harwolfson said while both men watched her progress.

"As Rhiannyn has told. But I believe you know who threw the dagger."

"At the time, I did not, but I know now."

Feeling the darkness in him uncoil, Maxen pressed it down, but still his voice was tight when he said, "Who?"

"Dora."

It was not the fit Maxen expected, but it made sense. He looked sidelong at the rebel. "The witch who tried to bury Rhiannyn alive."

Harwolfson returned the sidelong look. "The one from whom you saved her, I am told."

"So I did, but not before killing two of the three who aided her."

Harwolfson nodded slowly.

"Where is she?" Maxen asked.

"It is months since last I saw her. And that is well with me."

Might she be dead? Maxen wondered. "Who is she?"

Harwolfson shrugged. "An old Saxon who longs to return to the days before your kind came to our shores."

Rhiannyn having gone from sight, Maxen turned his face to the rebel. "'Tis obvious she is far more than that."

"True. It was she who saved my life and claims to be gifted with the sight of things not yet visible to others. But whether she foretells or but guesses well, long days past, she revealed your sister would bear me a son."

There was more. Maxen was certain of it when he caught a flicker of fear in Harwolfson's eyes. "What else did she tell?"

"The child must be killed to cleanse it of its Norman blood. And that is where Dora and I came to an end. And shall remain at an end."

Then justice might never be given. Maxen slowly released his breath, silently vowed that, providing the hag nevermore threatened any he loved, he would not pursue her. With Rhiannyn at his side, he would live this day forward.

Harwolfson sighed. "And now the day must be decided."

"All of Etcheverry," Maxen said. "I shall put it to the king, though I do not think it possible."

"But the battle is more than possible, Pendery. Deliver me these things, and I will submit to the usurper. Deny me and…"

Maxen inclined his head and turned his horse, but before he could dig in his heels, Harwolfson tossed at him, "Why is this so important to you?"

Maxen peered across his shoulder. "Because it is important to Rhiannyn." Though once he had wished peace to unburden his soul, now he also wished it for the woman he loved. And soon it would be their babe in her arms.

"A lowly Saxon who is but your leman?" Harwolfson scoffed.

"Nay, a Saxon who is my equal. And now my wife."

Maxen did not think the man's eyes could grow wider had a dagger been thrust through his chest. But though prepared to glimpse anger and resentment for what had been lost to another man, it was something else. Possibly approval. Assuredly grudgingly given.

Without further word, Maxen spurred away.

45

MILK WAS RELUCTANTLY provided, and as Rhiannyn peered into Elan's downturned face where the young woman lay on her side feeding her child, she was further convinced the best thing for Edwin's son was to be with his father in the absence of his mother.

Whereas Elan seemed not to want any part of this child, Edwin had long wanted one—so much there had been no question he mourned the lost opportunity of a son more than the death of the woman to whom he had first been betrothed, so much he had readily replaced the lady with Rhiannyn.

Still, the question must be put to Elan.

Rhiannyn glanced at Christophe who stood outside the tent staring at the battlefield. Since her return a half hour past, several times he had stuck his head in, interrupting her prayer to assure her all was yet still while his brother and the king conversed. God willing, it would remain so.

"At last," Elan said in a quavering voice and drew back from the babe who had drifted into sleep.

Rhiannyn touched her sister-in-law's shoulder. "Elan, do you think…" She swallowed. "Do you think you will come to love this child?"

A sickly laugh burbled from her. "I wish to begin anew—with Guy."

Would it be any better with him? Might a child made of their union be loved unlike this one Elan did not want to love? And why did she not? What had made her this way? Was something broken in her, the pieces so far separated they could not knit themselves back together? Was it because, as an only girl amid an abundance of brothers trained hard into warriors, she had been regarded as too delicate to have anything asked of her beyond the effort to look beautiful? Had she never learned that strength and courage hid in hard places that required effort and sacrifice to pull one's self out? And now, finding herself—albeit by her own making—amid those hard places, could she only flounder, too desperate to return to life as she knew it to grow into someone better?

Rhiannyn sighed. "Elan, you must be sure of what is best for your babe, because what goes upon what could become a battlefield has much to do with this child."

She squeezed her eyes closed. "I want only to start anew."

"Without your babe?"

Her lids slowly lifted, bloodshot eyes shifted to her child. With what seemed effort, she raised a hand toward his face, let it hover above his cheek, and lowered it back to her side.

"I want to be happy," she said, "and he will not make me happy. Guy will." She looked up, and Rhiannyn thought it a good thing the young woman's eyes were deeply wet, evidencing she felt some loss. "Aye, without the babe."

It seemed the best answer under the circumstances, but it made Rhiannyn ache knowing she could so easily turn from her child. "Edwin Harwolfson wants his son. Are you well with it?"

A frown so deep it might ever line her skin grooved Elan's face. "Is he truly a good man? Will he make a good father?"

"He is, and I believe he will."

Her nod was slight. "I am well with him. And if not him, the Church." She drew a long breath. "Now, will you take him away?"

Rhiannyn opened her mouth to answer, but it was not her cracked, crumbling voice that said, "I will take him away."

Rhiannyn jerked her head around.

The one who had tried to bury her alive stood just inside the tent, her aged figure holding Christophe before her with a blade to his neck.

"You should be dead, Rhiannyn of Etcheverry," Dora said. "And you will be, but first I will have that babe. Bring him to me."

"Wh-who is she?" Elan whispered.

"All things bad," Rhiannyn breathed, and out of the corner of her eye, saw her sister-in-law slip an arm around the infant and pull him close.

"Do it, betrayer!" Dora jerked her hand, causing Christophe to yelp as a thin line of blood appeared beneath his jaw. And yet for all the fear in his eyes, he gave a barely perceptible shake of his head.

"Do it," Dora repeated, "else I will bleed this whelp just as I bled his brother."

Rhiannyn gasped. "Thomas? It was you?"

"It is always me, and shall always be 'til England is Saxon again."

Here was how she had known of Thomas's curse when Rhiannyn had entered Andredeswald to warn Edwin about Maxen. Dora had not felt it as she had wished all to believe. From the wood where she had thrown the dagger that had spilled Thomas's life upon a dirt road, she had witnessed it.

"Bring me the harlot's babe!" she demanded.

Dear Lord, what am I to do? If I do not give her the child, she will kill Christophe.

That was not true, she realized as she held the crazed woman's gaze. Regardless of whether or not the babe was given her, Dora would kill Christophe, had already said she would kill Rhiannyn, and would surely make an end to the unresistant Elan. And though this child was the son of the man Dora believed to be the savior of the Saxons, she would likely kill him as well.

"What do you intend?" she hedged.

Dora drew more blood from Christophe's neck, but this time the youth was silent, and Rhiannyn saw the cause in his narrowed eyes, flared nostrils, and thrust jaw. He was too angered to remain afeared, a state rarely more than glimpsed in him. But it would be of no benefit if Rhiannyn did not move.

She raised a staying hand. "I will bring him." She bent over Elan whose eyes were large, breath sharp. As she slid a hand beneath the infant, she whispered, "With my life, I shall protect him."

Elan whimpered but loosed her son.

Rhiannyn pulled the babe into her chest, and as she straightened, he made sweet little sounds and nudged her breast. She turned to Dora.

"Here!" the old woman ordered.

And when I am near, Rhiannyn thought, *she will slit Christophe's throat, and I will be all the more vulnerable to the same fate whilst I hold this child.*

"Release Christophe," Rhiannyn said, "and I will come to you."

The bit of color in the woman's pale, gray face spread. "Bring him to me!"

"First, Christophe."

Dora's eyes moved between Rhiannyn, the babe, Elan, and her captive. But then she laughed, swept the blade from Christophe's throat, and brought its hilt down on his temple.

The youth's eyes went wide, lids dropped, and he fell at her feet.

"Christophe!" Elan struggled to sit up.

"He will live," Dora said.

Only for the moment, Rhiannyn knew. "For what do you want the babe?" she asked.

"Ah, Rhiannyn, you know for what. As he is tainted, he must be purified."

Rhiannyn held the child nearer. She knew the woman was mad, but here was greater evidence of evil. *Please, Lord,* she prayed, *let me keep her distant until I can think what to do.*

"Bring him!"

"Edwin wants his son," Rhiannyn grasped the only argument she could put her mind to.

A twisted thing that could not be called a smile, reshaped Dora's mouth. "He will have his son, but not this one."

"Do not!" Elan cried.

Rhiannyn dropped her chin toward her sister-in-law and caught the slight movement of the one at Dora's feet. Through the hair falling over her eyes, she looked nearer upon the youth. He lay on his chest with his face turned toward her—and stared at her. Rather than render him unconscious, the blow had dazed him.

"My babe is innocent!" Elan cried.

"The better to pay for its mother's sins," Dora snapped. "Now should I finish off your brother, or will Rhiannyn deliver me what was promised?"

Though the old woman no longer had hold of Christophe, he remained too near to escape the thrust of her blade. Ignoring Elan's cry, Rhiannyn moved forward, each purposeful step giving herself and Christophe time to take stock of all that was available to them. There was not much for Rhiannyn with both arms filled, but below her right hand supporting her left arm's burden was the meat dagger on her belt. She could turn her fingers around the hilt and pull the blade from its sheath, but how to protect the babe while she fended off the attack to come?

Feigning defeat, she lowered eyes that asked of her brother-in-law, *How, Christophe?*

He thrust his lower jaw forward again, shoved his upper body up off the earthen floor, and slammed his back into Dora's legs.

The old woman flailed in an attempt to recover her balance, but it was out from under her, and her blade sliced air as she fell backward.

She might have regained her feet, perhaps quickly enough to do what she had come to do, but the crack resounding around the tent told she would not soon rise. If ever.

As Rhiannyn held tight to the babe who had begun to wail, Christophe lurched to his feet. His own meat dagger in hand, he lunged at the old woman.

A step from where Dora slumped against the chest with her neck upon its edge, he halted, and Rhiannyn saw him quake. "I think I have killed her."

It was not enough to think it, not with one such as she.

Rhiannyn hastened to Elan and passed the babe into her reaching arms before coming alongside Christophe.

As told by the twisted angle of Dora's head, the slack mouth from which her tongue bulged, and her unseeing stare, she was dead.

Rhiannyn put an arm around the youth. "You did not kill her. That is what *she* came here to do—to kill the babe, me, and likely, Elan and you."

"I did not wish her dead," he whispered. "I just did not want her to…"

Rhiannyn stepped in front of him and clasped his face between her hands. "You saved us. Thus, the only thing for which you are responsible is that we live. This is Dora's doing, she who either had something foul in her or naught at all. The world is a better place without the darkness she cast upon it."

He swallowed what sounded like a throat full of tears. "I am not my brothers. I do not want to be."

"Of course you are not. You are Christophe." She smiled. "My wonderfully brave brother."

He closed his eyes long, and when he opened them, his mouth lifted in a sorrowful smile. "What do we do with her?" He jerked his head at Dora.

A good question, but the answer was better—a use for the old woman in death.

Rhiannyn looked to Elan who held her fussing babe close, her eyes yet wild with fright. "'Tis over, Elan," she said. "You and your son are safe."

"She is dead?"

"She is. Now Christophe is going to help me with something, but he will be back shortly." Rhiannyn nodded at the babe. "Methinks the breast might soothe him."

"What would you have me do?" Christophe asked as his sister set to quieting her son.

"Help me get Dora onto your horse."

He frowned but did not ask her purpose.

The king was adamant. He would pardon the Saxons alongside their leader, yield up Harwolfson's son, and had himself offered Elan in marriage in spite of her betrothal to Sir Guy—and the fit her father had thrown which had seen him dragged from the field. But William would not yield Etcheverry Castle and its immediate lands. They were to remain Pendery. But the king did make further concessions.

Hoping they would be enough, Maxen returned to Harwolfson. "King William will pardon your followers, grant custody of your son, and award a demesne of a size to accommodate your people."

"But?" the rebel leader said, knowingly.

"Not Etcheverry Castle. Blackspur Castle, but rather than a quarter of the Etcheverry lands, he will grant you half."

Harwolfson's eyebrows rose. "Etcheverry is not negotiable."

"The king will give no more."

"Then I regret we are where we were ere Rhiannyn brought the babe to me." He jerked the reins to turn his horse.

Maxen grabbed his arm to stay him, causing Harwolfson's soldiers to react with a clatter of weapons answered in kind by William's soldiers.

"Think, man!" Maxen said. "Consider the lives spent for something that can never be. And if that is not enough, think of your son growing up without his father, his only title that of being misbegotten. Can you live with it—likely die with it?"

All of Harwolfson tense, so much he began to tremble, he jerked his arm out of Maxen's hold. "Your problem, Pendery, is that you love, and it makes you more a fool than I."

"If a fool, one who is blessed as never will you be if you stay this course. Accept Blackspur. The castle nears completion, the land is fertile, and there is water aplenty."

"And ever I shall be under your watch."

"As the demesnes border, it is natural our goings-on will be seen by each other, but you will answer to the king, not me."

"Ah, but should I overstep my bounds, you will be there to rein me in, aye?"

Sensing Harwolfson had shifted nearer Blackspur, Maxen did not rise to his bait. But as he waited him out, a murmur rippled through the ranks on both sides.

"What is this?" Harwolfson demanded.

Maxen followed his gaze around and wished to know the same. Rhiannyn came, this time flanked by two knights, surely ordered by the king to accompany her. But more curious was that though she held no babe as she walked her mount forward, someone was over the back of her horse.

"I do not know," Maxen said, hating that she had left the safety gained in returning to Elan. "Will you allow my wife and her escort to draw near, or should I ride to her?"

"They may come." Harwolfson signaled to his men.

When Rhiannyn was fifty feet out, Maxen saw whom she had brought with her, but before he could speak, Harwolfson exclaimed, "'Tis Dora!"

Maxen looked sharply at him. "You told you had not seen her in months."

"I have not. I did not know she was here. Is she...?"

"So it appears." And Maxen did not think it a bad thing, bad being reserved for what had transpired to return Rhiannyn to the field bearing the old witch. But as she neared, he saw no evidence she had suffered harm.

He captured her gaze, and as she came alongside, she said low, "The worst is over. You are to be proud of Christophe."

Surely she did not mean the youth was responsible for the body draped over the horse?

Rhiannyn shifted her regard to Harwolfson. "Edwin," she said, "I know 'twas not by your order, but Dora entered Lady Elan's tent to slay your son and myself, and 'tis likely she would have stolen the lives of my husband's brother and sister as well had she not been stopped."

The horror in Harwolfson's eyes seemed genuine, and when he spoke, his voice was choked. "What of my son?"

"Christophe Pendery defended us well. Thus, the babe was no more harmed than the rest of us. Though I know not where you are in your negotiation with King William, I ask you to consider if you truly wish to stay the course set by Dora."

Harwolfson's lips thinned until they were more pale than the rest of him. "Her course is not my course."

"Not entirely, Edwin, but they converge. Just as she was willing to spill your son's Norman blood alongside his Saxon blood, so is your army and King William's willing to spill the blood of your own people alongside your enemy's."

He stared.

"Better that, Dora believed," she continued, "than the two meet and become something wonderful as they have in your son. But I know you do not believe the same, Edwin. Pray, make your peace with William so a better, stronger England can be knit from our two peoples."

Moment after moment breathed its last as Harwolfson considered her words, but finally he swung his gaze to Maxen. "Blackspur," he said with a nod. "Tell your king I agree."

It was heavens more than Maxen had believed possible when he had earlier awaited the sounding of trumpets. Still, there was regret for Guy. But at least he would live and Elan would be his as promised. "The bargain is struck," he said.

Harwolfson shifted his regard to William. "Peace for as long as he keeps his end of it."

Rhiannyn sighed. "I thank you, Edwin."

He jutted his chin at Dora. "Leave her so we might see her properly buried."

"Ride with me, Rhiannyn," Maxen said and reached to her. She came into his arms, and as he settled her on the fore of his saddle, he said, "We will speak again, Harwolfson."

"Certes, we shall."

Drawing Rhiannyn back against him, Maxen turned his mount and started back across the field with the king's knights following.

"It is truly done?" she asked.

He gazed into her upturned face and wished he could say it was so. There would be other uprisings, possibly for years to come, but the end of Harwolfson's rebellion would likely take the heart out of others that aspired to such size and strength.

"It is not done, *fricwebba*, but the end is nearer."

"Then I must content myself with that."

Thinking he owed Christophe more than he could repay, Maxen put heels to his mount. As they crossed the field that, God willing, would only ever know the colors of earth and foliage, the burden that had once felt like the weight of a thousand years lifted further, and he marveled at how light abundant hope felt. And sent up a prayer of thanks that his life with Rhiannyn could truly begin.

Epilogue

❧

Blackspur Castle
April, 1070

EDWIN HARWOLFSON WAS restless. As he should be, Maxen supposed. These past months, the Saxon had chafed at his yoke while the Norman army devastated the north in a cruel winter campaign to put down rebellions.

Though Maxen did not believe Edwin would rend the bargain made with King William, chiefly because of what he now had to lose, the lord of Etcheverry had been charged with ensuring his neighbor and those who had settled with him at Blackspur remained rooted to what had become Norman soil. And mostly, they had.

The ones who believed their people still stood a chance of reclaiming their country had slipped away in the night, and neither Maxen nor Edwin had moved against them. Now many of those hopeful men whose lives had been spared the year before were surely dead. William had England by the throat and would not loosen his hold.

But despite the unease hanging about Edwin like a rain-heavy cloud, he had planted himself at Blackspur for the sake of his son, whom he had named Harold after the king whose death had ended Saxon rule. Though not yet one year aged, the boy was of good size. With a serious, contemplative face and out of eyes as blue as his mother's, he stared down at the shifting bundle from where he straddled his father's hip at the center of the hall.

"Your cousin, little one," Rhiannyn said. "She is called Leofe."

Harold raised his upper lip to reveal a row of tiny teeth, turned his head aside, and dropped it onto his father's shoulder.

"'Twould seem," Maxen said, "we need not worry they like each other more than they ought to—for now."

Rhiannyn laughed softly and stroked the flushed cheek of their four-month-old daughter who showed even less interest in Harold than he had in her. Sucking a wet fist, her eyes were all for her father. And, as ever, it was no easy thing for Maxen not to become absorbed in the beautiful child Rhiannyn had gifted him.

He gave Leofe a grin that made her smile and coo around her fist, then returned his attention to Edwin whose gaze was on Rhiannyn, the mother of another man's child. But though Maxen steeled himself for it to be longing reflected on the Saxon's face, and to be doubly offended considering the man was also wed, it seemed more like sorrow. And he could hardly begrudge Edwin.

He was again the lord of a worthy demesne, albeit half the size it had once been, and he loved the son given him by a Norman, but this was not the life for which he had been prepared to die. But with the further passage of time and fewer uprisings to weigh upon his conscience, he could come out the right end of a world much changed.

"The demesne looks to be flourishing now winter is past," Maxen said.

Edwin turned his gaze to his neighbor. "Because it does," he said sharply, though not as sharply as he had spoken during Maxen's visits those first six months after Edwin had taken possession of Blackspur. He did not welcome a Norman on his lands, and he made no pretense otherwise. Still, his resentment had lightened, so much Maxen had finally agreed Rhiannyn could accompany him to Blackspur.

Edwin looked to the babe. "Your daughter is beautiful, Rhiannyn."

"I thank you." She glanced around the hall. For all its simplicity, it was of a grander size than the one at Etcheverry Castle. "Your wife, Edwin. Is she not here?"

"She is, and has been made aware of your arrival. But come, sit and refresh yourselves while we wait on her." He gestured to the high table, moved Harold to the opposite hip, and strode to the dais.

"How long will you be with us?" he asked when they were seated, their goblets filled and platters of bread and cheese set before them.

"Two nights, if it is well with you," Maxen said.

Edwin broke off a hunk of bread and yielded it to Harold's eager hands. "As you will."

A quarter hour, marked by strained conversation, passed. Then the creak of wooden stairs was heard.

Maxen looked across the hall, but before he could direct attention to the brightly garbed woman descending the last steps, Rhiannyn called, "Elan!" and passed Leofe into her husband's arms.

She ran to her sister-in-law who halted just off the steps. Moments later, her arms were around Elan, and with gasps of delight, they embraced as if feeling every one of the months since Harold's birth beside a battlefield whose bloody destiny had been thwarted.

Maxen shifted his gaze to Edwin and was comforted that the dislike that had shown from the Saxon most times he looked upon the woman who had deceived him was not much more than a flicker. Or might it no longer be dislike? Perhaps something more scaleable. Wariness?

Edwin had not wanted to wed Elan Pendery any more than she had wanted to exchange Guy for the rebel. But when it was time to hand over her babe, she could not. With beseeching and sobbing before King William, and despite their father's objections, she had gained their liege's consent to remain with her child as the Saxon's wife—providing Edwin Harwolfson agreed. Though it was with obvious distaste he did so, there had been relief about him to find his son's mother was not entirely without substance.

Guy had been hurt and angered to have been promised so much and to have it all given elsewhere. Still, in confidence, he had confessed that had Elan easily abandoned her child, it would have made him question if she was the woman with whom he wished to spend his life.

Thinking to distance himself, he had decided to leave Etcheverry. Though Maxen hated losing him, he had known it was best for Guy and the family Elan was making with Edwin. Thus, he had approached the king on his friend's behalf. It was agreed the knight would join William in further campaigns against the rebels and, if he proved himself as he had at Hastings, be awarded land upon which to raise a castle—a lord in his own right.

More for Elan's sake than the watch he was to keep on Edwin, Maxen had journeyed to Blackspur each month, several times in Christophe's company. Though certain his sister was under no threat of physical harm, he had feared for the emotional state of one so foolishly young, heartbroken, subject to the demands of a babe, and hated by the one with whom she would spend her life.

But tick by tick, husband and wife seemed to be making peace with each other, and Maxen thought it possible their marriage would be tolerable enough to raise their son without inflicting wounds so deep Harold would suffer. It was the most he hoped for, and he prayed that if one or both strayed from their wedding vows, it would be done with discretion. Again, for Harold.

"I have missed you!" Elan exclaimed, still holding fast to her sister-in-law. "You know not how!"

As Rhiannyn returned her embrace, feeling the fullness of the young woman Maxen had assured her was not wasting to skin and bone, her worries receded.

Elan seemed in good health, and there was lightness in her voice. Though she and Edwin might not be happy, if they could maintain civility, it would not be a miserable existence. In years to come, they might even settle into a kind of friendship.

Rhiannyn pulled back slightly and smiled. "I have missed you as well, and I am pleased to see how Harold has grown—such a healthy, handsome lad."

"Though my father would not agree," Elan said, "Harold is of good stock. As shall be our next."

Rhiannyn frowned. "I do not—"

Elan captured her hand and drew it between them and onto her abdomen.

She was not adequately fleshed merely because she ate well. As evidenced by the bulge that, though not yet visible, should not have escaped notice while they embraced, she was with child.

"It was but the one time—again," she fiercely whispered, throwing her eyes wide with exaggerated frustration.

"Oh," Rhiannyn whispered back, "I did not think you…he…"

"As I did not, but one eve we were much too civil with each other." A satisfied smile rose to her lips. "'Twas right after I sent Theta away. Maxen told you of it?"

He had, and been proud of his sister. He had not witnessed the confrontation, but as Elan had related and Edwin had confirmed, Theta had made derogatory remarks about Rhiannyn in her mistress's hearing. Elan had confronted Theta, and what had ensued sounded much like Rhiannyn's long-ago brawl with Meghan.

"Maxen did tell me of it," she said, "and I thank you for defending me."

Elan shrugged. "You *are* my sister. And as ugly as my cuts and bruises were—Edwin tended them—I was rather proud of them."

Edwin had tended them…And now his wife was with child. "Tell," Rhiannyn said, "does he know he will be a father again?"

Elan leaned near. "I was so ill with worry when I missed my monthly flux. All I could think was that he would not believe this babe was his— that I had cuckolded him."

"But he does know," Rhiannyn pressed, "and he believes he is the father?"

"Aye, he knows and seems to believe."

"Seems?"

Maintaining a whisper, she said, "He keeps a near eye on me and, for once, I am grateful. Otherwise, I might be bruising my knees praying this one also lacks a toe."

"Is he pleased you are to give him another child?"

She gave a soft snort. "A fortnight past, he said I should begin sharing his bed, and after several days' thought, I did. But the only time he intentionally touches me is to lay a hand on my belly—and once the dreaded *wolf* even pressed an ear to it."

Rhiannyn caught laughter behind her lips, and when it was back where it belonged, said, "Surely he is pleased."

She sighed. "At least he is not ever glowering at me. And when I am of a mood, I spare him my own displeasure."

"Mayhap one day you will discover you are happy together," Rhiannyn submitted, only to regret words sure to bring Guy to mind were he not already there.

Elan's gaze wavered. "You dream where I dare not."

"Permit me the indulgence. And know I also pray for you and Harold and Edwin."

"I do that sometimes myself." Elan removed Rhiannyn's hand from her belly and, keeping hold of it, pulled her toward the dais. "Brother," she called, "I would see your Leofe."

Maxen stood, and when his sister came alongside, kissed her cheek and passed the babe to her.

Elan's delight in the infant appeared as genuine as Harold's jealousy.

Straining toward his mother, the little boy reached with splayed hands and demanded, "Mama!"

Gently jostling Leofe who had begun to fuss, Elan stepped alongside her husband's chair and tapped her son's nose. "Be big, Harold," she softly rebuked. "You must become accustomed to mama holding another."

As he continued to protest and reach to her, Rhiannyn gave Maxen the gaze he sought. In answer to the question in his eyes, she nodded.

His smile was uncertain, but when she brightened her own, he relaxed into his and said, "It appears I must congratulate my sister and her husband."

"So it does," Edwin said with what seemed a determined lack of interest, then shifted his attention to the big man who entered the hall. "All is in readiness?"

Aethel halted just inside the doors. "Aye, my lord," he said and glanced at Rhiannyn.

As when he had greeted her and Maxen upon their arrival in the outer bailey, there was a gruffness about him, but not the angry one that had made her ache for the Aethel of old. He would never again be that, but enough of him was returned that he was recognizable. And it made her heart feel more sweetly full.

"If we ride now, Pendery," Edwin said, pushing back his chair, "we should be able to visit two of the four villages ere nightfall. And the sooner you can satisfy your king as to the state of a demesne lorded by a Saxon."

Not *his* king, but hopefully it would come with time.

"Rhiannyn"—he stepped toward her and held out Harold—"your nephew."

Who should have been our son? she wondered as she opened her arms to the little one. Was that what Edwin was thinking? If so, it was not apparent in his eyes.

She took Harold onto her hip, and for a moment there was such outrage in the boy's regard she thought he might bundle his chubby hands into fists and strike her. But then he looked to his mother, and catching her gaze, dropped his head beneath his aunt's chin and began to stroke the hair on her shoulder. Surely he was not now trying to make *her* jealous?

Rhiannyn rejected the thought, but after Maxen and Edwin took their leave and the two women settled before the hearth, Harold vehemently shook his head when Elan attempted to exchange children to allow Rhiannyn to nurse Leofe. Finally, Harold was convinced to stand alongside his aunt while she put the babe to her breast. And after many a glance toward his mother that turned flirtatious, he walked on surprisingly steady legs and climbed onto her lap. Her betrayal forgiven.

That eve, when Maxen lay down beside his wife after supper, he considered the sleeping babe between them, touched Leofe's cheek, and smiled at Rhiannyn across the dim. "Methinks I shall have to bring you more often to Blackspur."

"Oh? Does absence from your wife and daughter pain you so?" she said, then added a note of teasing. "Or is it that you have never been offered the lord's chamber?" She had noted his surprise when Edwin relinquished it to one who, in the order of nobility, could not be said to be his superior.

"Above all, the first," he said, "though I can hardly protest the comfort of the latter." He patted the mattress Elan had proudly told Rhiannyn she had seen stuffed twice as full before taking her place in this chamber. "Too," he continued, "you are good for my sister, and I thank you."

"Do you think it will come right for them?"

"I do, though how right, only they can say."

"Then not as right as it is between us?"

He pushed up onto an elbow, and peering down at her, said, "Though 'tis hard to believe any man could be happier than I, only God knows what is ahead for Elan and Edwin. Indeed, when we first wed, I did not even hope it could be like it is between us now."

Rhiannyn wondered if she would ever become so accustomed to the leaps of her heart that she would no longer notice them. "We are blessed," she said.

"Aye." He lowered his head and kissed her brow. "*Fricwebba.*"

Peace weaver.

He kissed her nose. "*Leof.*"

Dear.

He put his mouth so near hers their lips brushed. "*Deore.* My beloved Saxon bride."

Dear Reader,

On the day I finished the first draft of Lady Of Conquest— *the last of my rewritten "Bride" books—I was so emotional that the writer in me attempted to convey some of what I was feeling in a note to my dear readers:*

I am wrung out, hand as tired of supporting my head as the desk must be of supporting my elbow, vision blurred as I reread the last line which requires no *The End* to alert the reader that at this time and in this place, the story ends—on paper. If I have written these lives well, the imaginations of those who have been the much-envied fly on the wall will take up what I have put down and fill in what comes after. And if the stress and sorrow amid the joy of non-fiction life make them long for a scenic detour, an extended *Happily Ever After* will put babes in arms, faith in uncertain hearts, and years in the lives of those who beautifully grow old together. I have been there. I have done that. I aspire to give what I have been given.

Hopefully, I succeeded in some measure, and you enjoyed Rhiannyn and Maxen's love story. Thank you for joining me in the age of castles, knights, ladies, destriers, deep, dark woods and—dare I mention it?—outdoor plumbing. Wishing you many more hours of inspiring, happily-ever-after reading.

BARON OF GODSMERE

The Feud: Book I

England, 1308. Three noblemen secretly gather to ally against their treacherous lord. But though each is elevated to a baron in his own right and given a portion of his lord's lands, jealousy and reprisals lead to a twenty-five year feud, pitting family against family, passing father to son.

The Decree

England, 1333. The chink in Baron Boursier's armor is his fondness for a lovely face. When it costs him half his sight and brands him as one who abuses women, he vows to never again be "blinded" by beauty. Thus, given the choice between forfeiting his lands and wedding one of his enemies to end their feud, he chooses as his betrothed the lady said to be plain of face, rejecting the lady rumored to be most fair.

The Enemy

On the eve of the deadline to honor the king's decree of marriage, the fair Elianor of Emberly takes matters into her own hands. Determined none will suffer marriage to the man better known as *The Boursier*, she sets in motion her plan to imprison him long enough to ensure his barony is forfeited. But when all goes awry and her wrathful enemy compels her to wed him to save his lands, she discovers he is either much changed or much maligned. And the real enemy is one who lurks in their midst. One bent on keeping the feud burning.

2

Barony of Godsmere, Northern England
Autumn's end, 1333

To stop the wedding, she would have to kill the groom. Or so Agatha sought to convince her.

Peering up from beneath the ragged edge of the thick shawl she had drawn over her head, Elianor of Emberly considered the man who approached astride a destrier blacker than the dregs of her ink pot. Though Bayard Boursier was fairly complected, he seemed no less dark than his mount. From his perspiration dampened hair that flipped up at the nape to his unshaven jaw to the merciless heart that beat beneath an ebony tunic, he was kin to the night.

El ground her teeth over the king's plan to ally the bitterest of enemies. Had Edward learned nothing from the mistake of five years past when her aunt had been made to wed into the Boursiers—one that had turned the families' hatred more foul?

"A pox on you, Edward," she muttered as she glared at the king's agent of misery, a man whose appearance hardly improved the nearer he drew, one made worse by the black patch covering his left eye.

A fearsome groom he would make for Thomasin de Arell whom, it was told, he had chosen to take to wife and would do so within the next six days to avoid forfeiture of his lands. But providing all went as planned, *The Boursier*, as he was better known—as if the whole of him could not be contained within his given name—would not have the De Arell woman. Nor would he have El, though until three days past, she had feared he would choose her. Thus, she had laid plans to avoid a sacrifice possibly greater than that offered up with her first marriage.

Despite the shawl's heat that was too much for a relatively warm day, she shivered as memories of her husband crawled over the barriers erected against them.

She shook her head. Murdoch Farrow, to whom she had been wed five years ago at the age of sixteen, was dead. And, God forgive her, she had nearly danced to be free of him. Just as Thomasin de Arell would rejoice in being spared marriage to Bayard Boursier.

As he drew closer, she lowered her gaze. But one peasant among the many who thronged the market in the town outside Castle Adderstone's walls, she feigned interest in the foodstuffs offered by a merchant—an old man whose bones and joints were prominent beneath a thin layer of skin. A moment later, his hands shot up and, in concert with his voice, expressed annoyance over his dealings with a stout woman whose heavily loaded cart evidenced she was from the castle kitchens.

El slid her gaze past unplucked chickens suspended by their legs to the riders who skirted the gathering, and hazarded another look at The Boursier. She groaned. Having only seen him from a distance when he had brought his men against her uncle's, he was larger than thought. Beneath a broad jaw, his neck sloped to expansive shoulders, chest tapered to sword-girded hips, bulky thighs gripped his destrier, hosed calves stretched long to stirrups.

Curling her toes in her slippers, she assured herself she could do this. Though he had chosen Thomasin de Arell, still her family—the Verduns—must ally with the loathsome Boursiers, meaning it fell to her uncle to wed this man's sister. However, if El's plan succeeded, the Boursiers would be expelled from these lands, as might the De Arells.

Pricked by guilt that the De Arells might feel Boursier's wrath for that which would soon be worked upon the latter, she reminded herself of the raid upon Tyne five months past. A dozen villagers' homes had been burned with half their crops, and all evidence suggested the De Arells were responsible for the atrocity visited upon the Verduns' people.

The flick of Boursier's reins drew El's gaze to tanned hands that appeared twice the size of her own. Familiar with the cruelty of which a man's hands were capable, she told herself this one would not get near enough to hurt her as her departed husband had done. Still, her heart pounded with emotions she had struggled to suppress since her wedding night when she had realized Murdoch found her tears pleasing.

Boursier was less than twenty feet distant when the sun came out from behind the clouds, and she was surprised to see his looks lighten. She would have said his hair was deepest brown, but sunlight revealed it to be darkly auburn. And the one visible eye was pale, though she could not tell if the gaze he swept over the town folk was blue, green, or gray. Regardless, his soul was black.

Doubt prying at her purpose, she silently beseeched, *Lord, can I do it?* Not that she believed God would condone her plan, but neither was she certain he would condemn her.

She shifted her regard to the diagonal scar above and below Boursier's eyepatch. Though deserved, he surely loathed the Verduns and De Arells for an affliction without end.

When he was nearly upon the stall behind which El stood and his gaze settled on her, she forced herself not to react in any way that would attract more attention—all the while praying the shawl provided enough shadow to obscure her face. Not that he had ever seen Elianor of Emberly.

Though questioning disturbed his brow, he urged his destrier past.

She eased the air from her lungs, swung around, and hastened to the hooded one who awaited her near a stall piled high with cloth.

Despite broad shoulders that fifty years of life had begun to bend, the woman who looked down upon El had something of a regal bearing. It was also present in high cheekbones and the dark, sharply arched eyebrows Agatha raised to ask what need not be voiced.

El glanced beyond her at the great fortress that flew the red and gold colors of the House of Boursier, and nodded. In the guise of a kitchen wench, she was ready to steal into Castle Adderstone. Or so she prayed—or should have.

Six days she must hold him. Then, for his refusal to wed his enemy, his lands would be forfeited. Unless she failed.

I shall not, she promised herself.

Even now Boursier was likely feeling the effects of the draught she had slipped into his drink a half hour past. That had been no easy task, one nearly rendered impossible when the cook had approached her. Blessedly, as she tensed for flight, someone had called him to the storeroom.

In his absence, she had stirred Agatha's preparation into the cup that was to be delivered to Boursier's bedchamber, the lord of Castle Adderstone's habit of wine before bed having remained unchanged since Agatha had endured a year in his household.

"'Tis just ahead," Agatha said low, raising the torch to burn away the cobwebs blocking their passage.

El peered around the older woman at stone walls laid not by man, but by God. Here was the place to which Boursier was destined. Carved out of the bowels of the earth outside his own castle, the shaft with its branching passages had been dug by Verduns and De Arells twenty years past when, for several months, they had joined against the Boursiers. El's own grandfather had assisted with the undermining that had brought down a portion of the castle's outer wall—a short-lived victory.

Months following the thwarted siege, she had visited Castle Kelling and bounded onto her grandfather's lap. Only one arm had come around her. Bayard Boursier's father had taken the other.

"This is it, my lady," Agatha said as she turned left off the passageway onto another, at the end of which lay an iron-banded door with a grate at eye level.

El considered Boursier's prison. "It will hold him?"

Agatha fit one of several keys into the lock and pushed the door inward. "'Twould hold three of him."

El accepted the torch offered her, stepped into the chill cell, and grimaced. The stone walls were moist with rainfall that seeped through the ground above. To the right, a rat scuttled into shadow. Ahead, three sets of chains and manacles hung from the walls. Were Boursier of a mind to be grateful, he would be glad he had only to endure this place for the six days remaining of the two months given him to wed his enemy.

As El turned out of the cell, she wondered again how Agatha had learned of the passage formed from the mine of that long ago siege, the entrance to which was a cavern in the wood. More, how had she obtained the keys? Unfortunately, the woman's secrets were her own, but El would not complain. While wed to Murdoch, she had benefitted from those secrets in the form of sleeping powders.

Meeting the gaze of the one in the doorway, she said, "Aye, it will hold him."

Agatha drew from her shoulder the pack that would sustain Boursier and tossed it against the far wall. "You are ready, my lady?"

"I am."

With a smile that revealed surprisingly white teeth, Agatha turned to lead her into the devil's lair.

"I know what you do."

Bayard had wondered how long before she stopped hovering and spoke what she had come to say. He returned the quill to its ink pot and looked up at his half sister who stood alongside the table.

Jaw brushed by hair not much longer than his, she said, "You will not sacrifice yourself for me."

He wished she were not so perceptive. Though she had attained her twentieth year, she regarded him out of the eyes of the old. Yet for all the wisdom to which she was privy, she was a mess of uncertainty—the truest of ladies when it suited, a callow youth when it served. And Bayard was to blame, just as he was to blame for her broken betrothal. Had he not allowed her and her mother to convince him it was best she not wed, the king could not have dragged her into his scheme. Of course, it truly was advisable that she not take a husband.

"Pray," she entreated, "wed the Verdun woman, Bayard."

He would laugh if not that it would be a bitter thing. "I assure you, one Verdun wife was enough to last me unto death." He curled his fingers into his palms to keep himself from adjusting the eyepatch.

Her brow rumpled. "Surely you do not say 'tis better you wed a De Arell?"

He shrugged. "For King Edward's pleasure, we all must sacrifice."

Her teeth snapped, evidence it had become impractical to behave the lady. "Then sacrifice yourself upon a Verdun!"

Never. Better he suffer a De Arell woman than Quintin suffer a De Arell man. Of course, he had other reasons for choosing Thomasin. The illegitimate woman was said to be plain of face, whereas Elianor of Emberly was told to be as comely as her aunt whose beauty had blinded Bayard—in more ways than one. Then there was the rumor that Elianor and her uncle were lovers and, of equal concern, that she had given her departed husband no heir. He would not take one such as that to wife.

"Hear me," Quintin said so composedly he frowned, for once her temper was up, she did not easily climb down from it. "As Griffin de Arell already has his heir, 'tis better that I wed him."

Feeling his hands begin to tighten, he eased them open. Regardless of which man she wed, regardless of whether or not an heir was needed, she would be expected to grow round with child.

He forced a smile. "'Tis possible you will give Verdun the heir he waits upon." And, God willing, she would have someone to love through what he prayed would be many years.

Quintin drew a shuddering breath. "I will not give Magnus Verdun an heir."

He sighed, lifted his goblet. "It is done, Quintin. Word has been sent to De Arell that I ride to Castle Mathe four days hence to wed his daughter." Though the wine was thick as if drawn from the dregs of a barrel, he drank the remainder in the hope it would calm his roiling stomach and permit a fair night's sleep.

He rose from the chair. As he stepped around his stiff-backed sister, he was beset with fatigue—of a sort he had not experienced since the treacherous woman who was no longer his wife had worked her wiles upon him.

"Make good your choice, Bayard," Quintin warned.

He looked across his shoulder. "I have made as good a choice as is possible." Thus, she would wed Verdun, and the widow, Elianor, would wed the widower, De Arell, allying the three families—at least, until one maimed or killed the other.

"You have not," Quintin said.

Pressed down by fatigue, he stifled a reprimand with the reminder she wished to spare him marriage into the family of his darkest enemy. "If I give you my word that I shall make the De Arell woman's life miserable, will you leave?"

She pushed off the table. "*Your* life, she will make miserable." She threw her hands up. "Surely you can find some way around the king!"

He who demanded the impossible—who cared not what ill he wrought. Though Bayard had searched for a way past the decree, it seemed the only means of avoiding marriage to the enemy was to vacate the barony of Godsmere. If he forfeited his lands, not only would Quintin and her mother be as homeless as he, but the De Arells and Verduns would win the bitter game at which the Boursiers had most often prevailed. Utterly unacceptable.

"I am sorry," he said, "but the king will not be moved. And though I have not much hope, one must consider that these alliances could lead to the prosperity denied all of us."

Her jaw shifted. "You speak of more castles."

He did. When the immense barony of Kilbourne had been broken into lesser baronies twenty-five years past to reward the three families, it was expected licenses would be granted to raise more castles. However, the gorging of their private animosities had made expansion an unattainable dream.

"Accept it, Quintin."

She opened her mouth, closed it, and crossed the solar. The door slammed behind her, catching a length of green skirt between door and frame.

Her cry of frustration came through, but rather than open the door, she wrenched her skirt loose with a great tearing of cloth—their father's side of her. Later, she would mourn the ruined gown—her mother's side of her.

Though Bayard had intended to disrobe, he was too weary. Stretching upon his bed, he stared into the darkness behind his eyelid and recalled the woman at the market. Not because of the comely curve of her face, but the prick of hairs along the back of his neck that had first made him seek the source. In her glittering eyes, he had found what might have been hatred, though he had reasoned it away with the reminder that his people had suffered much amid the discord sown by the three families. And that was, perhaps, the worthiest reason to form alliances with the De Arells and Verduns.

Curiously aware of his breathing, he struggled to hold onto the image of the woman. As the last of her blurred, he determined it was, indeed, hatred in eyes that had peered at him from beneath a thick shawl. A shawl that made a poor fit for a day well warmed by sun.

3

⁓⊙⊱⊰⊙⁓

THE SQUIRE MADE a final, muffled protest and slumped to his pallet.

"Now The Boursier," Agatha said, pulling the odorous cloth from the young man's mouth and nose.

For the dozenth time since slipping out from behind the tapestry, El looked to the still figure upon the bed. Though the solar was dark, the bit of moonlight filtering through the oilcloth showed he lay on his back.

El crossed to the bed. "Does he breathe?"

"Of course he does." Agatha came alongside her. "Though if you wish—"

"Nay!" She was no murderer, and holding him captive would accomplish what needed to be done.

"Then make haste, my lady." Agatha tossed the coverlet over Boursier's legs so they could drag him down the steps of the walled passage. And drag him they must. Though the older woman was relatively strong of back and El was hardly delicate, there was no doubt Boursier would still outnumber them.

El put her knees to the mattress and reached to the other side of the coverlet upon which he lay. As she did so, her hand brushed a muscled forearm. She paused. It should not bother her to see such an imposing man laid helpless before his enemies, but it did. Of course, once she had also pitied Murdoch. Only once.

Returning to the present, she began dragging the coverlet over his torso. When she reached higher to flip it over his head, his wine-scented breath stirred the hair at her temple and drew her gaze to his shadowed face.

By the barest light, something glittered.

She gasped, dropped her feet to the floor.

"What is it?" Agatha rasped.

El backed away. "He…" Why did he not bolt upright? "…looked upon me."

Agatha chuckled. "It happens." She pulled forth the cloth used upon the squire and pressed it to Boursier's face. "But let us be certain he remembers naught."

Would he not? Of course, even if he did, the glitter of her own eyes was surely all he would know of her. Heart continuing to thunder, El watched Agatha sweep the coverlet over Boursier's head.

"Take hold of his legs," she directed.

El slid her hands beneath his calves. Shortly, with Agatha supporting his heavier upper body, El staggered beneath her own burden. Boursier seemed to weigh as much as a horse, and by the time they had him behind the tapestry, he seemed a pair of oxen. Perspiring, she lugged him through the doorway onto the torchlit landing.

"Put him down," Agatha said as she lowered his upper body.

With a breath of relief, El eased his legs to the floor.

Agatha closed the door that granted access to the keep's inner walls and jutted her chin at the wall sconce. "Bring the torch."

El retrieved it, and when she turned to lead the way down the steps, a thud sounded behind. She swung around.

Agatha had hefted Boursier's legs, meaning his head had landed upon the first of the stone steps. "Nay!" she protested. "We must needs turn him. His head—"

"What care you?" Agatha snapped, lacking the deference due one's mistress. But such was the price of her favors.

Still, El could not condone such treatment, for a blow to the head could prove fatal. "We turn him, Agatha. Do not argue."

"My lady—"

"Do not!"

Agatha lowered her eyes. "As you will."

El assisted in turning Boursier and, shortly, Agatha gripped him about the torso. His feet taking the brunt of the steps, they continued their descent. At the bottom, Agatha dragged him through the doorway that led to the underground passage.

"Give me the key, and I will lock it," El said.

Continuing to support Boursier, Agatha secured the door herself.

Trying not to be offended, El led the way through the turns that placed them before the cell.

When Agatha dropped Boursier inside, once more having no care for how he fell, El glared at her.

From beneath a fringe of hair that had come loose from the knot atop her head, Agatha raised her eyebrows.

El held her tongue. She supposed the rough treatment was the least owed one whose grievance against Bayard Boursier was great. Agatha had spent a year in his household serving as maid to his wife who had also been El's aunt. For one long year, Agatha had aided Constance when Boursier turned abusive, and comforted her when he took other women into his bed. Given a chance, it was possible she would do the baron mortal harm.

El fit the torch in a wall sconce, then aided in propping Boursier against the cell wall. She tried not to look upon him as she struggled to open a rusted manacle, but found herself peering into his face. And wishing she had not.

She returned her attention to the manacle and pried at it, but not even the pain of abraded fingers could keep from memory her enemy's dimly lit face—displaced eyepatch exposing the scarred flesh of his left eyelid, tousled hair upon his brow, relaxed mouth. All lent vulnerability to one who did not wear that state well.

"Give it to me." Agatha reached for the manacle.

El jerked it aside. "I did not come to watch," she said and glanced at Boursier's other wrist that Agatha had fettered. Wishing the woman would not hover, she pried until the iron plates parted, then fit the manacle. As she did so, his pulse moved beneath her fingers—weak and slow.

Alarmed, El asked, "How long will he sleep?"

"As I always err on the side of giving too much, it could be a while. Perhaps a long while."

"But he will awaken?"

Agatha shrugged. "They usually do."

Murdoch always had.

"And most content he shall feel," Agatha added.

As Murdoch had felt, which had many times spared El his perverse attentions, just as what she did this night would spare the De Arell woman Boursier's abuse.

El extended a hand for the keys and, at Agatha's hesitation, said firmly, "Give them to me."

The woman's nostrils flared, but she surrendered them.

El met the upper plate of the manacle with the lower. It was a tight fit, one that might make it difficult for blood to course properly, but she gave the key a twist. As she rose, she looked upon Boursier's face and the eyepatch gone awry. She struggled against the impulse, but repositioned the half circle of leather over his scarred eyelid.

Behind, Agatha grunted her disapproval.

El considered the pack of provisions. There was enough food and drink to last six days, after which she and Agatha would release Boursier.

Though she wished she did not have to return to this place, Agatha was of an uncertain disposition—not to be trusted, El's uncle warned. Not that the woman would harm the Verduns. She simply did not take direction well, firm in the belief none was more capable of determining the course of the Verduns than she. Thus it had been since Agatha had come from France eleven years past to serve as maid to El's aunt.

"We are finished," Agatha pulled her from her musings.

El knew they should immediately depart Castle Adderstone, but something held her unmoving—something she should not feel for this man who had stolen her aunt from another only to ill treat her. "What if he does not awaken?" she asked.

"Then death. And most deserving."

Once more unsettled by Agatha's fervor, wishing it had been possible to take Boursier on her own, El frowned in remembrance of how quickly the woman had agreed to help—and how soon her plans had supplanted El's. Grudgingly, El had yielded to Agatha, who was not only conversant in this place, but had possessed the keys that granted them access to Castle Adderstone.

"Do not forget who he is," Agatha said, eyes glittering in the light of the torch she had retrieved.

El peered over her shoulder at Boursier who was no different from Murdoch—excepting he was mostly muscle whereas her departed husband had been given to fat. And that surely made this man better able to inflict pain and humiliation.

Lord, what a fool I am! she silently berated herself for feeling concern for one such as he. *It is no great curiosity that Murdoch made prey of me.*

"Never shall I forget who he is," she said.

Agatha lowered her prominent chin, though not soon enough to obscure a childlike smile.

Telling herself she did not care what pleasure Agatha took in Boursier's suffering, El stepped from the cell.

As Agatha pulled the door closed, she beckoned for the keys.

"Nay," El said, "I shall hold to them."

The woman's lids sprang wide. "You do not trust me, my lady?"

El longed to deny it, but said, "Forgive me, but I do not." She locked the cell door.

Feeling Agatha's ire, she followed the woman from the underground passage, taking the light with them and condemning Boursier to utter darkness. A darkness that would not lift for six days.

All of him ached.

With a breath that tasted foul and a groan that bounced back from walls that seemed too near, he opened his eye and blinked in an attempt to fathom the bit of light provided by torches lit about the inner bailey. But no glow penetrated the window's oilcloth. All was black, as if he were blind.

He wrenched a hand toward his right eye and jerked when a rattle resounded around the room and metal links struck his forearm.

Disbelief slammed through him, then anger. Shouting above the clatter of chains, he thrust his arms forward. If anyone was near, they would know he had awakened from whatever had rendered him senseless.

A memory—there one moment, slipping away the next—stilled him. Was it something he had seen before whatever had drugged him had taken full effect? Something heard? Felt?

He groped backward, but that which he dragged forth had little form due to the darkness in which it was bred. There *had* been a glimmer as of one whose eyes gathered bare light. And a scent. But that was all he had of the one who had stolen him from Castle Adderstone. How—?

The wine! After all these years, had Agatha returned to make good her threat of ruin?

Forgetting his aches, he bellowed and strained against the manacles, but no one came to part the darkness that was so complete it returned him to the question of his sight. Had the last of it been taken from him? Was there light upon his face he could not see?

He touched his right eye. It was there, but in the presence of light, would it yet see him through the world?

He clenched his hands. Had Agatha stolen him from his bed? Likely. But it might also be Griffin de Arell who would not wish his daughter wed to a Boursier, regardless that his illegitimate offspring could not be dear to him. Then there was the possibility this atrocity involved both Agatha and the De Arells. Though the woman was occasionally seen on Verdun lands, Bayard's men had caught sight of her on De Arell's barony. Thus, Bayard was likely imprisoned at Castle Mathe.

He pressed his palms to the wall at his back and groped along the slick surface, but that beneath his fingers revealed nothing of the place at which he was held. His right hand brushed something. Another prisoner? If so, either dead or unconscious to have not been awakened by Bayard's raging.

Grudgingly grateful for the length of chain that permitted movement on both sides, he felt a hand across what turned out to be a pack. He dragged it onto his lap and tossed back the flap. The first bundle he pulled out smelled of dried fish, the next was a loaf of bread, and there were two large skins of wine.

Provisions? Meaning none would be coming for him soon? Meaning he was not meant to die? Why? For the suspicion his death would cast upon the De Arells? For how long—?

"Six days!" he shouted and continued to shout until his throat felt as if sliced through.

He dropped his head back. If he did not escape before the last day of autumn, he would not wed the De Arell woman and Godsmere would be forfeited.

"Lord!" he called upon the one to whom Father Crispin would counsel him to turn. Even so, it was more a cry of anger and frustration than an appeal for aid.

Perhaps I should have chosen the Verdun woman, he silently seethed. It was as Quintin had pressed him to do. Quintin who was alone except for her needy mother. Quintin who did not always act upon the wisdom gifted her.

Staring into darkness, Bayard ignored the voice that told him to pray and, instead, vowed that the De Arells would answer for what they had done. Then he cursed them, strained against his chains, and felt one give.

About The Author

Tamara Leigh holds a Master's Degree in Speech and Language Pathology. In 1993, she signed a 4-book contract with Bantam Books. Her first medieval romance, *Warrior Bride*, was released in 1994. Continuing to write for the general market, three more novels were published with HarperCollins and Dorchester and earned awards and spots on national bestseller lists.

In 2006, Tamara's first inspirational contemporary romance, *Stealing Adda*, was released. In 2008, *Perfecting Kate* was optioned for a movie and *Splitting Harriet* won an ACFW "Book of the Year" award. The following year, *Faking Grace* was nominated for a RITA award. In 2011, Tamara wrapped up her "Southern Discomfort" series with the release of *Restless in Carolina*.

When not in the middle of being a wife, mother, and cookbook fiend, Tamara buries her nose in a good book—and her writer's pen in ink. In 2012, she returned to the historical romance genre with *Dreamspell*, a medieval time travel romance. Shortly thereafter, she once more invited readers to join her in the middle ages with the *Age of Faith* series: *The Unveiling, The Yielding, The Redeeming, The Kindling,* and *The Longing.* Tamara's #1 Bestsellers—*Lady at Arms, Lady Of Eve, Lady Of Fire,* and *Lady Of Conquest*—are the first of her medieval romances to be rewritten as "clean reads." Look for *Baron Of Blackwood,* the third book in *The Feud* series, in 2016.

Tamara lives near Nashville with her husbnd, sons, a Doberman that bares its teeth not only to threaten the UPS man but to smile, and a feisty Morkie that keeps her company during long writing stints.

Connect with Tamara at her website www.tamaraleigh.com, her blog The Kitchen Novelist, her email tamaraleightenn@gmail.com, Facebook, and Twitter.

For new releases and special promotions, subscribe to Tamara Leigh's mailing list: www.tamaraleigh.com

CPSIA information can be obtained
at www.ICGtesting.com
Printed in the USA
LVOW12s0125261016
510289LV00002B/373/P